VANISHED!
MORLAH'S QUEST

May all your adventures be magical

David E. Daigle

DAVID E. DAIGLE
THE FRONTMIRE HISTORIES – BOOK IV

Copyright © 2010 David E. Daigle
All rights reserved.

ISBN: 1451551703
ISBN-13: 9781451551709

Other Works by This Author

Novels:
The Frontmire Histories:
Prince of the Elves
webpage: princeoftheelves.synthasite.com
The Rise of the Dark Queen **
webpage: darkqueen.synthasite.com
Kravorctiva
webpage: kravorctiva.synthasite.com
Vanished!
webpage: vanished .synthasite.com
Blog: davethedc.wordpress.com

Magic Kingdom: Foreclosed ***
A spoof based on Terry Brook's Magic Kingdom: Sold

Short Stories:
A Loon Called From the Opposite Shore ****
A Prayer for the Barley ****
Lily *

Plays:
"It's a fetish, Jerry!" ****

*Yet to be Published
** Also published on Kindle
*** Published on Kindle only
****Published on Kindle only in Two Short Stories and a Play by David E. Daigle

Mount Bahal

Frontmire Deserts

N

Parnham Bay

Land of the Dwarves

Land of the Gift

Korkaran Sea

Barrett's Fall

Dwarf's Pass

Frontmire

Parintia

Greater Continent of Canterhort

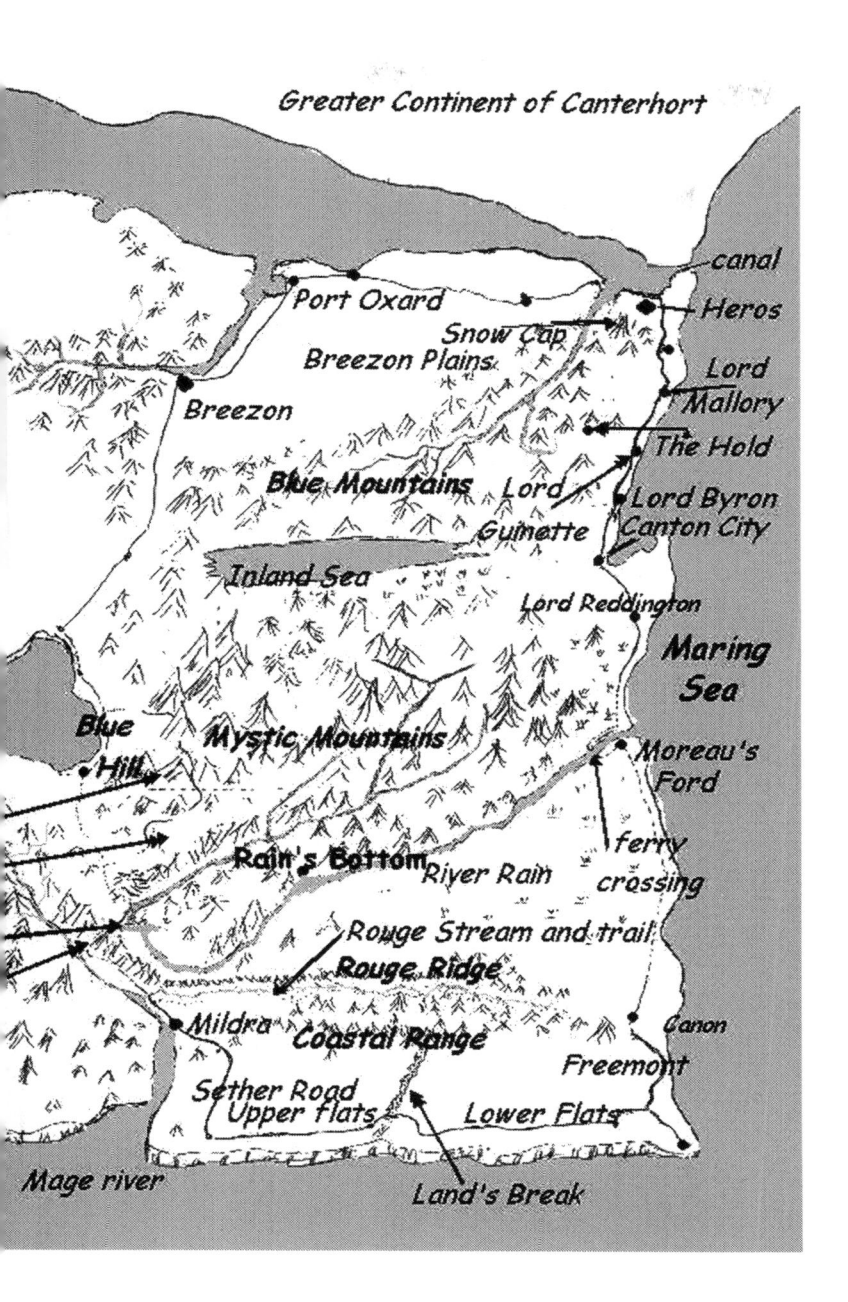

- canal
- Port Oxard
- Heros
- Snow Cap
- Breezon Plains
- Lord Mallory
- Breezon
- The Hold
- Blue Mountains
- Lord Guinette
- Lord Byron
- Canton City
- Inland Sea
- Lord Reddington
- Maring Sea
- Blue Hill
- Mystic Mountains
- Moreau's Ford
- ferry crossing
- Rain's Bottom
- River Rain
- Rouge Stream and trail
- Rouge Ridge
- Mildra
- Coastal Range
- Canon
- Freemont
- Sether Road
- Upper flats
- Lower Flats
- Mage river
- Land's Break

Tables of Measure

Time

- Course of the sun: the time from sunrising to sunsetting. In Frontmire, this is approximately a 12hour period depending on the season.
- Quarter course of the sun: the course of the sun is divided into four quarters of about 3 hours each.
- Quarter of the moons course: the moon's course is also separated into four roughly three-hour quarters depending on the season: one week.
- Moon's course: the time from sunsetting to sun rising.
- Moon's cycle: time from full-moon to the next full moon
- Spans: roughly one hour whether of the moon of sun.
- Cycle of the sun is roughly equivalent to one year.

Distance

- Span: a rough measurement approximately the width of a hand, generally accepted to be about five inches. It is from this measure that the measure for time is derived – one holds his hand to the sky and measures the time involved for the sun or moon to travel that distance.
- Pace: approximately three feet.
- League: approximately seven miles.

Weight

- Stone: approximately two pounds.

Foreword

❦

Many thanks to all who have assisted in this coming to a conclusion. First and foremost, my wife Eileen who was very patient and tolerant of the whole undertaking.

Second, I would like to thank those who have read and enjoyed my work, as crude as it may be, and for those who have let me know that they liked it: to all who encouraged me.

This is Book IV, the last of the series. Thoughts of a Book V exist, but to date, I doubt that it will come to pass.

Book IV's story line may surprise most who have followed the series, yet it is my best work yet. I hope you enjoy it.

A special thanks to Jerry Halkyard of Dragonfrog's Gallery of Renderosity.com. Firewing the flaming Phoenix on the cover is his work; Jerry graciously donated the artwork for this cover in exchange for a signed copy of the Frontmire series.

And though the manuscript has been read and re-read and edited and re-edited…the typo gnomes continue to ravage its pages. Your tolerance is greatly appreciated.

THE FRONTMIRE HISTORIES - BOOK IV:
VANISHED!
MORLAH'S QUEST

Chapter 1

❧

The Druid suddenly opened his eyes, staring up into the bleak darkness. The only sounds he could hear were his own breathing, and the resonance of his heartbeat in his ears. But where was he? There were no stars to be seen, no breezes to be felt, no familiar night's stirrings to be heard. Reaching out, his senses sought to lay hold of some kind of beacon to help him identify his situation, some strand that would permit him to understand his circumstances. It took him a few spans of heartbeats to remember where he was, in the deep recesses of the Druid's keep, under guard, lock and key. In the distant past, these rooms had been used as a prison. The castle fortification was named *seilstri*, from the ancient Elven word meaning knowledge or learning.

But what was it that had roused him from the Druid Sleep? Morlah waited. At first, memories stirred slowly. After all, he expected that he had slept the prescribed ten cycles of the sun. Nothing beckoned to him, nothing rang out in warning. Perhaps it was merely time to awaken from restoration. Light sprang to life within the silver-white orb on his black-polished-oak staff, his magic readily responding to his intent as he rose. His long, drab-brown robes and mantle flowed behind him. Moving and appearing like a man of forty cycles rather than his some six hundred, he strode to the thick-planked door that hung on heavy iron hinges. Twice, he rapped at the impregnable door, as he had always done when he awoke from the Druid Sleep. As Morlah undid the latches on his side of the door, he expected the guard would be shortly doing the same on the other side.

When using the Sleep, the Druids took no chances at being vulnerable. They slept under guard in the keep's depths, just above the caverns that housed the archives. The Sleep chambers' walls were solid granite, and the doors' thick Black Oak planks were cased with iron. Enchantments were set for protection. Ever since Daektoch's, the malevolent Black Mage's, attempted genocide on the Druids, they left nothing to chance but were cautious and vigilant in all things.

Everything was as usual. First, the Druid would awake, not sure as to where he was, but soon memory would stir and his thoughts would turn to the *what* or *why* of his awakening. The Druid Sleep was a combination of herbal potions and Gray magic. Its original use had been to stay deterioration and death in the mortally wounded, but later, it was used to renew, revitalize and restore the Druids, thus extending their lives indefinitely.

This time, however, something was different! There was no response to his knock and no undoing of the locks.

Normally, by now, Morlah would have heard the bolts being pulled back by the guard; perhaps he was not quite alert enough yet. Perhaps he had not knocked loudly enough. Using the metal orb formed of the Faerie element of magic that sat on the staff's top, he rapped again at the door and produced a loud thudding.

Still nothing stirred.

This was most peculiar. Never in all his time of undergoing the Druid Sleep had there been a lapse in response. It felt as if fear seeped out of the suddenly close walls of the crypt-like room, attempting to take hold of him, as if to entomb him. Stepping back from the door, his staff blazing with the argentus orb, he hurled a bolt of power. The door blasted off its hinges. Argentus was the source of the most powerful magic known throughout the planet; it was the very life and source of the Faeries' magic and existence.

Morlah the Druid shielded himself to protect against physical or magical attack. Slowly, he stepped out into the hallway, using his staff to light the darkness that had now turned ominous before him. No one was in the hallway. A thick layer of undisturbed dust coated the floor and cobwebs filled the passage. With his back to the cold stone wall and his staff held out before him ready to strike, the Druid made his way toward the exit; clearly the area had not been disturbed for a long time. Passing through the doors that led toward the main hall, he found debris and discarded objects strewn about. There were no signs of life beyond that of the small rodents and birds using the chambers as nesting sites.

Finally, stepping out into the courtyard, relieved that there apparently was no imminent threat, Morlah observed that the formerly polished and meticulously clean structures were overgrown with weeds and vines. The time-stained stone walls and buildings were in disrepair. Overhangs and roofs were collapsed. Wood was rotted, crumbling to the touch. *seilstri's* gates were rusted so badly that the once-solid-ironclad-maple doors, still standing and closed, looked like the skeletal remains of some gigantic fowl. Tall grass pushed through between pavement slabs of pink granite. It felt as if it were but yestercourse that he had gone down to the Sleep chambers.

Where was everyone? What had happened to the thousands of other Druids who had once lived and prospered here? The fortified castle must have been abandoned for at least two hundred cycles of the sun for decay to deteriorate it to this extremity of waste. Morlah released his hold on the magic and headed for the caverns where the libraries and archives had been housed. If he were lucky, he would find his answer there. Hunger began to gnaw at him.

Four spans of the sun's course later, Morlah was sitting in the caverns, a globe of white light floating over his shoulder as he read; the orb was conjured by a spell shown him by Master Filinhoff in cycles past.

Filinhoff! he thought. *He wouldst most likely be dead now.* Tears welled up in Morlah's eyes. Many of his friends and family were likely dead also. He breathed deeply, recomposing himself, attempting to accept circumstances as they were. He continued his reading.

Morlah was relieved to find the extensive libraries still intact, though shocked to find volumes that were written two, three and four hundred cycles of the sun past the time he had last been awake.

Four hundred cycles! How is it that he hadst not awakened in that time?

Normally, a Druid only slept twelve to a score of cycles of the sun at the outermost before waking from the Druid Sleep, unless he was roused earlier by some specified spell; Daektoch's movements in the land had always been the key for Morlah to awaken. Four hundred cycles without Daektoch exerting himself! Was it possible that the Elves had actually managed to kill the wicked mage in their last engagements or that the wizard had finally succumbed to death?

Using the catalogs, Morlah located a book that might help him. It was one of the last history books entered into the libraries. He blew the dust from the cover and read the title on the leather-bound volume: *The Frontmire Histories - A Synopsis by Esther Miller, daughter of the Master of **seilstri**, Barnes Roget, in the cycle 6053.* The black leather was cracked and the fragile sepia parchment brittle.

6053! That was over six hundred cycles past the beginning of his last Sleep! His hands trembled as he leafed through the history that was known to him. Finally, he found the period that covered the time after he had last been in the land:

"...and legend hast it that the Kingdom hadst prospered long under King Jerhad the Great. But in the cycle 5853, at the age of four hundred fifty-four cycles, he didst call his family to his chambers and spoke to them of taking the Final Journey, to follow his mate, Andreanna, who hadst done so one hundred cycles earlier. The King, who wast in excellent health, having drawn up his affairs and set his house in order, didst retire to his bed attended by his closest living relatives, and died. Kendra, mate of Elfstar, son

of Lehland the Captain of the King's Guard, in her four hundred and twenty second cycle, was named as heir to the throne."

The light orb over Morlah's head went dead. He gasped, taking in deep breaths. Jerhad and Andreanna were dead!

...And how many others that he had known? His use of the Druid Sleep came up as a bitter bile in his mouth. How many had he outlived in over sixteen hundred cycles' of its use? How many people had he loved and lost? Anguish and sorrow crashed down on him as if the very cavern's roof were collapsing. Pushing away from the table where he had been reading, he sat in the blinding darkness. Bending his chest down to his knees, Morlah wailed with grief.

Later, after the sunsetting, he rose from the floor, empty and numb. He rekindled the light orb and sat at the table again, salvaging himself, shoring his defenses against gloom and despondency, hoping to find what had become of the Druids. He read on, turning a page, which whispered with a crackle:

"...even if it were true that the Elves didst posses great and powerful magic under King Jerhad the Great's reign, there remains no evidence of it at this time. The capitol, Mildra the Magnificent City, doest lie in abandonment, while the small population of Elves on the south coast art fishers and farmers, showing no traces of what legend speaks of in relation to magic."

Morlah turned a few pages and found a reference to the Druids:

"...and though the Druid libraries doest have extensive volumes on the Black, Gray and White Arts of magic, no one doest know what they mean or how to use them. Even so, in the first cycle

*of Master Landancer's rule in **seilstri**, he didst add such volumes to the List of Forbidden Books and hadst them locked in the archives with other such works. Now times, scholars doest scoff at the mention of magic and state that legend and mythology shouldst not be confused with fact and science."*

Morlah skipped ahead, his anger beginning to rise.

*"...in the cycle 6001, with the Banantiand Party in control of the Parliament of **seilstri**, it wast passed as law that study, being an unproductive pastime, wast to be limited and that every individual's access to the libraries wouldst be restricted to one course of the sun out of every ten. The remainder of time wast to be spent in labor at one's craft, for the finances of **seilstri** were to be regarded as a priority. The Mandolt Party didst rebel at this and threatened to leave **seilstri**, which the Banantiand Party wast only too glad to facilitate. With the use of **seilstri's** militia, every last member of the Mandolt Party wast ousted from the keep, barred from ever entering its walls again, and to their dismay, forever banned from the libraries and archives.*

*On the fourth course of the sun after the spring equinox, the Mandolt Party didst make a futile assault on **seilstri** in attempt to regain control. After three courses of battle, the Banantiands, with the use of the militia, didst make a sortie, and the Mandolts were slain to the man. Of those from **seilstri**, casualties were light. Further descriptions of these events art catalogued in Manlin's Account of the Battle of the Banantiands, Library No. 438AEK9600B1 0".*

Morlah was stunned.

seilstri had fallen victim to political and internal striving. The Druids, who had been the example of tolerance, benevolence, harmony and education, had become everything they had been the antithesis of. How could this have happened? There had been no politics in his time! There had been no parties. And where had a parliament come from?

He turned to the last pages of the volume and read:

"...and when Minus, Master of the Heralds, didst hear of it, he hadst all two thousand of them put to death. With this new alleged treachery and subsequent executions, the Druid population is but four thousand thirty-six in contrast to the eighteen thousand three hundred thirty-nine of but ten cycles ago, diminished primarily by execution."

Morlah went on reading, overwhelmed by what had become of his people:

*"...it wouldst appear that the end of the Druids is at hand, for Minus' Party numbers but a few score, most dead by starvation from the six cycle siege, while the Canharts have somehow bolstered their numbers to the hundreds. We doest have water but no food. Master Minus hast decreed that he willst personally execute any who even but use the word' **surrender**'...."*

Having walked two-quarters of the sun's course in a mind-numbing stupor, Morlah finally arrived at the docks of the natural harbor that had been used by the Druids in the past. His heart leaped in anticipation and hope as he saw his first signs of Human life. The organic scent of the sea air helped revive him. The small port had several decrepit fishing vessels moored to the docks, waves lapping against the wooden hulls. Fishermen were mending their coarse, brown-hemp nets as others went about various activities; the bustle of goings-on acted to silence Morlah's turmoil. Perhaps here, he could learn a bit more about the fate of the Druids.

Morlah approached an old woman dressed in dark brown robes, her face crevassed with age and her hands work-worn.

"Couldst I take a heartbeat of your time, Gram?" Morlah asked.

She stopped and, abruptly turning him an evil eye, backed away from him.

"I wouldst like to inquire pertaining to thine knowledge of those formerly known as Druids who didst live in the abandoned...."

Morlah did not get to finish his question, for the woman gathered herself up, spat on the ground at his feet and hissed a venomous sound, moving away as quickly as her arthritic legs would allow. Morlah was puzzled: was it something he had said? How he had said it? Perhaps the ancient dialect of the Common Tongue had made her wary. He could speak the modern version; he would try again.

This time, Morlah approached a thin, middle-aged man who was mending nets; he would go slower.

"Greetings, friend," ventured the Druid.

The man looked up with a glance, nodded an acknowledgement and returned to his labor, his hands skillfully working the coarse meshwork that provided his livelihood.

"How's the fishing been?"

The fisherman shrugged his slender shoulders noncommittally. "Seen better."

"What you catching?" continued Morlah.

"White Throat an' herring mostly."

"It's been a while since I've been here," the Druid continued, feeling his way with the fisher and keeping an eye out for the old lady, lest she cause trouble for him. But she had moved on and was occupied with her work. "I knew some who fished these waters many cycles past; used to catch Blue Gill if they weighted their nets and fished off of the deep side of the reef. Ever try it?"

The fisherman's interest lifted with a genuine look of curiosity. "Say, how did you say?"

"Weighted the nets and trolled the bottom just off the reef, on the deep side. Had to watch close not to get hooked up on the coral though. Sometimes they'd put a boy floating in the water to watch the net; would hold on to a rope and tow behind the boats. If the waters were clear and the sun bright, he'd be able to watch the net and warn if they were too close to the reef. They'd catch Blue Gill."

The fisherman's head pivoted like a Keese Owl's, peering about, hoping nobody else was hearing what he was. "No, never did hear of it done. Blue Gill? That fetches quite a price. When was this done? I've fished here all my life an' never heard tell of it. You sure 'bout that?"

Morlah nodded. "It was the only way to get a boatload of Blue Gill, I heard tell."

"Boatload!" sneered the fisherman. The man frowned and gave Morlah a good eyeing over, his interest turning to skepticism.

"Lived here all your life?" Morlah attempted to divert the man's thoughts. The fisherman nodded and returned to his mending, his eyes at times glancing up to catch a look at the stranger, doubt clearly written on his weathered face.

"Must know a lot about the history of it?" Morlah set his bait.

The man nodded and relaxed a bit.

"What's that abandoned castle up in the hills back there?"

The fisherman stopped abruptly, his eyes narrowing, and Morlah thought he was about to have a repeat of the old woman's behavior.

"Not much to talk about." He peered around to see if anyone was listening. "Some folk called Druids lived there," he said in a hushed voice. "Got to fighting among themselves. Hired out mercenaries an' turned the whole island to warring. Brought down all kinds of nasty plagues an' pestilences with their magic earlier on, on each other an' even on island folk who just tried to mind their own business. Almost ended all existence here. Gone now. Long gone...a couple hundred cycles or so, but their name remains as a curse an' a festering hatred generations later.

"Not that we're still not without their curse…. Some large parts of the lands won't grow crops. Hardly any wildlife. Fish is all we got." He spat at the ground. "Cursed wizards!"

It took a bit of self-control for Morlah not to correct the man and tell him that the Druids were not wizards, but he found the strength to manage himself in light of the fisherman's emotion.

"Is there any ship traffic to the mainland?" asked Morlah.

Again, the man eyed him suspiciously. "How'd you come here if not by ship?"

"Sailed a small vessel but tore her bottom out on the northeast coast. She broke up on the reef and sank," Morlah lied.

"What you come here for?"

"I wanted to explore Parintia. Had been here a long time past and wanted to see it again."

"Where you from?"

"Northern Canterhort."

"Long way to come just to look. Parintia. Ain't no one call it that no more. Don't give it a name since..." He looked around to see that no one was within earshot. "...since that *Druid thing*," he finished in a conspiratorial whisper.

"I need to get back to Frontmire. Any way of getting there?"

"Nope," the fisherman mumbled, once again intent on his nets, as if he were finished with Morlah.

"No ship traffic?"

"Nope." The fisher paused for several spans of heartbeats. "Ain't nothing for them to get and no one with much coin to buy with. No one comes, not since...you know."

"Do you own your own boat?"

"Yup." He indicated a one-masted trawler, using his eyes to point. "Built her myself." Again, he looked around.

Morlah sighed. The laborious process of obtaining information was beginning to grate on him.

In a low voice, leaning toward Morlah, the fisherman said, "Went up to the castle when I was a boy. Big no-no! Found a place with books...thousands. Can't read, but I found one with pictures on building boats. So, I started with a few smaller rowboats. Made them crude on purpose so no one would suspect. Then, I kept getting better an' better, an' finally, I built *Mandy* over there. She's the finest vessel on the island. Jes' like in the book."

"Think she'd sail across to Frontmire?'

"Sure would! Had her twenty leagues out in a gale once. She's true as the night is dark."

"Could I get you to take me across?"

"Nope."

"Why not?"

"Need to fish. Mouths to feed." Rising, he began rolling his net.

"I'd pay well."

"With what?"

"What would you prefer?"

The man stopped and straightened himself, his well-worn leather loincloth the only garment he wore. "You come from the other side, do you?"

Morlah nodded.

"Got coppers?"

Morlah shook his head, causing the fisherman's eyebrows to rise up a bit.

"You got silver...gold!"

Morlah nodded. "I'll pay you two large golds to take me across."

"Naw. You's mocking me. Ain't nobody got gold.... Come to think of it...couldn't use it here."

Morlah jingled his oiled-leather purse, hid within his tunic. "I have both golds and silvers."

The man frowned. "No one has much coin anymore, but I'd take the same in silvers an' maybe you could let me jes' take a look at a gold." His eyes turned dreamy, as if there could be no greater pleasure on earth, his face breaking into a pleasant smile for the first time since Morlah had spoken to him.

Morlah's hand returned from under his garment and extended it to the man. "What's your name?"

"Jat."

"I'm Morlah. Here, keep this one, just for helping me. I'll pay for your time in silver."

Jat extended his palm, and Morlah dropped something into it. Then, the man closed his hand, brought it up near his face and peered in. He gasped, like a child beholding a joyous sight. He looked up at Morlah, his eyes sparkling with excitement.

"Is it real?"

Morlah nodded, amused by the fisherman's elation at the sight of the coin. "It is tested for purity by biting in with your long-tooth. If it sinks in a little like it would in lead, then it's pure. The more alloy found in it, the harder it gets. If you can leave a tooth mark fairly easily, it's pure."

The man's eyes darted about as he snuck the coin between his teeth. Glancing at the coin, his grin broadened immensely. "She's a real one alright!"

"When can we leave?"

"Help me get this net back on board an' cast off her lines. We's agoin' sailin'!"

"Don't you have to tell anyone you're leaving?"

Jat appeared puzzled. "They'll know when they see I'm gone...."

Morlah secured the mainsail's boom, using magic from the sliver of argentus, embedded in his left fifth rib. He had put on a good show for Jat's sake, making it look as if he toiled, but the reality was, he had not come near raising a sweat. He waved back to Jat, who was at the tiller. Jat signaled that Morlah could relax for a bit, so Morlah turned and looked out at the warm, green waters of the Korkaran Sea, watching the billowing white clouds that were sparsely scattered across the pale blue sky. The air was thick with the scent of the marine brine, and the warm wind breathed new life into the Druid as Jat brought *Mandy* about for their run into the mouth of the Mage River where Mildra, the capitol of the former Elven Kingdom, lay.

How had things come to this after cycles and cycles of effort, wars, battles, fights, pain and death? Blood, sweat and tears had been shed to see the Kingdom of Mildra, the Kingdom of the Elves, established, and...it had all come to naught. Still, Morlah reveled in his senses, the heat of the sun, the feel of the sea and the smell of the salt waters. He used them to ward his spirit against the dark sorcery that threatened to consume him, the morbid and overwhelming sense of loss, futility and defeat.

How far in the past was it that he had accepted the Faeries' charge of returning the magic to the Elves? Where had his labors gone?

Mandy crossed the river's bar at the Mage's mouth without incident, for the tide had turned, and the river's waters were low. Jat was again shouting orders, arousing Morlah from his reflections and threatening despondence; though a Druid and of powerful magic, he was still not immune to the frailties of Humankind. Running forward and dropping the jib, Morlah secured it as they entered the natural harbor that had been the Port of Mildra. *Mandy* eased her way toward the docks, the midcourse breeze blowing inland, chasing them toward their destination.

A span later, *Mandy* lay at her anchors, a stone's throw from the old broken-down docks. Barely a board remained on the decayed pilings that resembled ancient teeth, as if threatening them, an ill-omen of the tidings that awaited. They lowered a dingy over the side with a small boom and a wooden block-and-tackle pulley, and soon, Morlah and Jat stood on shore.

"You know anything about this place?" the Druid asked Jat.

"Only that they was Elves, an' now they's mostly gone."

"Do you know what happened to them?"

"Nope. You come from this land; how's it you don't know?"

"Come from up north. Just another visit." He handed Jat a fistful of silver coins, gave him thanks and made his way up the steep incline that led toward the city.

"Hey!" called Jat.

Morlah turned and faced the fisherman.

"You're one of *them* ain't you?"

"One of who?"

"The Druids."

Morlah paused, surprised at the fisher's intuition. "How could that be? They've been gone for hundreds of cycles."

"Yeah. That's what I thought." He launched the dinghy with a practiced heave, boarded it in a hop when knee deep in the water and slowly rowed back to *Mandy*.

Chapter 2

Star, a Human female in her twenty-third cycle, lay beside the man who had just paid to have her. He was snoring now that he was satiated. *Another of the fat, sweaty hogs who's unleashed his vile lusts on me,* she thought. Ye gods, she had lost count of how many so long ago. She took the ropes off her wrists and ankles.

Bastard!

Downstairs, the crowd in the large smoke-filled hall could be heard singing and laughing, talking and dancing to the music of a fiddle, as the other girls attempted to lure business to their rooms.

They had barely entered her room. She had turned toward him only to be met between the eyes by a set of massive, hairy knuckles. She had awakened a while later, gagged and bound to the bed. From there, her customer had had his way, inflicting her with pain, abuse and a beating. That had not been the agreement. In fact, it was against house policy, and more importantly...*hers!* But bound and gagged, she could do nothing to alert the bouncers. When he was through, he had cut the ropes that secured her, rolled over and gone to sleep.

Star slipped out of bed and got dressed. She packed her few belongings into a threadbare carpetbag and readied to leave. Then, she walked over to the bed and looked down at the odoriferous brute lying there; he was hairy as a bear and ugly as a Troll. He did not smell any better than either. Leaning over, she kissed him on the forehead. She left, emptying the coins from his purse into hers. As the latch of the door secured itself behind her, the blood spurting from the man's slit throat tapered to an ooze.

Nobody hits me! Nobody!

⁂

Morlah stood by Mildra's city wall. The hard, gray stone quarried locally had been turned white by a magical removing of the gray color, leaving a sparkling aggregate. The stone had been infused with the properties that produced a soft luminescence as people walked by at night; and it also kept the streets and dwellings warm in winter and cool in summer. The Druid put his hand to the wall by the western gate. The smooth, polished stone blocks were warm to his hand. The wall was still alive with Elven magic. Mildra had been a bustling city full of peace, harmony and the power of Elven magic. It was a true utopia, at least as close as one could get in a world beset with evils. Now she lay abandoned.

Morlah stood looking through the gate; the lumber of the doors was so rotted that the only remaining evidence of its existence were the few pieces left around the bolts on the hinges; the twisted, rusted iron hinges were the only other indication remaining that there had been doors in the opening. He entered the city, the streets resounding with emptiness.

Morlah moved through the streets as if in a dream, as if walking into a mirage He headed toward the castle, still not cognizant of what he was seeking. Perhaps, he simply needed to see its deserted state for himself, not taking the record that he had read in the libraries as fact. Perhaps, he needed to see it as truly abandoned.

How is it that it is abandoned?

Even if the Kingdom had fallen, surely some would have remained; someone would have seen use of such a haven as a home. Magic kept rodents out and kept weeds and brush from growing though cracks between the stone slabs of the pavement. The gardens and fountains were overgrown with edible vegetation planted by the gardeners several hundreds of cycles past.

Cool in the summer, warm in the winter, no weeds no vermin, rich soil in the lush gardens. Surely, someone would have seen its advantages. With his senses, Morlah's heart sought the comfort of the familiar Elven magic as if to ward off the emotional brambles that sought to choke his heart.

Heading toward the castle, Morlah meandered through the streets lined with stone-block buildings. He did not take the direct path but wove unpurposefully though a maze of lanes that had once been well known to him, that had once been teeming with life and vitality.

Ye gods, where hadst it all gone?

Morlah had watched it all come to pass. He had been witness to the Dwarves' construction of the castle and city, assisted by the Elves. The Dwarves had been used extensively for the stonework, the Elves shoring their labors with finishing touches of magic. Morlah had observed as Jerhad, the King, had grown in the wisdom and the power of magic. The Druid had monitored how the King had come into possession of much of the land about the Kingdom, and yet, had caused the people to prosper exceedingly as well, making them rich in employment, magic, happiness and life. Jerhad had also successfully undertaken the defenses of the Kingdom against the Black Mage and other threats, keeping the Elven Army intact, strong and ever vigilant.

The castle gates leading to its public areas were wide-open when Morlah arrived there; these were sheltered from the elements and had not suffered decay. The castle had housed the King's Guard, thousands of servants, gardeners, Healers, cooks, caretakers, and stables with their staffs. Now, it seemed to groan under the weight of its bareness.

Where is everyone?

Knowing that they would reveal no information, Morlah went up to the Royal Suites in spite of himself. Perhaps just to look. Perhaps just one more time to see where those he had loved so dearly had lived, those whom he had found, protected, nurtured and helped to mature into the Elven Royalty. Yet, he thought, Fate might have played a stronger hand in the matter than he had; he had merely pointed them in the right direction.

The apartments were bare, obviously looted, stripped of all belongings, furniture, art and the like. Other homes he had looked into had revealed the same. He stepped out onto the patio off of the Royal Bedchambers, high in the castle. This was Jerhad's and Andreanna's favorite upper garden.

He gazed out over the majestic city, which extended almost as far as the eye could see.

Morlah could see the original walls of defense, primitive and hastily thrown up as a bulwark against a Troll invasion. The old wall still existed, left intact as a tribute to those who had died in protection of their people. The gray stone defense lay well within the confines of the city, for Mildra had been but a small town of three thousand then. Later, it had blossomed to nearly one hundred thousand.

Morlah was startled out of his reflections. He had seen movement in the distance in one of the streets below. Then, he saw it again, a lone hunch-backed figure moving along and then turning into an alley. Should he pursue? It would take too long to get there; he decided to forget it and rather go down to the King's Libraries to see if there was some evidence that would reveal why things had come to this end.

Finding the Royal Libraries intact, tracking the King's journals, Morlah sat down for a long session of searching and reading. It was dark outside, almost as dark as he felt within, when he returned to the King's Bedchambers. His search had proven futile. He sat on the railing of the garden patio and gazed westwardly to the mountains on the opposite side of the Mage River, the mountains that bordered the Korkaran Sea. He ate of the provisions that he had received from Jat, despondent and failing to notice what he was eating. Setting a few wards to protect himself and alert him of intrusion, he conjured up a large cushion and lay down to sleep for the night. The stone walls would keep him warm.

At sunrising, he woke to the sound of heavy rain; the dark gray sky only assisted to solidify his solemn mood.

After eating a bit, he returned to the libraries and spent the remainder of the course reading, searching. Just before sunsetting, he returned to the upper castle, ate and slept again, the rain now reduced to a heavy falling mist in the chilled evening air.

On rising the next morning, the rain still dropping lightly from the dismal overcast sky, Morlah decided to try a new avenue for his exploration. He went down into the depths of the castle to the place where he had convinced Jerhad, in the distant past, to hold Daektoch as a clandestine prisoner. Later, after the mage had been moved to *seilstri*, the chamber was used as part of the castle's archives.

But a full course of the sun of reading only brought dismay and frustration to the Druid, for there was no record whatsoever about any decline of the city or any reason for its abandonment. He stopped and gazed for a span of heartbeats at the walls before returning to the upper castle. The stonework reminded him of the repairs to the mended hole back in the Druid Keep where Daektoch had, like a worm, slithered out of captivity. The Black Mage had been more resourceful than Morlah had given him credit for, even in his irreparable insanity.

The sun shone brightly and hotly the next course. Morlah left the castle and went north to see what could be found of the remnant of Elves. Then, he would go to the Dwarves; they would know. The Dwarves and the Elves had been allies and closely knit with a great love for one another. But what if the Dwarves were also gone? His heart threatened to fall into despair at the thought.

Then, there was movement ahead of him at the end of the street. The same severely-stooped figure moved around a corner and out of sight. Morlah ran after him, hurrying as fast as he could. He needed to catch this individual if only for the sake of contact with another living being. Not knowing what to expect, he cloaked himself with a spell of invisibility and silence until he could know who or what he dealt with.

From around the corner, Morlah witnessed the figure entering the same alley where he had seen him two courses earlier. It implied that the creature lived here. Was there only one solitary being living in Mildra?

Morlah slowed to a walk, allowing himself time to catch his breath, feeling winded with the effort of running. Not that he feared being heard, for his spell would cover that, but he wanted to be in full control and ready for anything.

Morlah arrived at the alleyway and peered around the corner, as if he could still be seen. He saw no one. Slowly, he moved along the alley. Caution took over, although he did not understand why he had become so wary. Arriving to an open door that led down into a basement, he paused and sent out a strand of argentus magic in search of his quarry. Yes. It was in there. He drew his feeler back and waited, augmenting his hearing with a spell from the Arts.

"...Elves."

Morlah's attention was pricked by the word, as was his soul.

"Have got to find...those blasted Elves.... Need to hurt them...make them pay. Think they have magic... Wait until they meet up with me...show them who has magic. Can't... find where I left them. Elves! Where...are you? Come see Master...Daektoch. Come out little...Elves, come out...." The voice raved on and on.

Daektoch! Ye gods, it canst not be. Daektoch? How...no!

Morlah could not contain himself. Warily, he crept down the stone steps and in through the doorway, still cloaked, hardly breathing, his defensive shields instinctively activating in response to his intent. He moved slowly in order to allow his eyes to adjust to the dim candlelight within. Just inside the door, he hesitated and peered at the author of the nonstop rambling about the Elves.

"...know they were here. Where are...you, my nasty little Elves? Come to Daektoch...won't hurt you a bit. Just... want to look at you." The room was dark, dingy and dirty. Crates cluttered the floor. Cobwebs wove a tangled maze.

Morlah could make out the stooped, emaciated figure now, though it had its back to him. The being went about working at a counter as if preparing food or some similar task, prattling continually. The figure was no more than half of Daektoch's former height and was withered beyond reckoning. His shuffling gait was slow as if balance were a problem, and the constant rocking foot-to-foot made him appear like a buoy on a choppy sea. Morlah cautiously slid in along the wall.

Daektoch stopped and sniffed at the air.

"Magic! Smells...like magic. Damned...Elves came back. Get out! ...Get out! Leave...me alone. Can't you damned... Elves leave an old man alone!" But the figure never turned toward the door or looked back; instead, he kept at whatever he was doing.

Morlah slipped into a darkened recess of the dust-ridden room, away from the little withered man, and sat on a keg.

The ancient wizard went on undeterred. Daektoch was old; actually, he was even older than Morlah. As a young boy, he had escaped from Pernham, City of the Mountain, when the naive population had paid tribute to a necromancer that had seduced them into thinking he was a god. The city's people had paid tribute to the necromancer with the blood sacrifices of their children. Daektoch had fled for his life. And although he had gotten away, Daektoch had never been the same since; he was corrupted with lust for the power of magic as he had seen wielded by the sorcerer.

It was as if the magic had sought him out, for no sooner had he arrived at the plain, later named the Breezon Plains, and passed near Mount Bahal, than he met a dark sylph who drew him to the volcano's interior maze. The sylph, who refused to be named, had introduced him to the Black Arts of magic and other evil ways. Twenty-eight cycles of the sun had gone by in the lessons in magic. Daektoch had now become an adult. One of the last spells he had been taught was the spell of longevity. Or, was it a curse?

After a lifetime of thousands of cycles of this enchanted existence, he was no longer really alive but merely a corpse indwelt by a mind and magic. His body went though the motions of life, his soulless heart beating in his chest, his fetid breath moving in and out of his lungs, but these were merely physical habit and served no purposeful function. His appearance was that of a mummified corpse; he forewent food and drink. His voice rattled in his chest. He was over seven thousand cycles old.

"Daektoch," spoke Morlah, throwing his voice to the opposite side of the cellar, using his magic.

"Go away. Stop...tormenting me, Elves!" The form went on in its work. "Elves won't let me sleep ...won't let me eat..."

"Daektoch, thou art utterly mad."

The little serpent of a wizard hissed. "I'll make...you mad! Take my Elves and...hide them from me. I hear...you, Druid. I hear you!" The mage persisted in his labors.

Morlah sent out an apparition of himself to engage the wizard. At this distance, he would not need to go into the trance that was required over extended distances; he appeared next to the mage.

"Daektoch," he said in an attempt to secure the wizard's attention.

"What!" blurted the withered mage. Daektoch raised his head and stepped back with a start. "Ah, Druid! What...have you done with...the Elves? Where...have you hidden them?"

"I wast hoping I couldst learn of their whereabouts from thee, Master Mage. I have been...away. I didst come back to find the city abandoned and only thee here. Thou doest not know of their whereabouts?"

"Useless! You're useless...then if you can't help...me. But there was something about you...something about you.... But I don't remember." He walked up to the Druid. The shrunken form looked up into Morlah's face while his index finger tapped through the apparition's sternum, apparently not noticing the lack of substance to his structure. "Yes, I...remember.... I didn't like you...in the past, and I think...I won't now. So be gone, Druid. Get...out!"

It appeared that the mage was quite lost to himself and the world. Morlah released his magic and allowed the apparition to vanish. Daektoch looked about, his eyes darting as if he expected to be attacked, but within a few heartbeats, he returned to his labors.

"Elves! Where are the...Elves?"

Morlah rose from his corner and crept out of the cellar. Daektoch was insane, and whatever information he had possessed was lost. So many times in the past, Morlah would have killed the mage in a heartbeat if he had been granted the chance. But now, to see the frail shell of a sorcerer, his mind gone and probably mostly defenseless, Morlah did not have the heart or malice within himself to kill the ancient wizard. The thought had crossed his mind for a heartbeat, but he could not bring himself to harm the miserable wretch, not even to simply put him out of his misery. The opportunity had been passed up on a couple of occasions in the past, always bringing its regrets, but Morlah had always deferred to what appeared to be a wiser course. And now, Morlah did not think Daektoch would have the ability to do much harm.

Morlah slipped down to the end of the alley and turned back to see if he were followed before dropping his cloak of invisibility. He was depressed. The Druids were gone. The Elves were gone. Even his old nemesis was basically gone. It had been almost heartening to meet up with someone he knew, but now, it was anticlimactic. He felt even more dejected than before.

Making his way toward the north wall, and stopping at the gates of the old battlements to reflect on the conflicts that had been fought there, the labors wrought and the victories won, Morlah felt his mood worsen. There had to be magic within Fate herself in those times. Everything had worked in the Elves' favor, regardless of what was thrown their way.

A span before sunsetting, the Druid left the city through the northeast gates of the newer north wall, what had been the woodworkers' gate, gloom filling him. He was overcome with a longing for death. The sky became as dark as Morlah's reflections.
Enough! Sixteen hundred cycles is enough! Too much!
Morlah yearned to be away from the situation, to cleanse his hands of the whole ordeal...the commission of the Faeries...his revenge on Daektoch's past attempted genocide of the Druids and his own parents. He stopped abruptly. He had forgotten about that. Somehow, he had been in his enemy's presence and forgotten why he had gone on cycle after cycle, seeking for vengeance upon the mage for having poisoned the Druids, his family and friends nearly sixteen hundred cycles past. Was he losing his mind also? To have forgotten such a thing? He wondered if he should go back, but the memory of the shriveled wizard made him keenly aware that he did not have the hatred or spite within him to do anything about it, so he moved on. Daektoch would go on for another course.

Chapter 3

It was a bit after the sunsetting of the next course of the sun when Morlah arrived at the first inhabited farm just east of Mildra. Twilight still hung on the horizon as if attempting to cling to the hope of light, but slowly, the sunlight was driven back by the night.

Morlah transformed himself into an old man and approached the Elves that were gathered about a bonfire. As he drew near, excitement overcame the depression that had been traveling with him. Elves! There were Elves remaining in the land! There were several adults and children present; they were apparently preparing for evening meat, the fragrance of life permeating the air by their very presence.

"Hail," he called in a feeble voice. "Is there any place for an old man to find shelter for the night?" he said, speaking in the Common Tongue.

"Come, old man. Welcome," said one tall, slender male, drawing forward to greet him. "You are welcome to share of our food and shelter. I am Nean of the house of Jandolain. These are my mate, my brother and his mate and our children and some friends. Well-met, friend. Where have you come from?"

"I am Morlah. I came to the port by a ship I had hired, crossed over from Karob on my way to the Homeland of the Giants. But I had a change of mind and decided to stop in Frontmire. I have a few interests that I would like to pursue. The ship I hired will stop for me in six moon's cycles for the return voyage. I had not been aware that the port was abandoned, for the ancient journals I read had it a thriving city and port."

Nean appeared surprised. "Those must have been quite ancient. The city and port have been abandoned for hundreds of cycles. But it is of particular interest, and it may be to you, that tonight is the Remembrance of the *salong*. It is the ancient Elven word for 'vanishing', the time set aside by the Elves that are left along the coast to remember the lost population of Mildra. Tonight, we gather in small groups throughout the South to eat and drink to the memory of the Kingdom of Mildra, its glory and to bring to heart the memory of the *salong* of the people of the city. Tonight, Brandier, my eldest brother, will recount the legend as we do every cycle at this season. Come. Come join us. Sit, rest and warm your bones, old man."

Somehow, just being in the presence of Elves, Morlah felt as if a great weight had been lifted from him. He took a spot near the blazing fire, on a well-wrought pole chair that was offered him, and he warmed himself in the cooling evening air. In turn, but without apparent order or design, the Elves came and introduced themselves to him, adults and children, and bade him welcome. Nean brought him a tall wooden vessel full of light ale.

"Made it myself...one of the better ales you'll find in the south...if you don't mind a bit of boasting" he said, laughing.

Morlah drank heartily, emptying half the tankard in one gulp; he needed something to quiet himself. He sat back and observed the activity about him. He could have wept for the sight of the children, gay bundles of joy running, playing and squealing with delight. The adults also appeared to be sharing the mood and spoke with joviality and intermingled laughter. Elves! Their long, slender, nearly lobe-less ears tapered to a point at the uppermost tips. They all had large almond-shaped eyes, most a radiant sky-blue, except for a few whose eyes were a striking marine-green color. Their skin was fair, their hair a golden blond or platinum color.

Mandalrin, Nean's mate, came over to Morlah with a plate of food. "I hope your appetite is good, Morlah. The food is plain but wholesome, and there's plenty of it." Morlah took the platter from her, thanking her, as she crouched, balancing herself on the balls of her feet, her head tilted to one side. She gazed at him with curiosity.

"What would you have been reading that is so old as to date before the *salong?*"

Morlah groaned within himself. He had simply wanted to maintain a low profile and not attract too much attention. He had found that it was usually easier to obtain the information he needed that way. Now, he was caught in having to perpetuate his lie. Should he simply come out with the truth? But he did not have the time to weigh his choices.

"Let me save you some embarrassment," she continued, her manner soothing. "You forget yourself, Druid..."

Morlah gasped! *How did she know?*

"You forget yourself. I posses the magic of *esord*[1] so I know you aren't an enemy. I also posses the magic *intalon*[2]. It took me a heartbeat to figure it, but it is the only conclusion that could be had. The argentus you carry cries of power. And your 'old man's cloaking' speaks of the magic of a spell of the Arts. They insist that you are a Druid. Exactly who, I cannot tell."

Morlah sighed, mostly in relief; he need no longer pretend. "Can I discard my disguise without alarming the others?"

"Yes. The children all saw you for what you are through the disguise; so did most of the adults. Our magic has evolved into a complex and fantastic phenomenon. Long ago, as I'm sure you're aware, most Elves only had one or two manifestations of the magic, but now, though we have only one or two powerful manifestations, most have a mixing of several others, giving a more balanced effect.

"The change happened after the *salong*," she continued "Some think it's to compensate for the loss of all the others. The magic of *acrch*[3] is the chief communal effect right now, and so, health and long life predominate rather than *igini*[4], as it did in the times of King Jerhad.

"And so, who are you, old man? You bear the name of one who has not been seen nor heard of in my two hundred cycles of life, but who fills the history and legends of our people."

---

1   *esord* – Ancient Elvish for **foe-finder**.
2   intalon – Ancient Elvish for **discernment**.
3   *acrch* – ancient Elvish for **Life and Health**.
4   *igini* – ancient Elvish for **harmony**.

"Two hundred cycles? My child, you don't look a course over twenty!" he said as he released his magical disguise and allowed himself to be seen as he truly was. Though he was nearly sixteen hundred cycles old, he appeared as a dark, short haired, middle-aged man of medium build, showing the evidence of early balding and graying. His face had a long, hawkish nose and sharply angulated cheekbones above a short, prematurely graying beard.

She laughed. "At two hundred cycles, I am hardly a child."

"At sixteen hundred cycles, I believe that I may call you a child."

"Sixteen hundred?" A bewildered look crossed her face as the other adults began gathering about them to listen. One child ran in, taking up a position on the Druid's lap.

"I'm Sannae," she giggled. "I like your old-man suit." Her charm drained the anxiety from his bones.

"How old are you, Sannae?"

"Eight cycles."

"Ah, one who is truly young. But to answer your question, Mandalrin. Yes, I am the Morlah your legends speak of. I was lost in the Druid Sleep and didst not wake, for some unknown reason, until but several courses of the sun past. The Druids art all gone, and now I find that Mildra is deserted. Everyone I knew, except for one, art quite dead." Casting his eyes down, he added, "And methinks that it is perhaps time that I doest follow after my ancestors into the Final Journey."

"Aww. Don't be sad," said Sannae. She reached up and touched him on his beak-like nose. *"acrch evandol, ponday cantalti.* Be happy, Morlah. Be glad of heart."

Instantly, Morlah felt magic infuse into him, strong and sure from the child's finger. It coursed through him in strength, revitalizing every nerve and tissue in his body, and with it came a sense of peace. Not giddiness or joy but heart-healing and soul-mending peace. Sannae smiled at him. She hugged him and jumped down to go play with the other children, leaving him perhaps more healed by her manner than by her magic.

Mandalrin smiled. "She has a very special way, that one. Steeped in the wisdom of the heart and its needs and with the ability to meet them."

"Another ale then, Morlah?" asked Nean, taking the empty vessel from the Druid's hand and replacing it with one topped with a rich head of foam; its full-bodied odor of yeasty fermentation reached up to his nostrils. "We will feast until the rising of the moon, for that is the time that the *salong* took place. Until then, you might interest us with a story or two of your own, for you are full of the knowledge of our history, and I perceive you are a man of truth."

The words stung Morlah; his ruse, his deception in having presented himself as an old man, made him feel like anything but a man of truth now.

"No, no, friend," said Nean, discerning the effect his words had on Morlah. "Your intent was harmless. We don't begrudge you such a trivial matter."

So, Morlah began from the beginning, his youth at *seilstri* and Daektoch's crime against the Druids, and he continued his story all the way to the last time that he had gone into the Druid Sleep. His story went on for nearly two spans, finishing with the latest events and, finally, of finding Daektoch in Mildra.

Talanila, Brandier's mate, spoke. "The mage goes on in his polluted form of magic, surviving course after course. We had at first brought him food and drink when it was found he was there, but then we discovered that he no longer eats to exist. Some had thought to assist him with *acrch,* but he ran like a beaten cur when he was approached with the magic. So, we leave him alone. He is quite harmless at this point.

"He was there the sunrising following the *salong*! It is thought that he has ties to the event, but he is mad and his memories of that night are lost. And even with use of magic, we were not able to discover what part he played.

"Sannae, who is my daughter, has befriended him and visits him regularly. He is quite taken with her and stops his rambling and muttering for the while she is with him."

"You allow the child to be with him?" Morlah asked in disbelief.

"Yes, under the supervision of one or two of the males who are powerful in the more aggressive or war-like types of magic. Though, I assure you, he has never raised a finger against her and actually behaves subserviently when she is about. Besides, she insists on it. And, to quote from an account from the *Elven Histories,* '*...one shouldst always give heed to the wisdom of the magic*'."

Morlah blushed, his own words returning to haunt him some eight hundred cycles later.

"Now is the time, for the moon rises in the east, to tell the tale of the *salong*," called Brandier. The children and the adults gathered in the darkness about the warm glow of the fire, and Brandier stepped to the far side of the fire pit, its low flames and bright hot embers glowing between him and his audience. The Elf was tall, slender and handsome. His voice and manner were gentle, even healthful, filled with the influence of Elven magic. His intense blue eyes were penetrating, and his long hair was platinum colored.

"Now, it is time, my children, to tell the tale of the *salong*. Mildra was a fair city in the southwest of Frontmire. Her beauty and might unsurpassed by any hitherto known. She was ruled, in those times, by King Jerhad, son of Lewin, son of Baros, descendant of another Brandier and Windemere, the last King of the old Kingdom in the north." The rising full moon shone brightly over his shoulder.

"The Elves had emigrated south after their last war with the Trolls and had hoped to find peace and safety to the south of the mountains, away from the troubles that had plagued them and their children in what is now the Breezon Plains. In the times of King Jerhad, in his youth, there came a Druid from Parintia who sent him on a journey...and in fact, as unbelievable as it may seem, my young ones, we have that very Druid here before us tonight. An omen of things to come?" There was a pause, and all eyes rested on Morlah.

"...Well, in perils and dangers, King Jerhad traveled the land of Frontmire, finding a mate, Queen Andreanna, and a friend, the future Commander to the Elven Army, Stanton Farrell. Together, they raised havoc among the Black Arts and the *dark ones* as had been prophesied by our friend, the Druid, at the forging of the Elven blade named *Gildar* in the Dwarf Tongue or *Ember* in the Common Tongue. Ember contained Elfstones, stones of great Earthen magic, a total of seven in number, and with these, the lost Faerie and Elven magic was restored to our people."

And so, for nearly a full span, Brandier, with great oratory and accuracy, recounted the history of the Elves and the coming of Mildra into her glory.

"...and then, on the fifteenth course of the four hundredth and twelfth cycle of the Kingdom of Mildra, under the reign of Mintiel son of Lehland and Kendra daughter of Jerhad, as the moon rose over the horizon...suddenly the Elves of the south coast, having survived attack after attack, cycle upon cycle, by magic and by beast, suddenly roused from sleep as an ominous pall of silence and oppression descended on the land. For several heartbeats, all felt as if they were suffocating, as if the air and magic were being sucked from them with great power. And then, in a blink, all was back to normal, except," his voice became low and hushed, "...except none of the inhabitants of Mildra the Magnificent City were left. *All had vanished*!" His voice was now a whisper.

It appeared that, in spite of all magical advantages, the Elves still loved a good tale.

"Not one was left! Disappeared into thin air! Never seen or heard of again! At the sunrising, when the people from outlying villages came to the city, they found *no one*. No one except for..."

"Master Daektoch," shouted Sannae with glee.

Brandier lifted himself from the stooped position he had slowly assumed through the telling of his tale and said, "That's right! Only Master Daektoch was there and is there to this very course."

A cheer went up from the Elves for a story well recounted, a story that had been told and retold. However, Morlah...was left somewhat stunned, for this was his first experiencing of it, and he was shocked to finally discover that there was no answer to the mystery, only the telling of it.

"Alright, all children to bed," Talanila called out, and they, as one, jumped up and ran into the house with the chatter, noise and laughter that accompanies any such group.

"Morlah," said Mandalrin. "We have room for you with the children in the loft of the house, if that suits you."

"Yes," he responded, drawn back from his thoughts. "Why Daektoch? What is the link? Does he have something to do with the disappearance? Had he been about before?"

"Not to the knowledge of any, but it is all speculation. Greater minds and magics have searched the matter out. The only thing that was ever discovered or thought relevant was that, in the first half-cycle of the moon after the *salong,* Daektoch repeatedly mumbled something about *soiccat*. But soon, it disappeared from his mind, and all trace of the event was lost to all.

"Oh, my!" exclaimed Mandalrin. "This is all new to you, Morlah...and painful. I am so sorry.... Please ask Sannae to hug you when you go to the loft."

"No, I am well."

"I must insist. It does no good for the heart to be heavy. In fact, it does ill to the body and mind. Promise me."

"Agreed. I shall speak to her before I doest sleep."

Chapter 4

Morlah rose early, while the others still slept, and crept down the ladder of the small farmhouse loft, using his magic to silence his movement. At the bottom, feet firmly planted on the floor, he congratulated himself on his undetected escape, even though he had cheated.

"Where you going?" asked Sannae, looking down at him from the loft.

"Go back to sleep, sweet pea. I'm just going out for a walk."

"I'm coming." She scampered down the ladder as quick as a squirrel and was standing next to him as his protest formed on his lips.

"Alright, then. Let's not wake the others."

In the early sunrising's light that filtered through the small windows, he could see the inside of the well-crafted house made of huge fir timbers. He walked to the wall, admiring the skill involved in the woodwork. A constant flow of water poured into a basin through a spring-fed cedar pipe, making a constant bubbling sound.

"Ah, look here, little one," he said. "This wood, if I'm not mistaken, is very, very old. See here...." He indicated a dark line in the grain of one board. "This is fire-scorch that the tree suffered while it was alive...and here another. If I'm not mistaken, this would have been made by a forest fire in the mountains in the second cycle of King Jerhad, and then, this one in the eighth cycle, and then, the tree would have been...." He counted the growth rings. "...It would have been cut at least one hundred cycles later."

Sannae put her hand to the wood. "Poor tree...there was pain there and there," she said tracing the scorch marks. "We don't cut live trees anymore.... Let's go outside."

Here, Morlah saw the flourishing, well-groomed vegetable and flower gardens about the grounds. The barn had a few dairy kine, a bullock used for plowing and drawing wagons and some fowl for eggs, since the Elves had long stopped eating animal flesh.

"Do the boats still go out to catch fish?" asked Morlah.

"No. It hurts them to be caught. We only eat eggs, plants and cheese."

Morlah was taken aback by the frankness and apparent intelligence behind her response.

"Come. Let's go see Master Daektoch," she said.

"I don't know..."

"It's alright," said Talanila, standing at the door. "Here, let me prepare some food to take with you. We *all* long to know where they went, what happened to them, Morlah. Maybe...." She turned and went inside.

As Morlah and Sannae walked toward the city, Sannae talked and talked, much like any female child might prattle on, but her wisdom astounded the Druid. She spoke to him of the flowers drawing up moisture through their roots, compartment by compartment as well as minerals and nutrients to build their leaves, and how the sun activated parts of the plants to change some components of air into their substance.

She stopped and spoke to a caterpillar and encouraged it on its journey to becoming a butterfly. She was able to tell what color it would become; she talked about the forces involved in the formation of different stones and how they had been broken down and polished by weather and time. All the way to the city, Morlah listened intently, caught within the spell of her being.

"Where did you learn all this, child?"

"I didn't learn it. Look! It is all there to see. The land speaks for itself. The magic is in the land as well as in the Elves and...in there." She pointed to the place under the Druid's mantle where his argentus knife hung on his belt. "Can I see it?" She looked straight up into his eyes.

He drew the knife. "Careful. It's very sharp."

Her eyes lit up and sparkled as they rested on the magical metal. "Oh, it's beautiful," she said, running her finger along the flat of the blade. "May I?"

Morlah handed it to her. The Druid could not resist her pleading eyes.

As she took the blade, a remarkable change visibly took hold of her, as if she were in the throes of ecstatic joy. She pointed the knife up to the heavens and threw her head back, eyes gazing up to the sky. She squealed with delight. An immense spire of flame erupted from the blade, up into the atmosphere, turning to snow and then falling back to the ground around and upon them. As the flakes landed, they changed into butterflies of an array of bright and unnatural colors, cobalt blue, mint green, flaming oranges and stunning reds.

"Butterflies are my favorite!" She handed the knife back to a dumbfounded Druid.

"What...how??"

"There are Faeries in it," she laughed. "I spoke to the Faeries, and they did it. Didn't you know?"

"Well, I knew there was magic...but not like that," he answered, slipping the knife back into its sheath.

Later, arriving at the alley where Daektoch resided, Morlah stopped Sannae.

"The mage didn't like me in the past. Perhaps I shouldst hide myself from him while you visit."

She nodded vigorously.

Morlah cloaked himself with invisibility.

"This is nicer than your old man suit," said Sannae looking him straight in the eye.

"Do you see me?"

"Of sorts. I see you as if you are a reflection on mixed up water."

Morlah sighed. This was a whole new realm of magical experience for him. The Elves had evolved, matured, in their magic, and now it was equal to them as their natural senses were, and they used it without thought or effort, like breathing.

"I will set a spell so you can hear me. Daektoch won't hear or see me."

"Hurry. Let's go before he sets out to his walking. He always goes about this time of the sun's course."

It was as she had said. Just as they arrived at the cellar, they met the wizard shuffling up the stairs. Daektoch stopped and looked up at Sannae. He resembled a smiling corpse. Morlah shuddered.

"Sannae, my...dear child," said the mage. "Come in. I have...something for you."

The three descended into the basement, Daektoch making his way to his work place with all the speed he could muster. He returned with a plate-sized butterfly made of pure silver, encrusted with gems.

"Oh, Master Daektoch. Oh, it's so beautiful. Did you make it?"

"Yes. For you, my...love. I *know* where...to find silver and gold and gems... hidden in the...city. I...made it for you."

"You shouldn't have gone through all that trouble, Master Daektoch."

Daektoch was reduced to groveling. "But it...is for you! A pretty butterfly for a...pretty girl."

"Thank you," she said. "You did an *excellent* work of it!" Daektoch reminded Morlah of a dog that had just been praised. The ancient wizard squirmed, bowed, and rubbed his leathery hands together.

"Does it...please you?"

"Oh yeessss! I will put it up by the window near my bed to catch the morning light. Thank you so much, Master Daektoch."

"Sit," he said, sweeping dust from a chair with his sleeve. "Sit and rest from...your walk. Can I get...you something to drink or...eat?" he asked, not aware that he was without either.

"No thanks. I have my own. Do you want some?"

A frown crossed his face, and he shuddered with revulsion at the thought of consuming food. "No, no," he said hurrying away as if disturbed by distant memories. "Elves. Where...are the Elves?" he said slipping back into his delirium.

"Master Daektoch!" Sannae said sternly. "You know you shouldn't do that. Stop it, please! Come and sit, and we can talk. I truly think the butterfly you made me is beautiful. Where are you going to go this course of the sun?" Daektoch came and sat on the stone floor at her feet, while Morlah positioned himself behind the Elf.

"About. Need...to get more silver. I want to...make you another...present," he said regaining the control of which she was the cause.

"Ask him about *soiccat*," said Morlah.

"Master Daektoch, do you know the Elfstone *soiccat*?" asked Sannae.

"Know where...silver is hidden..."

"Master Daektoch, what about *soiccat*?" she repeated.

Morlah slipped the argentus knife into her hand, which was hidden by the small food sack on her lap. Daektoch suddenly looked about.

"Elves!" he hissed.

"Master Daektoch," she giggled, "It's only me. Remember? I am an Elf."

"No! Other Elves..."

"Master Daektoch, *soiccat!* "

He looked at her. "*soiccat?* "

"Yes, *soiccat.*"

Daektoch looked troubled. He writhed about and squirmed.

"Master Daektoch. Shhh. Be still. Quiet your heart. Be as happy as is possible for you. Shhh." The mage quieted and looked back at her with a hideous smile, the only smile he could produce.

"Master Daektoch. What about *soiccat?*" she said, her voice rising to an intensity that made Morlah step back. The room took on a potent air of power that only the argentus could have produced. Yet, Daektoch appeared to be undisturbed by it now.

"Be happy, Master Daektoch. Be at peace..."

Daektoch sighed. "Oh, but I do...love you, dear child. When...you are here, it reminds...me of my youth in ... Pernham, City of...the Mountain...." Morlah thought that if Daektoch's body had not been so long in its deterioration, sustained only by magic, he would have had tears in his eyes.

"*soiccat,*" repeated Sannae.

"She was quite...a stone. Stole her from...the Elves," he said with delight. "Stole it right...out from under their little Elf...noses," he cackled.

"What did you do with her? I would be very pleased to have her as a gift."

The mage fidgeted again. "Can't. She's gone. Someone stole...her from me!" he hissed.

"Shhh. What did you do with her while you had her? You must have had a reason to steal her." He looked at her with suspicion in his otherwise empty eyes for a few heartbeats, wondering why he felt compelled to divulge so much.

"Shhh, you're safe, Master Daektoch. Really. I won't tell. It will be the secret of those who are here only." The wizard relaxed, but his mind was obviously working feverishly. His eyes narrowed and scanned about the cellar.

"Shhh. Be still...be quiet in yourself." He looked back at Sannae, and she raised the butterfly he had made for him to see. This calmed him some, and he settled down again.

"*soiccat?*" she asked again.

He giggled insanely.

"Nooo! Come back to me, Master Daektoch."

"Damned Elves...they got what they...deserved," he spat in a fury. "Tormented...me cycle upon cycle. Killing... my servants. Hurting...me at every turn. I got them back. I made them pay...." His intensity rose with every word. Sannae let him continue.

"Took *soiccat* from under their nose. Made them pay..." chuckled the insane mage.

"How?" asked Sannae.

"Opened the rift...into the Netherworld and let it... swallow them. All gone. Elves are...all gone. Into the Netherworld." He started laughing madly.

Tears flowed down Sannae's face. She snuffled them back. "Master Daektoch," she whispered, the argentus rising to a new pitch of power. "Sleep.... Rest.... Forget. It does your head and heart no good to remember this. I am sorry. Sleep."

Daektoch suddenly went silent and rapidly grew drowsy. He rose, turned and went to the corner of the room, lying down on a straw mattress and went to sleep. The sense of magic in the room abruptly ceased. Sannae hung her head and handed Morlah his knife.

"I feel dirty." she whispered.

"It hurt him to remember! It made his heart sick to remember the ill deeds of his past." She went silent, got up and left Morlah standing, stunned, bewildered and in awe of her.

Morlah caught up to the Elf at the end of the alley.

"Sannae..."

"It's alright, Morlah," she said, hugging her silver butterfly. "It had to be done. There is hope, but I don't know of what. There is purpose I don't understand. But there is also much pain and evil on Master Daektoch's part and in your future in the knowledge you gained."

Then, with words that completely shook Morlah, she looked into his eyes and said, "I'm *just* a little girl, Morlah. I should have been able to live my life without this. But it is done, and I did it of my own choice. *But I'm just a little girl!*" Tears flowed down her face. She turned and walked out of the city, Morlah following behind at a distance, feeling as if he had murdered her.

It was sunsetting when they arrived at the farm. Sannae handed the silver butterfly to her mother, who stood outside. She walked into the house without a word. Morlah stopped while still at a distance, lost and undone, as if he had to tell Talanila that Sannae had died.

"Peace, Druid," she said while he fumbled to find the words. "Do you think I don't know everything that has passed with my daughter, my flesh and blood? I am an empath to my family. Not one hair falls from their heads that I do not know about. Her father is with her. He will comfort her and remove the pain. She is wise beyond all of us; she did what was wise and right. There is no fault, and we do not blame you. You are welcome. Peace."

Morlah sank to his knees and wept. He sobbed great choking sobs until he thought he would die of grief. He sobbed the pain of the centuries that he had lived and for the corruption and evil that he had seen. He grieved the loss of loved ones as tears flowed like a river that sought to drown him. He wept for the loss of the Kingdom of the Elves and the futility of the cycles of his lost labors. He ached mostly because he had been the cause, the instrument, that had brought pain to a pure spirit such as Sannae.

When he finished crying, it was dark. Night peepers and crickets sang, and the night's chill was descending upon him rapidly. He lifted his head to find the Elves in a close circle around him, all on their knees and sitting on their heels, all looking at him. Then, he recognized Sannae just before him in the darkness.

She came forward and hugged him.

"Don't cry, Morlah. I'm better now. Father shared his *acrch* with me, and I'm all better. It was the Faeries in the knife, not you, who asked me to do it. Not you. It's alright. Shhh," she whispered into his ear, putting her arms about his neck. "Shhh, *acrch evandol, ponday cantalti.* Be comforted. Be glad."

The magic that flowed from her would have swept him from his feet had he been standing. Her power was astonishing, having been intensified by the argentus' transfer of its own strength into this little being. For some unknown reason, Morlah again handed her the argentus blade. She pointed it to the sky, and it erupted with the flame of a thousand bonfires, filling the darkened sky and bursting into countless twinkling stars of every possible color; each star then exploded into immeasurable numbers more as they danced in the heavens until the night became as under the midcourse sun.

She turned and handed the knife to her mother as the blade shone with the power of the silver-white metal. All eyes were drawn to it and they basked in the healing, wisdom and life-giving effects of the Faerie magic. As the blade dulled and returned to its usual state, the sun rose over the eastern horizon.

Morlah closed the door behind him two risings later. He would not have been able to face the Elves had it not been for the healing that Sannae had given him. He would have felt like a murderer, a defiler, hiding in their midst. Yet, they all had known when he had returned from Mildra. They had all known what had transpired as if in some conspiracy. No one had further spoken of the matter, and he had just felt grateful to be accepted by them again. His conscience had wanted to nag at him, but the Elven child and the adults had soothed him at every turn. He looked back toward the house and at the silver butterfly hanging in the loft window.

"Leaving?" asked Sannae, perched on a fence rail nearby.

Morlah's eyes moistened for intense joy. Perhaps the Kingdom was gone, but the magic in those who remained prevailed and made the Elves a living utopia, collectively and individually! If the Kingdom had somehow failed, the magic and the remnant of the Elves had not.

"Yes. I doest need to go north and see what transpires there."

"Come, kiss me before you go," she cried out insistently, her legs kicking and arms extended.

He went to her, taking her into his arms and lifting her from the fence, hugging her with a deep stirring of love in himself for the little Elf. He placed her back on the fence, fumbling under his mantle and withdrawing the argentus knife.

"A gift for you, little Elven princess."

She took it, her face beaming. Closing her eyes, she swung it about over her head. She laughed as she swept the blade around in a circle until the entire field about them was thick with blossoming flowers and butterflies. She handed Ember back to Morlah.

"You will need it in the future. You keep it for me. But the gift and its power remain in me and in my heart. You have severe trials that lie before you, Morlah. *acrch evandol, ponday cantalti.* Be comforted...Be glad."

As Morlah journeyed toward Dwarf's Pass, he felt overwhelmed by his experience with these Elves, with Sannae. The Elves he had met here had shored his sagging defenses, especially Sannae. Yet, her admonition about to his future need for the argentus blade was a source of trepidation.

Over the next few courses of the sun, Morlah traveled north on the western coast of Frontmire, heading to the land of the Dwarves. He bypassed the Land of the Gift of the Elves to the Giants, thinking there was probably nothing to be gained in meeting with the Giants who were there, for they did not leave their land and kept to themselves. They were not customarily abreast of the news of Frontmire's comings and goings. At least, they had not been in the past. Who knew, they might not even be there anymore. He did not want to know!

Journeying on, reflecting on his visit and experience with these new Elves, Morlah wondered at how sweet of disposition and refreshing a people they had become. A people without malice, guile or harm. A forgiving people. Not that the Elves of old had been otherwise, for they had always been the flower of the land, the cream on the milk, the nectar of the races. But these excelled!

However, it now appeared that Daektoch might indeed have had a hand in the loss of the Elven population of Mildra. Could he have, by *soiccat*, sent them into the Netherworld? The possibility nearly stopped Morlah's heart! *soiccat* had been used to send some there in the past. But bodily? Those sent there in the past were the dead, and if they inhabited bodies on this side of the rift, those bodies had been left behind, dead. But the Elves had disappeared completely, bodily, the whole of the population of Mildra!

And then, how couldst the mage have used an Elfstone? The Faerie magic was diametrically opposed to his very existence. *If he had...were the Elves in the Netherworld there bodily now? Alive? It couldst not be!* The Netherworld was a place for the spirits who could not make the Final Journey because of their evil deeds; they were forever trapped in the Nethers, doomed to stew in their evil temperaments, never finding rest for themselves.

These thoughts reminded Morlah of the crew of the *Druid Queen*, spirits of the dead, murdered Druids who haunted the waters near Heros, waiting, seeking and pining after vengeance against Daektoch. Perhaps he should see if they were still there. Perhaps they would have information. But to the Dwarves first. From there, he could go to Parnham Bay and attempt to call the *Druid Queen*.

But would they respond? He had infuriated them, snatching Daektoch from under their very noses when they were heartbeats from their goal of being set free to make the Final Journey. They would not forgive him; perhaps he best let things lie. But now to the Dwarves.

It was sunsetting when Morlah arrived at the foothills of the mountain that the Dwarves called home. The soft, peach-colored evening sky seemed to promise better things to come. Behind the mountain named *Dolan* (Dwarf for rock or fortress) was a large valley that was cultivated and settled by the Dwarves; it was inaccessible except through the tunnels in the mountain, surrounded by sheer cliffs that were hundreds of paces in height. The mountain housed the Dwarf Army, one of the three strongest forces in the land.

Finding the Dwarves was like finding Faeries; one did not find them, they found you. It was a matter of walking into their territory and waiting for them to reveal themselves. It did not take long. Morlah had barely set foot across the invisible boundary when a squad of heavily-armed, powerfully-built Dwarves surrounded him.

The short, stout, muscular, bearded folk looked grim and dangerous, but Morlah had many dealings with them in the past and had been a strong ally to them. The Druid expected that this would be a mere formality.

"Identify yourself and state your business here!" ordered the Dwarf Lieutenant.

"Mine name is Morlah the Druid, and I have come to see the King!" announced Morlah.

The Dwarves stepped closer, their weapons ready.

"Off with you, troublemaker! Next time we find you on our land, you will be killed on sight," spoke their leader. With that, Morlah was pushed at spear point, back over the boundary. Morlah allowed himself to be hurried along, sharp steel poking into his skin to the near drawing of blood, for he was confused at his reception. Resistance would not gain him access to the King.

When the Dwarves stopped, Morlah turned back, asking, "What is the problem? I have visited the Kings in *Dolan* for generations and wast always welcome. How have I offended thee?"

"Morlah the Druid is a name out of history and legend. Be gone, beggar!" growled the Lieutenant.

"But I...." His head dropped. How could he expect these Dwarves to acknowledge him after eight hundred cycles of absence? No one would be left that had known him. He walked away with a bilious bitterness rising in his throat. The sky and his mood darkened.

Later, after the sunsetting, with his body hidden in the rotted out trunk of an old Live Oak, warded for protection, Morlah went to the King's chambers by apparition. He materialized where the former Kings had usually spent their work time. There at a hardwood desk sat an old Dwarf, appearing ancient and weary, his gray beard drooping to his ankles.

"Peace, King of the Dwarves. I come in peace. It is I, Morlah the Druid. I have returned and...."

The King was up, war-axe in hand, quickly advancing on Morlah with broad, powerful strokes and crying out to his guards in a booming voice.

"Peace, King!" Morlah cried as the axe swung through the apparition without effect.

The King's Guard burst into the chamber and rushed Morlah with sword, spear and axe. They swept right through him before they realized what was happening. Back they came, the King having withdrawn. Over and over, they swung and stabbed at him, as if they were slaying Trolls by the score. But as they realized that they were not hurting him, instead of quitting and reassessing the situation, they became all the more agitated and riotous.

"Peace! Please! I need only...." But his voice was lost in the din and after several score of heartbeats of this activity, Morlah withdrew from the mountain in apparent defeat. Now, the Druid knew that he did not have the heart left in him to attempt to call for the *Druid Queen* and be treated in like manner by his fallen brethren.

But a trace of good fortune was with him, for when he came to the Human village of BlueHill, he found that the formerly devastated town had been rebuilt and, upon inquiry, learned that he would be able to purchase passage on the *Korkaran Seal* to Breezon. There he could find allies among the Army Commanders and city leaders and through them gain an audience with the Dwarves.

Chapter 5

Star slipped along the rubble-ridden streets of Breezon on her way toward the gates. If she managed to get through quickly enough, she would not be in danger any longer. Not that she actually needed to leave, for this was not the first time she had killed some abusive bastard client; it had happened more often than she cared to remember. The city bands consisted of a multitude of factions camped in Breezon; they did not tolerate a prostitute killing her clients, regardless of the reason. Those who did were promptly hanged.

In the past, she had simply moved to another section of the city where the patrols would not follow onto another gang's turf. But now, it was getting more and more difficult to remember where she was wanted and where she was not. Also, on occasion, the boundaries changed for one reason or another; turf wars were forever modifying territories. Breezon was becoming too complicated. It was time to leave.

Star had spent her entire life here. She remembered her early childhood living within the destitution of the city walls with her mother, never having known her father, who had been but a fleeting fancy and the source of money for another few courses' food.

Then, when Star reached thirteen cycles, her mother had taken ill with consumption, and her condition had rapidly deteriorated, leaving Star alone within the stark stone walls of the dingy one-room apartment that they called home. Around her neck, Star carried two polished, non-precious stones, the only possessions she had from her mother, the only gift ever given her. Her mother's corpse had lain there for three courses of the sun, Star not knowing what to do. Appearing much older than thirteen cycles, she learned how to survive and make her way by using the only resource she had as a female living in a decaying city.

The first time had bought her mother a burial outside the city walls. Afterwards, she had locked herself in her one-room residence and sat in the corner, in a stupor of shock and revulsion. She opened the window of the third story apartment and attempted to vomit into the streets below without success. She could not throw up, for she had not eaten in a few courses.

Finally, hunger and thirst drew her into the streets again. She walked as if she herself were dead, not knowing where she went, but knowing what she was about to do. Things took an even worse turn, for she was snatched from the street, beaten, molested and left lying in an alley. Her mind was clear, and she was aware of everything, yet she felt removed from herself. It was then and there that she vowed that no one would ever lay hands on her to abuse her in that way again and live.

She rose and walked along the stench-filled streets, back toward her home, stopping along the way in front of a building full of men and women who were laughing and dancing. What stopped her was the smell of cooking food from within. In the doorway stood a heavyset woman with a bottle in her hand. The woman leaned with her back to the doorjamb and one foot up against it, and she had taken a couple of hits from her corndrippings bottle as she had watched Star approach.

"Hello, girl."

Star stood silent.

"You don't look too good." An understatement. "You alright?"

Star stood, eyes filling with tears.

"Hey, aren't you Lacey's girl?"

She nodded.

"How's your mum?"

"She's dead. She coughed until blood came out of her mouth, and she died," Star sobbed.

"Oh! ...I'm sorry to hear that. You? What are you going to do?"

Star shrugged her skinny shoulders. They stared at each other for a score of heartbeats.

"You hungry?"

Star nodded.

"Why don't you come in? I'll give you something to eat. When did you eat last?"

Again, Star shrugged.

"How old are you?"

"Thirteen."

"A bit young still, but you do look older...hmmm. Come on in, and lets get some warm broth into you. I'm Sally."

And so, Sally had taken Star in and revived her as best she could. Sally had scrubbed the girl down and found some clean discarded clothes for her, discarded meaning they were no longer fit to wear. After four courses, Sally set forth her proposition to Star: she could stay on and work for her as one of her girls, and she would get room, board and twenty percent of what she earned in addition to the protection offered by the house bouncers. There was no such safety for a girl working the streets on her own.

Star thought she would be sick even as she nodded, accepting the offer. She wondered what the point was of having food to eat if what you did to get it made you vomit. But loneliness, fear and hunger forced her to accept, knowing she had no other way of surviving.

She was an intelligent girl and learned quickly. With good food (for Sally took better care of her girls than most) and a bit of teaching, she soon became a popular beauty. She had ink black hair that with nurturing became thick and flowed to her waist. Her almost black eyes contrasted against her fair skin, and her sharply cut cheekbones made her striking to look at. Sally taught her to use a bit of soot from the fire to accent her eyes. Star also took to her work, its recurring pattern soon giving her a platform to develop from, and she became quite outgoing and as happy as one could expect to be in such circumstances.

Star enjoyed meeting different men and learning all she could from them. She had many regulars, among whom were several from the local patrols. From them, she learned some weapons use, having a strong desire to learn to protect herself and not have to rely on others for her own safety. Under the circumstances, it could have been said that she blossomed. Sally probably had a lot to do with it, for she did take the girl under her wing and gave her love and care, which she had never received, not even from her mother.

Then one night, the first of many to come, she had been beaten by a customer who stuffed a rag in her mouth to keep her from crying out. Having kneed him properly as he tried to mount her, she rolled from the bed, fell to the floor on top of his clothes and quite deliberately took her time turning on her back as he lunged from the bed onto her, impaling himself on his own dagger that she had retrieved from his belt. She had stuck him exactly the way she had been taught, and he hardly even quivered as the knife sank into his heart.

It had taken a bit of effort to get the damned tub of lard off of her. She cleaned the blood off herself, not aware that she was streaking much of it across her face. Clothed in a robe, she ran to Sally.

"Ye gods, child. What's happened?" Sally gasped.

"He beat me." But she would not weep. She hardened herself against the memory of the beast's abuse.

"But all the blood on your face..."

"It's his!"

Sally gasped. "You didn't! You killed him?"

Star nodded. "Son-of-a-Troll had it coming. No one... No one hits me!" She spat the words out with a vehemence that caused Sally to flinch.

"Oh, child...You'll have to go. I can't protect you anymore. You know what the patrol will do to you. You know what the punishment is if one of the girls kills a man.... Oh, no, baby." She took Star into her arms and wept.

Star hardened herself all the more.

Sally told Star to wash more thoroughly and sent one of the bouncers to lock the room. After gathering the girl's scant possessions, Sally took her to the back door and gave Star her pay and a bit extra. She gave her instructions to go to another brothel on the other side of the city and never to return, for the city guard would put her to death if they ever caught her. The door was opened, and Star fled into the night. That had been the first of many such times. She would just get settled in, get to like the place, get a regular clientele that she liked, and then some drunken scum would beat her, and she would have to flee again.

Now, Star decided to leave Breezon. Maybe she could do better elsewhere. She knew how to take care of herself, having learned to fight with sword and throwing knives. She even had some fair skills at hand-to-hand combat. These had all been taught to her by some of her clients at her pestering. Obtaining lessons usually had called for a few freebees away from the place where she worked; soon, Star was considered to be fair or even good by those she trained with. She still carried the dagger of the first man she had killed.

She brushed up against someone as she exited the city gate. One hand instinctively went to the handle of her dagger and the other hand to the two stones about her neck, the mementos of her mother. But looking at him, all she saw was an old filthy beggar whose stench was far worse than most. The odor emanating from him was like a mingling of Human excrement and vomit. He appeared...diseased. He stopped and looked at her as if he were about to speak, but just then, the gatekeepers engaged him in discussion, asking for his toll money. She went on, leaving him behind.

The beggar, a ragged, old man, filthy even by Breezon's standards, with rags tied about his hands and feet for warmth, stood before the northeast gate for a few heartbeats. Then, attempting to hobble past the toll-collectors without stopping to pay his tariff, he bumped into someone leaving the city. He looked up to see a girl wrapped in a well-kept mantle. There was something familiar about her...something that caught his attention, but something that he could not identify.

Two brigands came forward to intercept him. The beggar coughed, blood staining his lips, his lungs rasping and bubbling as if he were drowning in his own secretions. The stench of death oozed from him. The brigands stepped back as the beggar extended his sputum-and-blood-stained hand that held two coppers. He coughed violently again, blood flinging out and speckling the clothes of one of the men. The beggar turned to locate the girl, but she was gone, lost in the crowd.

"Go on! Keep your coin. Get away from me!" the man said tearing his shirt off, casting it to the side and cursing. "Go on, get through." They had no thought for the safety of the city, for allowing plague within the walls, or for their toll. The beggar inched through the gate. At one point, he stopped, just within the walls, turned back as if to speak to them, but instead coughed again, blood spraying into the air.

The brigands retreated with grimaces of disgust on their faces.

He turned and went down a nearby alleyway. Then, slowly, the old man transformed, and Morlah stood in the darkened passage.

⚜

Morlah had made his way to the northeast gates from the docks, for none but sailors were allowed entry into the city via the riverside. So, walking along the waterfront and then the city wall, he had at long last arrived to behold the sight. The doors to the great gates hung askew on their hinges; traffic in and out of the city had to make its way around the edge of one of these doors that jutted out into the opening. Tents had been erected outside the wall, and it appeared as if a small community had established itself there.

Brigands occupied the entryway to the city. This moon's cycle, a group known in the streets as Harland's Band occupied the gate. There was constant struggle and fighting among the street gangs as to who would control the gateway, for he who occupied the opening got to collect the tariffs that were levied to enter the city. Harland's Band was a ragged looking bunch, armed to the teeth, loud and obnoxious. They harassed all those who entered and levied high tariffs according to what they expected each one entering was able to pay.

Morlah had assessed the situation for a heartbeat and gone back the way he had come. He pushed through a crowd of people and emerged on the other side as a very beggarly looking, diseased old man. He turned and, with magic wards in place to prevent taking physical damage, approached the entrance to the city. He did not know why he sought to enter it. The city was in obvious political, economic and moral decay. But for some reason, he needed to see it firsthand. Perhaps. He still could not believe that it had fallen into such a state.

Breezon had once been a prosperous city with a fair and strong government, a strong military and affluence only rivaled by the capitol, Heros. To see it in such disrepair was unbelievable.

Chapter 6

Morlah made his way down the streets, witnessing the degradation and squalor of the formerly affluent citizenry, not knowing where he was going. He stopped and gaped at the hordes of prostitutes, a number large enough that it could have replaced the former army; he saw the rubble and smelled the stench of garbage and excrement. He saw the Humanity that littered the streets, tattered, misplaced souls, observing that there were no children playing or about except for the abandoned and destitute orphaned. Beggars, blind, lame, maimed and diseased folk were as abundant as the prostitutes.

He witnessed two fellows robbing someone in an alley, slitting the man's throat and leaving him gurgling in his blood. For nearly half the sun's course, Morlah walked, moving along in a state of shock. How could Breezon have come to this? She had been the pearl of Human inhabitation in Frontmire. He decided to leave, not wanting to spend the night in its filth.

As Morlah passed yet another blind and ragged beggar, the man lifted his face up toward him and spoke.

"Brother...."

Morlah, frustrated, dropped a copper into the man's cup.

"...thou art a far distance from thine home. Art thou not?"

Morlah had taken three or four more steps before he realized that the beggar had spoken to him in the ancient version of the Common Tongue, the language of the Druids! He spun about, confronting the man, alarm mingled with rising hope.

"What did you say?"

The beggar smiled, his eyes frosted over with age. On closer inspection though, the man's clothes were not as tattered as they had initially seemed; he actually looked clean. The man got to his feet.

"Come with me. I willst lead thee to the others and our hiding place," he said.

"Wait! Who are you? What others? And why do you think you know me?"

"I am Taland of the Parintian Druids. We hadst not been acquainted when in *seilstri*, but I wast familiar with thine face. Though that is meaningless now that I am blind. I am sixteen hundred cycles of age. There art seventy-three of us who didst leave when the fighting began, and we didst come to Breezon where we doest dwell to this time.

"Thou art a Druid. I doest sense the power of the argentus that thou doest carry, Morlah. We hadst wanted to attempt to rescue thee from the Sleep-chambers. Most thought thee to be dead and the risk wast too great, for thou hadst not wakened in a hundred cycles when we left. But come. It is not wise to speak of such matters in the streets. Follow me."

The old man led him down a darkened, dead-end alley and then turned to a boarded doorway. He mumbled a bit, and the door opened, planks and all, and let them in. Once within, the beggar mumbled to the door again and it closed behind them.

"A horse couldst not kick it down. White magic."

Taland and Morlah walked in the dark, down a narrow hallway, finally, coming to another boarded door. After repeating his previous incantations, they were in. They stood in a very large area, perhaps the old dining hall of an inn, lit by white magical orbs that floated about, some stationary, some following men or women at their work. Refreshingly, there were also children present. The room was drab but clean and without the putrefying odors common to the streets. Instead, there was the smell of cooking food. Everyone was involved in some kind of labor, and none had bothered to look up as they entered.

"Campall," called the beggar. "There's someone here to see you."

A man stood and approached them. He was tall and thin, and his hair was dark, his face was appearing dirty from his short, thick, black stubble. Abruptly the man's demeanor changed to that of concern, then disbelief and, finally, joy.

"Morlah! By the gods, can it be? Morlah?" he cried, beckoning to the others to join them.

"I am Campall, son of Solland the smith."

"Son of Solland?" Morlah eyed him suspiciously, looking to see if he recognized his old friend's features in this man. Then, he saw it. There in the man's eyes, the very image of his ancient friend. As recognition appeared in Morlah's eyes,

Campall extended his arms, and when Morlah responded in kind, Campall stepped forward and embraced him.

"Well-met, Morlah. Well-met! Where hast thou been? And more so, what doest thou here?"

Morlah suddenly felt light headed. He swooned, hunger and this event climaxing his emotional strain since his awakening. Or was he being subdued by some spell? He fought to keep his senses but felt himself slipping away from consciousness. Maybe...maybe he could raise a defense in time and lash out at them, he thought, as darkness closed in about him.

Morlah opened his eyes, his vision blurry, not remembering where he had been.

Druids? Had there been Druids? Or wast I attacked? Perhaps just a dream. His memory stirred him to action, but his attempts to move were foiled by bands holding his arms and legs. Someone came into view, and he realized that he could hear the bustle of many moving about him.

"Oh, so thou hast come to," said the woman, who stood over him. In her hands, holding it with a cloth, was a steaming ceramic cup. "Wouldst thou like some broth?" She lowered herself beside him onto her knees, placing the cup on the floor. "Here, let me help you loosen this blanket. In his zeal, Campall wrapped thee as if he were binding thee in thine grave clothes."

Morlah looked down to see tightly wrapped blankets. They pulled away easily once he moved his weight off the edges that restrained him.

"Art thou hungry? I am Selenci, Campall's daughter."

Morlah nodded and sat up. "What didst happen to me?"

She shrugged. "It doest appear that thou didst faint. Perhaps the shock of finding friends thou didst believe to be dead...." She handed him the cup. "Careful, it is hot."

Morlah eyed Selenci over the rim of the cup as he blew on it to cool the broth before drinking. She was pretty but, in some ways, much more attractive than her face warranted. The way her dark hair fell and the depth of her brown eyes against a slightly pale complexion. He sipped at the broth.

"It is good. Thank you."

"Take thine time. When thou art revived, Campall wouldst like to speak with thee."

He nodded, and she rose and moved back to a stove that burned hot by magic. Later, with the children bedded down and the course's labors done, the adults sat about the magical smokeless but very real looking fire, soaking in its heat.

"Morlah," spoke Campall. "Thou hadst been left for dead. After one hundred cycles without thee awakening, it was presumed that thou hadst died as others in the past. But then things didst change in *seilstri*, with some becoming ambitious, and soon the whole situation became factious, and those who were in the Sleep-chambers were forgotten by most.

"A few didst attempt to open the chambers, with great difficulty, for thou doest know how well protected and sealed they were, and didst find the occupants dead. They didst not have the heart to open them all.

"We didst flee when things looked as if they would become violent, though, it didst take nearly five hundred cycles for actual fighting to come to pass. Until then, the politics didst grow fierce and deceitful with posturing and manipulations and such as politicians doest. We didst have no stomach for the matter. And with the outlawing of magic, we didst decide we were better off leaving.

"Breezon wast still thriving then, so we didst settle here. Made our own Sleep-chambers and didst continue in the Druid way to the best of our abilities. In later cycles, people didst become suspicious of us and shunned us because we didst not age as they didst, and so we didst withdraw from our former interactions with them and didst change our speech when about in the streets. Eventually we were forgotten."

"But what happened to the city?" inquired Morlah.

"The city...a dreadful shame," continued Campall with a scowl and a shake of his head. "About two hundred cycles past, Daektoch didst rise again after many cycles of dormancy. He didst want his revenge against Breezon for their part in his defeats of the past, and so, he didst raise Heros up again to take up the old lie pertaining to the ownership of the plains.

"The Breezon Army refused to fight Human against Human. Heros ended up laying siege to the city for six cycles."

"But what of the Dwarves. Why didst they not render aid?" inquired Morlah.

"They didst offer, but Breezon didst refuse to take up arms against Heros; therefore, the Dwarves didst hold their peace. Then, when supplies didst start to become dangerously low, and it became evident that the siege wouldst not end, there wast no way to get a message to the Dwarves. We didst not become involved, being that we were so few and we didst not want to war against any.

"Finally, Breezon's Army didst sortie, and the battle wast engaged, but Heros didst outnumber them four-to-one. Breezon's army wast driven back within the city at great loss. Then, the siege engines didst come and breached the gates, and the city wast overrun in a last fierce battle. In the end, Heros' army simply departed and left us in ruin. They had no intention of occupation or governing. They simply didst pack up, and at the next sunrising, they were gone.

"The city wast left in a desperate state and without government, for all city and military officials were executed by Heros. Small military groups didst attempt to salvage things, but envy and greed were also common, and soon we were left with all manner of factions, each hoping to possess small portions of the city. The result wast that Breezon wast never able to rise again. The groups that didst try to revive her became the very instruments that prevented the reestablishment of a central government. Each didst want to be the leading entity. So, they didst set out warring and fighting each other and finally didst establish their territories in the city.

"There wast talk of returning to *seilstri* for a time, for we knew of its abandonment and the death of the remaining Druids." He spat! "If thou canst call those damned politicians Druids! But when we didst attempt to hire a ship to return, we were refused passage for unknown reasons. Besides, the Parintian population wast hostile to the Druid cause by then. Finally, we didst settle in and never left. We doest have it good here, better than most. The magic allows us to survive where others canst not."

Silence hung heavy for a while, every man and woman lost in their own thoughts pertaining to the matter, reflections recalling somber times.

"And thee, Morlah? What of thee? How is it that thou art found among us this night?" asked Campall.

So, Morlah recounted the events since his waking from the Sleep. "...And now, somehow it doest appear that by use of the Elfstone *soiccat,* that Daektoch hast sent the Elves of Mildra into the Netherworld, though it is very curious that the mage shouldst have been able to use an Elfstone, for his magic is Black and contrary to Faerie or Elven magic.

"But is there no hope for them, Morlah?" asked Selenci.

He turned and looked into her eyes, which were full of compassion and concern, and he found himself moved by her.

"I doest not know. I doest have no more knowledge of this matter than the rest of thee. Canst a living being exist in the Netherworld? What doest thou say?"

There followed a long discussion about the Netherworld and its inhabitants and the little that was known to be as close to fact as is possible pertaining to the matter. They gleaned common thoughts from what they knew of myth and legends. Finally, it had to be concluded that it was not possible for the Elves to be bodily alive in the Nethers.

"But, brothers," Taland, who had been silent, finally interjected. "Thou have not taken into account one thing...."

All heads turned to him.

"Thou hast forgotten that the Elves were strong in Earthen magic."

For a span of heartbeats, nobody spoke, and then realization dawned on them as one.

"Thou doest have cause, Taland! Magic! The possibility mayest exist that they were able to do something to protect themselves. But what? I doest not know. But the possibility doest exist," spoke Campall.

"Oh, no!" cried an older female, Marril, with despair. "No! If it is so, they have been in the Nethers for hundreds of cycles and without hope. How awful!" She covered her mouth with her hands. She nearly wept.

The realization of what she said shocked Morlah as if he had been hit by lightning. His mind and body went numb; he could not feel his hands or feet, and for a few heartbeats, he thought he might black out again.

But then Taland spoke. "Brethren, if this is so, we shouldst see what canst be done."

Morlah revived a bit. "Done?" he said. "There is only one thing that canst be done and *only one*. The Elfstone *soiccat* wouldst be needed to open the rift and allow them to escape. There is no other way. But the stone is lost. Daektoch didst have it but doest claim it wast stolen. Whether it is true or not, I canst not tell, but that is all that his demented mind doest know. And yet, there doest now appear to have been purpose to those events that didst lead me to the knowledge of this...mayhapst..."

"*soiccat*? What do we know of it?" asked Selenci.

"An Elfstone with a long history that hast endured thousands of cycles.

"I doest believe I didst observe one of thee drinking wine?" inquired Morlah, in hope of obtaining some.

"Our secret is out," laughed Campall. "If the city didst know, we wouldst be overrun within the span. Bring the Druid some wine, Selenci, my girl, that he may tell us his tale."

A bit later, Morlah settled himself down with a vessel of red wine. After a few sips of it, which were surprisingly pleasant, he began his account. It was evident he was not going anywhere this night, and so, he took up to the telling of the story with all its merit, not only to pass the time with the telling of tales as a Giant would have done but also to give opportunity to his fellow Druids to examine all details. Perchance they might find clues within his story to solve the Elves' plight.

Chapter 7

Morlah spoke, "I doest begin my tale some ten cycles after the last Troll war in the early reign of Jerhad, King of Mildra. This is how it dist unfold:

"Daektoch hadst found how to rest his spirit and essence in the Netherworld to heal from wounds of magic that he sustained in battle. His body need not heal for there is no true life within. While in the Nethers, Daektoch didst become familiar with some of the inhabitants, one of them being a powerful sorceress, *Kravorctiva*. With the ability to transfer a spirit from the Netherworld to his, Daektoch didst bring her and three of her servants, also powerful in magic, and implanted the three into the bodies of Trolls and *Kravorctiva's* spirit into the body of a girl whom his dark servants abducted from Heros.

"The mage wast lost in an irreparable insanity at that point; it wast the product of magic keeping him alive for thousands of cycles, his intense hatred of the Elves and the overwhelming frustration at having been thwarted at every turn. Fate didst seem to have set her hand against his ambitions. Time and time again, throughout the ages, he didst raise the Trolls up as an army to attempt to destroy the Elves. Time and time again, something didst intervene and lay his devices to waste. He hadst been close once, but Queen Andreanna had risen in the power of Elven magic, a power hitherto unknown, and with one blow, she dist bring all to an end. His existence hadst almost ended, too.

"Much of what I doest tell thee about Daektoch, I didst learn from him during those hours I spent with him, attempting to learn his spell for crossing spirits to and from the Netherworld. I never wast able to retrieve that information.

"But *Kravorctiva* dist have no intention of listening to the lowly worm of a wizard. As an afterthought, she readily didst subdue the mage, his servants wisely giving her their allegiance, and *Kravorctiva* didst begin to plan her own reign of terror upon the Elves. The first attacks were trials to test their powers.

"The magic of *esord*, foe-finder, hadst instantly alerted the rulers in Mildra of that first attack. The Queen, also a possessor of *monit*, didst take on the form of a horse-size, pitch-black owl and flew to the scene, found the child Seleniah, the sole survivor of the raid, and brought her back to the castle. There the King's magic didst allow him to view what Seleniah had witnessed.

"Time and time again, the Boys didst attack, their powers far surpassing that of the Elves; they didst slaughter entire communities, using Daektoch's flying servants as a means of escape and return. The Elven Army wouldst have been a sufficient force to deal with these foes, but since they didst not know where attacks would occur, they couldst not be at the right place at the right time. With great difficulty, the Elves didst finally rally, abandoning the smaller villages, and in larger forces were able to hold off the Boys, *Kravorctiva's* assistants, from committing further atrocities.

"*Kravorctiva* didst keep hold of Daektoch, hoping to extract his secret of crossing from the Nethers. Bahal wast home to a recently awakened Dragon; the beast's existence hadst *Kravorctiva* on edge. Having battled Dragons in the past, she wast not anxious to repeat the task.

"The Raven, the flying Bornodald and I, didst rescue Daektoch from the sorceress, using her fear of the Dragon as a ploy to catch her off guard lest she obtain his secret of crossing to and from the Nethers. Also, I, through studies of the *Elven Histories,* didst discover that in the twenty-first cycle of the reign of Elven King Pavillione, Windermere's great-great-grandfather, a rift appeared in the boundaries of the Netherworld and all manner of foul spirits crossed over to this world.

"After many moon's cycles of battle with these creatures, the Faeries didst intervene, for it was about to become a situation that could have been the end of their world if any more of these spirits crossed over. They didst give the Elfstone *soiccat* to the Elven King, for the Faeries and Elves had regular goings and comings in those times. The translation of the name of this Elfstone wast lost, and it is not known what it means, but as to its use, the *Histories* doest state that the stone had been used to hurl these spirits back to the Netherworld and seal the rift. The *Histories* didst state that *soiccat* wast lost to the Elves shortly thereafter. It wast stolen by a group of Elves who claimed lineage to the throne. Of course, the genealogies clearly doest show that this wast not so. Nevertheless, they didst steal the stone, escaped to the northwestern deserts, and were never heard of again.

"So now, the Elves and I didst see this as a possible answer to return the sorceress and her companions back to whence they came.

"Queen Andreanna, in the form of the Dark Queen, didst visit the Faeries to seek their assistance in the matter of finding *soiccat*. They didst tell her that a form of magic known as *the seeker* existed. They didst name it *ti-ord,* a very rare expression of magic that gave the possessor the ability to find things. There wast no Elfstone manifestation of this magic, and an individual possessing this power wouldst be needed to wield it even if there were one. More so, the Faeries didst say that Seleniah possessed both *monit* and *ti-ord*. The Faeries, after deliberation, didst determine that if *Kravorctiva* were able to cross her cohorts from the Nethers, it wouldst prove a significant threat to the world, and so produced an Elfstone of the magic of *ti-ord* and gave it to the Elves.

"Also, the Faerie King had given her the advice that the Dragon was anathema to the sorceress, and if it were possible, that they should recruit the Dragon into their service, for it would prove to be an invaluable asset. King Jerhad refused to send the child in search of the stone. After suffering much weakening of will from Andreanna's persistent urging and the non-ending assaults by both the Boys and *Kravorctiva*, he was worn beyond resistance. A quest for *soiccat* was undertaken; it was filled with perils and difficulties of its own, with many of its members lost, including Seleniah. The few survivors returned to Mildra without *soiccat*.

"And so it wast that Stanton and Ahliene eventually didst return to Mildra with all hopes of finding *soiccat* lost."

Morlah began bringing his story to its conclusion.

"It wast a great blow to the morale of the Elves, and for six cycles of the moon, the attacks continued, *Kravorctiva* involving herself in the fighting and forcing a confrontation with the King and Queen themselves on a few occasions. But the Elves couldst not deliver the final blow.

"Then one night at the city gates, the guard wast alerted to the presence of a lone child outside the gates. There stood Seleniah, and in her possession, *soiccat*. Unfortunately, neither the King nor the Queen were able to wield the Elfstone.

"The King and Queen, by some accidental combination of their magics didst transform into the Great Dragon Ka and with their army forced a confrontation with the four from the Netherworld. The Dragon Greensmorld didst join the foray, for the Dragon hadst a bone of his own to pick with *Kravorctiva*. Then, quite unexpectedly, Raven didst fly in with the King's son, Rolann, upon his back, wielding *soiccat* in all its power. The rift to the Nethers wast opened with a great stroke, and perhaps with aid from Destiny. Rolann didst drive the evil creatures back into the Netherworld, the rift sealing itself behind them. Lanti, the girl inhabited by *Kravorctiva*, wast buried in the Elven cemetery.

"Within the cycle, Daektoch, who wast imprisoned in *seilstri,* didst disappear, escaping his confinement. Shortly thereafter, *soiccat* didst vanish. Neither hadst it been seen nor heard of again."

"Daektoch must have stolen it," suggested Campall.

"Mayhapst. But now, canst it be found...canst the Elves be rescued if they still doest live? And where is it to be found? The only means of locating it in the past wast with the use of the Elven magic of *ti-ord*. *ti-ord* wast in Mildra. Canst it be found? Couldst any be found who doest posses its magic in such a small population, for it wast exceedingly rare? And then to what end?" The discussion went on for a spell, and finally, Campall concluded that they should retire, for rested minds would think better.

The next rising, having finished break fast, a young Druid approached Morlah. "Greetings, Master. I am Easom. It is mine to keep what genealogies art possible in these times. Come see what I doest have." Easom brought Morlah to a chamber of books, a fragment of what was housed in *seilstri*. He opened a large wood-bound volume. Having turned several pages, he pointed.

"Here we doest have King Jerhad, his descendants, Kendra, Rolann and Inolandi. Kendra didst take the throne, being the eldest, and her heir survived until the vanishing of Mildra's population, the *salong,* as the Elves name it. All her heirs and Inolandi's art thought to have been in the city that night. But here we doest have Rolann's daughter who married Boronn, son of Pleier the farmer, who lived in Klisterie. They didst wed and live there. They didst have one son who remained on and farmed the land with his father. And here I wast able to trace the lineage to this one living heir who didst disappear during a raid by some pirates on Mildra after the *salong,* not but four cycles ago. Her name is not known to me.

"The remaining Elves didst not defend the city, for the possessions within were of no importance to them; however, a little over two hundred cycles later, this heir wast in the city, unbeknownst to her parents at the time, who both have since died. She didst disappear and wast assumed to have been kidnapped by pirates. My point being, Master... there mayest be a *living heir* to the throne. She wouldst be fourteen cycles of age. What is more, it wast rumored that she hadst recovered *Gildar* on one of her forays into the deserted city. That gives us an heir in possession of *Gildar*!"

Morlah fell back into a chair with a thump.

An heir! The lineage of the King alive! All might not be lost. But then, the very thought of the trials and energy it had required to see the Kingdom established tore the very heart out of him. *Perhaps he should let it rest.*

Morlah spent the next half-cycle of the moon with the Druids of Breezon. It lifted his spirits greatly to be among his people again. He thought he might just stay and live out the remainder of his time with them. He wondered if it might be possible to get them back to Parintia; their lot would be greatly improved. He had the magic that could make it possible as they only had the magic of the Arts, but he possessed the power of the Faerie element.

Late in the course before one sunsetting, Campall brought him to the rooftop.

"Morlah, I doest remember when thou used to search out the land with thine orb. Let us see what can be seen."

Morlah pulled his staff that held the argentus orb from within his mantle. "What art we looking for?"

"The Hope of the Elves! Canst thou find the King's heir?"

"No, I doest need to know the person to find them in such a manner. I doest need to have seen them but once.

"Canst thou find *Gildar*?"

"Yes, that is possible." Morlah called up the magic, the silver-white orb becoming a crystalline transparency that somehow appeared clearer than the air about them. It was but a few heartbeats before they beheld *Gildar* on someone's belt.

Morlah's heart leapt at the sight. *Gildar*! The Ember! The knife that he had forged with AlhadStone, King of the Dwarves in *Dolan,* by the hand of the Dwarf smith, Derrin son of Kalborn, the Elven blade containing seven Elfstones of power, the blade used of the Faeries to return the magic to the Elves. The history behind it fills volumes.

Morlah expanded the viewing to include its bearer. It was a female with long golden-blond hair...not an adult, but a girl. They could tell so by her stature; but they could not see her face. And for every effort that Morlah made, he was unable to turn the view to catch a glimpse of her face or profile, as if *Gildar* itself forbade it. Viewing further out, they beheld a caravan in a desert.

"The Gypsies!" exclaimed Campall. "She is traveling with the Gypsies. They art a nomadic people, Humans who doest travel the deserts between Frontmire and the cities of northern Canterhort.

Morlah released the magic that was keeping the view alive.

"Morlah. Thou must find her! If there is hope, it doest lie there."

"But without the Elfstone *ti-ord,* there is no hope. We doest not know how to find one who doest posses *ti-ord*, and hence, we art without *soiccat*. What is the point without it?"

"Morlah, thou doest surprise me. Thou wast of a greater heart than this in times past."

"Mayhapst. But time and trials doest seem to have worn me down, and the knowledge of what I didst wake from the Sleep to find hast been as a final blow. I doest no longer desire this of quest mine, for it hast wearied me and mine heart to the bone."

"Go. Find the heir. There is no harm to it. Find her that thou mayest know her. Let the future care for itself thereafter. Meanwhile, we willst send someone of our fold to the Elves to see if perchance we mayest discover one who couldst locate *soiccat,* and having done so, we willst also go to the Mystic Mountains to see if help may be had of the Faeries."

"The Faeries! That may be a fool's mission. The punishment for going to their land is death unless they have purpose."

"It doest appear, from the story thou hast told, that there mayest be purpose to it all. We willst chance it, for there art many of us who art convinced of it."

Morlah reached within his mantle and removed a small leather pouch. "This doest contain the remaining dust from the argentus ore given me of the Faeries. It is such a small amount that it hast no practical use, yet I have been loathe to discard it. Have those who go to the Mystics bear it if perchance it might gain them favor with the Faeries or at least draw their attention to its bearer.

"As to finding the heir...I willst think upon it."

Later that night as the Druids settled down, Morlah sat off in a corner by himself and nursed a sullen mood. Marril came to him.

"Morlah, please. My heart cries for the plight of the Elves. Please do not abandon them until thou hast proven that there is no hope," she urged.

He began to speak, but she put her fingers to his lips and, rising, left him alone again.

Chapter 8

Morlah arrived in Heros on a small merchant vessel, making his way from the docks to the aptly named Bourbon Street, where the sailors drank and sought the fairer sex. It had been a rough neighborhood in the past. It did not look the better for wear of the cycles. Actually, it appeared plainly dangerous. Making his way into a tavern that had the odor of cooking food wafting from it and finding a table where he could place his back to the wall, he sat, ordering the only item on the menu - fish stew.

Morlah needed information, and the sailors and those that frequented such places were probably his best bet. He finished eating and ordered two ales. When the crudely-fashioned tin tankards were on the table, Morlah motioned to a lone man who sat and gazed into an empty pitcher and tankard before him, as if they held some hidden secret to his future...or maybe...his past. The man rose and moved over to Morlah's table.

"What can I be doin' fer ya, friend?"

"Sit and talk with me.... That one's for you," said the Druid, indicating the second vessel of ale.

"Sure, friend. Always room fer another ale. Wha' is i' you be needin'? I don' s'pec' you wan' me fer me company," the fisherman smiled, revealing a mouthful of teeth that were in serious disrepair and decay. His face was several courses unshaven, and his hair was long and oily, while his body, clothes or both put off a pungent fishy odor that was seriously bothersome.

"I need to know something about the nomadic tribe that goes about the deserts to the north of here."

"Ah, the Gypsies.... They's a bad lo'. Nasty a' tha', me friend," he said, swallowing his ale in one gulp and setting the empty mug back down with a meaningful thump.

Morlah motioned to the barkeep to bring the man another.

"They wander abou' the deser' from the ou'side o' the teritry all the way to northern Canterhor'. Sometime they come as far south as Heros. Usually to ge' supplies or sell stuff they steal. No' tha' they's totally bad, though," he said, dropping some of his bravado. "They be a close kni' group and don' take much to ou'siders. They're hones' folk in lots o' ways, bu' i' don' bother 'em none to take wha' they find... any place they find i'. Go' a reputation tha' they take anythin' no' nailed down. Rumor has i' tha' they loathe magic with a passion...something about no' taking in a witch. Bu' ifin you ask me, they's be the ones who's witches.

"Why if a fella like you or me take up wi' 'em, you come back changed! Heard say tha' some men come back from travelin' wi' 'em, all they do is si' and stare. Never ge' a sun's course work ou' o' 'em again. Some grown men come back and all they do is cry, stare in the fire a' nigh' and wander abou' all the sun's course long and cry. Somethin' ain' natural abou' 'em ifin ya ask me." He downed his ale in a gulp.

Morlah motioned to the barkeep.

"They live by a se' o' laws they have, real strict abou' 'em, though one can' tell tha' they have any by lookin' a' 'em. Bu' they be like bees in a hive movin' the same way and together all the time. Real stric' abou' anyone breakin' 'em laws. Kick 'em righ' ou' o' the group they do. Some say tha' 'em who's gets kicked ou' usually kills 'emselves." His drained mug banged down on the table, whether to emphasize the suicide or need of another ale Morlah could not tell, so he motioned to the barkeep again.

"There be several bands o' 'em travelin' abou', comin' and goin' all over, all one tribe bu' they spli' up and ge' back together and then spli' up into new groups and off into the deser' agin. I's said tha' there ain' no one who can find their way through the deser' like 'em. Can live off cactus an' stinkweed."

"How's one hook up with them?"

"Ain' you gone and heard me, man?" the fisherman said incredulously, leaning forward, his fetid breath causing Morlah to turn away. "They can be a mean bunch, and *no ones* come back righ' in the head."

"I don't have a choice," said Morlah, motioning for two more ales.

"Well, i's like I said. They come to Heros by and by to sell and ge' provisions. Do mos' o' their business abou' this par' o' town. Jus' a few o' 'em come in while the others wai' on the north side o' the canal. Can' bu' spo' 'em; all dressed up in colors like flowers. One would think a man would be 'shamed to dress wi' colors like tha'. I hear the females is worse, and they ea' the hearts of outsiders, the women do, if the men folk 'ill le' 'em. Anyway, you se' youself up and stay pu' in one place. Then le' i' be known abou' the taverns and docks tha' you' lookin' for 'em and tha' you'll pay coin to anyone who can se' you up. Then wai'. Bu' you makin' a big mistake, man," he insisted, reaching across the table and poked Morlah's breastbone with a gnarled finger to emphasize his meaning. "**A big mistake!**"

Morlah pushed two silvers over to the man and took the stairs to the room he had rented.

The Druid had been in Heros for two score courses and was starting to wonder if he would ever get to meet the Gypsies. During his wait, he learned much about the changes that the cycles had wrought in the city. Though not to the extent of decline that Breezon had been subject to, the city was not anywhere near its former affluence and social order. Times were tough, and nobody spent more coin than they needed to. Poverty abounded, and the trash that had formerly been removed by the city and burned outside its limits was now burned within the streets by the populace, if at all. The city guard was lax and corrupt, and prostitutes, thieves and murderers were now tolerated and found in abundance, while the government was hard and self-serving.

It was no longer safe to be about at night if several men did not accompany one. The guild that had formerly run the port was no longer in existence, and now there were several small operations that tended to the port's needs. Prices were high. Service was poor. Heros still boasted a population of some six hundred thousand, an impressive number for any city.

Morlah was finally considering changing his tactics. He was still in the same tavern that he had been in, course after course, his clothing permeated with the rank odor of the place. The smell of the dingy, dirty, smoke-filled room, heavy with the stench of stale beer, seemed to cling to his nostrils. Reduced to twiddling his thumbs, Morlah sat there. Then, he noticed someone standing next to him. Looking up, Morlah saw a small man, whom he vaguely remembered. He nodded a curt greeting.

"You still lookin' fer the Gypsies are ya?"

Morlah nodded.

"You said you'd pay a small gold?"

Again, Morlah nodded.

The man stuck out his dirty hand, palm up, toward Morlah.

"Where are they?"

The little man looked over his shoulder and turned back with a shocked look on his face, as if he had lost something. Then, he looked over the other shoulder and finally turned all the way around. "Oh!" he said to someone behind him. "I thought you'd gone." He moved aside to let Morlah see a well-groomed man, dressed in flamboyant colors of immaculately-maintained, fine silk. He was clean-shaven except for a thick black mustache that matched the color of his hair, and a broad smile lit his face. The man had sat down and propped his feet up onto a nearby table.

"That's him there," said the small man, sticking out his hand again. Morlah tossed him a gold, and the man ran from the tavern.

The Gypsy lost his grin, narrowed his eyes and said, "What you want with the Gypsies?"

"I need to go north to Mallion," he lied. "I was hoping I could travel with you to get there, since I've never been there before and am not used to desert travel."

"Sure. Why not?" Then dropping his feet to the floor and leaning close, the sweet scent of fennel on his breath, he said to Morlah, "Are you not afraid?" His broad smile returned. "First you buy me two or three ales. Then you pay me in gold. Hmmm...." His hand went up to his chin and eyes turned toward the ceiling. "One small gold! Yes! Then you pay the lead-post one large gold and tell him you paid me one silver if he asks." His eyes sparkled at something that deeply humored him.

"The price includes food and water. You worry about your own bed. Some wagons have beds made of boards that hang on ropes beneath them that can be rented. That will cost more."

Morlah did not need to cue the innkeeper; he came to the table with four tankards of the warm ale that was served there. Morlah pushed three of the vessels across the table, followed by a small gold. The Gypsy bit the coin.

"I am Martino, one of the posts to the caravan. Welcome, my friend. Welcome!"

"What's a post?"

"Ah, yes.... The post...is a position like that of what you would call a sentry, only it carries much importance and dignity. There are eight posts to every caravan. One lead-post who is the leader of the whole band and seven others. Four ride by sunlight and four watch in the night. We get our pick of the finest and fastest horses that are bred by our people. It is a position of honor and is highly sought after.

"We leave at sunrising, for we have finished our business here. The caravan is north of the canal. I will come by and get you one span before sunrising."

Morlah reached across the table and retrieved his gold. "I'll pay you then."

Martino laughed. "Not as foolish as I had first thought. Very well." He got up, leaving Morlah and the three empty tankards, but not before reaching across the table and finishing Morlah's ale. Then, he was gone.

One span before the rising, Morlah stood outside the inn waiting for Martino in the pale gray predawn. He had not been there long, wrapped in his drab-brown mantle against the cold morning mist, when he sensed someone creeping up behind him. A normal man would not have noticed the stealthy approach, but Morlah was not a normal man.

Just when the stalker was near striking range, without turning Morlah said, "Martino. Are we ready to go?"

The Gypsy laughed. "Got eyes in the back of your head, outsider?"

Morlah handed him the gold coin, and they walked down to the docks where an oared tugger waited for them with four men at the oars, unlike the eight or twelve that would man them when the tuggers moved ships in and out into the harbor.

At sunrising, the sun now a brilliant-yellow orb sitting on the dark-blue waters of the Maring Sea, they landed on the north side of the harbor where another Gypsy waited with three horses.

"You can ride?"

Morlah nodded; he had ridden Bornodalds, a feat few could perform.

One-quarter span later, they arrived where the caravan was waiting for them. As they galloped up, one of the posts released a high-pitched whistle, and the wagons started moving. The covered wagons were painted in brilliant colors; stretched out in single file, the caravan resembled a rainbow. The front and rear ends of the wagons were framed in wood and boarded, with a door hung on each end. The framing also extended a pace out beyond the wheels providing much needed space within. From there, the canvass sides went up and followed the arched front and back ends of the wagon. Martino leaned over and took Morlah's reins.

"You walk from here unless you can buy space under a wagon. Mamma Cituro!" he called to an old lady on a nearby ox-drawn wagon. "You want to hire out your boards to this outsider?"

She nodded. "One silver for seven courses. Pay in advance!"

Morlah gave her enough for one moon's cycle.

Does she look like she might eat a man's heart? he wondered.

"If you are smart, you will walk a while. Keep the blood in your head clean," she instructed. "Later, you come from behind the wagon and climb on the bed. I will not stop. You need to learn to move quickly. I stop for this one time. Stow your pack and bedroll. Keep your walking stick."

Midcourse of the sun, the heat became intense, so Morlah hopped aboard his "bed" under the wagon to get out of the sun. His bed was comprised of a few thick planks nailed together and suspended by coarse ropes. There were canvas drapes hung about to keep the worse of the dust out. The Druid had noticed that the whole of the caravan moved as if in a trance. Drivers slept at the reins, while riders slumbered in their saddles. Some slept in or under wagons, and others appeared to sleep as they walked. Except for the posts.

Two posts were out ahead or were coming and going from behind, while the two others traveled along a few thousand paces out, always moving forward and back, investigating every possible site for an ambush or danger. These men were in a constant state of alertness.

Soon Morlah was rocked to sleep by the swaying of the plank bed.

Then, as darkness closed about the camp, after an unrestful course of being jostled beneath the wagon, evening meat over with, pots and pans washed and stored, two boys appeared and sat on some short-legged stools. One held a twelve-stringed lute, a high-pitched instrument, and the other a six-stringed lute of a lower pitch, used for rhythm. Behind Morlah, a panpipe began a haunting melody. The twelve-stringed lute began to play, strings picking their way through a swirling of evocative notes, while the six-stringed lute wove its own song amidst the first's voice.

Somewhere on the opposite side of the bonfire, Morlah heard the woeful lamentation of a fiddle, weeping its song into the night and joining the other instruments. In the darkness, he could see the fiddler standing, lit only by brief flashes of firelight, moving as if he were making love to the violin. Castanets entered the harmony, clapping their way into the Gypsies' incantation. Elsewhere, a tambourine joined in, sending its rhythm into the night.

Each instrument sang its own song of life and death, of rivers coursing their way through valleys, of waters that cascaded down snowcapped mountain ranges, of pain and sorrow, of pleasure and ecstasy. Each instrument intertwined with the other. Pain was joy and sorrow a celebration. The music, though sad and eerie, was at the same time lively, joyous and filled with laughter: a celebration of life, erasing the pain and severity of the Gypsies' existence in a harsh and desolate wilderness.

The music went on into the night melody after melody. It was not possible to tell where one started and the other replaced it, yet all wept the same plaint, sang of similar celebrations and told a familiar tale in varying ways.

Soon, the music became intoxicating, mesmerizing, more so than the wine, which was too strong. Couples moved about the bonfire, dancing slowly, circling each other as if about to enter into combat. Heads were held high, and arms swayed to the rhythm as if blowing in the evening breeze, while lively colors from the females' skirts swirled, flashing in the firelight, dazzling the eye. The women whirled and turned to meet the men who swept about from the opposite side.

The men strutted with confidence and assurance, leering lustfully at the women who led them about the roaring fire. The scene wheeled. The music moved and breathed with the dancers and those who looked on. As the fervor increased, those who were lovers pressed closer and closer, hands caressing bodies now turned sweaty in the cooling night.

Morlah was enchanted. Had he faced Black magic, he could have protected himself, but now he was defenseless, caught up in the spell of life, love and lust. The bewitching that was being played and danced before him was that of being alive, of being Human. The music told him of his pains and joys, of his hopes and fears, of his triumphs and discouragements.

Then, *she* was before him, dancing alone with her back to him, her body swaying to the rhythm of the night. Long black hair flowing thick and lusty swayed to the barely perceptible shakes of her head. Rich dark brown eyes, which were half-closed, watched him from over her shoulder, her hands as if following some unseen pattern etched in the starlit sky above. Tiny bells that were tied to her fingers tinkled in time to the music. Her feet stamped the hard sun-dried earth, yet without making a sound. Her twirling hips were round and her breasts firm, her lips lush and her skin vibrant with youth, life and health.

Intoxicated with music and wine, Morlah became lost within her movements. His eyes followed her well-formed calves up to her skirt's fringes. Things stirred within him that he had not known in hundreds of cycles. His loins filled with the ache of want. Her hand swept down, and a finger lingered, slowly tracing across his cheek. Her skirts brushed against his face, the fragrance of sweet sweat mixed with musky perfume filling his nostrils and lungs and making his senses reel.

Morlah became light-headed, and his body moved with the living tempo that embraced him. Perfect white teeth flashed at him from her seductive smile while the other dancers rocked to the gentle beat. Music undulated throughout the camp. Old and young *danced!*

She reached down and took Morlah's hand; it felt as if he were levitated up onto his feet and carried to a tent off in the darkness. The music went on as the lovers, the Gypsy and Druid, worked in the hot night, bodies writhing in ecstasy, lost in the lamentation and rhythm of the music, lost to the reality of the world that they lived in, lost to all but each other.

Night after night, the scene was played out. Night after night, the dark-eyed female danced for him, luring him deeper and deeper into herself and into the web of her spell.

Chapter 9

One night after they had joined up with another caravan, she danced yet again for him as he watched, his life now drugged with sensuality. His purposes were forgotten, his history gone. He lived for her, for her love and his lust for her. He was lost, not knowing where he had been, not knowing where he went. Her body swayed, drawing him, pleasing him, as the strings sang in the hot night. It was all as it had been and as it promised to be. Death would come and claim some. Birth would replace those. And the Gypsies would *dance*. They would continue living for their music and song. And they would *dance!*

And then, as a young girl walked by, he saw it! He became deaf to the music. Blind to his lover. Numb to his emotions. His heart beat violently within his chest, and his breathing became ragged. He had seen *Gildar!* There on the girl's hip, he had seen the unmistakable handle of the knife that had been forged with Faerie magic. The seven stones, Elfstones, within the handle clearly declared that this was indeed *Gildar*.

His lover, for he knew not her name, stopped dancing and kicked the wine glass from his hand.

"What? Do I not please you?" she pouted. She reached down, drawing him after herself. "Come, I know other ways to please a man." She led him to her tent, but he was not with her. For he had seen *Gildar*, the Ember. The knife forged by the Dwarves. The blade instilled with the Faerie element of magic. The handle that contained the seven Elfstones of power. The object at the very heart of his quest. Morlah was sober now, awakened from the trance he had been bound in.

Later, the Druid's tears flowed, mingling with his sweat as the two lovers danced the dance of love with each other, hungry mouths locked together in passion. She did not know that he wept. His hunger for her, his hunger for the life he had missed, burned hotly within, the hunger of hundreds of cycles of denial. The music outside played on as he unleashed his lust, as he consumed her passion.

*But he had seen **Gildar**.*

He mourned, he wept, he died as his reality came crashing in on him, as he found himself torn out of the fantasy that he had become enthralled within.

How many sunrisings hast gone by? How many nights hast we been lovers? How many times hast the sun set? How many countless leagues hast been traveled? All were lost in a blur, lost and uncountable.

*But he had seen **Gildar**.*

Outside, the fiddle took the lead, its strings weeping with melancholy, the crying instrument singing his song, recounting the Druid's tale. It grieved with him. It cried with him. It wept for him. It promised him love. It promised him death. It called him back as a child to its mother's arms. It promised to take away his pain, to soothe the hurt, and to quiet his brain.

*But he had seen **Gildar**.*

Then, later in the night, she drove him from her tent. "Go away! You don't love me anymore," she pouted. But she was without pain, for tomorrow night, there would be another. The music would again play to lovers' movements in the darkness. And once again, the Gypsies would *dance!*

The sunrising found Morlah on his plank bed under Mamma Cituro's wagon. He felt hung over, but he had not had all that much wine, not like the other nights. As the caravan prepared to move on, he remained where he was and watched the activity about the camp. His heart was sick, sick for having lost her and sick for having forgotten why he had come to be with these people. Now he was torn. He could take up a life like this and remain lost to the world, lost to the Faeries' purposes and his quest. Here he could live out the remainder of his courses in song and dance...and *her,* if she would have him back. He would no longer trouble himself with the business of the rest of the world. He would forego the Druid Sleep and die a natural death as a natural man.

But the Faeries' commission haunted him. He had devoted most of his life to it; it would not be easily forgotten.

Is it possible to forget it? Can I walk away and not look back?

Then, she walked past the wagon where he lay. Morlah recognized her walk, her dress, her legs. Rolling out of his bed, he emerged from under the wagon, a ruined man, ready to follow her to the ends of the earth, knowing that he was a fool. Hundreds of cycles spent in exercising the power of his mind, in self-discipline and focus had all vanished. He understood that she changed lovers as often as the moon changed its phases; still, his self-control was gone.

The lead-post whistled, and the wagons began moving on, heading north. The other caravan that had joined them for the night turned westward. Morlah noticed that there had been an exchange of some kind. Several wagons that had accompanied the train that he was traveling with turned and went west, while some from the second caravan joined the northbound train, waiting to pull up the rear. *She...*went north, walking, as was her custom under the early sun, at the side of her wagon.

Morlah fell into step alongside Mamma Cituro's wagon, his eyes burning holes in *her* back as her hips swayed as only a female's could. He wondered where *Gildar* was.

*Was the girl who carried the Elven blade going north or west? Had she been with their group or had she come with the others? Will I see her again! Will I see **Gildar** again! And what of the girl? How had she come by the Elven blade? If she traveled with the Gypsies, she could have bought it, stolen it or found it.* It dawned on him that finding the knife might not put him any closer to fulfilling his quest, that of finding the Elven heir.

Damned Faeries!

Morlah had fulfilled his purpose in the past. He had found the heir to the Elven Kingdom. He had helped the Elven heir come into the magic and had seen the Kingdom reestablished in magic, power and might not ever known or seen before. Then, after countless cycles of the Druid Sleep, he had woken to find it all gone. He could have wept for the tragedy of it all but was too desolate within himself to do so.

Why should I pick up the torch again? It could be another six or eight hundred cycles to see things only partially restored.

The sun grew hot.

About one span later, he mustered up the courage to come up and walk beside her.

She looked at him and laughed.

"You are not experienced in the ways of our people," she smiled, her smile fueling his need for her but also cutting him deeply. "You look like one of the outsiders. Once they have tasted of Gypsy love, they are as those who eat desert mushrooms and have them suddenly taken from them. You are also not experienced in the ways of a man with a woman, are you?"

He shook his head.

"You could always kill yourself," she mocked him. "It would be easier on you, for you love like it was your first time, and you look as if it is the first time that you have lost your heart."

"Actually, it is," he mumbled.

Then, she reached over and touched his arm, and with compassion in her voice, she said, "I am sorry. I know that it is a painful time, the first loss."

"I don't know your name."

"My name? Ahhh, but a name is a very powerful thing," she said taking on her indifferent air again, resuming her march. "There are times that a name should be guarded and kept. To give your name to the wrong person can be to one's demise. It is said that among the wizards of the South, that one can simply speak his true name and render the mage powerless."

"I have heard that it is so, too. I am Morlah." The air had grown dusty from the tramping of a multitude of feet and turning of wheels.

With mischief in her eyes, she glanced at him. "I knew not your name, but I think that I have rendered you powerless." She pouted to hide her smile. "Lohlitah is my name. It means *Flower of the Desert*. Do you think it suits me?" she asked, continuing to taunt him, but not in malice.

"Yes. A beautiful, fragrant flower at that."

"Not exactly...for it is a shrub that grows thick with thorns as well as the sweet and fragrant blossoms."

"Then, I am sure it is a fit name for you."

She burst out laughing. "Well done, Morlah! A well placed knife into the prickly shrub."

Her laughter captivated him and made him lust to possess her for his own and forever. She was indeed the *Flower of the Desert*. But he loved her. He loved her spirit, her brazenness, her fire. It was such a contrast to what he was and had been. He would gladly impale himself on her thorny branches if only he could once again smell the fragrance of her passion.

"Would it be possible...I mean would you...I would like you to.... No." He sighed deeply. "I *need* you to dance for me again," he finally managed, not able to tell if he had begged, pleaded or merely stated a fact.

She stopped, staring at him with her dark eyes, hands on her rounded hips, head tilted to one side. "I thought you did not love me anymore."

Her pose slew him.

"I was distracted by something else. It wasn't you. And as for me loving you...." The words stuck in his throat.

Lohlitah turned and followed after the caravan, leaving him standing in his adolescent-like awkwardness. Catching up to her, he spoke, trying her name on his lips.

"Lohlitah." The name came out in a whisper. "Though I am a fool and I am not sun-crazed, I know you have had many lovers and that you will most likely have many more. I know men have sworn their undying and eternal love to you almost as many times as the sun has risen. I would be more of a fool to speak the words to you, only because you have heard them too many times and without meaning... but...yet, I am enough of a fool to do so anyway. I love you with all of my heart, soul and being. I will love you forever. I have never been in love with a woman, and I have never lain with a woman before you.

"But I have never smelled the *Flower of the Desert* before either. I have seen many roses and other flowers whose sweet fragrance didst turn the heads of many men." His speech slipped back into the ancient form of the Common Tongue. "But not until now hast mine head been turned by any flower, nor didst I desire any. Until now."

She stopped again, her full lips forming the pout with which she said and hid many things. She spoke, sternly. "Then you still love me?"

"More than life."

"Alright. I dance for you tonight...maybe." She jumped up onto the rear of the wagon she travelled in. Just as she disappeared through the flaps, she turned her head, looking at him from over her shoulder with half-closed eyes, in the way she had the first time she had danced for him. "I sleep now. You should do the same. Oh...and *if* I dance for you... you should get some real clothes. The desert is not a place to wear those dark robes. Besides, they do not become you, and they stink."

Chapter 10

⚜

Morlah lay awake, thinking of Lohlitah and rocking in his bed under the moving wagon until the sway left him to doze. He finally fell asleep as much from emotional exhaustion as from physical fatigue. The caravan moved on. He understood why everyone traveled as if in a trance. They slept as they journeyed, whether walking, on horse back or in their wagons, resting up for the night and *the dance*.

It might have been three-quarter sun's course when sharp whistles awakened Morlah. Lifting the cloth drape, he peer out from beneath the wagon and attempted to see what was happening. The lead-post's horse galloped by, flying toward the rear of the train, his whistles repeating over and over.

Suddenly, Lohlitah appeared next to the wagon. "Bandits! Stay where you are. You will be safer." Then she was gone.

The wagons quickly formed a circle as the men pulled bows from them. Morlah heard the thunder of horses from behind him and turned to see more than four score riders closing in on them, all brandishing longbows, some with arrows whose oiled cloth tips were aflame.

Morlah did not stop to think what he was doing. He did not consider that a display of magic would alienate him from the Gypsies; the old Morlah was back. Reaching into his mantle, retrieving his argentus orb and attaching it to the staff that he kept in his bedding, he dropped to the ground. Emerging from between the wagon's wheels. The Druid stood up and took off in the direction of the Bandits.

"What are you doing? Fool!" called the lead-post.

Calm and composure claimed Morlah. Strength, determination, and focus returned, as if he had awakened from a dream, the magic within the argentus orb leaping alive, responding to his intention. Stopped and down on one knee when some sixty paces from the caravan, with his staff firmly planted to the earth, Morlah raised a magical shield to protect himself from arrows.

How serious art these Bandits? I mayest only have to scare them off.

Morlah eyed the lead horseman over the top of his orb, as if taking aim with a crossbow, although aiming was not necessary. The Druid released a surge of magic that would hit the man like a stone. A couple of heartbeats later, the Bandit's feet flew up into the air, and he rolled off the horse's haunches, falling to the ground. He was nearly trampled by those who followed. The man lay unconscious with a goose egg forming on his forehead.

Stopped, the Bandits glared angrily at the circled wagons and then back at their fallen leader. Another of them went down, then another and another. Fury rose in their faces, and their cries were filled with murder. They turned and rushed on toward the caravan. Now, they fell two and three at a time, until there was only a handful left, and they still were out of bows' range.

Halted, obviously wanting to forge on, their good sense finally took over. Their curses could be clearly heard even at that distance. They turned, went back, stopping at each fallen band member. They tied the unconscious men up on their mounts, which were being gathered, and, eventually, with six long strings of horses secured to each other, escaped the way they had come.

Behind him, Morlah was aware of the ominous silence as he stood and stowed his staff beneath his mantle. As he approached Mamma's wagon, the eight posts met him.

"I willst get mine belongings and go. I wouldst appreciate it if thou wouldst allow me to fill mine water skin." He gathered his bedroll and few belongings. Everyone stood back except for the posts, who scowled at him, arms folded across their chests.

"Wait! Morlah. Don't go!" Lohlitah rushed to his side.

The lead-post glared at her. "Get away from the witch, girl," he spat.

"He saved our skins, and you would turn him out? It is you who is a witch then! Besides. I *claim* him and *place my cover* on him!"

"You do what?" the post hissed. "You cannot do it. I will not permit it."

"But she has. The words are spoken and cannot be revoked by any but she," said Mamma Cituro, confronting the post, poking him in the gut with the handle of a whip. "It is the law! Will you go back on the law, Petrosis? You who are sworn to uphold it?"

"But he is a witch! The law clearly says we are not to house a witch."

"But the law does not say she cannot *place her cover* on him. And once that is done...then he is one of us and one of ours."

"No!" cried Petrosis, turning to look for help from the others, but they cast their vote against him, turning their backs to him, heads raised high in defiance.

The law of *placing one's cover* on someone was most sacred, pardoning murderers, rapists and those guilty of all manner of vile deeds if someone stepped forward and *claimed* the guilty party and *placed their cover* on him. In ancient times, it had been done literally. The one *claiming* the accused would cover them with their own body or a large basket to protect them from assault. In this present age, the words were sufficient, or rather, the sanctity of the law was.

Once *claimed,* the accused had to be accepted back into the tribe, and that without prejudice. The accused also became the property of the one who *claimed* them until a release. The law limited the practice to that of once in a lifetime for both offender and the claimer; Lohlitah had just used hers.

"Methinks, that I hadst best just leave," whispered Morlah to Lohlitah who stood between him and the clan.

"Leave?!" she cried, turning on him and striking him stiffly on the chest with opened palms, shoving him back forcefully. "You belong to me, witch! If you leave, it will be the tribe's duty to hunt you down and bring you back in chains or to kill you if they cannot. You are my property, witch. Stay put! Besides," she whispered, drawing nose-to-nose so that only he could hear, "I had hoped to dance for you tonight. Come into my wagon, and I will explain the custom.... All is well."

"Petrosis," Mamma continued, rounding on the lead-post, preventing him from following Morlah. "You will abide by the law or lose your position as post. Do not force my hand in this. You are a strong-willed child, but I will beat this out of you if I must. Go now. We still have one-quarter span of sunlight for travel. Tonight, the *whole* tribe dances again, and because *the witch* was here to fight for us. Be glad!!"

Inside the wagon, Morlah said, "I shouldst just go. Mine presence willst only cause trouble."

Lohlitah put her hand through a pocket in her dress and pulled out a long slender dagger that she carried strapped to her thigh.

"I hadst not seen that there before," he said, somewhat puzzled.

Her dark eyes turned hard and evil. "There are many things you do not know, witch. But this you should know.... If you leave without my release, I will hunt you down and kill you myself. My honor among my people is at stake. I will not be put to shame by you now that I have *placed my cover* on you," she said as she pressed the knife's point to his throat, pushing it through his skin and drawing blood, but not doing any real damage. "I have killed men...even lovers before. Do not test me, witch! And besides...." She withdrew the knife and kissed the wound she had made, licking at the blood, "tonight, we *dance!*"

That night, the Gypsies danced with a renewed intensity and fervor. The events of the course and their near catastrophe inspired them and renewed their zeal.

Again, Lohlitah danced for Morlah, and she even got the Druid to join her in the circle for a while. It was evident that he was not one of them. Later, she led him to her tent and began removing his clothes. He stopped her.

"Just doest lay with me for a while," he said lying back and pulling her down so that her head rested on his chest. Her perfume made his head swim with desire.

"But you are strange, witch. No man has ever asked this of me, knowing what he *could* have."

He ran his fingers through her thick black hair. "Tell me about yourself, Lohlitah," he said, changing back from his native speech of the ancient dialect.

"About myself? I am Lohlitah. What else is there?"

"I expect that there is much more. What do you like? What makes you happy? What do you want from life?"

"Again I say, witch.... You are a strange man."

"Morlah, please...."

"Morlah. That is a funny name. What does it mean?"

"I don't know if it means anything. It's just a name."

"Ahh, that cannot be. All names must mean something. We have a custom among my people that if the meaning of a name is not known, that we should give it a meaning, for all names should be with a meaning. If we do not know it, we make it up whether it be true or not. Let me see...Morlah.

"My father used to call me Moe."

"Is he alive?"

"No. He died a long time ago."

"Morlah...I think it means hidden. Yes, that is it. Your name means hidden, for you are a man who has many things about him that are hidden," she said, her face becoming suddenly joyful in the darkness of night.

"Tell me about yourself, *Flower of the Desert*."

"What is there to know? I am Lohlitah...I dance, I love and I travel by the sun's course. What more is there?"

"What is your favorite color?"

"Red. Crimson, passionate red!" Outside, the music played in the still desert night.

"What is your favorite food?"

She paused for a few heartbeats, thinking. "The salty goat cheese made by the Mallions to the north."

"Would you like...or do you have children of your own?"

"I do not have children. You make me speak of things that I have not spoken of in this way. The men I have known have not asked such of me...I drink the elixir of the stinkweed, which prevents me from bearing. But maybe, some course, I would like to have a little Lohlitah," she said, smiling to herself. "I would dress her in red and teach her to *dance*. Her hair would be long, black and straight, and she would steal all men's hearts."

And so, Lohlitah talked on, Morlah having opened her heart with a few uncomplicated questions. She talked on into the night, sharing her dreams with him, telling him much of her past, speaking until the three-quarter mark of the moon's course. Finally, she fell asleep in his arms.

The caravan ambled on northward. They were in no hurry, the Gypsies coming from nowhere and going nowhere. They lived onto themselves and were without the constraints of time.

On the fourth course since the Bandits' attack, Petrosis rode up to Morlah as he walked in the early sunlight, stopping his horse uncomfortably close to the Druid. The lead-post leaned down from his saddle and said, "Listen, witch. I do not like you. I do not like your presence among our people. But it will take more trouble than you are worth to do anything about it. So we call it a truce, eh?" He reached down and gave Morlah a couple of firm, but painless, slaps on the cheek. The broad grin that was so common among the Gypsies spread across his face.

Serious again, he said, "Only...no more witching. Truce? No more witching and I can live with you." He turned his horse, not waiting for a response. He maneuvered his horse's haunches to push Morlah aside, and he sped off to the rear of the caravan.

That night they sat about the bonfire; Morlah had the presence of mind to ask Lohlitah of *Gildar*. Wood was abundant in the desert, for it had not always been a desert. One could always find timber a little below the surface of the sand or where the wind had again exposed it. As she danced before him, Morlah pulled her down to himself and drew her close with her back to him, his arms lightly wrapped about her. After he paid the necessary tribute of kisses and nibbles to her neck, she settled down. Again, he paid his dues and told her that it was a transgression for her to so cruelly slay him with her beauty.

Then, he breached his subject. "Have you noticed a young girl about with a knife that has seven stones in the handle?"

Lohlitah suddenly struggled to rise. "What do you want with her? Were you going to have her dance for you? Let me go...."

"Shush, mine love, mine *Flower of the Desert*. Shush, now," he said, securing his hold on her. "There is no flower I doest desire but thee. There is no passion but thine. There is no beauty but thine." He bit her ear lightly.

"What do you want with her, witch?" she demanded, allowing him to keep her seated.

"I noticed the knife she bears. It reminded me of another I had seen in the past. One that was like it." He waited, not daring to ask more questions, yet baiting her with his silence, having learned quickly that she was a jealous lover. Though she eagerly consumed and discarded men, Lohlitah would not tolerate the same usage herself.

A while later she said," She is Petrosis' *kino*...."

"*Kino?*"

"Outsiders!" she spat. "You have a different word for everything! *Kino*. She is one he bought from the outsiders. She belongs to him."

"A slave?"

"No, witch! The *kina* is a slave. The *kino* is different in that they are taken in as one's child and enjoy all the privileges of family. He bought her from some sailors in Mallion."

Morlah's heart leapt.

Perhaps the girl could be the heir. She was not Gypsy. O ye gods! He felt electrified by the information, but he suppressed his thoughts lest he provoke Lohlitah. Instead, he said, "Come, mine thorny bush. Come into the tent, and let me show you what a witch can do to a girl's heart."

She laughed and sprang up. Turning, she took his hands and pulled at him. "Quickly, before you grow too old."

His mind raced as she led him to the tent. Lohlitah laughed and talked, but he was too busy plotting. He needed to know if Petrosis intended to go to Mallion and if Lohlitah would be traveling the same way. The fortunate thing was that he now knew that wherever Petrosis was, *Gildar* would be there also. Now, it was just a matter of seeing to it that Lohlitah went the same direction.

But enough of that, he thought as they entered the tent. He did not have the luxury of being distracted, for Lohlitah was sure to notice and accuse him of thinking of another woman...and then there would be demons to pay. *What a snare I have gotten mineself entangled in.* But for now, he would gladly allow it to strangle him and deal with the rest later.

Chapter 11

❦

After the next rising, at midcourse during travel, the posts abruptly stopped the caravan and whistled, signaling a stop for the night. Morlah rolled out from under Mamma Cituro's wagon to see what was happening. As Martino rode by, Morlah signaled him to stop.

"Why are we stopping so early?"

Martino grinned and pointed east to a forest that grew a few thousand paces away, jutting from the desert like a mirage, a lush tropical-like jungle. Morlah stared at it as if it might disappear at any heartbeat.

"*Gatalopie*! You come?"

Regaining his true intent, he asked, "Is Petrosis going all the way to Mallion?"

"Definitely!" answered Martino. "Definitely...maybe." Laughing, he rode off.

There was a sense of excitement among the men as they gathered in groups and looked out toward the forest. They stored their weapons in the wagons and armed themselves with flexible wooden rods, round at the handle and tapering to a flat span with a thin board-like end.

Petrosis rode by at a gallop, passing very close to the Druid.

"Catch, witch. *Gatalopie!*" he threw one of the "boards" to Morlah who caught it with ease but received a sharp thwack to the thigh with the other one that Petrosis carried. The men all turned in his direction at the sound and roared with laughter.

Morlah ran to Lohlitah's wagon and stuck his head through the rear flaps.

"What's going on? What's *gatalopie?*"

"Witch! I was sleeping. What do you want?" she moaned in frustration at the interruption.

Morlah repeated his question.

"*Gatalopie* is a large cat. Very ferocious. Every time we go by *Testal*, Petrosis stops, and the men go torment the cat. They arm themselves with the *chopa*. It is a meager defense against the cat, but the noise of a blow frightens it, and it flees rather than fight if it is struck with the *chopa*. If the striker is too late…you are dead. The men think it is great sport, for the cat is a man-eater and will take every opportunity to engage them. Men! More like boys when it comes to the *gatalopie*."

"What does the cat look like?"

She shrugged. "I don't know…let me sleep. I don't chase after him."

"What's he look like?" insisted Morlah. "Answer, and I will let you sleep."

"Grey with light brown stripes. Big like a first-cycle bullock. Now leave me alone, or I will not dance for you anymore."

Reaching into the bed, he gave her leg a squeeze above the knee, making her squirm.

"Alright, alright. I will dance. Let me sleep!" she barked, her hands pushing at his.

Morlah emerged from the wagon. A large gray cat with light brown stripes. The *gatalopie* was a damned Moor Cat! *What kind of moron goes out chasing a damned Moor Cat?* The most dangerous and aggressive predator known! A man-eater! Morlah sighed and looked at the *chopa* in his hand.

Petrosis rode up again. "You come? If you do, you leave your witching behind. Man against cat," he laughed. "Come, witch. It will be a great time. It will improve that bucking you call dancing. No one hunts the *gatalopie* and remains the same."

"What do we do?"

Petrosis dismounted from his horse, a beautiful, chestnut stallion. The excitement in Petrosis' eyes was clearly evident as he placed an arm about Morlah's shoulders.

"It is easy," instructed Petrosis, his free hand punctuating his words. "We go into the forest. The *gatalopie* comes to eat us." He laughed loudly. "If you hit him with the *chopa* before he eats you, he runs.... If not...you die. Very easy!"

"And this is for fun?"

"It makes you feel alive!" he bellowed, pounding his chest with his fist. "Your heart races, and the blood surges through you. If you live, you feel like a man, for you have looked death in the face and laughed and lived to tell about it. It is great fun! You come?"

"I'll give it a try," Morlah said doubtfully.

"No witching!"

"I'll leave my staff behind. I promise." But he did not say anything about his long slender knife that was also made of solid argentus, the magical metal. Nor would he mention to anyone about the sliver of argentus imbedded in his fifth rib just over his heart. He would name himself a son-of-a-Troll before playing with a Moor Cat without his magic to protect him!

Yet the Gypsies are going to do just that. Are they crazy? Maybe they spend too much time out in the sun. That has to be it, he decided. *Too much time in the sun.*

The men stood at the forest's edge in a long line. It was a dense, lush forest comprised of towering trees, unfamiliar to Morlah. The canopy was rich with all manner of vines, leaves and flowers and inhabited by all kinds of wildlife. Thick and lush as the canopy, the jungle floor was unlike anything Morlah had ever seen, broad leaves and vines of all shapes and thick broad grasses growing everywhere. The sounds of birds and other creatures could be heard all around..

"How is it this grows in the desert?"

"It rains here," said Martino with a shrug and a broad smile. "Nowhere else. But it rains here, heavily and every course of the sun. The forest, she is full of life and also, we think, one...maybe two *gatalopie*. The forest, she is named *Testal* in our tongue. It means to swallow. You will understand when you enter." Martino began to show Morlah how to hold the *chopa*; Morlah, however, was not paying attention, as he was in the process of setting up a spell to protect himself.

The men spread out at about ten paces apart from each other and slowly disappeared into the forest.

"Witch, come. You hunt with me," called Petrosis.

Morlah followed the lead-post in, the verdant maze closing about them as they stepped past *Testal's* boundary. Green! Everything was too green!

Is it the sun filtering through the foliage? Or just mine adrenaline coursing though my veins?

They could not see much farther than two spans in any direction, the forest seeming to want to claim them and entangle them in its growth.

"If you need to get out, go west, witch," said Petrosis.

With the forest already disorienting him, Morlah looked about. The overhead density of foliage obscured the direction of the sun. Petrosis pointed to the leaves of a low growing shrub.

"They all point south, see. Or is it north?" His grin widened to a broad toothy smile, and he winked. "South! Silence!"

"Are you going to Mallion, Petrosis?"

"Definitely! Maybe. Absolutely! Now silence! We do not want to be a meal for the beast. Keep your eyes and ears sharp."

Carefully, cautiously, they stepped through the vines and around low bushes; the rich odor of plant decay rose from the spongy ground with each step. Morlah saw large serpents poised in the trees up above. They took great care to detour around them.

Thwack! Thwack! resounded the sound of a *chopa* through the trees, its sound somehow carrying well in the dense growth.

"Ahieee! Ahieee!" rang a high-pitched call from one Gypsy.

"Ah, Tolato has scored a hit. The *gatalopie* is about and was waiting. She will return quickly, for the blows only deter her for a bit. Be alert!"

Morlah was seized with fear. His heart raced. His breaths became as if each were his last. He was close to becoming paralyzed with terror in spite of the fact that no Moor Cat could touch him through the magic. His eyes darted about. Every sound became a threat. This was worse to him than going to battle against the Black Mage and his servants.

How in the gods' names didst I get mineself into this? Yet, the Gypsies do without magic. Sun-crazed, it has to be that!

So intent, so focused was Morlah on the forest itself, that he did not know what was happening about him. He saw great green leaves striated with purple veins, little geckos feigning the color of bark, clinging to trees. He saw vines strangling gigantic trees.... Every tiny detail caught his attention, as if they threatened his existence.

Petrosis, in a flash, moved around to the left and behind Morlah. Thwack! Thwack! cracked the *chopa*. An enormous cat brushed passed Morlah at a blinding speed.

"Ahieee! Ahieee!" cried Petrosis.

Falling backward to the ground, Morlah snapped out of the trance he had been in, and Petrosis extended his hand.

"Great sport! Ahieee! Ahieee!" cried the Gypsy, pulling Morlah to his feet. "Do not let her take you in, witch. *Testal*, she will lull you to sleep and draw you into herself. She is a friend of the *gatalopie* and will bait you for the *gatalopie* to take. Beware!" His eyes sparkled, and his grin broke into the broad Gypsy smile once more.

"Definitely...maybe," said Morlah, at which Petrosis laughed loudly and cried again.

"Ahieee! Ahieee!"

Well, enough of this! Morlah decided that if he were going to play, he would equalize this a bit more in his favor. He drew from the magic. He heightened his senses and reflexes, making himself keenly aware of his environment, but on his own terms, not willing to be cat fodder. Feeling himself relax as argentic power flowed through him, being on familiar ground again in the magic, Morlah followed Petrosis. Morlah had fought wizards, mages, Trolls and demon-like creatures in the past; he should be able to handle a cat.

Thwack, smacked the sound of a more distant and muffled *chopa*, followed by the familiar call; whether a cry of victory and excitement or a way of letting the others know one was still alive, Morlah did not know.

Morlah's enchanted hearing let him know the cat was coming. He reached out and rested his hand on Petrosis' shoulder. Petrosis froze. The cat was moving fast, though silent as the breeze. Morlah sidestepped the Gypsy, lunged straight through a bush and caught the *gatalopie* smack on the flank with the *chopa*. The cat roared and fled back the way it had come, the roar standing the hair on Morlah's arms and neck.

"Ahieee! Ahieee! Ahieee! Ahieee!" Morlah looked about for Petrosis but could not see him. Then at his feet, he saw Petrosis bent in two, clutching at his belly and writhing about.

"Petrosis! What? What's wrong?" Morlah fell to his knees, holding the Gypsy by the shoulders.

The lead-post looked up, breathless. "Witch...witch," he gasped.

Then Morlah saw that Petrosis was laughing.

Damned Gypsies! He let the post drop to the ground.

"Witch!" he laughed and rolled onto his back, gasping for each word. "You howl like a Gypsy. Ahieee! Ah, great sport. Great sport! It lets you know you are alive."

Morlah stood, extended a hand to the lead-post and helped him up. The realization dawned on him that he had been the one calling out the victory cry. "It does at that, Petrosis! It does at that," he said, and his mouth broke into a broad grin.

Thwack! "Ahieee!" came the sounds from the distance.

"The cat will grow more cautious now she has been hit so many times. She will try to set an ambush rather than rush in. She will become...more dangerous," stated the Gypsy. His eyes sparkled.

They moved through the forest more slowly, examining every leafy shrub, every gnarled tree, every branched limb, searching for the cat who, when still, was all but invisible. Later, they came upon a bloody *chopa*.

Petrosis stopped. "The cat has won," he said with disappointment in his voice, not grief. "She will not hunt again this course of the sun." He picked up the *chopa*, wiping the blood off on some leaves. After examining a bush for a heartbeat, he took off in a westerly direction. He called "Aya, aya, aya," which was answered by others from off in different directions.

The hunt was over, and they were returning to camp. Just about to release his magic, Morlah, suddenly became aware of the biggest Moor Cat ever on a thick branch just in front of them, a branch they were about to walk under. At first, all he had seen was the trees and leaves. Then

Morlah saw two large yellow eyes as if suspended in the air, glaring at him. And then, materializing like some magical apparition, there was the *gatalopie* as clear as if it were whitewashed. Not understanding how he had not seen it before and without thinking, he hooked Petrosis' foot with his own and firmly pushed the Gypsy forward, headlong onto the ground.

Thwack! Thwack! Thwack! Thwack! resounded Morlah's *chopa*.

The cat's angered roar was deafening as it leapt high over Morlah's head and disappeared into the greenery.

"Ahieee! Ahieee!" cried Morlah, adrenaline coursing through him.

Petrosis rolled onto his back and looked up at the Druid. "Witch," he said seriously, his face pale and eyes wide. "Witch, that is as close to death as I have ever come. I never saw the *gatalopie* until it was too late. And...death did not look so pretty from so close.... Like a woman you see in the distance. You say to yourself 'Oooo, mamma!' And then you see her close, and you say, 'No, no, later'!" He laughed. "Four! Four blows you struck. Ahieee! Ahieee! Aya, aya. Enough of the hunt. Let us be gone before we are eaten! Aya, aya." Morlah extended his hand and helped the post back to his feet.

When they left the forest, it was sunsetting; they had spent almost a half-course in the jungle, yet it had felt like less than a span of heartbeats. The men gathered a safe distance from the darkening jungle and discussed the hunt. Petrosis dominated the conversation. Twilight began to supplant the sunlight.

"...and the witch, he hits the first cat so hard that he makes it growl! He makes it growl! Have you ever heard of such a thing? Then, we are walking out, and this cat the size of my horse is right there in my face, and I do not see it, and the witch he pushes me down like he was a *gatalopie* chasing a deer, pulling my foot back as I go to step, and his hand on my back, and then before I know what is happening...thwack, thwack, thwack, thwack. Four times, right in the jowls of the cat the size of my horse. Four times! I tell you, Lohlitah's loving has turned him into a Gypsy! It has to be that!"

The Gypsies howled with laughter, and then each who had scored a hit on the cat recounted in minute detail every move that had led to the blows, every detail of the cat's reaction, every emotion that they had felt. No mention was made of the missing man. There were no strange looks or darting eyes as if something were amiss. When the story telling was over, they headed back to the caravan.

After dark, while they were eating, Lohlitah approached and sat next to Morlah, which she did not customarily do.

"I hear you are the prize hunter this hunt."

"Just luck."

She looked at him doubtfully. "You have scored more than in the hunt. You have made a great mark among the men. It is a worthy prize you have won. You saved Petrosis' life, a great prize!"

"He saved me first."

"That was expected."

Morlah's eyebrows lifted in surprise.

Lohlitah laughed. "You were brought to be tested. Maybe to be lost to the cat, maybe not. Maybe...definitely." She looked at him with all solemnness but then broke into laughter again. "Definitely!"

"Lohlitah. No one mentioned or spoke of the man who was lost."

She shrugged.

"The cats follow us when we come this way. Each time we come, *gatalopie* almost always eats regardless how hard we try to stop him. Sometimes a man or a woman. Sometimes a child, or even worse...they kill a horse or an ox. They will eat. Why not have sport while waiting." But then she said, her eyes turning mischievous. "Wait to see what it does to the *dance*! The nearness to death changes a man when he again tastes of life. Tonight we *dance*!"

Morlah sighed. Then coming to himself, he asked, "Do you think Petrosis will go all the way to Mallion, or will he turn and go some other way?"

"Petrosis? The gods do not know where they go and what they do. How should Petrosis? Definitely!"

He threw her an annoyed glance, but then, broke into a broad smile. "Definitely! Maybe."

That night when the music started to play and the camp settled in for the night, Petrosis suddenly stood before Morlah, as if the Moor Cat had materialized before him again.

"I have come to thank you, witch. You allow me to live for another *dance*."

"You did the same for me."

"I am experienced. You are not. Mine does not count."

"Alright."

"Here. I bring you a gift," he said, handing Morlah a bottle of wine. "The best I own. In it, you will find the capacity to not stomp about but to *dance*." He smiled and left.

"Did he give you that wine?" asked Lohlitah, appearing from behind as Petrosis left; it appeared to be to be a course of the sun for 'apparitions'.

"Yes, he did."

"Ohh," she cooed. "That is good wine. Maybe not to taste but in your head and your feet and...well...." She gave him a meaningful look that made him blush. Under the cover of darkness and with his back to the fire, it went unnoticed.

"Here, I will open it, and we will drink. This is an honor Petrosis does to you. This is a peace offering. Do not take it lightly. You should repay with a gift of your own in due time. Definitely! ...Maybe." She laughed, and he was under her spell once more.

Ahh, sweet Lohlitah!

As a few men led a lame calf out toward the forest he asked Lohlitah, "Where are they taking it?"

"They go to bait the *gatalopie*. The calf is hurt. The *gatalopie* will feed, and we will not need worry in the camp."

"Why not just kill the cat instead of hunting it with *chopas?*"

"You eat turnips. They do not hunt you and kill you...."

He laughed. "Maybe...."

Chapter 12

The caravan stopped at a desert oasis, intent on spending the next moon's cycle there, sunlight temperatures having grown far too hot for travel. There was plentiful water available from the fresh spring that bubbled zealously on the bottom of the small, pond that had formed about the water source. And after a careful scouring of the area to ensure it was free of snakes, they settled in for a rest. The women gathered the ripe dates that were bountiful in the palms growing about the water's edge. The Gypsies slept and swam by sunlight and, by night, they *danced*.

Morlah woke sometime about midcourse, restless, and feeling as if he were suffocating from the heat. He rolled out from under Mamma's wagon and looked about to see if there was room in the shade of the trees, which might be cooler; he saw that the shade was pretty much occupied, strewn with resting bodies that sought refuge from the scorching heat. The children were playing in the pond, and after a bit, in desperation, Morlah decided to join them to cool off so that, perchance, he might live to see the night.

Walking to the water's edge and dropping his clothes, for it would have been considered rude to wear clothing to go swimming, he dove into the water. Shock registered in his brain as he hit the surprisingly cool water. He swam underwater toward the other side of the shallow pool; he felt the hotness sapped from his overheated skin. Breaking the surface, his lungs now hungry for air, he surfaced and found himself face-to-face with a young Elven girl. He stared into her eyes longer than was polite, stunned by her presence, even though she was what he had set out to find at some time in what seemed like the so distant past. But time had just swept by and was lost in the wind that blew the desert sands from drift to dune.

Finally, the girl broke the trance. "Greetings."

"Hello," he responded.

"The water's nice and cool," she said.

"It sure is. Do you know that I can't remember the last time I went swimming? It could be a matter of some thirteen hundred cycles."

She splashed water in his face. "You're silly," she said, disappearing underwater.

Desperately wanting to talk to her without drawing attention, especially from Petrosis or Lohlitah, he submerged himself until only the top of his head and his eyes were above the water's surface. He swam a circle, innocently scanning the area to see where Petrosis and Lohlitah were – they were not in sight. Morlah casually looked around. The Elf was nowhere in sight either.

Then suddenly, someone was on his back, and he went under just as he had been about to come up for air. He broke the surface sputtering and turned to see the Elven female again, laughing at him.

"What's your name," he inquired.

"Andreanna."

His heart almost stopped! Andreanna, the same name as that of the girl he had helped train at *seilstri* hundreds of cycles past. The girl that had made a man out of the young male who became King of the Elves. The girl who became Queen of the Elves and one of the most powerful magical forces ever to be known in all the land. Morlah slipped underwater in a futile attempt to cool his thoughts, that he might behave and speak so as not to concern her. Surfacing a short distance from her, turning onto his back with his head held high enough that he might see her, he asked, "Did you know there was a queen by that name among the Elves a long time ago?

"Yup."

His heart pounded in his chest. He felt his skin flush with the heat of nervous excitement. "Did you know that you're an Elf?"

She giggled. "Of course I know. But Petrosis says I'm not an Elf anymore."

"Do you think you might be related to the ancient Queen Andreanna?"

"No, I don't *think* so." She dove back under water and reappeared near the shore. She ran out of the water and wrapped herself in a towel, leaving Morlah baffled by her response. If she were the heir, surely she would have known that she was descended of the King and Queen.

Perhaps not. Many counted such things trivial as the generations passed, and such information was often lost, as it had been in Jerhad's time. Still, Morlah wondered. Surely, this was Petrosis' *kino*, for she spoke of him in a way that implied some kind of union. She had to be the bearer of Ember.

There couldn't be two Elf girls in the camp, could there?

From that time on, Morlah watched for another opportunity to meet up with the girl. It took four more courses of the sun before he awoke one midcourse to see her swimming again. Rolling out of his bed, he causally made his way to the water. After a cautious surveying of the area to see that his jealous lover was not around, he slipped in and swam about for a while, feigning innocence and purposelessness. Finally, he swam near the Elven girl and stopped.

"Hello," he said.

"Greetings."

Heartbeats slipped by, and he found himself at a loss for words. He slipped under water and came up a little distance away.

"What's your name," she asked.

"Morlah."

"Are you the witch?"

He sighed, resigned to his fate.

"Yes. I guess I am. You? Are you a witch?"

Her reaction surprised him, for she frowned deeply and her eyes narrowed. Quickly, she looked about, dove underwater and emerged near the shore, running from the pond as if pursued.

So much for their second meeting! Whatever had transpired had frightened her; he worried that she might now try to avoid him.

It was their third-quarter moon's cycle at the oasis at about three-quarters of the sun's course, when Martino flew through the camp on his horse, whistling an alarm. The Gypsies roused, women and children running to the wagons and men for their weapons; it could only mean Bandits!

Morlah made his way to Mamma's wagon and retrieved his knife, leaving his staff behind lest it draw the Gypsies' attention. But he did not know what to do. Petrosis was willing to abide his presence if he refrained from magic, but could he refrain? *Can I stand by and allow the Bandits to hurt my people?* The thought struck him. *How is it I thought of them as my people, as if I were a Gypsy?*

Petrosis, on his horse, galloped by and threw a longbow and quiver at him. "Make yourself useful, witch. And remember...no witching!"

Morlah took up a position by Lohlitah's wagon. An attack would have to come from the east, for the camp was on the eastern side of the pond. It would be too cumbersome an effort to make a successful attack from the west. He looked about to locate Andreanna but could not. He stuck his head through the wagon's rear door.

"Lohlitah, do you have any weapons in here?"

She showed him a bow and quiver of arrows.

"Give me the arrows and stay down behind the bed."

"Witch! Since when do you tell me what to do?"

Having glanced outside to see if anyone was near and sticking his head and one arm back into the wagon, he caused his hand to glow with power, wrapping her with it and holding her paralyzed for a heartbeat.

"Right now, I tell you what to do. Tonight it will be your turn. Let's just get through this alive." He released her.

She glared at him for a score of heartbeats. "It would seem that my bewitchment on you is wearing off, witch. ...Maybe." Then she laughed. "I will obey, my witch. I will obey."

From the distance, Morlah heard the thundering of hooves approaching.

"No witching," came Lohlitah's voice from inside as he took up his position by the wagon's end. He could see the Bandits now as they bore down on the Gypsies, longbows in hand, some with arrows that had fire burning on their tips. Casting a solid invisible barrier about Lohlitah's wagon and extending it over the wagon tops, hoping any arrow launched from a distance would simply look like it overshot its mark, Morlah prepared to defend.

The gods take Petrosis, and the Gnomes eat his heart! Morlah was not about to stand by idly! *But how to help and not be obvious?* Subtle uses of magic in battle were not what he was accustomed to.

In the next heartbeat, arrows filled the air. Morlah raised small invisible shields at intervals to protect some of the Gypsies. He took a handful of arrows and, having checked to see that no one watched him, launched them without use of his bow toward their marks, mingling them into the flight of the band's arrows. A dozen Bandits fell. Two wagons down, a canopy caught fire, and Morlah was there with a bucket of water in his hand and a spell on his lips, dousing it before it could cause damage. As he looked down the line of wagons, his eyes met Petrosis' who gave him a "thumbs-up."

The Bandits swept by, launching a rain of arrows before turning off and riding on their horses' sides to avoid being hit. Several Gypsies fell. Down the line, a few men were attempting to put out the fire in a wagon. Morlah turned to see two Bandits making a run on the Gypsies' horses. These were more precious to them than their very lives. Morlah released two arrows in one shot, guiding them to their marks. He also tangled the reins of the riderless Bandits' horses by magic, so they would stay within the camp.

But the Gypsies were taking too much damage, and now, three wagons were burning. Several men and women lay on the ground.

Damn it, Petrosis!

If only he could act freely, he could stop this. Morlah picked up the arrows from the quiver of a dead Gypsy and sent them out to find the thieves' hearts, but it was not enough. Now, fire was spreading from wagon to wagon and even more of the men were wounded or dead. Morlah ran down to the last of a row of wagons that were untouched by fire, gathered a group of men, and together they pushed the wagon away from the fire to break the chain, though Morlah and his magic actually did most of the pushing.

Morlah was becoming angry. *This is a waste of time. Damn it! Should I just do it and suffer the consequences? But I would be banished, and the Bandits would be back another course, and the result would be the same. Damn it!* He turned and met Petrosis face-to-face.

"See, witch. We can hold our own without witching...."

That was the last straw for Morlah! Striking the leadpost in the forehead with his opened palm, he screamed, "What? Are you stupid? You've lost six wagons, almost half of your men are dead or out of action, and the Bandits aren't finished! I could end this in a heartbeat if you let me! Damn it, Petrosis, look around you and see what's happening to your people." He grabbed the post by the hair, forcing him to look at the slaughter that was taking place.

Petrosis broke free and laughed. "Got some fire in you, witch. Keep it for the Bandits." He turned to leave but stopped short. For a heartbeat, he appeared to grow taller. The lead-post fell back against Morlah with an arrow protruding from his chest. His eyes were rolled back, and his breathing was suddenly shallow. Morlah lay the lead-post on the ground.

Enough!

He strode like a Giant through the soft-green oasis grasses. He stepped past the wagons out toward the Bandits. His breathing slowed, deep and hard. His heart pounded in his ears, and his anger rose dangerously. The Bandits swept in for another strike, finding one man standing between them and their objective, one man walking out to meet them with raised hand, palm forward as if to stop them.

Some of them laughed just before fire roared out from his palm, while he drew hard on the argentus blade in his hand. The fire roared as if belching from a volcano, turning to ash rider and horse as the Druid swept the sands clean of the attackers. The fire was too hot and swift to even allow its victims to cry out in pain, the intense pain that lasted but a heartbeat before they went into nonexistence. Lasting a few score of heartbeats, the whole scene played itself out quickly. To those who watched, it was as if it went on forever.

Morlah thought the earth had stopped. His anger fueled his adrenaline so that he felt his every heartbeat distinctly. He felt every particle of air moving into his lungs. The riders seemed to barely move before him. Horses' nostrils flared as they breathed hard in the hot desert air. Granules of sand were suspended in the air, thrown up by pounding hooves. And then, they were all gone. All dead. Ash!

The Gypsies had watched in fascinated horror to see such raw power erupting from Morlah. Time had stopped for them also as they fell under the spell of the witch's display. The Gypsies watched as the witch strode out before them, leaving them puzzled and causing them to stop their attempts at repulsing the Bandits. Bows were lowered. Water buckets dangled while fires raged a few steps away. It was as if the witch had grown in stature as he rounded the last wagon. His steps were long, slow and deliberate. He appeared to cover ten paces with each step. The aura of his power pulsed about him, causing the Gypsies to sway to its rhythm as if it were the *dance*.... And then, with his hand outstretched, he had unleashed an inferno that resembled a forest fire in time of drought, driven by high winds, the flame appearing to have burned the very screams from the air as they formed in the Bandits' mouths.

Still. All was still now. Except for the crackling sound of fire burning the wagons. Even the wounded were silent. Morlah kept walking. Walking away from the caravan. Walking away from his lover.

Lohlitah watched him go, but held her peace.

Morlah walked and did not look back. He walked with no place to go...no one to go to...alone again.

The blood-red sun set on the stricken caravan. The dead were buried a distance into the desert as not to pollute the water of the oasis. The injured were cared for, but the music did not play, the *dance* did not begin. When the Gypsies looked out into the distance, against the darkening horizon, they could see the form of a man, the form of Morlah, sitting on a boulder and staring out away from them.

Chapter 13

Star walked the remainder of the course after leaving Breezon, heading north along the road that followed the Breezon River to Port Oxzard, traveling alongside an ox-cart full of freshly scythed hay. She walked as if she journeyed with it in order to draw less attention to herself. The road was fairly busy with traffic that moved back and forth between the cities. That did not necessarily make it safe, for brigands and thieves had few deterrents from committing their crimes when and where they would.

Having no provisions, she grew hungry. The dust from the poorly-maintained, wagon-wheel-rutted and marred road caused her mouth to feel parched and pasty. Her feet became blistered from walking in ill-fitting, black leather boots reaching to her knees, better suited for fashion and dancing. Come sunsetting, she hobbled painfully and was exhausted.

The wagon she walked alongside of on the open prairie road turned off onto a broken trail and went south, leaving her on her own in the diminishing traffic. Star journeyed on, but she was now in sight of Port Oxzard, the port situated at the mouth of the Breezon River and on the shore of the large bay that opened into the Korkaran Sea to the west. The city was a clean and upright community, not having suffered Breezon's fate and having escaped Daektoch's attention in the past. Hence, it had also not suffered Troll attacks. It was prosperous and without the level of crime and prostitution of the neighboring Breezon; it would not be a good place to attempt to settle down at her trade.

Star approached a small inn along the road and stopped for the night. The inn, the Trader's Haven, was a one-story rammed earth structure with an old gray slate roof, speaking of a former affluence. The inside was finished with axe-hewn boards, and the interior was open to the roof, exposing the beam framing and boards that supported the slate. Only over the bedrooms were there finished ceilings, leaving a large open loft on each side of the dining area and kitchen.

Star procured a room and soaked her aching feet. She found a table in the dining area in order to eat evening meat, ordering the Blue Gill. When it arrived, she was amazed at the tastiness of the meal. Her experience with food in Breezon was limited to eating ill-prepared, frequently spoiled provisions prepared without spice or care. For the first time ever, she tasted quality wine and not dregs. She had a sweet, cinnamon bread pudding for dessert; she had never in all her life eaten such wonderful fare.

The simple but good meal and the clean, well-groomed establishment opened her eyes to a whole new world, a world that she had never imagined. She had heard of better circumstances and had dreamed of them, but somehow they had never been real and were more mythical than factual in her mind.

What possibilities existed out here if even food and dwellings could be so different? There were no beggars, no refuse, no prostitutes littering the streets. What type of work would one do if they did not sell themselves or steal from others? Of course, there would be the basic vendors in the markets, bakers and sellers of wares, but that could not account for the employment of an entire populace. *Could it?* Star hardly slept that night, her mind racing at the possibilities that lay before her.

Come sunrising, having eaten break fast, procured a water skin, some hard cheese and fresh bread for travel, she stood on the porch of the Trader's Haven ready to resume her journey. She looked up at the sky. It promised to be hot.

"Traveling alone?" asked a man's voice from behind her.

Star turned to see an old, baldheaded man, bent with age, rise from a bench. He was clean-shaven; his clothes were a bit tattered but fairly clean and without the stench that such a one would have carried in Breezon.

"Yes...I am," replied Star.

"Which way?"

"Heros."

"Going that way meself," cackled the old man as if there was something funny about going to Heros. "Room for you up on my wagon if you need a lift. Two silvers...up front."

The old man looked harmless, and she did not doubt that she could handle him easily enough if he tried to cause her trouble. Besides, riding would be safer and less painful than walking, at this point.

"One silver and five coppers," she countered from habit.

"Three silvers then!"

She chuckled. "Two silvers it is."

"Wait here," he responded, going down the foot-worn-plank steps leading off the front porch. He walked around to the back of the inn and returned a bit later, driving a two-mule wagon loaded with woven baskets.

As Star got up onto the wagon and sat next to the man, he indicated the baskets with a movement of his head.

"Me and the missus sells them in Heros. Gets a good price."

Star nodded without interest, noting the loaded crossbow and extra bolts at his feet on the wagon's floorboard.

"Name's Emmit," said the man.

"Star," she said as the wagon started out with a jolt, traveling toward Heros at a slow pace, creaking, rocking and wrenching along the creviced road.

A while later, Emmit asked, "S'at your real name?"

"No. Just something my ma gave me when I was a kid. Haven't gone by my real name in cycles."

"You been to Heros before?" asked Emmit.

"No."

"Got any family there?"

"No."

"What are you going to do there?"

She shrugged.

"Where are you coming from?"

"Breezon."

"Plan on going back?"

"No."

"Know how to drive a team?"

"Nope."

"Well, here. Hold the reins a few heartbeats. Don't have to do nothing. Just hold them loose." Emmit gave her the reins and turned to the rear of the wagon. He searched his bags behind the seat. "Ah, there they are." He turned again and took his seat, holding two shiny apples in his work-worn hand. "Want one?"

"Sure," she said doubtfully. "How much?"

"How much? No, no. Just to give...no cost."

"No cost?" That was unusual. Never had anyone give her anything for free, except for Sally; there was *always* something expected in return.

"No cost?" she repeated.

"What? Can't give you an apple for nothing?" puzzled Emmit. "It's just an apple. Ain't gold or nothing." He did have a point. She took the apple and bit into it. It was deliciously moist and sweet. An apple could sell for as much as one silver in Breezon.

"You hear about the ol' sea captain without legs in Port Oxzard. Had some ruffians take his ship. Took 'em before the magistrate."

She shook her head.

"He didn't have a leg to stand on. Haw, haw, haw," he laughed and slapped his knee. "Didn't have a leg to stand on." He shook his head in amusement and slapped his knee again.

Star glanced at him and smiled.

"What's a pretty filly like you doing out alone?" Emmit continued.

"I'm leaving Breezon."

"What's your family think about you leaving?"

"I got no family. My ma's been dead a long time."

"Your pa?"

"Never knew him."

"That's right sad," said Emmit, shaking his head. "Down right sad. Ever sell baskets?"

"No," she smiled. "Not *baskets*."

"Pretty easy; set them up in the market, and folk just buy 'em up. Takes no talent, except to do figures for coin. Can you do that?"

"I can do figures. I'm used to making change for coin."

"You sell something?"

She nodded, sighed a slow sigh and rolled her eyes.

"What?"

"Stuff."

"My wife and me, we sell stuff, mostly baskets or anything we can find at a good price. The inner markets in Heros, you have to pay to get a table or a booth. But you can double your prices too, and folk will pay if they need what you sell. The outer markets don't charge, but mostly the poorer sorts shops at 'em." After a pause, Emmit asked, "Ever think of selling baskets? My wife is getting old and a bit feeble. Maybe we could set you up selling with her if she doesn't git too upset at the thought."

"Maybe," said Star, rather than giving him a plain no.

"We ain't got no children of our own. Sure would be nice to have someone young around."

"Maybe."

The wagon moved along, jolting through the hardened mud ruts, following the traffic heading toward Heros. The conversation ended, and the two traveled on, arriving on the outskirts of Heros long after the sunsetting.

Stopping by an old warehouse, one street over from the docks used by fishermen and the smaller vessels, Emmit asked, "You got a place to stay?" The lane was lined with run-down buildings.

Star shook her head.

"We got room in the shed. Cramped, but safer than the street."

"How much?" she replied.

"Oh, no, that's alright. Me missus'll be glad of the company." He got off the wagon, walked to the large barn-door-like panels and pounded twice. "Open up, Greita. It's me." Shortly the door opened, revealing a thin, elderly woman.

"Who's that?" asked the old woman, suspiciously eyeing Star, her menacingly thin lips expressing her doubt.

"Picked her up in Oxzard; needed a ride. She needs a place to stay for the night. Thought we might put her up in the shed."

"Hmmm," growled Greita as she considered the matter.

"Got food for us?" asked Emmit, as he returned to the cart and climbed up into it.

"Yeah, yeah! It's ready. Hold on! Just have to serve it up," she said gruffly.

"Don't go minding her," whispered Emmit. "Seems to think growling is the way to talk." He drove the wagon into the warehouse, got down and started unhitching the mules.

Star climbed off of the wagon.

The old woman returned and set a large stew bowl containing a foul smelling concoction next to the oil lamp on a large crate. Star had eaten worse in the past. The old lady pointed to the crate.

"Use that for a table and find a keg or something fer a seat! That un's yours." She turned and left.

Emmit was further back in the structure, tending to the mules as Star sat and ate. She looked around at the mostly empty building, not seeing far for the lack of light. She saw a few pairs of large wharf-rats' eyes at the darkness' edge.

Heros at last, she thought, hoping things would work out better for her here than they had in Breezon.

A bit later, Emmit returned, closed the doors to the warehouse and walked over to Star, pulling up a small box for a seat. "I'm ready!" he called back into the dark.

"Yeah, yeah!" sounded the distant barking answer from the rear of the building.

"Have to house the mules inside; they'd be gone afore sunrising if stabled in an open corral. Probably be eaten afore this time next rising. Got to watch the thieves and hooligans; always watch your back in a town like this. One can't be safe just no place. Gotta keep your wits about you."

Star nodded, finishing the last of her meal, although she had failed to identify the contents thereof. The slop was a striking contrast to last night's feast at the Trader's Haven.

The old lady returned and glared at Star, dropping a bowl in front of Emmit. "You staying?"

"How much?"

The old man coughed and glared at his wife across from the oil lamp on the crate.

"Ah...it's alright, I reckon. Come with me. No charge." She turned with her lantern in hand and disappeared into the dark. Star followed.

"You have a name?" asked the old woman.

"Star."

"Humph!"

The old lady did not appear to be very friendly, but life was hard. Sometimes it made people hard.

"I'm Greita." She led Star out the back, through a small door, outside and to a small shed. "Safe as anything you'll find. No one comes back here. I'll lock the door just to be sure." Greita reached into her apron pocket and removed a short candle. Holding the candle's end over the heat of her lamp's chimney, the wick lit. She handed the lit candle to Star.

"There's a blanket and a straw mattress in the corner. Slop bucket too. I set you a cup of water if'n you get thirsty."

Star nodded and entered. The door closed behind her and she heard the sound of the lock turning. She found the pallet, and after dripping a bit of wax on a small crate top, she set the candle on it and held it for a heartbeat until the wax set. Examining the pallet and blanket, she found them infested with vermin. The place stank.

Damn it. She would be picking them out of her hair and clothes for weeks. *But at least it's a safe place to sleep.*

The air near the bay was cold and damp; Star could smell the fog rolling in from off the water. She would have to sleep with her clothes on for warmth in addition to using the tattered blanket left for her. Once settled in, Star blew the candle out and lay back on the pallet.

145

What would life in Heros bring? Should I look to set up with an established brothel or work on my own? The former would most likely be safer. A new start. She always hated starting over, the uncertainty, the unfamiliar places and faces. New rules, new rates, new customers. Yet, she felt hopeful.

Staring through a crack in the roof at the one lone star that she could see, she rested. *A lot like me,* she thought, *one lone star.* She thought of Emmit and Greita. *How did people get to the point of actually getting married? An actual couple!* She did not think that she knew anyone who was actually married, or at least, she had never met them with their wives. This had to be the first actual couple she had ever encountered! They were a good match somehow, though Greita was a bit sour. *She's alright,* Star supposed. *Met worse.*

Star awoke. It was still dark. She listened. It took a few heartbeats for her to remember where she was. Then, she heard voices outside. A key slipped into the door's lock.

"It's just me," Star heard Greita say in a strained, sweet voice. "Was up and thought I'd look in on you to see if you needed anything."

The door opened. The darkness outside was less oppressive; the moon on the fog gave the outdoors a silver-gray hue. Then, a form moved into the doorway; Star could tell it was a big man, not Emmit.

"You awake?" asked Greita's voice.

Star did not answer. Her hand slipped toward her dagger.

"She's in the corner on the left," whispered Greita, but her voice echoed in the night's stillness.

The man took two quick steps, kicking to locate the pallet. He threw himself, full-weight, onto Star, letting out an *oomph* as her dagger sank into his chest, his own weight driving it to the hilt.

"Bring the light," called another man who rushed in and threw himself on top of the dead man and Star. Star was unable to move or retrieve her weapon because of the mass on top of her.

"She's killed Raddu," he called, as two more men entered the shed, with Emmit and Greita pulling up the rear with lamps.

"Get hold of her arms," he insisted still on top of Raddu and Star.

The men rushed to the pallet and secured her arms. The man on top of her rose and pulled the dead Raddu off.

"What are we supposed to do with him?" barked Greita.

"Dump him in the bay. Get the wagon, Emmit. We'll load him up for you."

"Lockart, you've turned this into more trouble than it's worth. If I have to dump him in the bay, I get to keep her stuff and any coin she's got on her," complained Emmit.

"Don't worry about it," replied Lockart. "Just get the wagon."

Star lay passively on the pallet. The two other men had their full weight on her arms; she knew that it was futile to struggle. She would wait for an opportunity.

As Emmit left, Greita asked Lockart, "Where's that gold?"

Lockart dug into his pocket and removed one large gold, handing it to Greita. She bit into it and then stuffed the coin into a purse hanging from a leather cord about her neck.

Lockart spoke to Greita, "Go ahead and check out what she's got that you want to keep. We've got to get going." Lockart went out. Greita eagerly frisked Star, discovering a small leather purse that contained two small golds and twenty silvers.

"Only one silver in here," she said, holding one up to show the men restraining Star. Greita quickly emptied Star's handful of coin into her skirt pocket, holding the one silver in her hand for show.

Lockart returned with some chains and shackles and secured them to Star's wrists. He bound the other end to one of the two men who held her. "You can let her up. She ain't goin' nowhere." Outside, the wagon pulled up alongside the shed. Lockhart and his friend lifted the dead Raddu and carried the corpse out to the wagon.

"Did he pay you?" called Emmit.

"Yeah, yeah. Git rid of the body and hurry back. Want to git some sleep tonight," growled Greita. Burd, the third man led Star outside, tugging at the chain. They all met at the wagon.

"Looks like a good one. She'll bring a good price," said Lockart. "Pleasure doing business with you again, Emmit."

Emmit laughed and stepped close to Star. He grinned wickedly, staring into her eyes. "Well, there! Hope you enjoyed your ride," he cackled. "Been running that same load of baskets back-and-forth for twenty cycles."

Star took a step forward and kneed him in the groin. Emmit folded in two. She kneed him in the face, and he fell over onto the ground, blood spurting from his nose. Emmit lay there, locked in his folded position. She spat on him. Greita hissed and stepped forward with a dagger in hand, but Lockart intercepted and disarmed her, throwing the knife into the shed.

Then he laughed, "He got less than he had comin' to him from her. She's our goods now; don't damage them or I'll be wanting that gold back. Get her out of here, Burd." Burd tugged at the chain and led Star away. "Let us know when you get another. Market's good for strong young men for the oars. Two golds apiece. See ya."

Greita grunted at Lockart. She stood next to her husband and watched the men take Star away. Then, she viciously kicked Emmit in the ribs, hard. "Come on in when you're done here. Stupid old fool," she muttered, returning to the warehouse, leaving him lying in the dark.

Chapter 14

Star awoke. A beam of light filtered through the open hatch in the ceiling of the ship's hold to which she had been delivered. Lockart and Burd had led her to the dock after leaving Emmit's place, loading her onto a small rowboat on the tranquil fogbound harbor waters. They had rowed through the mist. The only sounds were those of the creaking oarlocks and the thumping of the oars as they worked.

Not only was Star angry, she was also embarrassed, taken in like a sot to the bottle. *Damn it! I don't have the time or the patience for this.* It was just a matter of time before she escaped. Still, the situation infuriated her.

Panic had taken hold of her when she realized she was to be loaded onto a ship. That meant she could end up leagues and leagues away; possibly in a place where Humans were a minority, stripping her of anonymity in a crowd. But then, she thought she remembered someone telling her that only Humans used slaves. She supposed it did not really matter where she ended up, as long as she was among Humans.

The hold of the boat stank of Human excrement and unwashed bodies, although there were but a dozen shackled there. She saw six rows of bunks stacked three high, but she could not tell how many there were in all, down the length of the hold. The bunks were crudely built of roughly hewn planks. The young man in the bunk next to her was dead. Streaks of dried blood from his nose and ears clung to his white flesh; he appeared to have put up quite a struggle. The ship groaned a bit as it suddenly jarred; the tuggers must be pulling the vessel away from the dock.

Bringing a hand to her mouth, she licked it the best she could with her parched tongue, folded her thumb into her palm and with a little effort slipped it out of the shackle. A hint of a smirk crossed her lips, and she slipped her hand back into her bonds. She would just have to wait for the right time; a boat out on the water was not that time.

About one span of the sun later, the vessel stopped moving, and Star watched as thick coiled ropes, whose ends were secured in the hold, were pulled out onto the deck through brass flanges in the ceiling. Shortly, she heard the call of a mule driver's *ha mule ha!* The boat began to move again. She assumed the ship was being towed through the canal that led from the bay to the Maring Sea.

Star felt more alone than she had since her mother died. It felt strange to her how alone and isolated one could feel even in the presence of others. This was different than being alone in a new place. Here, she was not in control; self-determination was very important to her. She did not even mind dying as long as she was given the opportunity to put up a good fight before she did. But to have her fate lie in the hands of others made her feel weak; she despised weakness and helplessness.

The sun stared straight in through the hold's hatch when she awoke again; it had grown stiflingly hot below the deck with the sun's heat pouring in. Flies buzzed around the dead man's mouth and nose. Someone across from her, a woman, moaned in pain. Further down, someone wept.

The ship lifted and sank as it moved across the sea's swells. Star watched the movement of the sails as they caught the breeze, filling to billowing and faltering as the ship dropped over the top of each wave. The vessel's movement mesmerized her. Star lazily watched, while billowing plumes of clouds drifted past the open hatch, and, had she not been hungry, extremely thirsty and a captive, she would have enjoyed the experience tremendously. It was so vastly different from being cooped up in a Breezon brothel. For a heartbeat, she forgot herself and smiled as a tiny breeze played across her face. For a heartbeat, being out of that decrepit city, away from her work, out on the sea...for a heartbeat, she felt free.

A long ladder slid down the open hatchway, and two men climbed down. They were sinewy, thin but well-muscled fellows. They wore no shirts, and their pants were cut just below the knee. Their skin was bronzed from long periods spent in the sun. Walking to the other end of the hold, one unlocked the chain holding a prisoner to his bunk. The other locked the chain to an iron ring on the hold's floor; the process continued until all the prisoners were secured to each other, in a row.

"We gots us a dead un," one of the sailors called up.

A big man, the tallest Human Star had ever seen, stepped into sight up on the deck.

"What?"

"I says we gots a dead un," repeated the slaver.

"Yer sure?" asked the man at the top. He was as wide as a Troll at the shoulders and muscled like a bull. His hair, sun bleached nearly white, was tied back in a tail that fell to his mid back. He was quite handsome and wore a waxed-handlebar moustache that extended a half-finger's length beyond the corners of his mouth. Otherwise, he was clean-shaven. His teeth were pure white, and there were none missing. Star gasped, for something about him struck a chord in her. For the first time in her life, she actually felt attracted to a man.

"Flies is laying eggs in his nose, Capt!"

"Which un?" inquired Capt.

"The un they knocked on the head."

The captain laughed. "Good. I paids Lockart a lead slug for him. Didn't think he'd last long." He turned and spoke to someone behind him. "Bring a rope."

A man appeared at the opening and dropped the end of a rope down below.

"Tie 'im, Martie," called the captain.

The sailor undid the dead man's shackles, dragged him to the ladder, slipped a noose around the dead fellow's neck and called, "Pull 'im up, mates."

Though not squeamish, Star turned her head, as did the other prisoners. She did not care to see the man hauled out that way. As the body got to the hatch, his head hit the edge of the frame with a loud thud that was followed by the sounds of the body bumping across the opening.

"Throw 'im over.... Bring 'em up, Martie," the captain called down into the hold.

The second sailor below deck went to the ring and unlocked the chain, gave it a good yank, and started up the ladder with the captives in tow. As they shuffled onto the deck, the sun blinded them; hands secured in irons and chains came up to shield the captives' eyes.

"Line 'em up, Pig," called the captain. The second sailor secured the chain to a brass ring by the foremast and the opposite end toward the stern so that the enslaved were in a straight line. Martie followed, emerging from the hold.

Capt walked down the line with a cane in his hand, using it to raise a young girl's chin so he might look at her face, lifting her skirt to the top of her thighs with it and prodding an older man at whom he sneered as if disappointed with what he saw. Walking down the row of prisoners, he inspected each one until at last he arrived at Star. An eyebrow went up as he surveyed her, and he smiled widely.

"How much I pay fer this un, Martie?" asked Capt.

"One large golds, Capt."

Capt laughed. "If Lockart had shown her to me in sunlight, I would have been willing to give him four. Listen up!" he shouted at the captives, walking down toward the other end of the chained row, "Turn around and look behind you."

Heads swiveled. Some of the captives turned completely. There on the horizon was a thin, dark line sitting on the water.

"That's land," stated Capt.

The prisoners frantically looked about at the horizon all around the ship, desperate to see something closer. One older woman fell to her knees and sobbed.

"Now, I've gots a fair bit of experience at this," continued Capt. "I've found that 'em who stays too long in the hold gets sick and don't bring as good a price. Some die. So, while we gots a small load of goods, I'd just as soon let yer all free to roam the foredeck and only chain yer at night. I make more money if y're in good health.

"But, if some dang fool jumps ship and thinks of swimming fer it or drowning hisself, well then, I'm out of the coin I've already paids. If we lowers a dinghy and goes fetch yer. Then, we whips yer good and leaves yer in chains for the remainder of the voyage. It's yer choice. Think about it for a while."

By then, all the prisoners were down on the deck, despondent, all hope seemingly as distant as the land on the horizon. Except for Star.

Star was invigorated by the sea, by the boat plowing through the great swells, by the clear-blue open sky and the smell of the seawater in her nostrils; she would escape later.

"Give 'em water, Pig," ordered Capt, and he climbed back up a short ladder and onto the wheel deck.

Pig returned with a bucket and ladle. They all drank greedily.

About one span later, Capt returned.

"Well. What will it be? The hold?"

No one responded.

"The deck?"

Heads bobbed vigorously.

"Remember," admonished the captain. "If I have to fish yer out of the water, yer get whipped and stuck back in the hold fer the entire journey. Yer can die down there if yer wants to. Take off their chains, Martie."

Martie, the first mate, gave the key to another sailor, who then went down the line and released everyone. They stood rubbing their wrists, some eyeing the horizon again as if they might consider attempting the swim; but the distance was daunting. No one moved toward the rail. Then, two sailors herded the group to the foredeck, instructing them to remain there.

Confined to the foredeck, Star separated herself from the others and leaned on the rail, watching the sea swell by. At times, she closed her eyes and just enjoyed the ship's movement on the water, the wind on her face and the smell of the brine.

"Moves like a woman under a man," said Capt's voice from behind her.

Star bolted about, her back to the rail, regarding him with an evil eye.

"No need to worry 'bout me," he said, coming to the rail and leaning his muscular forearms against the glossy, oil-polished wooden bar. When Star felt that he was not about to attempt anything, and having covertly surveyed his rippling muscles and bronze skin, she turned back to gaze out at the water.

"Ye're a whore, ain't yer?"

She was, had been so since the age of thirteen cycles, had been called such as an insult without ever having considered it. Coming from him, somehow, the word stung her.

"How'd you know?" she asked.

"Whores gots...attitude. They don't cow like common women. Holds their heads up proud. Knows when to fight and when not to. I can make this easy or hard fer yer. I heard what yer done to Emmit." He laughed. "Wish I could have seen it. My boys don't touch the merchandise unless

I lets 'em. Behave yourself and they won't. Cause trouble, and yer'll wish yer were swimming with the sharks. Just a friendly warning, miss."

Dolphins rose on the wake behind the ship, following along, leaping and playing.

"What are those?" she asked Capt.

"Porpoises. They like to play. Smart too. Not like regular fishes or animals," he responded absently, looking back at them.

There was a period of silence.

"I could make yer life lots easier," Capt said after a while. "Ye're a real beauty. Might want to keep yer for myself, fer a while at least. Maybe a long while. Ye're worth six or eight golds in the right market, but I might like to keep yer fer myself.... Only...I'm not interested in fighting fer it, if yer knows what I mean. Think about it. I don't beat my women. I treats 'em proper. One man, no beatin's, no work. Plenty of good food and good wine. There be many a free woman who'd jump at the chance. Think about it." He turned and left.

Star remained at the rail, glancing back after him, at his wide, well-muscled shoulders and narrow hips as he walked away; not like most of the hogs she had endured. *He's not much different than me. One who deals in Human flesh in order to feed himself. Admittedly, a bit cruder of a trade, but then, not all that different.*

A while later, Martie came by with a tin of salve. "Here," he commanded. "Hold still." He smeared the salve onto her skin. "The sun will burn yer bad if yer don't cover up with clothes or ointment. We haves thirty courses of sailing ahead of us. If yer ain't careful, you'll look like yer were in a fire, being out on deck all course long. Use this, or cover yourself with clothes. There's some extra in the box by *Lady's* foremast."

"Lady?"

"Yeah. The ship. Her name is *Capt's Lady*. We jus' calls her *Lady*. An she's a fine one at that," he added, eyeing Star down to her feet and back up to meet her eyes. "A fine one at that," he repeated dreamily. "Capt's got his eye on yer. Yer'd be a fool to turn him down. Slave market ain't no picnic. Never know where you'll end up or what will happen."

"I can handle myself."

He drew close, face-to-face. "Don't be stupid! I've seen prettier girls than yer have their legs cut off at the knees just to prevent 'em from running off. Used and abused till they was ragged and broken in spirit. Then, thrown out in the street for the dogs to eat after the beggars was done with 'em. Some men'll go to the very end of all decency to make a bit of coin."

"And you?" she asked with a sneer, brazenly pushing closer to him. "You don't think slave trading is the end of decency?"

Now, he was nose to nose with her!

"Capt runs a decent ship. Nobody gets hurt if they behave. Yer gets drink and food and air. There's much worse. Much worse!" He turned to leave but stopped and came back just as close. "Some of what we do makes a man have bad dreams. But we're free. We lives on the sea. No one bothers us. It's a good life, and Capt looks after us good. Yer've seen worse, whore. Yer've seen much worse." Then he left.

Turning to face the sea again, Star felt liberated!

The wind swept her face and hair. She breathed deeply. She loved the smell of the sea. She loved the movement of the boat racing along its surface. *Yes, something like a woman moving under a man.* And, she had just been given more dignity by these two men than she ever had received in her entire life. It was not much, but it was *more*! It felt as if she had been lifted to a new height. As if she really mattered somehow. She had never been given a **choice**! It was startling! Inside herself, she *danced*.

As the orange sun set and melted into the sea, all the captives were chained again and brought back to their bunks in the hold. Though used to filth and stench, Star thought that this was a bit more than she cared to endure. Besides, she could be sleeping in the captain's bed!

Chapter 15

❦

"I brought you this," said Lohlitah's voice from behind Morlah in the darkness. "...your cloak."

Morlah did not respond. He was an alien in this land. A freak. Everywhere he went, his magic made him an outcast. He had wanted to hide himself in the Gypsy way of life, but now he knew it was not possible.

They art different. No, rather...I am different. I am the outsider. A witch! Where willst I go from here? Back to Breezon? No. The Druids there art too zealous and idealistic. The Giants? I couldst buy fare on a ship and go to the Homeland of the Giants. They have no aversion to magic. They art tolerant of other races and peoples. Mayhapst I willst go there.

"I brought you some water," said Lohlitah, breaking the silence, handing him a skin.

But he did not take it.

"You will need to drink...."

He did not respond, his heart breaking because he would have to leave behind the only woman he had ever loved. His throat closed tightly, making it hard to breathe or swallow, and the night hid his eyes, which were filling with tears.

"Petrosis wants to see you...."

The words did not register in Morlah's mind.

Pain!

Is that what this existence was for? To experience pain? Is that the purpose of life? Not to live, not to laugh, not to love, not to eat or drink but to experience pain? Physical pain? Spiritual pain? Emotional pain?

"Petrosis wants to see you. He is not well. He may not live until morning."

More pain. Though Petrosis had been antagonistic, he had come to rather like the man. Now, the Gypsy would die. More pain. Death.

Damn it!

Lohlitah took his hand in hers. "Come, witch. Petrosis wants to see you."

She pulled at him; he followed because it was easier than resisting. Walking through the darkness toward the firelight of the camp, Morlah realized that he felt like a serpent waiting to strike. He felt raw. He felt anger writhing just beneath his skin, as if all his defenses and patience were stripped from him.

Or am I just protecting mineself from the pain that hovers over me, waiting for its opportunity to strike me again. But it willst not have the opportunity it doest seek. I willst harden mineself. I willst not let mineself become involved again. The damned Faeries can look to their own problems. The Elves...they art dead. Nothing canst be done for them.... No there is not! he tried to persuade himself. *I willst not be hurt, for I willst not become involved.*

Lohlitah led him into the camp. Voices hushed as the pair went by on their way to Petrosis' wagon. Morlah shielded himself with his anger, with his new resolve. Lohlitah stepped up into the wagon and spoke in soft tones to someone within while Morlah waited outside. Opening the door and indicating that he should come in, she moved aside as Morlah climbed the two steps up into the wagon and found himself face-to-face with Andreanna.

It killed him.

The little Elven girl. Her face was long with sadness; her eyes were swollen from crying. She was in his heart, as were all the Elves. He longed for Sannae, for Jerhad and Queen Andreanna, for Kendra and Rolann, for all the Elves he had known.

So much for mine defenses!

Morlah could protect himself from magic, but he could not defend himself from being Human. As he brushed past the Elf on his way to Petrosis' bedside, he heard her gasp. He ignored her.

Petrosis lay in his bed, his woman, Syndrill, at his side. His face was pale and sweaty, looking already dead even as his open eyes moved to meet Morlah's.

"Witch," the Gypsy whispered, the famous broad grin crossing his lips. "I thank you for coming. I want to thank you for what you did for my people. I have been a stupid man. Forgive me, witch, that I may die in peace."

Morlah sighed deeply. He had not expected anything, but if he had, it would not have been this.

"Some laws can be changed if the whole of the band agrees," whispered the man. He coughed feebly. "I am sure you can find a home among these people. Perhaps even be post...lead-post, eh?"

Morlah was too shaken to be able to respond, to find words, to find a way to back from his commitment of noninvolvement.

"Witch? Do you hear me?"

"I hear you, lead-post. I hear you."

"Do I get your forgiveness before I die? It would mean much to me. Truly!" He coughed weakly and blood oozed through the dressing on his chest. Sweat beaded on his skin.

"You know, Petrosis, there are some witches who could heal that, but I am not one. My magic is not given to healing. There is nothing to forgive; you were looking out for your people...I don't begrudge you that." He put his hand on the Gypsy's. "I will be leaving with the rising. I am no Gypsy. I don't belong here. I was using you to find your *kino*, Andreanna," the Druid confessed.

"But why?" asked the Gypsy in true bewilderment.

"I was looking for the heir to the throne of the Kingdom of the Elves. The heir to the magic of the Elves. I thought it might be your *kino*."

"But...?" whispered the post.

"I expect she would have known if she was descendant of the King and Queen. I guess I have the wrong *kino*."

"But I am," responded Andreanna's voice from behind him.

Morlah turned to her. "You said you didn't think you were."

"That's right. I don't *think*...*I know*!...that I am descendant of King Jerhad, son of Lewin, son of Baros, descendant of Windemere. I am the only living heir to the throne of the Kingdom of the Elves," she declared with surety and confidence.

Morlah fell back, sitting on the floorboards of the wagon, staring at the Elven girl whose hands glowed with the aura of magic. She reached behind her and pulled *Gildar* from its sheath.

"Behold, Ember, the King's blade, encroached with *acrch, esord, balan, urcha, igini, acdec,* and *licri!* Elfstones of power and Elven magic." And suddenly, Morlah saw in her all the pride and regal carriage that belonged to a queen... *Queen of the Elves!*

"Only," she finished in a weaker voice, "I don't know how to use it." Morlah motioned her to come closer and took hold of her hand, the hand that held *Gildar*.

"My dear child," he whispered. "How I have longed to see you. Is this what you felt when I entered the wagon?" he asked, pulling his knife from its belt.

She nodded. "I felt its presence and power as if they spoke to me."

"Take it. Hold it."

She took the argentus blade from his hand, standing with Ember in the other, both hands and knives glowing so brightly that the light could be seen through the canvas by those on the outside of the wagon-tent.

Morlah pointed to the silver-white Elfstone at the pommel. "This is *acrch*, Elfstone of Life and Health. The Faerie manifestation names herself Nan, and she can guide you in the use of the magic. Only remember that it is always wise to give heed to the wisdom of the magic."

Andreanna gasped and took a step backwards, the light about her growing in intensity with each heartbeat. "Oh,

I see you Nan. Oh, you're so beautiful. Oh Nan...!" she whispered, staring beyond to what the eyes of the others could not see.

What passed between the Elven Princess and the magic was not perceived by those present, but it was obvious that she was no longer with them and had gone to some distant place. She continued to look the same but was at the same time transformed in some indefinable way. After a while, her spirit returned and she became conscious of their presence once more.

"Morlah, Nan sends her greetings and asks you to take heart. She says *'acrch* to you Morlah'. Now, please stand aside." She made her way in the narrowness of the wagon to Petrosis' side. The floorboards creaked beneath her feet.

"Petrosis," she said. "You have always been good to me...as a father. You bought me from the pirates and gave me a home. You returned my knife to me after you bought it from the pirates, just because I asked it of you. But I have always had a secret that I kept from you, and I always felt as if I were betraying you by hiding it. I am what you would call a witch.

"Not like Morlah but simply an Elf with Elven magic. I'm sorry I lived a lie before you, but I didn't want you to send me away, so I lived the lie. Forgive me. Now I will repay you for your kindness to me even if you might not like it." She placed her hands on his chest, still holding both knives, the argentus and Elfstone *acrch* burning fiercely with power. She whispered in the ancient Elven tongue, which was actually unknown to her, *"acrch evandol, ponday cantalti."*

The glow from her hands spread to Petrosis. Color returned to his face. The sweat ceased to bead on his skin. Strength visibly returned to his body. He suddenly sat up and said, "I think I feel well enough to dance." A broad grin inscribed itself upon his face. "Ah, I think this witching could be for good. Andreanna, my love. Do you think you could do the same for the others who are injured?"

She nodded.

"Go then. Go quickly. Lohlitah, take her and go with her. Hurry. Hurry." Lohlitah and Andreanna left the wagon to tend to the others who were wounded. Petrosis pulled a bottle from under the bed, uncorked it and offered it to Morlah. "Beware! It is very strong."

"Why not?" responded Morlah, a broad grin breaking out on his face. He put the bottle to his lips and poured it in until Petrosis began to protest.

"Hey! Hey! Hey! Witch! Save some for me. What are you doing? Hey!" Petrosis retrieved his bottle, which was substantially reduced in content, and looked back at Morlah to see if perhaps the witch might choke, cough or fall over. When Morlah did none of these, Petrosis sneered. "Witches!" he hissed, and then proceeded to empty the bottle down his own throat.

Chapter 16

The sunrising after Morlah left Breezon, Easom, the young Druid, began his journey in search of a possessor of the magic of *ti-ord*. Departing in the early light, heading south toward the coast and the homeland of the Elves, he walked with a pack of provisions, a three-quarter staff, a bedroll and an oiled-canvas cloak. Nean and a few others had accompanied him to the gates to see him safely away, since his gear would attract attention.

Easom was a young Human, young in that he was but eighteen cycles and had only undergone the Druid Sleep once in his lifetime, the time he had contracted River Fever. He had been born in Breezon and had never been beyond the gates alone. He had traveled to BlueHill three times, twice to the Elves' country to work on their genealogies and to Heros twice. His mission was simple: to go to the Elves and discover if they knew any with the magic of *ti-ord* and return to Breezon with the information. Though a valued member of the Breezon Druid group, his time was given mostly to study. After much discussion and over the protests of his mother, the others had finally allowed him to undertake the journey alone.

Tall, lightly muscled, with dark brown hair, fair skin and with no facial hair showing, Easom was a handsome young man. He was somewhat practiced in the Arts of White magic and of defensive weapons. It was expected that he should be able to fend for himself and that the errand was expected to be uncomplicated.

For Easom, it was a quest. Long had he studied the *Elven Histories,* and he had acquired a fascination, if not a love, for the race. And if at all possible, with this new information at hand, he hoped against hope that the Elves of Mildra might actually be found and rescued.

However, he was still much of a novice in the ways of the world. He knew how to survive the streets of Breezon, but that was mostly done through remaining inconspicuous in a place where he was a familiar sight. The Druids had adapted to life in Breezon and had learned to be like a known tree or rock that one no longer sees. And, in spite of the vulgar and dangerous life in this degenerate town, his home-ground advantage there had not prepared him for all he might encounter on the outside.

Easom reveled in being out of the city as he walked along the road that led to BlueHill He was outside its walls, away from the vermin infested cesspool and out where nature was the dominant force. Making his way south, he stopped at midcourse to refresh himself with food and water under a large White Pine standing on a hill a short distance off the road. He rested briefly and resumed his journey.

Easom spent his first night under the stars, for it was warm and cloudless. He watched as meteors burned themselves out as they plummeted through the atmosphere. In some way, he felt as if he were off on an adventure, much the way the former King Jerhad had, the times he had gone out on Morlah's errands. The story was incorporated into the books of the *Elven Histories,* a volume of the *Frontmire Histories.* Easom had read them many times, giving him the feeling that he was already quite familiar with the south coast. He had studied its people and maps of the region, and twice, he had visited there with some of the Breezon Druids. He had gleaned much information from the volumes. Watching the stars, he soon fell asleep.

Sunrising brought him up with a start; it took a few heartbeats to remember where he was. He had forgotten how uncomfortable sleeping on the ground could be! Soon, he was on the road again, heading south under what promised to be a second lovely course for traveling.

The third sunsetting brought Easom to the town of Arbor, one of the towns that had been razed to the ground in a former Troll uprising. It had been rebuilt. Though not as dangerous as Breezon, it still was a place where one needed to be careful. The three courses of the sun of walking had taken a subtle toll on Easom, however, and he somehow felt as if he were among his own as he entered the small, clean, beggar and prostitute free town.

As darkness claimed the final span of the sun's course, Easom made his way to the only inn, Potter's Pride. The only inn along the road to BlueHill, it had been constructed by a Breezon merchant. Though worn with age and weathering, it remained a sturdy plank structure, clad with a new cedar-shake roof. A bright light shone through its turbid glassed windows.

Standing just within the doorway, marshaling his bearings as he entered, Easom found few patrons present; most were drinking warm mead and smoking or chewing tobac. The furnishings spoke of a past prime, with whitewashed walls sorely sooty from oil-lamp fumes and smoke trickling into the room from a hearth with a chimney desperately overdue for cleaning. Just beneath the odor of stale, spilled beer and smoke, Easom detected the smell of cooking food, stirring his gut into activity. He headed to a table near the kitchen door and sat. Eyes followed his movements as he made his way through the dim dining hall.

A weathered, pasty-skinned, middle-aged woman approached him, eyeing him up and down as if she might be interested in having him for evening meat.

"What'll ya have, boy," she said, smiling through a distressed dentition. "Something to eat or drink?"

"What do you have?"

"No choices, love. Mutton stew and hot rolls. Water or mead to drink."

"How old a mutton?" Easom asked, not relishing the choice.

"How should I know? You gonna eat?"

"Yes...one mutton stew. And mead."

The "old girl" looked at him wantonly. "Anything else, love?" she inquired, drawing closer.

He choked. "No.... One mutton stew is plenty." She returned to the kitchen, not sure whether she had been insulted or not.

Well, his intuition about the stew had been accurate, but it was warm food. He secured a room for the night and bedded down. Come sunrising, having finished his break fast, packed and replenished his provisions, he set out on the road.

Colors of salmon and peach lit the bellies of the scattered clouds at the sunsetting. The clouds appeared determined to follow the sun as it journeyed beyond the horizon.

It was dark when Easom made camp in a copse of oaks. There were plenty of dead branches around for him to make a fire. Having set the small pile of wood ablaze with steel and flint, he settled in for the night. Weariness stole over him. He had been lucky so far: the weather had stayed good for traveling. Just as he was thinking of turning in, he heard footsteps approaching.

"Hello, in the camp," came a husky male voice out of the darkness. "Mind if'n I join ya?" Easom felt a bit uneasy but figured that since the person had bothered to call out, he was probably harmless.

"Come on in," he answered, preferring to have stayed alone.

A large figure approached out of the darkness, making his way to the fireside.

"Hey," he greeted the young Druid. "I be Matt. Mind if I warm meself by the fire and use it to cook m'self some meat?"

"Help yourself. I'm Easom," answered the Druid uneasily.

The broad-shouldered man dropped his pack to the ground and sat on a log by the fire. "Ya out here on y'own?"

Easom nodded.

Matt did not make any moves to begin preparing his food, which gave Easom even more hesitation about having him there.

"I was travlin' north. Goin' to Heros when I saw ya fire. Where ya fixin' to be goin'?"

"Down to the southern coast."

"Elf country?"

"Yes."

"Was down there weren' several moon's cycles back. Went to see the city. Mildra. Sure was a fine place. Nothin' left to pilfer. Some says that there's still lots of silver an' gold hidden there, but we uns didn' fin' none. Ya been there afore?" Matt spit a thick wad of tobac juice to the side and continued to chew on what was still in his mouth.

"Twice. Came down from Breezon."

"Breezon? That's a fine place. Man can get all the woman he wants there for cheap. Ya live there?" Matt asked, staring into the fire.

"All my life."

"Funny about fire, like that. Sort of draws un in. Hypnotizing."

Easom looked into the flames, as Matt threw a handful of powder into them, something that burned green for a score of heartbeats, the breeze carrying the smoke toward the younger man.

"What kinda business would ya be havin' down there, if'n ya don' min' me as'in?" The flames played before Easom's eyes, and he began to feel the weariness of his travel more than he had on previous courses.

"Going to see the Elves. Thought it might be more interesting than Breezon," he said, presenting his fabricated story.

"Ain' nothin' but a bunch o' farmers. Good crops they do grow though. Fire sure is warming for a body."

Easom had to agree. He was feeling quite relaxed and comforted by the small fire.

"They don' let out their women folk though. Never did have an Elf girl." Matt's voice sounded distant as he kept talking, continually bringing Easom's attention back to the flames. His voice began to drone on, and soon Easom realized he had not followed what the man had been saying for a while. He thought he should get his bedroll set up for the night but did not move to do so. He was too sleepy.

Then, Easom noticed that Matt was not speaking anymore and that he could not see the fire. His eyes were closed. He tried to open them. They were too heavy. He heard Matt speaking again.

"Like pickin' eggs from a dove's nest," he was saying.

"Sure makes i' easy," sounded a voice from behind Easom. "Less chance o' gettin' hurt or havin' him put u' a fight."

Alarm rang through Easom! He struggled to open his eyes and managed to get his head up only to be met on the back of the head with a thump from a heavy wooden club. Everything went dark as the night.

Towering and billowing clouds bobbed in a bright-blue sky, floating by, as Easom lay on his back. He had never been to sea, but he thought it might have felt like this if he had. Everything moved in ways he did not expect, and he felt as if he were rocking about as he went along. The motion made him queasy. Soon, he fell back to sleep.

When he opened his eyes again, Easom was inside a dimly lit stone chamber. He tried to lift his head, but it hurt too much and made the room whirl. He was warm and dry; his mouth was dry too. His lips felt cracked and his tongue parched to the point of being stuck to the roof of his mouth. His body did not respond well to his attempts to move, though he did not sense anything was broken. He could not figure out where he was. The strain of trying to move was too much for him, and he soon drifted back to sleep.

"Oh, there you are," spoke a female voice as Easom opened his eyes again. "We thought we were going to lose you."

Easom turned his eyes to see a young, soft featured (for a Dwarf), female Dwarf. She was clothed in a simple, long cotton dress, had long brown hair tied back in a braid that fell to her knees. Her look was very pleasant and friendly. He tried to speak, but it split his lip and caused his throat and mouth intense pain.

"Open," spoke the Dwarfess. "I have a mixture that will soothe your mouth, and maybe we can get a bit of water into you." The potion burned for a few heartbeats, but then his mouth went mostly numb. The Dwarfess lifted a polished stone bowl to his lips, and he sipped at the water it contained.

"Easy now. You have not had much for eight courses. Go easy."

He heard the words she spoke but they did not register.

"Where am I?" he managed in a thready whisper.

"You are in *Dolan*. Does that mean anything to you?"

He nodded, knowing it was the name for the Dwarf Nation's home. The motion produced a splitting pain in his head, and it was revealed on his face by a contorted grimace.

"Hurt?"

He squeaked a "Yes."

"I am not surprised. You took a nasty blow to the head and were probably left for dead. I expect you were robbed, for you had no possessions when the patrol found you."

"How long?"

"Eight courses ago. You might have been there for one or two longer. I have managed to keep you alive with a bit of water I could get into you by putting wet napkins in your mouth. It was not much, but it was better than dying."

"Not sure."

"Here. Drink some more. Just a couple sips. I am Oreleana. Do you have a name?"

"Easom," he whispered.

"Well, Easom, let us not tax you too heavily. A couple of sips of water, and you should go back to sleep. There's herb in the water for sleep and pain," Easom heard her say as darkness closed in about him again.

It was sunrising when Easom awoke. His head was throbbing and his vision blurred, but he felt somewhat better. Lifting his head immediately set the chamber to spinning. He had just enough time to see that he was in a small rock-hewn hollow just off of a large cavern before he had to lay his head back down. He assumed he was in the military area of *Dolan*, which he had read about. The entire place was lit with light from bluish-white magical orbs. No one knew where they had come from or who had made them, but it was commonly accepted that they were made of a lost, ancient Dwarf magic.

"Awake again!" said Oreleana as she came into the chamber. "It has been another two courses of the sun. Let us get you to drink again." This time Easom was able to drink a fair amount of the broth that she offered him.

"Well, this is encouraging," she said.

"What happened? How did I get here?"

"As to what happened.... We assume you were robbed. Quite common in the area you were found. Someone is using a mixture of copper and arsenic powder in the campfire to knock out their victims. You can tell by the smell left in the ashes of their fires. It's quite toxic when one breathes the smoke, and it alone can kill you, even without the blow that you took in addition to it. One of our patrols out investigating reports of Troll activity found you and brought you in. They normally would not do so; but you being so young.... I guess they had pity on you."

"Hungry," he said, as visions of Matt returned to him.

"Good. I will be back in a bit with some more broth."

"Why still in cavern?" he whispered. The scant activity was tiring him.

"Oh. It is forbidden to have outsiders in the living area of the valley. You have to stay in the military quarters for now, where the males can keep an eye on you. I will get some more broth and be back soon."

Three courses later, Easom was sitting up and eating thickened soup; he was even able to remain seated for a span at a time. Oreleana was at his side by sunlight and by night; every time he opened his eyes, she was not far off.

Eventually, he opened his eyes to find a male Dwarf standing over him. The Dwarf was the height of a ten-cycle-old Human male but of a thick muscular build, and with a thick beard that hung to his knees. His features were coarse and his nose pronounced. Both his hair and beard were braided into thick weaves.

"Where you from, boy?" he asked in a deep, gruff voice.

"Breezon."

"Hmmm. Sort of a long way from home. You going to live?"

"I am not sure I want to, the way my head feels most of the time," he said speaking in the Common Tongue, rather than the Druid dialect.

"You know you are not really welcome here. We have no use for strangers. As soon as you are up and about, you will have to leave. Already in enough trouble for having brought you here." He turned and left.

Oreleana entered the room. "I see you met Bone-Breaker."

"Real pleasant fellow."

"Oh, do not mind him. He is just a bit sour because the Captain tied his whiskers in a knot for bringing you here. It is all just a formality. Policy and politics. At heart, they are glad you survived. Just need to keep a good front. Goes with the male image they have of themselves." She smiled warmly at him. "Well this course, I believe, we will see if you can walk. Think you are up to it?"

"We will know when we try," said Easom. He slowly sat up, for he had discovered that if he did not move too fast, the room usually stayed put. Sitting up, he thought that he might be feeling stronger. "Why are you doing this, Oreleana?"

She looked at him, puzzled.

"Taking care of me like this?"

"Is it not the way of the noble races...to help those who are in need? Do not judge us too harshly. The Dwarves withdrew from the affairs of the other races because they seemed bent on destroying themselves. It was a measure of self-preservation...only, it sort of became political over the cycles. But at heart, the Dwarves are still the same. They just need a little motivation now and again to let it show."

Easom made his way to his knees and finally, with Oreleana's help, to his feet. He swirled like the handle of a butter churn for a few heartbeats, before the floor stopped heaving under him.

"Our goal, this course, is to that wall and back to your pallet. Do you think you can manage?"

He started to nod but thought better of it. "I think so." By the time he returned to his pallet, he was thoroughly drenched with sweat and exhausted.

"It is a good beginning," said Oreleana. "I think you will recover."

"Oreleana. How is it I'm clean and dry..." he asked somewhat embarrassed, expecting he knew her answer.

"I have taken care of that for you. One cannot be expected to lie in his own waste and get better, now can he?" she said matter-of-factly. Easom was embarrassed.

Chapter 17

It was a full cycle of the moon more before Easom was able to move around on his own and not become drenched with sweat or tire excessively. He walked as much as he could, pushing himself that he might recover. His dizziness and vertigo diminished course by course, and he ate moderate amounts of solid food at each meal. His thoughts began turning toward his quest; he needed to head to the south coast soon. Besides, the Druids in Breezon would be expecting him back, and he had not even achieved the first leg of his journey.

"Oreleana," he asked her one night after he had eaten. "How long before I canst go?"

"Are you well enough?"

"I doest not know. I just doest need to be going soon. I am already too far delayed."

"But you are alive! What business could you have that would be so important?"

"I doest need to go south to the Elves and see if I can find a *seeker*."

"A seeker?" She eyed him suspiciously because his speech had slipped back into the Druid dialect, with which she was not familiar.

"One with the magic to find something that wast lost."

"And what would you be looking for with this *seeker* of yours?"

He hesitated for a score of heartbeats, but decided it would be safe to tell her. "The Elfstone *soiccat*. Morlah and the other Druids doest believe it is possible that the Elves of Mildra mayest be found with use of the stone."

"Found? But they have been gone for hundreds of cycles."

"It mayst be possible that they are alive in the Netherworld. Morlah wast able to get information from Daektoch that leads him to think it is possible."

"Morlah and the Druids? Are you sure you are not suffering from delusion or dreaming?"

"Look," he said, raising his hand. He mumbled the words of a spell and caused a white light-orb to appear. "I am a Druid."

Oreleana's face changed to a look of concern. "Enough for now. You rest." She quickly rose and left.

Later, Easom awoke to find several male Dwarves standing around him. With care, so as to not set his head to spinning, he rose to a seated position. Oreleana stood behind them.

"Oreleana says you are a Druid. Is this true?" asked Bowdin, Captain of the King's Guard and the Captain of the Captains.

"Yes, I am."

The Dwarves stared at him for a few scores of heartbeats. "And you say the Druid, Morlah, is about?" continued Captain Bowdin.

"Last I didst see him, he wast leaving Breezon and heading toward Heros."

"Why did he not come to the Dwarves instead of to that filthy city?"

"He didst."

"He did not. I would have heard," exclaimed Bowdin.

"He didst, and he wast treated the beggar by the patrols outside. They didst send him on his way. Then, when he didst attempt to appear to the King, it didst raise such a ruckus that the only thing he couldst do wast to leave."

At the mention of Morlah's visit to the King, understanding registered on Bowdin's face and laughter danced in his eyes, but he squelched it. "And you say there are Druids in Breezon?"

"There art."

"Why is it we never heard of them?"

Easom was beginning to tire of the senseless interrogation. "Well, we hadst never heard of the Dwarves, but here thou art anyway."

"Never heard of...," the Captain huffed into his beard. Bowdin eyed Easom, knowing that he just had his beard pulled by the youth. He turned to the others. "Back to your duties. Mendalow, get our young friend here some ale." The Dwarves departed, and soon, Mendalow returned to deliver Easom his ale, and then, he took up position outside the chamber. Bowdin sat on the ground.

"I do apologize...Easom. We have grown more than cautious through the cycles, and I do think at times that good sense has left us. We spend too much of our time within *Dolan* and have contact with none but our own. Methinks that it shrinks the head and wisdom. Peace. I mean you no harm.

"Your tidings are somewhat outlandish if one goes by what is known to us. But we are out of touch with the outside, except for what goes on immediately about our lands. Pray, forgive me and answer my questions if you please... and the ale is a peace offering, not a ruse to loosen your tongue." His smile was genuine and warm.

"Yes. Everybody within *Dolan* is still talking about the ghost who visited the King," he chuckled. "And you say it was *the Druid?*"

"It wast."

"Tell me, are you quite sure it is him?"

"Without a doubt. Mine uncle wast a boy, the son of Morlah's closest friend, back in Parintia. He didst recognize him the heartbeat he saw him. Others of our group also didst recognize his face and his magic."

"You are telling me that there are those alive that were at *seilstri* that long ago?"

"Yes. We still doest use the Druid Sleep...the same way that Morlah doest to still be alive."

Bowdin picked up a stone and pounded it on the floor, causing a hollow thudding sound to echo in the cavern. In two heartbeats, a Dwarf ran into the chamber. Bowdin said to him, "Find out who was Captain of the Watch on the west side the night the ghost visited the King and send him to me, now!"

"Yes, sir!" The Dwarf rushed off with all speed.

"Well, mine friend, if what you say is true, and I do not doubt you, though there are many who would, then this may truly be tidings that could cause quite a ruffling of the 'great minds' among us. There are those who believe they know much and have answers for all things...but they keep us locked in this hill until many of us think (even for Dwarves!) that we will go mad for not having seen the sun in so long. They think the best way to live is to hide like rats in a hole and not know and not see anything or anyone from the outside.

"I am not one who agrees with this. I think we need to extend ourselves to the races and together rise to new heights. The mere presence of Druids, especially Morlah, could be reason for a beginning to open our doors once more." The Dwarf that Bowdin had sent off returned, followed by another Dwarf.

"TenOres," said Bowdin. "You were Captain on the west side the night the King saw his ghost?"

"Yes. What of it?"

"You had a visitor who asked to see the King?"

TenOres stopped and thought a bit. "There was a beggar. We threw him out."

"Human?"

"Yes."

"Why was I not told?" growled Bowdin.

"I saw no need. We saw him to the boundary and sent him on his way. There was no further trouble."

"And is that how you deal with all who come to *Dolan*?"

TenOres began to grow uneasy. "Those we do not know."

"And are those my orders?" the Captain huffed.

"Ah, no...but RedBeard says that we should...."

"Ahem! Is RedBeard the Captain of the Guard?"

"No, but...."

"No but nothing!" barked Bowdin. "It is not yours to screen those who would come to us. In the future, you will follow my orders, or I will replace you with someone who will. Is that understood?"

"Clearly, Captain! Will that be all?"

"No. TenOres, describe the man you saw to this Human."

Easom gulped because of the severity that Bowdin had used with TenOres. It intimidated the Human. If the Dwarves were half as stern in physical confrontation, he would want to remain on their better side. Having finished his description of Morlah, TenOres went quiet again.

"Is this your beggar?" Bowdin asked Easom as the Dwarf Captain threateningly surveyed TenOres from under a heavy brow.

"Could be. Sounds right," said Easom.

"You are dismissed," growled Bowdin to TenOres. The Dwarf saluted Bowdin with a thud of his fist to his chest and left.

"Well, then. I think that I should go to the King. Is there any way of getting in touch with Morlah?'

"He hast gone to Heros and then wast to go north. I doest doubt that he willst be seen for a while."

"Tell me about the Elves as you told Oreleana."

Easom relaxed enough to take a long draw on his vessel of ale. He now trusted Bowdin and was willing to tell him everything.

Easom stood at the opening to one of the secret entrances at the foot of *Dolan*, not having seen the sun in what felt like ages. He was about to set out toward the land of the Elves. Since he was six moon's cycles off schedule, he was quite depressed about his mission. Not only was he way off plan, he really was not up to traveling yet, but he could lie about the Dwarves' caverns no longer, concerned that time might be a factor in the returning of the Elves to Mildra. He did not know why he felt this way, but he did.

Oreleana was with him, as were several soldiers assigned to watch the entrance. The Dwarfess had insisted on accompanying him south, not believing that he should be departing so soon, since he still suffered from spells of dizziness and nausea and would break into a sweat if taxed the slightest bit. Her brother, Laskey, was accompanying them also, for he would not hear of her leaving without a Dwarf's protection; the outside world was not a safe place. Laskey had desperately tried to deter her, but she was her own person. Unless one of the rulers forbade her, she would go. So, the only thing left for him to do was to go with her.

Chapter 18

༺❦༻

Easom, Oreleana and Laskey left not long after the sunrising, the sky a brilliant blue and without a trace of a cloud. They planned to take their time heading south. It was doubtful that Easom would travel far each course of the sun. Heading down toward the road that connected to the trail that led to Barrett's Fall and south and arriving to the boundary of the Dwarves' lands bordering the Land of the Gift of the Elves to the Giants, they were surprised to see Bowdin sitting on a stone, as they came around a bend. He was whittling away at a branch with a broad-bladed knife.

"Thought you were going to sleep throughout the sun's course," he grumbled, dropping the stick, sheathing his knife, picking up a pack and throwing it onto his shoulders."

"Going somewhere?" asked Easom

"With you. I want to see Elves and Druids and whatever else there is to be seen. Been in *Dolan* with nothing to do but to play make-believe soldier for too long."

"What of your duties?" asked Laskey.

"I am due some leave. Had not taken any for ages. Good a time as any."

"Why art thou doing this?" asked Easom.

"I am one who has studied the *Histories* of all races more than most, methinks. Three things I have observed: that is to expect the unexpected. And, that things are rarely what they seem to be to the masses. And lastly, that change is inevitable. Those who are not ready get swept away or left behind. I have had a long talk with the King in secret and hope that I have made these things clear to him.

"Though his counselors are old hens who want to stay hidden within *Dolan*, I think the King agrees with me that if the Elves of Mildra may be helped, as do think the Druids who are in Breezon, then perhaps it is time for the Dwarves to look about and see what may be done to render assistance and to see what is happening to the races and in the land. For now, it is evident that things are not as we thought. And so, the advice that has been given over the cycles is not as wise as it originally was thought to be. Besides, you children need someone to watch over you on your journey. There are still brigands and derelicts about, as you have found out, Easom."

Laskey appeared a bit put off by Bowdin's referring to them as children, but did not respond. It would not have been his place to question or reprove someone of Bowdin's status, though Bowdin was not one to have taken offense.

It took them three courses longer than it normally would have to reach Barrett's Fall, for Easom was not able to travel for long periods at a time and needed to stop at regular intervals to rest. The Dwarves did not mind. The weather was warm, and it was a welcome change to be out on an "adventure."

Having set up camp above the falls in order to distance themselves from its roar and to keep away from the dampness about its waters, they left camp and went down to see the great waterfall. The waters of the River Rain plummeted down some two hundred paces and thundered into a small lake at its base.

In the past, the River Rain had flowed through the mountains and merged with the Mage River, which flowed past Mildra and out to the sea. But an earthquake in ancient times had altered the terrain. As a result, the falls had been formed, and the river was turned, now coursing its way to the east coast. The falls, it was said, were named after one Barrett who had discovered them too late and gone over, hence, Barrett's Fall.

The view of the cascading waters and the sound of the thunderous roar it produced instilled life and hope into the travelers. Its grandeur and potency were immense, and something about witnessing the raw power and beauty of nature sparked dormant seeds within them.

Easom, who had spent most of his life within Breezon, was ecstatic with joy at the sight. He felt like a bird that was freed from its cage, and so, he spent the remainder of the course watching the water as the others returned to camp to prepare evening meat. Night arrived, and the sound of the falls changed from a roar to a hiss. The night brought its own peculiar stillness and tenor. The travelers lay awake long after they had gone to bed, listening to the water.

Bowdin took the first watch and at half moon's course turned the duty over to Laskey. Laskey, like most male Dwarves, was trained as a soldier and took up such tasks without resentment or resistance; he was glad to have Bowdin along to share the watch. Easom was not fit for the task, and Oreleana did not think it was important.

Sunrising dawned, its warmth raining down on the Human and the Dwarves. A low-lying fog appeared to want to turn to rain clouds, but as the sun heated the land, it burned off, leaving a clear blue sky. The heat intensified the scent of the forest's conifers. The travelers soon departed and set off along the road that led south. It was an ancient highway, and had it not been paved with stone blocks by the Dwarves long before the time of King Jerhad, it would have been overgrown and lost. But the thoroughfare, instead, was a clear way with dense brush, thickets and trees growing on each side, providing shade from the sun and shelter from the wind, making for a pleasant lane to travel. The way would lead south into the mountains that separated the two rivers, and then, through the channel that the river had once used and that eventually had become Dwarf's Pass.

The pass was a road carved out by the Dwarves along a gulch that led through the mountains in the time the Elves had first migrated to the south coast. An earthquake had collapsed the mountain walls at a later date, and the pass had not been reopened until after the renewing of relations between the Elves and the Dwarves in the early time of King Jerhad.

The Dwarves had tunneled through the rubble and shored it up as an arched way, travelling beneath millions of stones' weight of rock debris. While the Elves had been in Mildra, there had been a lively trade between the two nations, and the pass was used extensively. Now, it was all but abandoned, and rarely did any ever travel there.

At about midcourse, they reached the first tunnel of Dwarf's Pass. They sat and ate, refreshing themselves and allowing Easom to rest. Then, they set out again. The pass was quite long, and the tunnel went on uninterrupted for a quarter league in three stretches, each open to the sky for a short distance.

When they reached the second of these opened areas, they stopped briefly to drink and to enjoy the sun. Bowdin went into the tunnel entrance of the next stretch and examined the stonework wrought by his ancestors. It was still solid and without evidence of weakening. He returned to the group as they put their packs back on and drew Laskey aside.

"There is a foul odor in the tunnel ahead of us. Like that of carrion and some animal that is not known to me. Methinks we may meet up with whatever is in there. Be on your guard and have your weapon at hand. I'll take the lead and you the rearguard. Say nothing to the others lest we worry them needlessly."

Moving into the tunnel, Bowdin used a magical blue orb to light the way as he had previously. They followed the gulch that went through the mountains, snaking its way along the foot of two steep peaks, which caused the tunnel to twist and turn as it went. After traveling for a while, Easom commented on the odor, but Bowdin did not respond. The odor grew stronger.

They traveled nearly one span of the sun's course. Abruptly, as they rounded a turn, Bowdin stopped in his tracks and let out a hiss, stepping back as the sound of a woeful moan from the distance echoed in their ears. Around this bend, they could see sunlight at the end of the tunnel, and silhouetted within its illuminated opening, stood a form on two feet. Its head was lowered slightly to avoid hitting the tunnel's ceiling. In one hand, it held the remains of a tree, as a club.

It was a Mountain Troll! Of the Trolls one could meet, this was the most dull witted, the slowest but also the biggest and strongest...and most dangerous.

The Mountain Trolls were a rare (not rare enough at this point) breed of Trolls usually only found deep in the Mystic Mountains. This one had obviously come down from there and had taken up residence in the tunnel, probably having an easy time of getting food by waylaying the few travelers or animals that traveled through the pass.

The Troll headed toward them as they turned and ran. Its long legs carried it faster than they could run, and it was soon evident that they would have to turn and fight. But how? How did one fight a Mountain Troll? It was almost the height of a Giant, twice the height of the average Human. It had leather-like skin, almost as strong as wood or stone, and it was highly territorial and had an immense appetite. It would not tire from the small exertion used fighting them.

Bowdin, who had been pulling up the rear with Laskey in their escape, stopped and turned to meet the Troll. The least he could do was to delay it to let the others get away; it probably would not be much of a delay. Laskey turned back and joined him.

"No. Go with the others," Bowdin commanded.

"Sorry, you do not get to pull rank now. We will be dead in a bit and you will not be able to put me on report."

To his dismay, Bowdin found that Easom and Oreleana had also stopped.

"Go," he cried, "Run! We cannot stand long against it." His war-axe was out, and he braced himself to deliver the only blow that he would have a chance at.

Easom did not move from his postiton next to the Captain.

"Damn it boy. Now we're all going to die."

"Not just yet, I doest hope."

The Troll was now but a few steps from them and slowing down as it raised its great club.

Easom cried, "Close your eyes!"

A bright flash of white light erupted before them. The Troll roared in surprise, and its club dropped to the ground as it covered its eyes with its huge iron-like hands.

"Let us get moving," called Easom. They turned and fled back the way they had come.

Unfortunately, Laskey and Oreleana had not obeyed the Druid and were both also blinded; they had to be led by Easom and Bowdin as they raced back toward the falls. They had not been running long when the Troll's mutterings turned to a roar of rage. They heard the scraping of the great club being dragged along on the ground and the thumping footsteps as it moved in their direction. However, its vision had not returned, and every few steps it took, they heard grunts and groans as it bumped into the walls of the tunnel, first to one side and then the other. Soon, the foursome outdistanced the Troll, who made poor progress with his meandering and collidings. They emerged from the tunnel, Easom pale, breathing raggedly and perspiring profusely. The Dwarves' vision was adequate for them to find their own way.

"Let us go up there where we can hide," Bowdin said, pointing to a spire of stones up the mountainside a short way.

Captain Bowdin, Oreleana, Laskey and Easom feverishly climbed as the Troll's groans rapidly drew nearer, and they soon found themselves at a guard tower that had been fashioned to look like part of the mountain on the outside and was of a polished sawn stone on the inside. Entering, they found it quite spacious, with light filtering through tall and narrow arrow ports set all along the walls. A great iron door stood open, and with a tremendous effort, the two male Dwarves were able to close it despite its well-rusted hinges, the sound attracting the Troll's attention and guiding him toward them.

Easom sat, panting, near fainting.

"Hurry!" cried Oreleana as she watched the Troll through one of the arrow ports. "He's almost here."

The door was closed, and with use of a sledge that Oreleana found, Laskey hammered at the pins that locked it just as the Troll arrived. The tower shuddered as the huge tree-like club smashed at the entrance. Everyone stepped back. Again and again, the Troll swung his weapon and battered the door, until everyone inside thought that he would bring the mountain and the tower down upon them. But after nearly a span of beating at the tower, the sound stopped, and the tower and its door stood intact.

"The gods be thanked for Dwarf stonework," Easom sighed from where he sat on the floor, his back against the rock wall furthest away from the entry. "There is not another race that couldst have built something strong enough to withstand punishment like that."

Laskey perked up at these words and said, "I think I may grow to like a Human who thinks so highly of our craft."

"Well, I was thinking quite highly of it myself, under the circumstances," quipped Bowdin. "Not to say I did not have my doubts for a spell. The work is very old and has not been tended to for hundreds of cycles.... I am impressed beyond reckoning. I do not know if we are building to these standards in our times. This is truly impressive craftsmanship.

"Damn it! Look at this, Laskey! Our own people's works. Have you ever seen this meshed lay of stone? It is pure genius. Look at how the hinges on the door are locked into the stone. The wall would need to come down to dislodge them. It grieves me that our isolation has kept us from seeing the work of our ancestors and that only a few leagues from our very gates."

"That is all well and good, but we still have a Troll to deal with," said Oreleana, who had continued to watch the beast through the slits. "He is still out there and sniffing around."

"Well, let him. I think we are safe enough in here for the time being. Tend to Easom. Make sure he eats and drinks a bit. I'm going down these stairs to investigate the cellars below. You coming, Laskey? Oh, that reminds me...what was that you were saying about putting you on report," Bowdin said quite sternly, but then he laughed and slapped Laskey on the shoulder. "Only 'tugging at your beard', old Dwarf'. Come along.

"Oreleana, you stay with Easom. I'm going to investigate what we have available here to deal with this problem".

At the arrow slits, the snuffing sounds from the Troll continued.

"Coming, Laskey?" Bowdin turned and descended the stone stair that led them to the foundations of the tower, pulling his blue orb from his pack for light.

The two Dwarves reached the cellar. In one corner was a well that could provide fresh water when besieged. There were old casks of food, which had turned to powder for age. There were a variety of weapons: war-axes, swords, spears, pikes, slings, and shields -- and more stores. The metal of these was not rusted, as the Dwarves used a trace of argentus in all their weapons and tools, making a rust resistant alloy. Off to one side, on the south wall, was a tunnel, which the two Dwarves followed. Every few paces they found arrow slits that looked out into the main tunnel of Dwarf's Pass.

They followed this passage for nearly one span before turning back; it went on uninterrupted except for the arrow slits and occasional shafts that they assumed were escape passages to the surface. Upon returning to the tower, they found Easom asleep, Oreleana preparing food and the Troll still moving slit to slit, snuffing at the scent of the travelers within.

"Should we discourage him a bit?" asked Laskey.

"How do you mean to do that?" questioned Bowdin.

Laskey ran back down to the cellar and returned carrying a spear. "It is the old spear tip in the nostril remedy," he said with a grin.

"Might just provoke him," muttered Bowdin.

"If I get the angle right, it might kill him."

"Naw.... He really is not malicious," said the Captain. "Just a beast doing what he does. Try it and see if you can offend him just enough that he decides we are not worth the trouble." Laskey went to the slit where the Troll was presently sniffing and slid the spear down the opening. The wall was surprisingly thick and the shaft was almost to its end before it connected with something.

The Troll howled, probably more from anger than pain, and it proceeded to beat the stone walls with its fists, causing the tower to reverberate.

"Powerful little demon, is he not?" said Laskey, looking back with a grin.

After a short season of this behavior, the Troll took to snuffing at the slits again, only to meet with the spear tip once more. This was repeated six or eight times, but each time, the Troll returned.

"He does not learn very quickly, does he?" said Bowdin. "Maybe we should change our tactic. We could leave something with our scent in a few ports and then go down the inner passage. My guess is that the inner tunnel will follow the Pass all the way to the other end.

"I am not sure what is to be done with our Troll friend out there, though. He really should not be left in the tunnel. Just trouble for any who look to get through. Wish there was a way to get him to move back to the mountains. We will have to think on it. Let us rest up and get fed, and we will leave after dark. Maybe he will be quieter by then."

So, they ate and then slept for a couple of spans of the sun, and shortly after sunsetting, they were all wide awake. Having left an old garment, which Oreleana was willing to part with, torn into pieces and stuffed into a few slits for the Troll to sniff at, they departed by way of the cellar.

Traveling for a few spans and finally stopping to rest, they were about to resume their march when they were suddenly startled, and dismayed, to hear the Troll snuffing at a nearby arrow port.

"Well, he will not be easily gotten rid of, it would appear," complained Laskey.

"I guess not. I expect we will find a tower at the other end. We should be safe enough for now," said Bowdin

"But what if the door to the tower is open?" asked Oreleana.

"We can deal with that later as long as he does not figure out that he needs to get there before we do. If not, I doubt he can fit into or move in this passage, and if he does, we will just have to go back."

It was somewhere near three-quarters of the moon's course when they began to see moonlight through the arrow-ports and guessed they were near the tunnel's end. Bowdin put his plan into action. Using the last piece of Oreleana's sacrificed garment, he tied it to the shaft of a spear he had brought with him and stuck it through almost to the other side of the wall, where they could hear the Troll.

"Easom, hold onto this and tease him with it, but do not let him get hold of it. Oreleana, come with us a ways so you can easily hear Easom and let us know if the Troll heads our way. Now, we must make no noise as to draw it away from here, except for you, Easom. You need to keep it occupied while Laskey and I secure the door to the tower. Everyone set?"

They nodded and took their positions. Easom sent the bait down the opening and soon had the Troll clawing and snuffing with excitement at the wall. But a short while later, the two Dwarves returned to report that the tower door on the other end was rusted solid and open. They were unable to budge it.

"Now what?" asked Easom, who was still teasing the Troll with his bait.

"We can sleep the remainder of the night here and hope that the sunrising brings inspiration or respite," said Bowdin. So, they bedded down for the remainder of the night, Bowdin and Laskey splitting the watch.

The next sunrising, the sky was dark and overcast, with a cold, heavy rain falling; the lack of sunshine appeared to have forestalled the inspiration they had hoped for. They moved their camp to the cellar of the southern tower, for the stair was too small an opening for the Troll to get through; the Dwarves agreed that it would be safe. The Mountain Troll, Bobo, as Oreleana had named him, followed. Once they were in the cellar, Bobo left the tunnel and started exploring the surroundings of the tower, and soon, his face appeared in the opening to the stair.

"Ye gods," exclaimed Oreleana. "That ugly snoot does make me uncomfortable even if I know he cannot get in here. What are we going to do?" No one had any suggestions. They could run from end to end of the pass, back-and-forth forever, and probably meet up with Bobo each time they tried to leave. Their provisions would only last them a couple more courses.

Bowdin sat on an oak cask and mumbled to himself. "A fine end for a warrior such as I to come to. Trapped like a rabbit in a hole.... Hole!" He got up and ran back down the tunnel causing Bobo to swat his arm through the opening in hopes of catching something before they all got away. They were, however, sitting far enough from the stair to be outside its reach. A span later, Bowdin showed up with a grin under his beard.

"We are going out," he announced. "Pack your toys, boys and girls, Uncle Bowdin has found a way." Refusing to waste time talking about it, he led them back down the tunnel, causing the Troll to whimper at the sight of his disappearing meal; he had not eaten in a while and felt that he was overdue for at least a snack.

Bowdin led them a short way down the tunnel and then turned to one of the ports that he had assumed led to the surface. Sure enough, after a quarter of a span of climbing on hands and knees, they found themselves outside on top of the tunnels. To their delight, situated a couple of hundred paces up alongside the gorge was a narrow trail cut into the stone that allowed them to travel along at a moderate speed through the pouring rain.

Following this path for a span, they found themselves emerging just above the road about one hundred paces south of the opening to the Pass. They could see the tower in the distance, embraced in clusters of foliage, but not Bobo. They began their descent to the thoroughfare. Suddenly, the Troll appeared on the road below them, gazing up at them and snuffing at the air. Oreleana stomped her foot in anger.

"Blasted beast!" she cried. "Can he not just leave us alone?" With that, she picked up a stone, about the size of a small melon, and hurled it at the Troll, smacking it square on the forehead. Bobo's eyes crossed, his legs grew watery, and then after a few rolls of his immense and ugly head, he fell over headlong backwards and lay full length across the Pass' road.

The three males looked at her, then at each other and back to the Troll.

"Oh, I hope I did not kill him," she lamented.

"You could not kill that thing even if you beat him on the head with a mace. Damned lucky shot, one in a hundred thousand. You could have saved us a lot of trouble if you had done that last night," grumbled Bowdin. Easom smiled. He had seen the gleam of mischief in Bowdin's eye as the Captain took off down the hill toward the road.

For the remainder of the course, the four made their way along the stone-slab paved way, and, come evening, they arrived at the Mage River. Bowdin went off into the forest a while and then returned.

"Let us camp back in there. No fire tonight. Do not want to announce to...*Bobo* where we are," grumbled the Dwarf Captain.

So they set up camp and ate bread and cheese for evening meat, except for Bowdin who went to work cutting driftwood timbers with his war-axe and dragging the pieces down to the water's edge, working long and hard into the night and leaving Laskey to the entire watch under the moonless indigo sky.

Come sunrising, when Oreleana and Easom rose, they found the Dwarf Captain sleeping on a raft that floated out on the river, secured to an overturned tree with a rope. A heavy mist of rain was falling.

As they boarded the craft, Bowdin woke and mumbled, "I hope you two can steer this thing because I intend to sleep." With supplies and everyone on board, they cast off into the current and let the raft drift on the slow waters. Only twice did they have to pole to get away from being caught up on a sandbar or snag. Bowdin and Laskey slept under their oiled-canvas cloaks. The rain continued to fall.

At about three quarter courses of the sun, the two Dwarves finally awoke and ate. Come sunsetting, they were making their way along the shore and to the deteriorated docks of the Port of Mildra. They went up into the city and found a small house, which they secured, and there spent the night, dry and warmed by the magic in the stone, and the stone's luminescence. They had arrived at the south coast.

Chapter 19

The following is a description of Mildra the Magnificent City, as found in *The Frontmire Histories, Vol. 3, The Elven Histories*:

> *Southern Frontmire has truly become a Kingdom of Magic. Small farming villages dot the entire land south of the Coastal Ridge, but the populace chiefly dwells in the Kingdom's only city and capitol, Mildra the Magnificent City. Mildra has taken on a new face, having become the center of the Kingdom's activity, and what had formerly been a mountain owned by a widowed Elf, has been carved by the Dwarves and fashioned into what is now an immense castle, home of the King and Queen of the Elves.*
>
> *The castle is twelve stories in height, with spires and towers rising far up into the sky. The natural stone has been, by magic, leached of its gray color, leaving a white speckled stone that glistens in the sunlight. There are gardens, courts, fountains with a constant flow of fresh spring waters and one small stream dancing through the middle of the castle's public center. There are servant quarters that house thousands, kitchens, dining halls, dance halls, ballrooms, storage rooms and more.*

And, of course, the central feature, almost a village onto itself, is the Royal Family Quarter. Most of the public areas are finished in the glistening white stone, though some are paneled with red cedars, some with oak, and others with rare woods brought as gifts to the Elves from foreign lands.

The Dwarves have faced some arenas, ballrooms and auditoriums in blue marble or pink granites, fossil laden sandstones or polished agates. Some are constructed of copper-plated or brushed-steel-plated stone block, while some of the stone is overlaid with wood finish or stucco. The overall effect is that of warmth, comfort and elegance. Gardens grow flowers of a multitude of varieties found in the land, and some from other lands, along with fruit trees, ornamental trees, mosses, ferns and even lichen. Hundreds are employed to daily nurture and tend these.

The castle, as are all homes, is heated by magic, which causes the stone to exude warmth, keeping all indoor areas at a comfortable living temperature, and even keeping stone paved streets and gardens warm during the colder winter months. The magic also cools the buildings in the hot courses of summer. The former village of Mildra has virtually been replaced and is now a city of stone, the rock having been mined by the Dwarves from the Coastal Range. Streets are paved with either stone or brick, fired at a local brick and pottery factory; the ovens are heated with magic and not with wood.

The original city wall, which once encompassed the entire city, stands as a memorial to those who labored and battled for Mildra during the Troll Wars. Its finished height had been ten paces and its width six paces.

The new city wall, which is really only ornamental in purpose, for none would dare attack the Elves, is built several score thousand paces further out and rises to the majestic height of thirty five paces and the width of twenty paces. It is built of the same white stone as the castle and city.

The space between the two walls has become home to spans of market places and bazaars, as well as a multitude of homes. Here local and foreign merchants set up their stalls and sell their wares: spices, clothing and cloth, tobac, fruits and vegetables, baked goods, preserved goods, jewels, song birds, plants and most anything one could hope to obtain.

But if that were not enough for a magic kingdom, in Mildra, there is no sickness and death is almost nonexistent. With the prevalence of the Faerie magic **acrch,** Life and Health, there is no disease or illness. All injuries can be healed, even the very worst, within a span of the sun to one or two courses of the sun. Death might take place if, for example, one fell from the city wall and there were none present with magic that could save them. The kingdom being only ten cycles in its establishment has not yet seen the progression of what in the future will become a natural cycle, pertaining to births and deaths.

Those gifted with foresight predict that in the future, the Elves can expect to live two to three hundred cycles of the sun in health and vigor. Then having reached that age, like fruit coming into its fullness, ready for the picking, they will pass quietly in their sleep and make the Final Journey. It will be an experience of joy and happiness, much as at the time of harvest when that which has long been labored for is attained. The magic will also eventually achieve a balance between deaths and births. For now, only a few of the eldest have passed on in this way, and the birth rate continues to drop closer to that of the rate of death. The entire Elven population is in awe of these happenings.

Magic permeates every facet of the Elves' lives, as it is in the nature of the magic to do. It is, of course, of argentus, the

*Faerie Earthen Magic. It is very, one might say, compartmentalized in that the magic is, as it were, faceted into portions that have specific functions, as we have seen in the case of **acrch** being the magic, the Elfstone and the ancient Elven rune of Life and Health. There are hundreds upon hundreds of these compartmentalized manifestations of the magic.*

Most Elves possess one or two, some even three or four. King Jerhad, son of Lewin, son of Baros, descendant of King Windemere, in short known as Jerhad en (meaning 'descendant of', after the ancient Elven tongue) Windemere, is unique in that he possessed seven qualities of the magic. Windemere possessed five, making Jerhad the most powerful king ever to have ruled the Elves.

*The qualities of magic possessed by the King are reflected in the Elven blade, Ember (in the Common Tongue) or **Gildar** (in the Dwarf tongue, for it was actually the Dwarves who forged it under the guidance of Morlah the Druid). The Knife was forged of steel with argentus sprinkled in and has seven Elfstones embedded within the handle. The stones themselves are nothing to look at, appearing as dull-colored, non-precious stones. They are, in order from pommel to blade, named with ancient Elven runes, the silver-white **acrch** (Life and Health), the yellow **licri** (strength or mighty), the blue **acdec** (flight or safety), the green **esord** (foe-finder), the pure white **urcha** (shield or defender), the purple **igini** (Harmony or unification) and the black **balan** (purification). Each of these qualities in the handle of **Gildar** are manifested within the King.*

Though existing in individualized forms, the magics can be used separately or woven proportionately to achieve the purposes of the wielder. The magic possessed determines what one can achieve. In the course of Destiny, fate would have it that igini is in her zenith during Jerhad's reign; hence, the Elven nation lives in Harmony.

The Harmony of the nation is manifest as follows. None work for pay, but, according to their abilities in magic; the populace makes a wholehearted contribution to their people. The concept of owning property or items has been forgotten, although gold, silver and copper coins are still used; they are more for the gesture than the value. The use of coin also keeps the avenues of trade open. The King's coffers are open, and any in need of coin can, upon request, be granted their need. More importantly, greed among the Elves, by Harmony, is unknown, as is sloth. The Elves labor and prosper, balancing ease and labor, sweat and rest, family and nation.

Work is almost exclusively done with the addition of magic. Farmers and gardeners urge and nurture seed and seedling with **petca** *(growth), and vermin are kept out of field and granary with* **werca** *(distaste or dislike). Hence, all work prospers and has excellence.*

More importantly, the Elves are at peace. After the last conflicts, Daektoch, presumably mortally wounded, has disappeared. The Trolls have returned to the Blue Mountains to live out their base animalistic lives, which they are quite happy with. Magic, like wildfire, has wakened in the Elven population and built the kingdom to its present glory.

※

It had been a clear, cloudless night, the night of the actual *salong*. The stars shone brightly over Mildra the Magnificent City. Magical light from the city's stone glowed softly along the streets and in the Elves's homes, where there was scant late activity. The kingdom was at its zenith, the Faeries' commission having come to pass; they had caused the magic to return.

Then suddenly, a surge of an ominous power was felt across the entire south coast. As one, the Elves awoke, struggling as if for breath. As suddenly as it had started, the power dissipated and the populace of Mildra was gone, the avenues and buildings deserted. Only the ringing of an insane cackling laughter could be heard in the streets.

Mildra's Elves found themselves in a darkness that transcended night; they felt no motion but were aware of being hurled through the cosmos into a timeless dimension. Fortunately, the magic, whose source is in argentus, has an intelligence of its own. It moved its wielders into action. Those among the Elves who possessed the magic of *igini* (Harmony) were quickly united by the force, their minds melding as one. They reached out and found those who possessed *urcha* (shield or defender) and then *licri* (strength or mighty), the magic in communion, in strength, in defense, creating a sphere that contained all the Elves, thus protecting them from whatever transpired.

Having secured themselves, the King had taken the lead and with the magic of *acdec* (flight or safety) in hand, attempted to return the Elves through the rift that Daektoch had opened to send them through to the Netherworld.

For a few heartbeats, it appeared they would succeed, but as Daektoch released *soiccat's* power, the rift closed, rending the King, his Guard, a battery of soldiers and those that were at its edge into shreds. Their cries were heard and their pain was felt throughout the entire Mildra population. All of the royal family and the remaining of the King's Guard had made a final rally in an attempt to save the king as the rift closed upon him. They had all been killed in the effort.

In a reflexive reaction, the Elven population had poured all *licri, urcha* and various magics into their defense, sustaining their lives within the sphere of magic that they drifted in. There was no sound, no sight, no gravity. They went on as if floating in a bubble of ink, drifting through an unearthly mist of darkness for what felt like an eternity...*for mortals are not meant to be within this realm!* It is a place for the dead, the evil dead!

Later, much later, the sphere arrived at its destination, the Netherworld, the habitat of the spirits of the dead who will never complete the Final Journey into the Final Rest. Its denizens consist of thieves, murderers, rapists, wicked men and women. Even worse, it also contains the spirits of evil wizards, necromancers, sorcerers and sorceresses, witches, goblins, demons, vile creatures and beast-like men from every world, planet and time.

The Netherworld did nothing to lessen its occupants' evil, malevolence or powers. If anything, it was as if they fed off each other and fermented in a bath of malice, festering in hatred, their evil souls stained with the malice of their co-captives.

As the globe containing the Elves arrived and came to rest in the Nethers, it was as if the entire population of spirits became aware of their presence. The evil denizens hurled themselves at the ball, wanting to take hold of mortal flesh, hoping perchance they could inhabit their bodies and once again feel with skin, breathe with lungs, see with eyes and hear with ears instead of experiencing the disembodied existence they languished in.

With a horrific clash, the first assault struck the Elves. Their magic failed for a heartbeat before it returned again, powerful enough to repel the transgression-stained spirits and to reinforce their shield.

With renewed fervor, the malicious citizens of the Nethers attacked, again and again, hungrily and without reserve, bombarding the sphere of Elven power. The process continued without respite for what felt to be forever, one hundred cycles as counted by those in the land of the living.

At last, all participants became weary and disconsolate, and the assault ceased. As time does not exist in this place, hunger, thirst and sleep do not exist; but weariness of such combat does. The Elves, with hollow eyes, gasped for air, though they did not breathe air. The spirits of the dead fell back to glare at them, reconsidering their manner of assault, watching the Elves as a Moor Cat glaring at prey beyond its reach.

The Elves collectively managed to send out one fiber, a strand of magic, and with tremendous effort, violently penetrated the barrier to the land of the living. They found an argentus vein in the Mystic Mountains and drew heavily on the magic, as a Mountain Troll sucking water from a cold spring in the summer drought.

This brought on a new flurry of onslaught from the Nethers' denizens, but with the Elves renewed in and by the magic, the evil ones soon fell back though not before breaking the tendril of life-sustaining might. Nevertheless, the Elves were revitalized and now had enough reserve to sustain themselves for an indefinite period.

Chapter 20

It had taken Star only the one night of sleeping on the plank bunk with no mattress and no blanket in the stench of the hold to make up her mind. She was an opportunist. Besides, she was looking forward to running her hands over Capt's arms and shoulders; she wanted to know what all that muscle felt like. The situation would be better than working in a brothel. There would be good food, drink and only one man to tend to. And, being out at sea thrilled, even aroused, her.

On the foredeck with the others, she looked out into the distance, all signs of land having vanished. The wind was gusty, driving great billows of white clouds swiftly across the sky, but the air was comfortably warm. The wind lessened the sun's heat on her skin.

Then, Capt was next to her, also staring out across the blue expanse. Glancing sideways at him, she moved in closer so that her clothes rubbed lightly against him. Capt's head turned. His eyes took her in. Slipping her arm around his, she continued gazing at the choppy waters. Her heart raced. She was nervous, and she found herself breathing deeply, as if she could not get enough air into her lungs.

His forearm felt like warm steel. No. Brass was more appropriate for the tanned skin.

Mother-of-a-Troll! What is happening to me? Her feelings toward this man were what she had feigned for countless others but had never truly experienced.

Capt reached out with his hand and took her chin, turning her face to meet his, and tenderly, briefly, kissed her on the lips. "Martie'll show yer to my cabin. Yer can wash up, and there's clean clothes there that should fit yer. I don't like a woman that stinks." He returned to his duties, leaving her breathless, electrified.

Twenty courses of the sun had passed since that first kiss. This course, Star was dressed much like the sailors, with knee length pants and one of Capt's large shirts, which was tied at the waist with a ridiculously large knot at the front. The long sleeves were rolled up to her elbows. She was in the crow's nest with Pig, who had gone with her at Capt's direction to see she did not fall or get into trouble with the climb.

A bit giddy with the height and the sway of the mast and boat, but not much giddier than she had been for the last twenty courses, Star gasped at the sight, her senses reeling. She had moved into Capt's cabin after that first night in the hold; the two had become like first-time young lovers, spending endless spans of the sun in bed together, by sunlight and by moonlight. Capt had suffered the brunt of the men's jeering, enduring names like *schoolboy* and *loverboy*. He was obviously very happy with himself and his situation and would have even tolerated a good mutiny at this point, not that one was imminent.

Since moving in, Star had barely emerged from Capt's quarters until this course. *Lady*, aside from her hold, was immaculate. The vessel was constantly being washed down and oiled, polished and buffed. The ship more resembled a royal galleon than a slaver. Capt's quarters were four fold larger than any bedroom Star had ever known. The woodwork was a polished natural mahogany and was edged with polished brass. There were crimson red curtains on brass rods over the windows that crossed the breadth of the stern. His bed was of a thick-planked oak. The plush, vermin-free feather mattress was suspended on a rope net and swung freely within its frame to accommodate for the boat's movements, with silk linens and a blanket made of the same velvety material as the curtains dressing it. In one wall was a rack of wine bottles and crystal glasses. There was also a pipe rack and a shelf for several large tins of sweet aromatic tobac.

The food they ate was even better than what she had eaten at the Trader's Haven in Port Oxzard. Capt's food was prepared separately from that of the crew's, though they fared better than anyone she had ever known. At one point, *Lady* had tied up alongside another ship they knew and taken on two sides of beef, which had then been roasted to a spiced perfection.

Star felt as if she were a queen. She had moved in with the captain and scarcely ventured outside for the next twenty courses, spending her time in leisure, sipping wine, napping, watching the sea through the large cabin windows and making love to Capt. Her passion for the man was acutely inflamed. This sunrising, Capt had demanded that she get some sun and air for a change.

Capt had given her a tour about the three-masted vessel, his pride in the ship evident, and when at the end they had surveyed the lookout, she had decided that was where she wanted to spend the remainder of the sun's course. Pig climbed the rigging alongside her, as Star made her way to the crow's nest. Never having climbed anything substantial before, the motion of the boat and the height of the climb set her adrenaline on a keen edge, but rather than fear, she experienced an intensifying of her last twenty-one courses' emotions.

Now, secure in the observation post, beaming like a child, she waved down at Capt. She saw his shoulders bouncing and knew that he was laughing at her. Wildly, she waved again. Then, she looked all around. The scene was as if she were upon a glass plate full of unending water. No land, no other vessels, no birds, just sky, clouds and water as far as she could see.

Ahh! She breathed in deeply and settled down with one arm wrapped about the mast. "Ain't it grand?" she asked Pig.

"Sure is, Miss Star. It sure is."

She turned and looked at him. *"Miss...Star?"*

"Capt's orders, Miss Star. One is to address the Captain's mistress with respect. That's how it's always been."

Always been, thought Star. It dawned on her that this might easily turn out to be another temporary position. Accustomed to living as an opportunist, she discarded the thought. *For now, **it – was - grand**!*

"How'd you get the name Pig?" she asked the sailor.

He grinned broadly. "We was in port fer leave, and I had been talkin' 'bout nothin' but findin' me a woman for the last fortnight. Well, I gots to drinkin' a bit too hard and wents out fer a piss. I found a pigsty and thoughts I would piss inter it. In the middle of me piss, I falls over inter it, passed out. Slept there the entire night. When the boys finds me in the morning, I was sleeping up against a friendly sow. Wells, you cans figure what's they be athinkin'! That's where the name Pig comes in.... Never did tells 'em otherwise."

※

Morlah traveled, rocking on the planks under Mamma Cituro's wagon; Lohlitah had her unwritten rules and would not allow him in her wagon. Morlah did not argue the matter. Things were back to a normalcy, and he was satisfied with that. Actually, things were better. Petrosis and the clan accepted him fully, including his magical powers. There had been no debate. After the Gypsies had witnessed Morlah defending them and Andreanna's abilities in healing, their views of witchery were forever changed.

The Gypsies had lost six of their twenty-four wagons in the assault from the Bandits. Fifteen of the eighty-two members of the caravan had died; more would have followed if not for the Elven Princess' powers. Since the attack, the Gypsies had joined up for a few courses with another caravan, and there had been a heated debate about Morlah the witch, but eventually all bowed to the new law. However, the new ruling only applied to Petrosis' band. Laws that were changed only affected those under the leadpost where the ordinance was enacted. Each caravan would have to decide about the change on their own; the positive aspect of the Gypsy ways was that they generally followed and accepted each other's rulings peacefully. While with Petrosis' band, there would be witching; elsewhere, there would not.

Ten courses of the sun later, the caravan camped on the outskirts of Mallion - *definitely*. There had been another exchange, and now Petrosis' group numbered thirty-seven wagons and one hundred twenty-six nomads along with the extra herds of sheep, goats and milk-kine. For now, they planned to remain encamped for one or two moon's cycles; they would restock provisions, and sell and barter blankets the women had woven, as well as saddles and leather goods the men had made.

Morlah had been advised by the lead-post to find himself some means of employment so that he might contribute to the general fund. He had taken to making wood carvings using the timber found hidden in the desert sands, of which much was cedar and easy to sculpt. The aged wood displayed fantastic imprints of time and lent itself to dramatic use.

Petrosis had scoffed at the idea!

"No one will pay for a piece of wood, witch. There is wood everywhere!"

However, after Morlah had finished a startlingly life-like bust of the head, shoulders and forelegs of a Moor Cat, Petrosis himself paid one small gold for it, mumbling something about how someone needed to buy the thing so that Morlah could contribute to the band's funds. Then, Petrosis had spent the remainder of the course showing the sculpture to everyone in the camp.

The second rising after arriving in Mallion, the majority of the Gypsies went into the city and down to the open market by the docks to sell their wares. Morlah accompanied Lohlitah, who had knitted shawls to sell. Morlah could not imagine where she had found time to knit so many, for in all their comings and goings and...other things, he had never seen as much so a piece of yarn in her hand.

The Druid sat in the shade and watched the Gypsies selling; they were the epitome of crafty merchants. Everything they sold was touted as extremely valuable, and they sold it all under great protest and lamentation, complaining that they were not even getting what the products cost them to make. The Gypsies were zealous barterers and would have been offended at selling at the asking price, for the dickering gave them greater pleasure than the coin they obtained.

Lohlitah had quickly sold all her shawls, for they were woven of combed lamb's wool, dyed in beautiful colors and very well crafted. Having finished with her wares, she went to help other women. Morlah drifted in and out of napping, propped back against some grain sacks by a warehouse wall.

At sunsetting, the Gypsies packed up what remained of their goods and prepared to return to camp. Morlah rose and went looking for Lohlitah, ambling about the market, searching for her, before encountering Petrosis.

"Witch, have you seen Andreanna and Syndrill?" asked the Gypsy.

"Nope," replied Morlah. "You see Lohlitah?"

"Not for about a span. Women! They must be out looking at trinkets in the shops. You go to that street," he said pointing at a narrow cobblestone lane, thick with shops. "I will go that way. If you find them, tell them to hurry, or they will have to fend for themselves."

Morlah searched in the direction Petrosis had indicated, asking the Gypsies that he encountered after the women, but none had seen them in a while. Morlah worked his way down the road, entering for a quick search through doorways of shops that were not yet closed for the night. At the end of the market area where the street only contained warehouses, Morlah turned up a side alley and circled back toward the square where he met Petrosis and Martino.

"Find them, witch?" asked Petrosis.

Morlah shook his head.

"This is becoming worrisome," said the lead-post, looking more bothered than concerned. "It is not like them to go off alone for so long."

"Follow me," instructed Morlah as he stepped into a narrow alleyway. Pulling his argentus orb from a pocket within his mantle, he screwed it to the end of his oak staff.

"What is it we do in here?" asked the lead-post.

"A little witching," the Druid whispered with a diabolical tone and a twinkle in his eye.

"What are you doing, witch?" asked Petrosis, more interested than put off. Martino peered over the lead-post's shoulder.

"Watch." Morlah stared into the orb for a couple of heartbeats, the silver-white globe transforming and becoming clearer than the air about them. The Gypsies' faces drew nearer and gazed into the orb with enchanted wonder.

At first, they only saw blue rippling within the sphere, but then a ship came into sight, as if sailing across the inside of the argentus ball. It was a small, dilapidated, one-masted vessel, and the shoreline indicated that it was sailing off the coast of Mallion. Morlah refocused the image within the orb, and they clearly saw the ship's decks with sailors securing the sails and riggings.

"She's just got under sail," mumbled Martino, a frown furrowing his brow.

Morlah nodded. He was having some difficulty finding what he sought.

"So what do we see this ship for?" questioned Petrosis, meeting the Druid's eyes.

"Looking for the women. They're on this boat."

Petrosis frowned, skeptical. Again, he peered into the orb.

The orb grew as dark as night, and Morlah backed his head away for a heartbeat, puzzled. But then a ray of light swept across the scene and back again. Again, the light crossed the orb and returned.

"It's the ship's hold and the hatch is opened. That's sunlight coming through as the ship rocks." Morlah muttered something and the view within the hold brightened. There for the three men to see were Lohlitah, Andreanna, Syndrill and another Gypsy woman lying in chains among other captives.

Lohlitah had one spectacular black eye, her hair was matted with blood and her temper was plainly displayed upon her countenance. Andreanna appeared unharmed, but she looked terrified. Syndrill's face was battered, and the fourth woman, Mannya, had a laceration across one cheek.

"Slavers," spat Morlah.

"Looks like they put up a good fight, though," grinned Petrosis looking up at Morlah again. Morlah turned him a look of disgust, which made Petrosis smile even more enthusiastically.

"Well, witch. Now what do we do? We have no boat, and they have a good start on us. Do we cut our losses and move on?"

"We could go after them," sighed Morlah, and he smacked the lead-post on the back of the head.

"How? We have no....," began Petrosis, undeterred.

"No boat! I know!" interrupted Morlah. "We hire one and get them back. They are not cattle!"

"Good," stated the lead-post. "That works also. Martino, get back to camp and tell the others what happens here. The witch and I will go get the women. Wait...three cycles of the moon...?" Petrosis glanced at Morlah as if to ask if that was enough time.

Morlah shrugged.

Petrosis looked back at Martino and said, "Three cycles. Then move on. You be lead-post while I am away. If it takes us longer, we will catch up to you later. Leave the usual signs of your travels." Without hesitation and without a word, Martino headed back to camp.

"Where is this boat we will sail"?

"Let's go look for one," responded Morlah.

It was dark when Morlah entered *The Bald Rooster Tavern* and scanned its occupants. The man at the bar looked as amiable as a *gatalopie*, though still appearing friendlier than most in the crowded, smoke-filled room. Prostitutes were entrenched in force, entertaining prospective sailor customers. Morlah moved to the bar, again surveying the rough crew and the shabby surroundings.

Why doest the smell of stale beer and smoke cling so heartily to these places? thought the Druid.

"Mead," said Morlah.

The barkeeper drew a tankard of the hazy unfiltered brew from a keg and slid it to Morlah who pushed two coppers back at him.

"Where can one find a fast ship for hire?" Morlah asked.

The man did not respond.

Morlah slipped him two silvers.

The barkeep inspected the coins and lifted his eyes toward the corner where a short, fat, bearded man sat with four whores. The ladies liberally poured corndrippings into the man, and all four appeared to be physically linked to him in one way or another. Morlah slipped the barkeep a silver and asked for a bottle of bourbon. He walked over to the corner, setting the bottle before the sailor.

"May I sit?" asked Morlah.

"Sure, friend, as long as you leave that bottle alone." He laughed a high-pitched wheezing laugh. "What is it you want from me, me good fellow?

Morlah sat. "I was looking for a boat to hire, a fast one."

"Well, maybe you come to the right place. And maybe you ain't. I be captain of a fast one, a four masted schooner named *The Sea Skimmer*. And what pray tell, me friend, do you need a *fast* ship for?"

"Does it matter if I pay your fee?"

"Ooh, yes it does! She does matter a great deal, me friend. I won't put *The Skimmer* in harm's way. No pirating. No smuggling. No slavery."

"Someone stole something from me. I want to get it back."

"Pirates?" asked the captain.

"Slavers," responded Morlah.

"Hmmm. Tell you what.... Do you know where they be heading?"

Morlah nodded.

"I'll take you, but we ain't gonna board her. First port they set in, I put you ashore and you be on your own."

"How much?"

"Six golds will take you on a journey of one moon's cycle. Pay up front."

"Done," said Morlah. "When can we leave?"

"At first light."

"Too late. I want to go now."

"Then find another ship. I got some ladies here that have missed me company terribly, as you can see. I needs be cheering them up." He wheezed another prolonged laugh.

Morlah sighed. "First light. Where do we meet?"

"Outside here." The *Skimmer's* captain reached for the open bottle and took a large swallow. "Now, move along, man! You be distracting me."

As the crimson-red dawn began to glow on the horizon and the gulls ventured out for their scavenging, Morlah and Petrosis stood in front of *The Bald Rooster*.

"Think we are able to catch up to them, witch?" asked Petrosis. "We have lost a lot of time."

"They'll put into port sooner or later. I can track them with my mag...witching."

A thin, bald man dressed like a typical sailor emerged from the alley next to the tavern and eyed them. "No one said anything about a Gypsy coming."

"Well, he is!" said Morlah in a foreboding tone that gave the sailor a start.

"Captain won't like it. Come."

Once they arrived at the ship, the captain stood at the top of the gangplank, barring the way.

"What's the Gypsy for," asked the captain.

"He's with me," replied Morlah.

"He wasn't in the bargain."

"What's the problem?"

"Gypsies – don't trust them. Don't like them."

"Told you it would go this way," whispered Petrosis to Morlah.

"I'll answer for him," said the Druid. "Besides, it's his women that the slavers have."

"So?" inquired the captain.

"What if I pay more?" asked Morlah.

"How much can you pay?" probed the captain.

"Two more golds," offered Morlah.

"Naw," said the captain, turning to spit tobac juice into the water, a good portion of it clinging to his lip and dribbling down his chin.

"Four more golds," Petrosis offered the man.

"Four...as in four large golds?" inquired the captain, running his sleeve across his mouth.

Petrosis held his hand out, revealing the four coins.

"Eh, mates?" the captain asked turning to his men. "Let you split them among yourselves."

The sailors looked at each other, exchanging some communication that evaded Morlah and Petrosis. One called out, "Sure, take 'em on, Captain. We can throw 'em over if they cause trouble." The others nodded in approval.

"Come aboard, then, me friends," called the captain with a changed demeanor. "Come aboard. Cast off the ropes, you sea dogs!" hollered the captain. "Signal the tuggers. Up the foremast sail." Turning back to Morlah he added, "I will hold you to your word about being responsible for the Gypsy, man."

Once on board, Petrosis suddenly stopped, turning pale, grabbing at Morlah's forearm to steady himself.

"What is it, Petrosis?" asked the Druid.

"The *dance*! How many courses must be endured without the *dance*?"

Morlah opened his mouth as if to laugh but stopped at the thought. "The gods have mercy on us," he said, planting a hand on the post's shoulder. "The gods have mercy on us."

"Definitely," said Petrosis, and, then, his broad grin returning to his tanned face. "Maybe you get a piece of wood and carve me a woman to dance with me, witch."

Morlah had to laugh but then said, "I think you best not call me that while we're on board. A Gypsy *and* a witch - we may walk the plank before too long!"

"Too true, Murlow."

"That's Morlah."

"That is what I said - Murlow," said the Gypsy, a bit irritably.

"Whatever. As soon as we get off this ship, I'd just as soon go back to have you calling me witch," Morlah whispered.

Once clear of the river's narrow channel and into deeper waters, all sails went up and *The Sea Skimmer* veered north. The seas put up a light chop, the wind was at their backs and brisk, and soon, the schooner demonstrated her namesake; she rode high but steady on the water as her keel bit deep into the aqua-blue sea, setting a wonderful speed.

Chapter 21

Easom and the three Dwarves stood at the southern entrance to the tunnel of Dwarf's Pass, looking into the passage. Their visit to the Elves had proven futile, and though the Elves had searched among their people for one with the gift of *ti-ord,* they had found no one. Their only suggestion was for them to seek out the Faeries. Being so far off schedule in returning to Breezon, Easom had decided to go straight to the Mystics in search of the Faeries instead of wasting time by returning to Breezon and then retracing his steps south.

From the tunnel, they could hear an enchanting voice singing, a sweet soothing lullaby-like song. The four companions stared into the darkness from within which they also heard Bobo grunting. Bowdin shook his head at the thought of the Troll, and Laskey was poised to run at the least provocation.

Shortly, a male Elf emerged, followed by Bobo. Bowdin, Laskey, Oreleana and Easom stepped back, away from the Troll.

"It's safe to be near him for now," said Loirein, an Elf of eighty cycles. He did not look a course over twenty. Loirein was taller than most Elves, a head taller than most Humans. He had the uncommon shade of marine-green eyes and typical Elven ears, and his flowing platinum-colored hair, tied back in a long tail, hung to his waist. His features were a distinct window into his nature and portrayed a gentle kindness but also revealed a quiet confidence of power.

"Only question is...what to do with him," continued Loirein.

Bowdin grimaced. "He does serve a purpose here. Deters that Human riffraff from coming through to your country, even if he has to eat them to do it."

Oreleana gasped. "Captain Bowdin!"

"Your decision, Elf," continued the Dwarf Captain, ignoring Oreleana the best he could.

"I'll leave him here for now. We can always send him back to the mountains if we want to reopen the Pass in the future," said Loirein.

"Done then," concluded the Dwarf. "Only...could you send him off a little ways until we get through?"

"No problem, my short, bearded friend," smiled Loirein. Turning to Bobo, he pointed up the hill. "*alatal crinsti olat.*"

The Troll turned and ambled up the mountainside.

"Aww," said Oreleana. "He's so cute."

The Dwarves and Easom exchanged baffled glances but reserved judgment. Loirein smiled at her.

It was nightfall when the travelers settled down above Barrett's Fall. Easom and Laskey gathered firewood as Oreleana prepared to cook evening meat. Situated on a tall boulder, Bowdin kept a close watch on the road they had journeyed for fear that Bobo might followed them. The night was warm and cloudless, the stars sparkling like glistening magic, and the roar of the falls complained in the distance. The Elf, Loirein, had returned home after having assisted the travelers in getting past Bobo.

Bowdin slipped off his perch when their food was ready, muttering to himself, "Could not see him approaching in the dark before it was too late anyway."

"I willst set a trap," suggested Easom.

"What kind of trap?" puzzled Laskey.

"Magic. What else. I willst set a spell that willst alarm the Troll with a show of flashing light, but it willst also be accompanied by sufficient noise to warn us of his approach."

"Whose approach?" inquired Oreleana, somewhat absently.

"Your Bobo," grunted Bowdin. "Who do you think I have been watching the road for and we have been talking about?"

"Oh," she said, returning to her stew. "He is really not mine."

Bowdin scowled at her, but the effort was wasted, as she did not look up from her work.

Laskey accompanied Easom back along the road of the Pass for a span's distance. After setting the wards, the two returned to camp and settled into their bedrolls for the night. Bowdin, still fretful about the Troll, took the first watch.

Easom was back to his former health, as the Elves had healed him completely during his visit with them, and it was expected that they would cover a considerably greater distance each course as they traveled.

As Easom slept, he experienced a disturbingly vivid dream.

Standing on the tallest pinnacle in the Mystic Mountains, Easom surveyed the entire peninsula of Frontmire, taking in the land from the cold, deep-blue Maring Sea to the warmer, marine-green Korkaran. The Blue Mountains were still snow-capped in their higher peaks, the Coastal Range of mountains was springing to life and the Mystics were displaying their usual gray bareness and snow-capped peaks.

A great cloud descended on the young Druid, not a cloud of mist but a cloud of Fate and Destiny, enveloping him, containing him. A sense of awe and wonder was upon him as he attempted to peer through the fog. He could not sense what purpose it held for him or his future.

Suddenly, he was caught as if by a great invisible hand and held. Try as he might, he could not break free. He thrashed about within his bond, held there by his destiny. Finally, he submitted to his restraints, exhausted from his struggles. Only then did the haze lighten, increasing his visibility and revealing in the distance a beautiful young Human female. Motionless, she stood, gazing at him.

She had thick, platinum-colored hair that flowed to the ground behind her. Her eyes were like pools of liquid argentus, silver-white and shimmering as if reflecting a distant moon. She was clad in a transparent gossamer silk robe, as if woven from spider webs; the cloth did nothing to hide her nakedness, revealing her perfect feminine form. Easom choked at the sight, for never had he seen such pure, stunning, feminine beauty. She seemed to penetrate the very depths of his very essence and being with her gaze.

For what appeared to Easom as cycle upon cycle of the moon, she stood, motionless, except for her breathing and the occasional slow blinking of her indifferent cat-like stare. Desire heightened within Easom by the heartbeat.

Finally, slowly, she sauntered toward him. His heart raced, and his breathing deepened. Lust, love, passion swirled within him. Again, he struggled to break free of his bonds but was limited to the movement of his eyes and his breathing.

Now standing only a few steps from him, she stopped, her lips pouting wantonly, her head slightly tilted to the side, her eyes purposefully sweeping from his face down to his feet and back. A head-spinning fragrance of sweet honeysuckle filled his nostrils, reaching out to him from the air around her, teasing his senses.

"Who.... Who art thou?" *he managed with a gasp.*

"Who am I?" *she repeated, as if puzzled.*

"Who art thou?"

"Easom! You have sought me with **great desire;** but not the desire you have for me now," *she smirked.* "Foolish boy. You have sought me and intend to seek for me to the ends of the earth, and you do not recognize me when you see me?"

"I have sought thee?" *the Druid begged, confused.* "I doest not know who thou art. How is it thou doest say that I have sought thee?" *His body burned with longing, and his mind craved for understanding.*

The dream siren moved again, drawing closer, gracefully walking past Easom and around behind him, brushing against him as she swept by, her hand lingering on his hip. His head swam with her scent. From behind, she pressed her warm supple flesh against him, her fingers playing lightly about his right ear. Her warmth drove him mad, as if he were being seared with a hot iron.

"Easom," *she breathed into his ear.* "I am **ti-ord**, your seeker, the one you seek. The argentus dust you carry caught my attention, so I came to find you."

"No! No!" screamed Easom. "Thou art but a dream...a deception...."

Her laugh stirred his passion. "I am?" she said.

"Yes. Thou must be..." Easom gulped. "I doest seek an Elfstone...the seeker, **ti-ord**."

"But I am she. Why do you doubt me?" she pouted, running her fingers through his hair. "You know that most Elfstones also have a Faerie manifestation."

"Thou art not a Faerie. Thou art not an Elfstone. Thou art a seductress!"

"In your eyes, perhaps. But, I really am **ti-ord**. Choose to believe it or not. You have sought me, and now you have found me. So now, you have me...what is it you **desire** of me?"

"I doest want thee.... I doest want **ti-ord** to seek **soiccat**, that the Elves might be freed from the Netherworld."

"I could reveal to you where **soiccat** is," she taunted.

"Where? I wouldst do anything...."

"Anything? How badly do you...**desire** this?" she purred into his ear, her breasts firmly pressing against his back.

Easom gasped, unable to answer.

"As much as you...**desire** me now?"

"No. I mean...no. I doest not know. I am confused. Yes, I want you...both ways, the same amount!" he cried as if in defeat.

"Only those who desire me with...great passion ever find me. And. You are Human," she said with calculated condescension. "The Elfstone does not concern you. It does not behoove Humans to pursue matters that belong to Faeries and Elves. I should not even be discussing this matter with you. The only reason I have come to you is out of curiosity and because of the argentus that you carry. Otherwise, Human, you would have never, never...never...

ever found me." She wrapped her arms around him, holding him, kissing the nape of his neck.

"How canst thou be a Faerie?" the Druid demanded.

"How can I be but a Faerie, for that is what I am? Do you love me, Easom?"

"Doest not toy with me. I doest mean, how is it a Faerie doest appear as thou hast appeared to me?"

"To test you. To tease you. To know all that is in your heart, Human. As I have said, only those who seek me with great passion do find me. And. I am willing to be found by you, for your... **passion** *is great," she ended in a whisper. Her lips brushed his ear with each word.*

"Seven trials I have laid before you, mortal. Seven trials you must endure...besides this one, of course," she laughed. "You mortals are so weak in the control of your desires; they wax and wane like the flitting of a butterfly. The first trial, you have already overcome, that of your near-death experience. You persevered where many would have turned back. Six more lie before you.

"If you endure, the time will come when you will lay your hand on me, **ti-ord**, *but not as you would now," she teased. "And when you find me,* **soiccat** *will also fall into your hand. And. You will have your desire for the Elves."*

"Why art thou doing this? Why the game? Why doest thou torment me thus?"

"It amuses me. It amuses me that you seek me. It amuses me to make you...," she nibbled at his ear, "...want me."

"Hast thou no care for the Elves and their...?"

"Yes, yes," she interrupted, a little impatiently. "I know all about the Elves. They are alive, you know," she whispered, her voice returning to its seductive tone. "The Elves will continue, with or without you.... Do not be so presumptuous, mortal. The Faeries

are not overly concerned with the affairs of mortals...especially Humans. We concern ourselves with the balance of things, of power and magic and the health of the land. Be thankful that I endure you at all. The course of time and destiny are not in your hands nor in mine." She traced along his arm with her finger until she touched his hand.

Easom shivered.

"What doest thou want from me, then? What is your price?"

"Price? There is no price. The price is **all**. There is no cost, but the cost is insurmountable. I ask for nothing, but you must give **everything**. It all depends on how much you...**want** me," she cooed, pulling his head back by the hair and biting his ear surprisingly hard.

"Yes!" the boy screamed in desperation. "I want you! I want **ti-ord...**" His last word was uttered faintly, "...desperately.

"And thee.... Willst I have thee?" asked the subdued mortal.

"Don't be foolish! Such things are forbidden!

"So then, these are my instructions," she said, pressing her knee between his legs from behind. "Persevere in your six remaining trials, and you will find me. I will be...yours! When you think of turning back, when you've had enough, when you want to quit, remember me as I am now. It will be a seed to fuel your heart to continue. And. Maybe. Maybe you will achieve that which you desire." **ti-ord** kissed him on the neck and disappeared. At the same time, the ground beneath the Human vanished also. Easom screamed out in frustration and fear as he fell for what felt to be forever, until suddenly, he was on hard ground.

"Are you alright, Easom?" asked Oreleana, her hand on his back.

Easom rolled onto his back, and groaned, "Yes...a nightmare. The mother of nightmares." It was sunrising. Laskey was out gathering firewood, and Bowdin was perched on his boulder again.

Easom spent the remainder of the course as if he were still in the dream he had experienced, reliving each word spoken to him by *ti-ord*, each thought he had known, every emotion he had felt and every...*desire*.

The Druid and the Dwarves crossed the treacherous path behind Barrett's Fall's thundering cascading curtain of water; Easom barely noticed. They made their way up along the portage, which was exclusively used by trappers. Finally, they arrived at the end of the portage trail, where canoes were returned or taken from the water. This was where voyaging became limited to river travel unless one wished to fight bramble and underbrush the rest of the way. The roar of the waterfall was a mere hiss in the distance.

"A canoe would have been welcome. I had hoped that we might find an abandoned one here in the portage," said Bowdin, grabbing his braided beard and giving it a couple of firm tugs as if to stimulate his thoughts.

"We can walk," said Oreleana.

"The brush is too thick; it would be a slow, difficult passage," mumbled Bowdin.

Laskey stood silent.

"What about a raft?" asked Easom.

"No good," replied Bowdin. "Current is too stiff. We would never be able to paddle it upstream, and poling would be slower than a foot march."

"I doest have a way to propel a raft upstream. Build it, and I willst power it."

The two male Dwarves set themselves to the task, and come sunrising, they had an impressive vessel, floating high on the water, with a platform lined with grasses for sleeping on and one for packs and provisions. They loaded their stuff on board and set up bedrolls on the platforms, for the two male Dwarves intended to sleep after their night of toil.

Easom stood on one corner of the raft muttering and waving his arms about while the Dwarves watched him doubtfully. He walked from the corner where there was a log for a seat to the opposite diagonal corner, working his way along each side of the raft. With his right palm extended to face their vessel's edges, he continued muttering and mumbling all the while. After one span of the sun, fatigued and pale, he ceased from his conjuring.

"Come aboard and doest cast off," he called to the Dwarves.

Skeptically, Laskey and Bowdin glanced at each other. Bowdin sighed and followed Oreleana onto the raft. Laskey and Bowdin pushed the craft away from the shore with long poles. The current quickly caught it and turned it downstream toward the falls. It was not long before the river tore any semblance of control away from the Dwarves, and they pulled their poles aboard, having nearly been torn from the raft by the water's power as they were pushing against the quickly receding bottom and intense current.

Laskey turned to Easom. "If you have intention, you had better execute it now."

Easom smiled, nodding, taking to his log-seat. He lifted his face to the horizon, closed his eyes and drew in a deep breath. For a span of heartbeats, nothing happened, and the male Dwarves grew restless.

"Easom!" growled Bowdin. "I can see the falls from here!"

The raft lurched, causing the Dwarves to stagger a step, and then, slowly, it ceased from its downstream sweep and stood still in the current. The corner diagonally across from Easom slowly swept about and pointed upstream. Then, with another jolt, the raft moved away from the falls, gaining speed by the heartbeat until water threatened to plow over the lead corner. Easom slowed the craft slightly to avoid plunging the prow underwater.

"A little rough getting started," said the young Druid. "I doest think I have full control of it now. Things shouldst be smoother from here on."

"How?" asked Laskey. "How are you...what are you doing?"

"Gray magic spell," replied the Druid, eyes focused straight ahead, chancing a brief glance at Laskey. "I have created a channel about the raft whereby I doest displace all substance from the forward point, and thus, create a void that thence doest draw the raft forward into the displacement of matter, which then moves down along the edges and reorganizes behind the raft, adding a forward thrust as the excess of matter doest accumulate and reorganize. The two, combined, doest form a propulsion requiring a minimal concentration to maintain."

"You never did this before, did you, Druid?" growled Bowdin with a scowl.

"No," returned Easom with a smile. "How didst thou know?"

"Just a hunch."

"How did you know it would work if you never tried it?" asked Laskey.

"I didst read about it in a book of spells."

"How did you know it would work?" repeated Bowdin.

"The basic premise is logical. The spell is straightforward and obvious. It didst have to work."

Bowdin sneered. "I do not understand how you knew it would work if you had never tried it, but it does, and so I shall accept it. Could have been the end of us all if it had not."

"But it didst have to. The incantation doest mandate its efficacy."

"Captain Bowdin, he is a Druid and you are a Dwarf. Perhaps you should leave the matters that do not pertain to you alone," suggested Oreleana in a submissive tone.

"*Not pertain!* Phaw! It is my beard that would have gone over the falls.... But I do see your meaning, and I will leave off."

"Captain Bowdin," said Easom. "Let us say that, being a Druid, I hadst never seen the use of an axe in warfare or the cutting of a tree for that matter. To thee, the principles of its workings art evident; that is, if the steel is sharp and swung with sufficient force and velocity, the end result is guaranteed. It is the same for one studying and utilizing magic. There art some basic reasonings that one doest take for granted, for they art self-evident."

"What do force and velocity have to do with cleaving a Troll?" asked Bowdin.

Easom sighed just before he noticed the mischief in the Dwarf's eyes.

"I see your meaning, boy. Just pulling your beard, 'old Dwarf'. I will leave matters pertaining to the raft to you, and you leave the cleaving to me."

The group journeyed up river, the two male Dwarves soon retiring to their blankets for sleep and Oreleana sitting at the prow, watching the water pass. Near midcourse, she came over to Easom.

"Do you need anything?" she asked.

"Water and a bit to eat wouldst be satisfying."

Oreleana retrieved a water skin, some cheese and Elf-baked bread, which was wrapped in an enchanted cloth that kept the bread fresh. Returning to Easom, she sat beside him.

"Can you not rest?" she asked.

"No, I must maintain the exchange of the displacement of water, though it is more a matter of direction now that the process is established."

They traveled on in silence for a while...silence, other than the snoring of the male Dwarves. Easom was able to relax for extended periods as they coursed though longer sections of the river. He and Oreleana sat, enjoying the riverside scene. Large old-growth cedars and firs lined the river's edge. The mountains grew taller, steeper and closer to the water's edge; the river grew narrower and became swifter.

"Easom?" asked the Dwarfess.

"Yes," he answered after a pause when she did not continue her question.

"Do you have a female...companion or mate? I believe the term used by Humans is a girl or a wife."

"No, I doest not. I doest assume that thou doest not have a mate...seeing that thou art here."

"That is correct," she smiled, turning back to watch the river.

Bowdin awoke and lifted his head. "Still heading upstream?" he asked. It was difficult to ascertain whether it was mischief or doubt that crossed his face.

Laskey woke at the sound of Bowdin's voice. "How are you, Easom? Need to rest?"

"Not yet, but soon. We willst pull into the next convenient cove that we canst safely land in and stop for the night. I doest estimate we have traveled four leagues while you slept, Master Dwarves."

"Incredible," replied Bowdin. "And so far, easier and safer than trekking through the forest."

A span later, they spied a stream joining the river and, up beyond the mouth, a small pond. Easom maneuvered their craft into the tributary's current, and shortly, they found a gravel shore to put in to and to camp for the night.

As they slept, Easom dreamed again.

Easom stood in the clouds on the Mystic Mountain's tallest pinnacle. He gasped. "Damned Faeries!" he muttered, cursing.

*"Shall I go away?" whispered the invisible **ti-ord**, as if deeply hurt.*

"What doest thou want now?"

"Just some instructions, lover," she said in a cheerier voice.

Easom sneered at the unseen Faerie.

"Turn your search to finding Morlah, the Druid. Continue on your present course and go to the northeast. Seek to meet up with him on the eastern coast of Frontmire."

"Where on the coast?"

But she did not answer, and by the diminishing of his passion that had been escalating with every word she spoke, he knew that she had gone.

Chapter 22

❦

It took two more courses of the sun to arrive at the point where the river was but a small stream no longer able to accommodate the raft. Putting in to shore, they secured the craft and prepared to journey on foot.

"Dwarf-Friends," said Easom. "Thine grace, kindness and help to me art immeasurable. However, now that I am whole again, thanks to Oreleana and our Elven friends, I doest think it is time that we reevaluate our association."

The three Dwarves grimly gazed upon him.

"What I doest mean is that...thou, Oreleana, didst come with me because of mine health. It is restored. The journey ahead couldst become dangerous. Perhaps it is time for thee to return home. And of course, Laskey willst accompany thee to insure thine safety. And, well, Captain Bowdin, I doest have no reason to dissuade thee from accompanying me other than thou hast already been too kind."

"Mother-of-a-Troll, what *are* you talking about, boy?" exclaimed Bowdin. "If you think I am going to let a greenhorn like you run off into the Mystic Mountains on his own, then you must have burnt out a nugget or two pushing that raft upstream. No, no, no! By my father's beard, I intend to see you safely home when this is over. And that is not open to debate, though I would thoroughly enjoy debating the matter with you in detail, at length and with all its merits as we travel."

Easom smiled. "I didst not expect otherwise, Dwarf-Friend. Oreleana?"

"Oh, dear," she said glancing from Laskey to Bowdin. "I had just assumed we were all going back to *Dolan* together. Laskey?"

Laskey appeared skeptical. "Well, Easom. I do think that you have a point about Oreleana's safety. If it was just me, I would love to accompany you, but my mother would beat me with her war-mace if something happened to Oreleana. I think we should go back, sister."

"No. No, I have decided," said Oreleana. "I am going on with Captain Bowdin and Easom. I have spent my entire life in *Dolan,* not that I dislike it. But this is perhaps the only chance I will have to see the outside world. No, I am going on, Laskey. And as to mother's war-mace, I hid that a long time ago."

Laskey laughed, but not convincingly, his eyes revealing his displeasure. "Well, once a female has made up her mind...as we say in *Dolan,* 'it is easier to befriend a Troll than to turn a female's intentions.' Easom, I guess we are all going."

"Alright, then," growled Bowdin, "Which way to Faerie Land?"

"That doest raise another problem I wast hoping to sidestep by having thee return to thine homes. Thou hadst better all sit down. In fact, we may as well camp here for the night that thou mayest reconsider the matter after thou doest hear what I have to say."

"Using a tone of voice like that, I would expect that the King's Guard is after thee," muttered Bowdin.

"Let us make camp, and then I willst explain."

Having caught and cleaned a beautiful string of trout, Laskey returned to camp where Oreleana prepared to cook them. Bowdin sat back against a sun-warmed rock and puffed great billows of tobac smoke out of a short-stemmed, fist-sized pipe's bowl. The night promised to be warm again, the orange moon, breaking over the horizon, was magnified by the heavy, humid atmosphere. The night peepers chirped in a nearby marsh. Easom lay on his back and watched an osprey circling, searching for fish in the remaining light.

"Well, let us have your worst, boy," called Bowdin from within a cloud of smoke. "No, let me guess...you are defecting over to the Trolls."

Easom sat up with a smile. "No, I doest think that this may be worse."

Pretending to be aghast, Bowdin asked, "You are getting hitched to Oreleana?" Oreleana turned the Captain a sour look but also blushed. Mischief and understanding showed in the Captain's eyes.

Oreleana turned to Laskey, "Are you going to let him say something like that about me?"

"What can I do, dearest sister? He is a Captain."

"That did not seem to bother you when we met Bobo."

"Well, he had words with me pertaining to that and got me all straightened out," lied Laskey, averting his eyes from hers and biting into his cheek. The males quickly exchanged glances and grinned.

"Fish are ready for cooking if anyone is hungry," said Oreleana, rising and walking away from her work.

"Soldier, see to our grub," Bowdin ordered Laskey, the Captain appearing quite pleased with Laskey's need to demonstrate obedience. He turned his attention back to Easom. "Let us have it, Druid. What is your problem? Deliver your report or be beheaded at sunrise."

"Yes, sir! Well, it didst begin the last time we camped at Barrett's Fall...." And so, Easom told them the entire story about his dream and of meeting *ti-ord*...well, not *everything*, but he told them the crux of the matter, during which Oreleana decided that Laskey did not know what he was doing and took over the cooking again. Finally, Easom finished his tale.

"So, there thou doest have it," concluded the Druid.

"Where do we have what?" grunted the Dwarf Captain. "I have known soldiers under duress who have had worse dreams, more bizarre nightmares. What are you driving at, boy?"

"The dream is real, sir!"

"Real?" gaffed Bowdin. "Sounds like sour pickles before sleep to me."

"Hast thou read the *Elven Histories*, Captain Bowdin?"

"Some."

"Remember the accounts of Queen Andreanna coming into her magic?"

"Yes. In fact, they are also recorded in the *Dwarf Histories,* as the outcome greatly affected our nation at the Battle of *Dolan's* Summit," said the Dwarf.

"Doest thou remember how she communed with the Faeries most of the time?"

Bowdin's brow furrowed and he chewed at his pipe's stem. "I do see your meaning, boy. What makes you think that this is the same kind of dream?"

"It is. There wast nothing about the dream that wast like a dream. It wast more like being branded with an iron. I willst not defend it, mine friends. Sleep on it and decide at sunrise. Mine road doest lie through the Mystics and to the coast. If I canst follow close to the path that Queen Andreanna didst take, then I expect to come out somewhere between Heros and Canton City."

"And the Inland Sea," Bowdin cautioned, disgruntled.

Later that night as they slept, Laskey having the watch, *ti-ord* appeared again in a dream...only...she appeared to Bowdin.

*Bowdin, Captain of the King's Guard, stood proud on the summit of **Dolan**, surveying the land, feeling as if he were the King of Dwarves. A great cloud descended upon him, a cloud of Faerie magic. He stood firm. He was also aware that he was having a dream similar to Easom's. Then, before him, the mist parted and a beautiful female Dwarf stood before him, her long rich-brown hair flowing to the ground, her silver eyes sparkling as if in the moonlight....*

*"Stuff the show, **ti-ord**. And put some clothes on.... Mother-of-a-Troll...you are an embarrassment parading around in that gossamer thing!"*

***ti-ord**'s form changed, and she reappeared as a small somewhat Human-like figure, only one-third the height of Bowdin and with three sets of wings on her back, which, though they hardly moved, kept her flying so she could remain face-to-face with the Dwarf.*

"Mother-of-a-Troll, does no one keep you Faeries in line?" demanded the Dwarf Captain.

"Lighten up, Bowdin. It was worth a try. I had a great time with the Human using the same approach."

"Well, you will have to do better than that with me. So, this is the dream that you Faeries appear to folk in," stated the Dwarf, surveying the scene. "I can see why they come away convinced that it is not just an ordinary dream. So, what do you want, Faerie? And do not go pulling my beard with your fool antics!"

ti-ord sighed. "Well, this is the last time I visit a Dwarf in a dream."

"Can I get your seal on a parchment stating that as fact?"

"Dwarves!" hissed **ti-ord**.

"Faeries!" spat Bowdin. "Can we get on with it? What do you want?"

"I need you to go with Easom. He will need your help on his journey."

"What's in it for me?"

"Well," she cooed. "I could grant you things that you have desired."

"Like?" grunted Bowdin.

"Your King is old, and his heir will be many cycles coming to the throne. It would be easy to see that you become regent until your death. You could be as...King! The Dwarf nation would bow before you...."

Bowdin lunged at the Faerie, who disappeared before he had taken a step. "Grrrr. Let me get my hands on you, **ti-ord,** that I might wring that little Faerie neck of yours."

She reappeared a few paces away from him.

"Do the other Faeries know what you are up to? Perhaps I should demand audience with your King. I believe, now that you have set your hand to this matter, that your law requires I be granted one upon request,"

"No. No! Don't do that. I'll stop teasing. Please don't! What can I do?"

"Rrummph," Bowdin grunted into his beard. "That's better. Tell me what you have brewing with the boy, you little witch."

"Nothing...I mean...well. Alright. This is the way it is. Everything he told you is true. Being Human and searching for me are exclusive to each other, and only by trial may he attain what he seeks. That is the nature of things and cannot be altered. The trials are already predestined in his fate, if he chooses to travel that path, though he may turn from it at any time. I didn't so much formulate his trials as much as foresee them. I wanted you to go along that he might have a small chance of getting near his goal...to amuse myself." She dropped her head as if ashamed. "I didn't mean any harm...though, much harm lies before him."

"And me?" commanded the Dwarf.

"Like I said, his chances are better with you along."

"Hmmm. Is that it?" asked the Dwarf, his hand stroking his beard.

"Yes."

"Can we end this foolish dream now? It must be time for me to take the second watch."

"Alright."

"Wait! Don't forget. I will demand audience with your King if I think you are playing this to your ends or it lends itself to your toying. **mansi porop hantlaisan coustamali...**" spoke Bowdin in the Faerie tongue.

ti-ord screamed. "No! Please don't!" she hissed, falling from the air to the ground. "How.... Where did you learn the request for audience with the King?"

249

"Ha. There is more to this Dwarf than you bargained for, Faerie! I also know the last word to the incantation that would bring us both immediately before your King. Beware!"

Easom woke the next rising, the sky a dark, gray and cloudy mass that promised rain. Bowdin sat by the fire, poking at it with a stick and grumbling to himself. Laskey and Oreleana slept.

"Awake, boy?"

"Only the left half. It willst take a cup of coffee to wake the other half. I willst tell thee, when in the comfort of home, with warmth and a soft bed, that sleeping out under the open sky hast a certain appeal that is lost once actually lying on hard ground."

Bowdin grinned from under his heavy beard. "Know what you mean. You'll get used to it."

"Didst thou consider the matter of our journey?" asked Easom, slipping his clothes on, rolling his blanket and rising.

"Yup," grunted the Dwarf, dangling a water pot from a stick over the fire.

"And?"

"Fool's mission! I would go home if I was you, boy."

Easom's face fell, his disappointment evident.

"I did not say I was not coming with you if you persist. Just said, 'I think you should go home'".

Easom's face lit. Oreleana and Laskey stirred, wakened by the talking.

"Thou willst come?"

The Dwarf nodded.

"Many thanks to thee, Dwarf-Friend."

"Still say that you should not go. Takes a fool to play in stuff that does not belong to him. Takes a bigger fool to do so when the matter pertains to Faeries."

"What about you?"

"I am just going along for a vacation. I am not meddling in nothing."

Shortly thereafter, with the foursome underway, the rain broke free from the clouds; big, heavy drops streamed from the heavens. The group traveled northeast, Bowdin taking the lead, claiming that Dwarves had built-in compasses and could not get lost. Though Easom and Bowdin both had tried to dissuade Oreleana, she followed. Laskey pulled up the rear, remaining with his sister. The rain poured down on them throughout their journey. Under their oiled outer cloaks, their garments turned moist with the humidity from the rain and from the wet grasses they walked through, soaking the legs of their pants. No one spoke, the weather dampening Easom and Laskey's spirits. Oreleana appeared oblivious to it, and Bowdin...Bowdin was Bowdin...like the peaceful quintessence of a rock that does not change.

Come nightfall, they stopped to bivouac. Laskey quickly erected a lean-to, covering it with heavy fir boughs, and lining the floor with a thick layer of the driest fir needles he could find. Bowdin set about getting a fire started but was unsuccessful at his first two attempts, the rain working against him. Easom came over to help, and with a brief incantation, he soon had a blue Druid flame burning hotly in the center of the stack of broken branches.

The group huddled about the fire, Laskey watching the water bead on his oiled-canvas cloak and then trickle down the fabric. "This stinks," he finally said, breaking the silence.

"It will do you good," responded Bowdin. "You are getting soft, living all this time within *Dolan*. It will build character...even if it turns out to be bad character." He glanced over to Laskey to see if he would get a rise out of the young Dwarf.

Laskey failed to respond.

"Well, I like it," said Oreleana enthusiastically. "It is very alive compared to living in a house. The elements are constantly at our fingertips. The smell of the forest is invigorating, and I just love the sound of the rain falling on me and around me." Laskey turned her a sour look, but held his peace. The fire crackled, the group staring into its flames, glad for the warmth it offered.

At sunrising, the rain was falling even harder as the group broke camp and moved on. They traveled through a dense fir forest, between massive trunks that bore no branches well up to the towering spires' three-quarter mark, the floor of the wilderness a dense carpet of fir needles and moss, and the canopy a tangled meshwork of interlocked and embracing boughs that closed out the light as well as some of the rain.

Two spans after the sun's three-quarter course, by Bowdin's estimation of time (he also claimed to have an internal timekeeper), the ridge they had been trekking along turned to a sheer cliff. With this change in scenery, they located a good site to make camp for the night. They found a ledge, some four paces wide and twelve paces long, set up at about the height of Easom's reach. The cliffs above sloped outwardly, leaving the ledge sheltered from the rain.

They sat in silence as they ate, and soon afterwards, Bowdin and Laskey went out to set a few snares, hoping that they might pick up a couple of conies to supplement their supplies. When the time to sleep rolled around, the rain began falling by the barrelful. Lightning and thunder followed. From the ledge, Oreleana and Easom watched the storm as trees were repeatedly lit up as if by sunlight and as quickly turned black again. Bowdin and Laskey slept. Thunder rumbled frighteningly close and loud, drowning out the Dwarves' snoring.

"Quite hair raising, is it not?" stated Easom.

"Oh, it is alright. I've seen worse from a tunnel entrance up near *Dolan's* peak. *That* was scary! Up there, you are right in the clouds and in the middle of the storm. The lightning is blinding and the thunder deafening."

"Well, this is the worst I have ever seen...or want to see," said the Druid. "In Breezon, the storms doest hang much higher in the sky, and the lightning always is off in the distance; usually the storms doest follow along the water of Nickolii Bay and move toward Heros."

Easom paused.

"Oreleana, why art thou doing this?"

The Dwarfess was silent for a long while.

"I am not sure. Back in *Dolan*, when the troops brought you in half dead, I had compassion for you and wanted to help save your life. Then, when you decided to go south... well, I was still concerned about you, your health being what it was. I had to go with you if I was to continue caring for you...and the journey to the Elves' country was exciting...."

"Well, Bobo didst see to that!"

She laughed. Her hand came up and swept a wet strand of her hair back beneath her cowl. "Well...then after the Elves healed you and we came north again...I guess...it just was natural to continue as things had been. It would have felt strange to go back to *Dolan* without you. And..." she said, pausing again, taking in a deep breath, "I think that...I like you...very much."

Easom choked. "Ah...."

"You need not say anything, Easom. You asked and I answered. Leave it alone. It is alright." The trees lit up before them again, appearing as an army of skeletal serrated wraiths, standing in ranks before the mortals. Finally, Easom spoke again.

"Doest the Dwarves accept matches with those outside of their race?"

"No. It has always been frowned upon in the past, and I would expect that it would be more so in these times." The incessant rain was as a wall before them, but the worst of the electrical storm moved off toward the east, the thunder reduced to a distant grumbling.

"I think I will try to sleep now," said Oreleana, rising from before the fire that they had kept well fueled. "Do not forget to wake Laskey for his watch when you bed down."

"Oreleana?"

"Yes?"

"I doest think that I like thee also."

She turned back to look at him. "Do Humans frown on the mixing of races?"

"I have never heard of it happening, I mean mixing the races between Dwarves and Humans. Humans and Elves do it without prejudice, but the resemblances between Humans and Elves are much closer. I read that some suspected that King Jerhad the Great's mother might have had Dwarf blood in her lineage, but no one ever searched her genealogies to prove or disprove the matter. But I wouldst have mine reservations as to the acceptability of Human and Dwarf uniting together among the Human population. Humans art...rather intolerant of much, including each other. Almost like Trolls."

"You are a severe judge of your people."

"Live among them a while, especially in Breezon. Thou wouldst probably have a severe outlook also. It is unfathomable what Humans will do to Humans."

"Good night, Easom."

"Sleep well."

Chapter 23

Dawn revealed a pale-blue sky behind swiftly clearing steel-gray clouds; the air was cool. Bowdin was sipping at the hot coffee in his tin cup when the Druid awoke. Easom rose, packed his blankets and canvas cloak and came over with his empty cup, dipping it into the boiling pot that dangled over the fire. Thin slices of rabbit meat were laid out on the hot stones around the fire, turning the snared catch to jerk.

"Snares were successful," Easom observed.

"Yup. Four. Got a bunch of Cucumber Root, too. Real nice, most as big as two thumbs. You ready to move on, boy?"

Easom's eyes met Bowdin's and held them for a few heartbeats. "Thou mayest turn back at any time, Bowdin, but I am going on. Actually," Easom said, glancing over at the sleeping Oreleana, "I doest wish thou wouldst take her back to *Dolan*."

"You would miss her cooking too much," grinned the Dwarf. "But anyway, she has a mind of her own, and I doubt any of us will change it for her."

Midcourse found the travelers making their way between the cliffs of a ravine so deep that it hid the sun from view, though the blue streak of sky overhead was a welcome sight. The air remained cool, bringing relief as they labored along the rock and boulder strewn way. Bowdin still led the pack; Easom followed with Oreleana, and Laskey had fallen back a little.

Suddenly, Oreleana screamed, and Easom and Bowdin turned back to see what had happened. Oreleana stood at the base of a rockslide she had just descended from, her back to them. On top of the pile of stone rubble stood a large Moor Cat. Laskey hung from its jaws.

A swing of an arm and five bounding leaps later, Bowdin stood next to Oreleana, axe at the ready; the Moor Cat turned and went the direction from which they had come. In two more leaps, Bowdin was on top of the mound and about to disappear over to the other side when Oreleana called out to him. Bowdin paused, looking back over his shoulder.

Oreleana shook her head.

"What do you mean, *no?*" growled the Dwarf.

"He is dead, Captain Bowdin. Please do not go and attempt to get yourself killed, too."

Bowdin stood in an obvious turmoil.

"He is dead! I saw...his neck was snapped," she sobbed. "Please! You cannot win against a Moor Cat...."

Bowdin looked to Easom. "Stay with her!" he commanded, as he bolted down the opposite side of the mound.

"No! Captain Bowdin! Come back. Please do not go!" she screamed.

By then, Easom, looking pale, stood next to her.

"Art thou sure...that he is dead?"

She nodded and turned to him, leaning her head against his chest, weeping.

"His throat was torn open and his head hung like.... His neck was broken, Easom. It was broken. He is dead...."

Easom put his arms around her head and drew her closer, great sobs breaking from the female's throat. They stood there for a long while. Finally, she pulled away from Easom.

"We had better go see if we can find Captain Bowdin," she said.

Easom nodded and took the lead, heading over the mound of stone.

The trail was marked by a continuous line of fresh blood that, after a few hundred paces, turned to a track of drops of the red life's fluid. They continued on for one span until suddenly, from overhead on the cliffs, they heard Bowdin call out.

"Ho!"

Easom and Oreleana looked up to the cliffs to see Bowdin sitting on a narrow ledge more than half way up to the top, gasping for air.

"Went up this way," called the Dwarf between breaths. "Could not find a way to the top. Tried four different routes. I lost him.... Cat ran right up the face of the mountain. Mother-of-a-Troll! I lost him!" With the severity of the cliff's rise and the meager holds available, it was amazing that he had managed one climb as far as he had.

Oreleana turned and sat on a rock, her head drooping. Easom went over and stood behind her, placing his hands on her shoulders.

"I need to rest," puffed Bowdin. "Too winded.... Too tired to try to climb down now."

"I am sorry," said the Human to Oreleana. "I am most truly sorry. This is all mine fault."

"No, do not," she whispered. "Do not do this. It is not your hand that...."

"It is mine fault," interrupted the Druid. "If I hadst not allowed thee...."

"No!" she shouted. "No! Do not make this into something that it is not. It is not your hand that did this. A cat can take one anytime and anywhere it chooses. You cannot take responsibility."

Easom did not answer, but neither had he changed mind.

Bowdin sat on his ledge, still catching his breath.

Oreleana gathered stones that carried the stain of Laskey's blood and set them in a heap, leaving a hollow core in the pile. Finally, Bowdin, recovered from the tremendous exertion of his frantic chase, descended the cliffs and rejoined Oreleana and Easom.

"Let us go," the Dwarf Captain grunted.

"Just like that, *Let us go!*" spat Easom incredulously.

Bowdin glared at the Druid. "What do you want? He is dead. Probably completely in the cursed cat's belly by now. It would be best to be out if its territory before it gets hungry again." Bowdin kicked at a boulder in frustration. He growled in anger from under his beard.

"He has reason," Oreleana put in. "There is nothing to be done." She appeared to be resigned to her brother's fate.

"It is mine fault," shouted Easom. "I canst not just leave him...."

"Your fault, boy?" growled Bowdin. "Are you the experienced one here? Are you the one who knows Moor Cats best in this group? Are you the one who missed the signs? Are you the warrior here? No! I am to blame. I should have sent these two back to *Dolan* while there was time...."

"I would not have gone," interrupted Oreleana. "Laskey would not have been here if not for me. I will bear the blame before my mother.... Though the tidings will break her heart." Great tears flowed down her cheeks, her grief etched upon each word.

"Well, then, let us be gone from this gods-forsaken gorge. We can fight over who is to blame when we are safely away," muttered a sour Bowdin.

"Easom?" Oreleana asked, "Could you burn a fire among the rocks with the use of your magic?"

"Why? What art thou doing?"

"A release of the dead. Though it should be done with a burial...we have no body. I would burn my brother's blood as a release that he might with peace and ease make the Final Journey."

"But how willst...."

"Please," she pleaded.

"It is the way of the Dwarves," said Bowdin. "We recognize our dead with celebration. I guess, under the circumstances, it is the best we can do. The custom allows the dead to leave us as we express their worth. It also allows the hearts of the living to grieve freely and to heal from the grief. Both the living and the dead benefit."

Easom drew close to the mound of death-tainted stones, each rock standing as an individual monument to the dead Dwarf, each holding the evidence of a finished life. With a spell, the Druid lit a fire of blue flame in the hollow in the midst of the mound. The flame burned hotly, licking at the bloodied shale shards, hoping to erase, as it were, the pain of the loss. Unlike normal ceremonies that accompanied this release, the three stood in silence, simply watching the fire.

The group traveled the remainder of the course in dead silence, except for Oreleana's soft sobs. Come sunsetting, they exited the confines of the ravine they had journeyed through and emerged into an open valley. Establishing camp for the night, they sat about the fire, each lost in his own despair and guilt.

The travelers did not move on the next course nor the one following. A dark mood had settled in among them. They spent their time separated by their own thoughts and remorse; no one spoke or ate.

Midcourse of the third rising after Laskey's death, Bowdin returned to camp after having spent the morning away from Oreleana and Easom, brooding.

"Well, are we going to rot here?" asked Bowdin. "Where to, Druid?"

Easom raised his head to meet Bowdin's stare. "I willst go on. Take Oreleana back to *Dolan*," whispered the Human.

"You cannot go on alone," contradicted the Captain.

"I willst...I must. There is no choice for me in the matter."

"If he goes on, I am going with him," stated Oreleana.

"No! Thou canst not," insisted Easom. "Thou hast done more than is required of thee. Thou hast cared for me above that which is reasonable and...thou hast given thine flesh and blood. I willst have no more upon mine head. Bowdin, please, I beg of thee, take her."

"You will have to carry me all the way to *Dolan* if you take me," protested the female.

"Come, children," pleaded Bowdin. "Surely we can be sensible about this. Easom, give up this fool's journey and return with us. There can be only more pain and sorrow... and death, awaiting us along this trek. Let the Faeries look to the Elves if they are concerned. We are but mortals. If we were at war, if our lives were threatened...I would be the first to lead you into death's jaws, but the matter is beyond us...."

"The Elf Queen, Andreanna, saved the Dwarf nation from annihilation in the Battle of *Dolan's* Summit," interjected Oreleana. "Do we not owe our very lives to the Elves?"

Bowdin's head dropped. He had no response; neither had Easom.

"Then, that settles the matter. We go on together or return together. I do know that Easom desires to see his quest to fulfillment, and he will not be deterred. I will accompany him and render him the assistance that I can. I will speak of it no more." She rose from her seat and walked away from the males.

"Easom? Will you not reconsider?" asked Bowdin.

But the Druid turned away and began gathering his provisions, threw his pack over his shoulders and left the Dwarf standing. Oreleana, seeing Easom leaving, quickly assembled her blanket and knapsack and followed. Bowdin glared at their backs in anger.

Sunsetting, with the sky cold and clear and stars shining brightly in the darkening firmament, Oreleana, closely followed by Bowdin, finally caught up to Easom as he sat by the fire he had just started.

"Thou shouldst not have come," stated the Human, not bothering to look up from the swirling yellow flames. "Is it not enough for me to have thine brother's blood upon mine head that I shouldst eventually have thine also?"

"Leave it, Easom. We all did make our own choices. Can we not allow each to bear his own burden?" she asked.

"Oreleana," said Easom with a sigh of emotional exhaustion, glancing for a heartbeat into Bowdin's eyes. "I doest care for thee, more than is right for a Human to care for a Dwarfess. I wouldst die if harm didst befall thee."

"I care for you too, Easom. I would die if I was separated from you. I want to be with you in life and in death. Please allow me to be with you."

Easom looked to Bowdin for help.

"Do not look at me. She will not listen to me or to reason. I am torn. I would accompany you without hesitation, Easom. In fact, I cannot allow you to go on alone. And, I cannot leave Oreleana to return alone. I cannot do both. The matter is in your hands." Again, the three spent the evening in silence, the mountains filled with an eerie stillness, unlike that of the forests they had previously traveled.

Easom was weighted down with guilt, feeling as if he were leading Oreleana to her own death, feeling responsible for Laskey's. What had been a pleasant fellowship had now turned bitter for him. He did not want Oreleana to continue; he did not want to see her come to harm. The weight he carried already pressed him into a spirit-numbing existence.

The flames of the fire held his eyes, and sadness permeated his being more than he had ever known. But what could he do? The Dwarfess would not be deterred, and she would not even allow him to own the guilt he felt was his.

Bowdin sat on a boulder a little way from camp, pretending to keep watch; the solitude allowed him to be miserable in private. He was mostly resigned to whatever was to happen, knowing he was powerless to alter what had happened, understanding he was impotent to change the two youths' minds, but claiming all blame for himself. *Yet, am I greater than a Moor Cat? Is my hand that which can turn Destiny, Fate or that damned Faerie's game? My "vacation" has turned sour. I should have pulled rank at the outset and forbidden them both to accompany me and Easom. I would have had the influence then.*

And, he could not keep watch by night and march by sunlight for more than three or four courses, for he would tire to exhaustion, leaving him unable to go on. At midcourse of the moon, Easom approached Bowdin in the dark.

"Easom," said the Dwarf as the Human sat next to him. "I do not begrudge you anything. You have a purpose, and you follow it. But, I want you to know that I had a dream... much like the one you had of *ti-ord*."

"Thou didst?" asked Easom.

The Dwarf nodded.

"And?"

"The Faerie was not completely honest with thee. There is more peril to your journey than she let on. She is also toying with you to entertain herself."

Easom sat silent for a long time. "It doest change naught. I doest go on."

"I thought as much. I am with you, boy. If only Oreleana were not with us, it would take the worry out of the matter. Then, my heart would be glad of the adventure. But now it is fraught with anxiety for her safety."

"With reason, Dwarf-Friend. But as for this night...go sleep, and I willst set up wards of magic about the camp. The enchantments I cast willst warn us of danger, and we willst all sleep."

"Are you sure?"

"Almost," smiled Easom in the dark. "They art spells that I have been rehearsing for a while. It didst take some time for me to remember them completely. I doest believe I have them correctly now. Sleep, mine friend, sleep."

Course after course, the trio traveled the treacherous terrain, exhaustion seeping into their frames with each step of the arduous path; and though the Dwarves had come to terms pertaining to Laskey's passing, the self-imposed guilt of his death kept all three isolated from each other, making them even wearier than they should have otherwise been.

To add to their ill-humor, black clouds rolled in, casting a bleak gray hue on the sky that complemented the desolate gray of the mountain's bare stone and seeped its melancholy into the mortal's hearts as they journeyed. Course after course led to moon's quarter-cycle after quarter-cycle. The hard granite pinnacles forbade joy, and eventually a cold wind blew down out of the northwest and chilled them to the bone, each member of the group numbed in body and spirit.

Food stores dwindled but nobody paid attention to the matter. Appetites were poor and bodies weakened. Yet, they went on, despondent. By night they warmed themselves by Easom's enchanted fires as there was no available wood, staring blankly into the flame as if bewitched, often failing to sleep until the night was far spent.

Then at midcourse of the third moon's quarter-cycles, having stopped for a light meal, Oreleana looked up from her pack.

"I have no food left," she muttered blankly, her gaze returning to the knapsack in disbelief. Bowdin and Easom quickly searched their possessions, their eyes meeting above the empty oiled-canvas sacks, despair written on their faces.

"Well, that is a fine Troll-hole we have gotten ourselves into," cursed Bowdin. "Not enough sense left among the three of us to fill my pipe's bowl! Not that I would want to smoke such a foolhardy mix."

"We willst simply have to hunt," suggested Easom.

"Hunt? When is the last time you saw anything but a beetle move on this desolation of a mountain. It barely is able to grow a blade of grass," spat the Dwarf Captain. "There are no roots, no berries, no herbs, no streams for fish...."

"He has reason," Oreleana put in. "There is nothing to be done."

Easom turned and ran off toward a higher elevation and climbed to the summit as the Dwarves stood and observed. Shortly, he returned.

"Off in the distance...that way." He pointed east. "There doest seem to be a valley with trees growing...I doest think."

"Worth a try," sighed Bowdin. They gathered their packs and headed east.

The valley Easom had seen was indeed there, deep within the Mystics; however, distance was immeasurable across this terrain, and by sunsetting, the valley did not appear any nearer. Maliciously, hunger crept in, more because of the absence of food than the presence of appetite. Tiny springs were in abundance, providing water for the asking, but that did not answer the need at hand.

Two courses they journeyed, weakness multiplying fatigue. Finally, just as sunsetting turned the gray sky to black, Bowdin, Easom and Oreleana stood looking down onto the forest that lay below the edge of the plateau they had traversed. However, arriving at this present destination did not hearten them. They were without a bow, though they did have wire for snares.

"Let us camp up here tonight," suggested Bowdin. "Lest we find something unwelcome in the darkness if we descend into the forest now. Sunlight will be safer." No one argued with him. They spent another bone-chilling night huddled around the magical flames Easom conjured.

Sunrising revealed a cleared sky, and the blue firmament promised better fortune, lending a bit of heart to the group. Descending into the forest, led by Bowdin with war-axe in hand, the great pines, their fragrance heavy in the air, sheltered the group from the cold wind, and the soft, pine-needled blanket that covered the ground breathed life and hope into the weary travelers.

Bowdin spotted a rabbit trail and set a few snares. He was reminded of Laskey's luck at procuring a meal for them in this way.

"Nothing to do now but wait. We could go down further and see if there is a stream that might have some fish," said the Captain. "If we are...." He stopped in mid sentence, staring down through a break in the trees, where, turning, the other two saw what the male Dwarf was looking at.

There in the clearing stood a great elk stag, antlers rising above its head in a display of dominant majesty. The stag stared back at them for a few heartbeats, and then, slowly moved off into the forest. With a stroke of his axe, Bowdin cut a sapling and proceeded to strip it clean of bark with his knife.

"What are you doing?" asked Oreleana.

"Making a bow, as best I am able. Oreleana, do you think you could make some arrows?"

"It would not be the first time, Captain Bowdin. Easom, light a fire so we can harden the tips, and see if you can find something to use to make the feathering."

"What?"

"Feathers of course, or anything else that is light and strong enough. I do not know, but look and see what is available."

It took them the remainder of the course to make their hunting weapon. Easom luckily found a dead raven, and so, that part of the puzzle was solved. Oreleana labored diligently and skillfully, producing a dozen straight arrows. Bowdin whittled away at his sapling, shaping an impressive and sturdy bow of a thick girth. The only thing they lacked at the course's end was a bowstring.

Not long after the next rising, Oreleana and Easom woke to find Bowdin sitting by a wood fire, cooking two rabbits and tearing strands of fiber from a wild hemp stalk, working as if renewed.

"Got a bowstring to braid, Oreleana," he said, indicating the pile of fiber lying at his side. "Easom, get a pot and melt the suet I managed to save from these skinny rabbits and render it on the fire. We will use it to oil the string. Then, all that will be left to do is...hunt."

The following rising, Easom and Oreleana awoke to the smell of cooking quail. Bowdin sat by the fire, watching the birds cook.

"Bow and arrows work well," said the Dwarf with a wink, indicating the roasting fowl as Oreleana and Easom got out of their blankets. "Only thing left to do is find something big enough to replenish our supplies with, and we will be ready to move on. Easom, if you could gather some roots with Oreleana while I hunt, we would have a better variety of food."

Toward the course's end, the three met back at their campsite, Easom and Oreleana having filled one of the packs full of a variety of edible roots; Bowdin had three more rabbits.

"Well, it will get us through the night," said the male Dwarf. "Only found one trail that the stag uses to come through here, though there has to be a herd nearby if he is staying in the area. I will follow his trail north tomorrow. The landscape gives itself to better grazing in that direction. I may not return tomorrow night if the situation looks promising."

"What are *we* to do, Captain Bowdin?" asked Oreleana.

"If I have not returned by sunset, then at the rising, follow my trail: I will leave it marked. That way, if I make a kill, you will be closer to me. But, be sure not to wander off my markings. We do not want to become separated out here. Meanwhile, you can fire-dry some of those roots and gather more, too."

"What if we doest become separated?" inquired Easom.

"Hmmm. We may be in trouble if that happens. But, do you see that tall peak off to the east?" asked the Dwarf.

Easom nodded.

"If we do, make your way to its base, and we will attempt to rejoin there. I want to cross the range there...on its southern edge. If my nose does serve me correctly, I expect to find one of the three passes that cross the range."

Chapter 24

Bowdin knelt in a thicket, watching the grazing elk herd, the cows and calves near and the young bulls together further off in the distance. It had taken him three-quarters of the sun's course to find them. The great stag lay off to the side, apart from the herd, dozing and basking in the last of the sun's heat.

The herd lay well out of bowshot, in an open field along a large stream where the ground was kept clear of trees by the spring ice flows, lending the area to lush growth for late summer grazing. The stag slumbered between the Dwarf and the herd. Bowdin did not want the bull, as it offered tougher meat and too much waste; the three could carry but a fraction of its weight. The Dwarf would wait until the rising. Backing into the cover of the forest, he settled in beneath the crown of a blow-down's roots, chewing at some of the dried tubers and strips of rabbit jerk that he was carrying. The ground was dry and covered with a crisp layer of beech leaves.

Fools mission indeed!

They had lost one of their party needlessly. Yet, no one could account for the comings and goings of a Moor Cat.

One could spend a lifetime in the mountains and not encounter one; they were extremely rare, the males of the species seeing that competition was kept to a minimum.

If I had been bringing up the rear...but I would probably be the dead one, the Dwarf sighed. It did not matter how he relived the event, how many *if's* he could muster, how many alternate scenarios that he conjured, Laskey was still dead. No amount of wishing or hindsight could change that. Nevertheless, Bowdin played and replayed the event again and again in his mind, imagining the possibilities that could have been. Bowdin grieved, needing to find absolution or release, forgiveness, pardon or an easement of the guilt that haunted him.

Moor Cats left little in the way of tracks or evidence of their presence; no one in *Dolan* would have expected Bowdin to know of its proximity. Yet, he did not accept that as an excuse. Somehow, against all odds, he demanded of himself that he should have known and should have stopped it all from happening, placing upon himself expectations that were far beyond reasonable.

Laskey had not even wanted to be on this journey; he had only accompanied them because of Oreleana. *Funny, the one who did not want to be here was the one to fall...at least...the first one to fall.* Though Oreleana did not blame Bowdin, he found it easy to heap blame upon himself, since he was the most experienced, the eldest, the skilled one in the group.

Bowdin's thoughts drifted through the night like a wraith, revisiting familiar haunts cycle after cycle. Sleep eluded the Dwarf until near the third watch, before he found rest in slumber for his aching conscience. Only in sleep did he find escape, and only if his dreams allowed it. Ultimately, though, it was not dreams of Laskey that haunted the Captain.

He saw himself as Captain of the First Dwarf Battalion, sending thousands of warriors into battle against Cave Trolls, the Dwarf ranks razed by their foe, he bearing the responsibility. Even though he was not the one who slew his fellows, his hand felt the taint of each death, as if he had plunged his own dirk into their hearts. Blood flowed from their wounds, their blank, empty eyes staring up at him in accusation.

Bolting up, unrested, Bowdin woke with the break of dawn, disheartened by his turmoil, wishing he could somehow find a release or *an end*.

Moving back to the pasture's edge, Bowdin saw that the stag had left his post. The herd was awake, grazing, meandering about the riverside meadow. A cow and calf moved within bow range. Selecting the calf, as it was as much meat as they could handle, he drew the bowstring back, having selected what appeared to be the truest arrow that Oreleana had produced. His breathing grew labored as anxiety rose, fearful of a missed shot or worse, a non-fatal wound, leaving the calf uncatchable but left to die a feverish death in the forest.

Holding his position and his breath for a heartbeat, Bowdin let the arrow fly; as if by force of will he sent it to its mark just behind the calf's shoulder.

The calf bellowed a loud low wail, raising the herd from its grazing. Again, the calf wailed, stampeding the herd to the opposite end of the field and into the forest. With head bowed low, in obvious pain, the first-cycle-calf gazed at the Dwarf as he emerged into the field and walked until he closed half the distance to the animal. The cow on the wood's edge watched him and her calf. Then, the Dwarf let another arrow fly, straight into his quarry's heart. It sank to the ground, relaxed and died.

Bowdin stood staring at his prey. Dead. Never in his life had he felt the taking of a life so keenly. It was as if he had been a god, the power of life and death in his hand, the instrument of death in his grip, another's fate under his mastery.

The Dwarf had hunted for the last sixty cycles of his life. This kill was different. This kill was Laskey's death, at Bowdin's hands. He doubted that he would ever kill again. He might choose to die of hunger before taking another life.

Oreleana and Easom found Bowdin in the field that sunsetting, a large fire burning, rocks lining the fire pit, with strips of meat on the hot stones as Bowdin worked at making quick-dried jerk. A hind leg was roasting on a spit. Bowdin sat silent, merely glancing at his friends as they approached.

"Captain Bowdin," cried Oreleana with joy. "You are fantastic! We should have enough meat to last us two moon's cycles."

Bowdin grunted.

"Where to next?" asked Easom.

Bowdin did not respond for a while. Finally, he spoke. "Across that range." His eyes pointed with a lift of his chin to the mountains in the distance. "Late summer like this, we should be alright."

Bowdin's eyes scanned the range of pinnacles that stood before him, a bleak, gray wall of creviced stone that jutted from the plateau as far as the eye could see to the north and south.

"She is climbable," he said, pointing with a gnarled and stubby finger to a fissure that ran to the top. "Doubt that we will find a better way. Nothing to do, but do it."

"It doest not look all that easy to me," muttered Easom. "Art thou sure about this?"

"Heard tell of it by an elderly Dwarf," said the Dwarf Captain, speaking as if from some distant memory, his eyes in reflection. "Said that there were three passes to the east across this range, that one was not better than the next, but that they all lead across, if one has the mind to attempt it."

The range was an eruption of bare stone, a geological plate that projected into the sky and forbad life itself, its peaks cloaked in clouds; not a shrub, grass or bramble grew from it. Rising from the ground for an eighth of a league almost straight into the sky, it would have been picturesque if it were not for the fact that they had to climb it.

"Ready?" asked Bowdin, shouldering his pack and returning his gnarly pipe to its case before tucking it within his tunic. The three set forward, making for the fractured stone face to begin the climb. Bowdin led. Viewing the pass from closer up, Easom saw that it had the appearance of a great stair climbing to a cloudy heaven. Within the crack, the mountain was littered with boulders, stone rubble, and ledges that dotted the path as far as he could see. From this vantage, the barrier actually appeared climbable.

The debris they ascended was of large stone shards, heavy and stable. Bowdin climbed, turning back to lend Oreleana a hand, heaving her to the next level of each difficult obstacle. At times, they scrambled on all fours, as if scaling a bull's forehead, almost standing straight up while the stone wall rose in front of their faces. Bowdin used a short span of rope, allowing the other two to pull themselves up.

As they traveled hand-to-foot for spans at a time, the plateau slowly sank beneath the travelers. At midcourse, beneath a warm, blue and windless sky, they stopped to eat. Fatigue kept them silent, and they paused to gasp for breath between bites of food.

By nightfall, they discovered a small crevice that was as close to a shelter as they would find. They bivouacked there as darkness descended upon them, enveloping them. The night air turned cold.

"Could use a fire, Druid," Bowdin casually grunted, not bothering to look at Easom.

"Yes," said Easom as if aroused from distant thoughts. Setting a few stones together as a reference for his spell to work from, he muttered the enchantment that brought forth the familiar pillar of blue flame.

"I will get us some food from the packs," said Oreleana, applying herself to what she could contribute.

"Only one problem with the fire," mentioned Easom. "The colder it doest get, the less time the fire willst last. I doest have to be awake to maintain it; otherwise, it willst go out within a span or two."

"It will have to do," said Bowdin. "I do not think we will need to set watch. Your Druid wards should suffice for this place. How is it that they do not stop working when you are asleep?"

"The ward is a passive spell, a spell that doest wait to work rather than to work at all times like a fire. Such an enchantment only doest need to be tended to every several courses of the sun. Thou doest see, time and energy in such an enchantment doest oppose each other, setting the laws of...."

"Did I ever explain to you exactly why an axe can penetrate into a Troll's skull?" interrupted Bowdin.

"No," replied Easom. "I believe that I doest...."

"Easom," whispered Oreleana. "The Captain is pulling your beard. He is not interested in trying to understand how magic works."

Easom looked from Bowdin to Oreleana and back again. Then he smiled. "A successful pulling it wast at that, Captain Bowdin," laughed the Druid. Bowdin remained silent.

"Captain?" asked Oreleana. "Can we expect to encounter any...Moor Cats up here?"

"Not likely. Not likely much living up here. If you are to feed a predator, you need to feed a grass-eater of some kind. Seeing that there is nothing to feed on as far as grasses or leaves, it is not likely. Nope," continued the male Dwarf. "Our biggest worry right now is falling...or a rock slide. Well, if you children do not mind, I am going to go to sleep as soon as I have eaten and had a bit of tobac."

Later, with Bowdin snoring softly, Oreleana and Easom huddled by the fire against the deepening chill.

"Easom?" said the Dwarfess.

"Yes?"

"Are you still feeling that it was your fault about... about Laskey?"

The Druid was slow to answer.

"Then, I take it that you are," she finished.

"Thou art correct. It wast mine journey to undertake. Thou shouldst not have accompanied me."

"But how was anyone to predict the outcome? It seemed like a perfectly harmless venture."

"True..." he sighed. "I doest not know."

"If there is blame, it should be mine. I am the one who insisted on accompanying you."

"No, do not..." protested Easom.

"Shush, Human," interrupted Oreleana, putting her fingers to his mouth, preventing him from speaking. "If it must be this way, let us bear the guilt together; if only for the love that I have for you, allow me to do so."

Easom looked into her eyes and smiled feebly. "Oreleana, I wouldst be dead without the care that thou didst render me.... Let it suffice then; we willst bear the burden together. But methinks that Bowdin may object to not having any left for himself."

Oreleana turned her head and looked at the sleeping male Dwarf. "A true warrior, that one. Only, a little too soft at heart.

"Easom?"

"Yes?"

"Do you love me?"

The Druid gasped. The night was soundless. An uncomfortable pause hung in the air.

"Forget it, I should not have asked."

"No...it is not that. Thou didst catch me off guard. I...I have never loved a female, but...I doest believe that I love thee, Oreleana. Yes. I do," he said, leaning over and kissing her on the cheek. The two paused, faces almost touching, adrenaline coursing through them.

"If you two are quite done," grunted Bowdin, "I think you should both get some sleep."

Midcourse after the next rising found Bowdin at the top of the fissure that led to the summit, standing, surveying the sight from the mountaintop.

"How about a hand, Captain?" called Oreleana.

"Hey? How's that?"

"A hand up this last rise...!" insisted the Dwarfess.

"Oh! Yes. Just admiring the view. Can see for leagues and leagues in most directions," said the Captain, taking in a heartbeat more of the grandeur before assisting his companions up next to himself.

With all standing on the summit, they stood gazing into the distance under the cloudless heavens, the sun warming them now that they were out of the fissure. The Mystic Mountains spread out as far as they could see in multiple ranges of peaks and ridges, a bluish haze hanging over them. In spite of the desolateness at this altitude, it was indescribably beautiful. In the distance, a lone eagle soared below them, yet its flight was still far above the earth below its circling.

"Well, children," spoke the Captain, "the worst of the climb should be over, but the journey is not. So, let us get our feet into motion once again, though the sight is as magnificent as any that I have seen. Methinks that I feel like a song to travel by. There is a legend that speaks of a mountain people that lived somewhere in the Mystics, a lost folk. Some say they were the ancestors to those we call Humans."

"Doest thou refer to the Pernhamites?" asked Easom.

"Yes," answered the Dwarf with surprise. "How is it you know of them?"

"Queen Andreanna. She didst write of them in her entries into the *Elven Histories* and didst visit the city in her travels to the lands of the Faeries."

"Makes sense. But as to a song, there is one in the *Dwarf Histories* that refers to them. It is thought that the Pernhamites carved the passes across this mountain, and that this was once an actual stair that we just climbed. Come, I will sing it as we travel," said the Dwarf, turning to continue the journey.

"In the Mystics deep,
Far from other civilizations' reach
In fertile valleys warmed by sun
Dwelt the Pearl, the One.

Pernham, City of the Mountain,
Thriving in knowledge as a fountain.
City of beauty, wisdom and wealth,
Life enduring, the habitation of health.

There sojourned the ancient race,
Living in an enchanted place.
Advanced beyond fellow mortals,
The way to utopia, a portal.

Her gardens were molded of stone,
Pillars sculpted of the mountain's bone.
Lanes paved of granite block,
Homes raised of solid rock.

Craftsmen, artisans, merchants and scholars,
The fair city's inhabitants there did prosper.
Wisdom, understanding in all did abound,
Their like never again to be found.

But woe unto them did befall,
A time that no race does recall.
In innocence of malice being beguiled,
In damnation all did die.

Weep, ye nations, for the blow,
How the necromancer did sow.
Seeds of malice and deception,
Pernham, City of the Mountain, left a desolation.

For the sorcerer claimed he was a god,
Ruled them with a bitter rod.
In gardens he caused to sacrifice,
Children of their houses, their delight...."

"Oh, no! Stop please, Captain Bowdin," cried Oreleana. "How awful."

"Well...yes. The tale is one without a happy ending. The Faeries swept in and put an end to the necromancer and the city, and so to his evil. I guess it is a desperate plight for a song. But the city, until the time of this necromancer, was one of splendor. It is said that the whole of the lower parts of the Mystic Mountains was a fertile, warm haven in those times. One would not think so to see it now. Anyway, it is thought that they are the ones who carved the stair and this path."

The pass Bowdin spoke of had indeed once been a smooth lane, but one would not now know it for the ravages that time had wrought upon it. It was now worn and broken, and to the nonobservant traveler, it would have appeared to be a chance of nature.

Bowdin, Oreleana and Easom trekked through the pass for the next four courses of the sun, cold by night and warm by sunlight. As they pressed on, a sense of foreboding grew as if the mountain was set against them, but this was not mentioned openly.

Late in the sun's course, after their fifth rising in the pass, dark clouds suddenly moved in, blotting out the sun and plummeting the temperatures to well below freezing. The group kept trudging along, but then, in a fury, a hailstorm broke, driving pea-sized ice pellets at them.

"Follow me," cried Bowdin, gathering himself and setting off at a run. Oreleana and Easom pursued him. Bowdin, a typical male Dwarf, quickly outpaced the other two in his frantic search for shelter.

Rounding a bend, Oreleana was the first to catch up to the Captain. Bowdin sat under a deep, rocky overhang, smoking his pipe. Easom followed a while later.

"We may as well hold out to see what becomes of this," he mouthed around the mouthpiece of his fist-sized bowl's stem. "Have a seat."

Oreleana and Easom removed blankets from their packs and sat on them just as the hail turned to egg-sized missiles of ice.

"Well, the gods be thanked for this overhang," muttered Easom. "That could have hurt."

"Likely to have killed us," mentioned the captain.

"Captain Bowdin, would it be possible to withhold on such poignant observations," inquired Oreleana.

"Say what?" asked the male Dwarf. But he saw her meaning when her brow furrowed angrily.

Bowdin went silent.

The storm continued for a quarter-span, and suddenly the air warmed as quickly as it had initially chilled, and the hail turned to rain, solidifying the blanket of ice into a frozen mass. Just when it appeared that the storm had come to an end, leaving them stranded on an iced mountain top, the wind picked up and began driving a sheet of snow down on the heights: a storm that promised not to end soon. Temperatures dropped again, plummeting to a severe and dangerous level.

The travelers huddled together for warmth, using all of their bedding to bundle themselves, the blizzard beating at them, snow blowing into their shelter, swirling, and melting on the blankets. Easom and Bowdin removed their oiled cloaks and used them to shelter the blankets from further snow.

"What about a fire, Druid," asked Bowdin.

"Yes, thou doest have cause, Dwarf-Friend. Get three piles of stone together...one before each of us, though this willst be a more difficult enchantment because of the wind and the cold."

Soon, however, there were three small heaps of stone, each burning with a flame that shot straight up, unaffected by the wind, casting heat on the huddled travelers. The storm intensified, heaping snow all about them, encasing them and the flames that kept them warm.

Darkness descended with no hint of relief from the storm. The snow about the shelter now enclosed the companions like a wall. The blizzard continued into the night, and finally, one by one, they fell asleep.

Later, Easom awoke, roused by an elbow in his side.

"Easom," said Oreleana, "I am freezing. The fires have gone out."

Easom trembled. "Yes, I willst rekindle the fire. Thou art correct. It is deathly cold."

Having re-ignited the magical flames they began to feel relief from the heat and were soon asleep again. Exhaustion claimed them, their strength sapped by the cold.

Somewhere near the third watch of the night, Easom woke to find the flames extinguished again. Attempting to rise to rekindle the fires, he found that his hands and feet were numb. He was trembling violently. It was cold enough to crack ice. But he soon had the flames up again, and he drifted into a sluggish mentation as is brought on by severe chill.

Chapter 25

In the morning light, Bowdin woke to find that their shelter was completely enclosed, encapsulated by the snow, a white wall rising to the overhang's edge. At least, it held out the wind. But the cold seeped into his bones, and ice from his frosting breath sheathed his beard. He elbowed Oreleana, who was sleeping between himself and Easom.

She roused. "Oh," she cried weakly. "It is *so* cold."

"How are the fingers and toes?" asked the Captain.

"They feel alright, but I am so cold that I can hardly move."

"Wake Easom."

Oreleana nudged the Human, but he did not respond.

Bowdin got up and moved over to Easom, shaking him. "Come on, boy. Wake up." It took an uncomfortably long time for the Dwarf Captain to wake the Druid.

"You alright, boy?" asked Bowdin with concern, when Easom finally opened his eyes and gave evidence that he was aware of his surroundings. The Druid's face was a pale bluish color, and it appeared he was having difficulty focusing.

"Canst not feel hands, feet," Easom whispered.

"Can you get your fires going again, boy," shouted Bowdin, attempting to keep the Human awake.

"Yes." But then Easom began to drift off.

"Come on, Easom. You have to stay with me! The fires! We need fire."

"Yes," mumbled Easom without opening his eyes.

"Come on, boy! Wake up!" demanded Bowdin. But Easom was obviously sinking back into his frigid sleep. Oreleana got onto her knees and elbowed Bowdin aside, startling the male Dwarf. Grasping Easom at the collar, she shook him.

"Wake up, Easom," she yelled. But there was no response. Winding up an arm, she let fly with three opened palmed blows to Easom's face.

Easom bolted upright! "What? What happened?"

"Fire! Now!" commanded the Dwarfess.

"Yes," the Druid whispered weakly. "We need fire... help me move to the stones."

Bowdin simply grabbed the Human by the back of his tunic and heaved him to the desired spot. Within a few heartbeats, the three flames burned, and Easom was asleep again.

"We had better put him between us. Humans do not weather as well as Dwarves," Bowdin muttered grimly. The shelter warmed nicely, but Easom remained asleep and his face blue, as the Dwarves watched the flames slowly recede to nothing over the next two spans.

"Time to wake the Druid again," muttered Bowdin.

Oreleana, not wasting time, slapped the Human again. "Up! Wake up!"

Easom moaned feebly, "Yes, get me to stones." Bowdin moved Easom to the stones and soon the flames were lit brightly and hot.

"Keep him closer to the fire, and I'll put the blankets on his back. See if you can keep him awake...a little more gently."

Oreleana blushed.

Propping Easom against her shoulder, she began talking to him in a low voice, patting his face with her hand, encouraging the Human. The flames endured longer this time and finally, Easom roused on his own. He re-intensified the fires.

"Bowdin, I canst not feel mine hands or mine feet," stated the Druid.

Bowdin grimaced.

"Not good," the Dwarf finally said. "It would be best if we warmed them some, but they will sting as if we had them in a hornet's nest."

"Do it," sighed Easom. "I willst lose them otherwise... if it is not too late already."

Bowdin and Oreleana removed Easom's boots and propped his feet up near the fire while the Druid held his hands close to the flames.

"Well, this is a fine mess that I didst get thee into," spoke a disheartened Easom.

"Stow it, Human," growled Bowdin. "We all make our own choices. Stop taking responsibility for what I do, or we will go to knuckles over it." After a half-span of warming Easom's extremities, sensation began returning to them.

"I canst feel mine fingers again," said the Druid, attempting a smile. "They willst become painful, for I doest already feel them turning as hot as pokers. I doest know a spell that willst take the worst of the pain away.

Unfortunately, that is the extent of mine knowledge for spells that doest pertain to healing."

"What of your feet?" asked Oreleana.

Easom shook his head. "I doest not hold much hope. As thou canst see, they do remain blanched. I willst at the least lose toes."

In the middle of the night, Oreleana awoke; it was bitter cold. Easom's flames were out again. She shook him, trying to wake him, but he did not stir. Waking Bowdin, both attempted for a few score spans of heartbeats to rouse the Druid but without success.

"Our time here draws short," muttered the Captain. "Without the Druid's fire, we will not continue long. The time has come for some Dwarfish intervention. Help me wrap him in all of the blankets and pack our provisions; we are leaving."

A quarter-span later, Bowdin broke out of the mountain shelter, with both his full pack and Easom slung over his shoulders like a sack of potatoes. With snow near chin-deep, the Dwarf took off down along the trail, plowing himself a track with powerful short strides and the use of his free arm. Oreleana followed.

For the next course of the sun, through deep snows and bitter freezing cold, Bowdin continued to plow his way through the storm's deposit, traveling by sunlight and by darkness, without stopping to take a break. Early, just before the next dawn, as the sky cleared but temperatures grew colder, he stopped to catch his breath.

"I do hope we get out of these mountains soon. This work is keeping me warm, but methinks Easom will freeze through and solid if we do not get him warmed." The Dwarf puffed for breath.

"Let me break trail for you, Captain Bowdin," said Oreleana. "You are working hard enough with what you carry."

"Alright then. Only hurry as much as is possible."

Oreleana nodded.

Taking the lead, Oreleana forged ahead at a run, opening the path with her short but strong Dwarf strides plowing through the snow.

Bowdin followed.

They continued their trek without rest on through the sun's course and into the next and the next night. At sunrising, they stood on the steep slopes looking down onto a green plain.

"I do not know about you," said the Captain, "but *I* am sliding down. Should get to the bottom twice as fast." Without hesitating, he hurled himself onto the mountainside and was off skating toward the base. It was a long, dangerous and tortuous journey down, but finally, the Dwarf thumped onto snowless ground, followed closely by Oreleana.

"Now to see if we can revive this boy," said the Dwarf, stopping and sniffing at the air. "Sulfur!"

"So?"

"Only place you get the smell of sulfur above ground is from lava or a hot spring. Let us get going!"

Easom opened his eyes; he was warm, very warm. Bowdin and Oreleana sat on each side of him. Easom suddenly noticed that they were all submerged to the neck in a pool of hot, steamy water.

"Hot springs such as these are said to contain many curative powers," said the Captain. "But unfortunately, I doubt it will help those." The Dwarf indicated Easom's feet.

Easom looked down where his feet floated in the misty pool, strong with the scent of sulfur. The toes on his left foot were turning black and those on the right foot were still blanched in spite of the hot bath.

"Oh, well, I wast not using them," replied Easom, shrugging and attempting a dismissive but unconvincing smile. "How long have we been here?"

"Two courses of the sun have passed since we came out of the mountains," replied Oreleana. "We had thought to have lost you." Her face was marked with concern.

"Too bad," said the Druid. "You could have gone home."

"Easom!" gasped Oreleana. "Do not speak such. You do take away the nobility of the higher races from us if you do not permit us to assist you in your need. You have a quest that is your very own, but to forbid us to help.... You would have died if not for Captain Bowdin. Do not belittle his efforts and worth as such!"

Easom lowered his eyes. "I doest stand properly reproved. Thou hast reason. I hadst only thought of thine safety, but thou art correct. I shouldst not belittle or take lightly thine kindness to me. Forgive me. I willst not think in like manner of the matter again. Only...Captain of the Guard, I may have a grim request to make of thee."

Bowdin looked doubtful. "Yes?"

"The toes...they doest need to come off, at least the ones on the left foot. They are dead; I have no feeling in them and canst not move them. The ones on the right foot art painful so there may be hope of those."

"What about the fingers?" asked Bowdin.

Easom raised his hands out of the water. "They doest burn like hot coals. I expect they willst survive. As to the toes...the sooner the better, lest some festering spread up my leg. I hadst seen such in an injured man once when I wast a lad. He forbade us to remove his foot. Two courses later, he was dead, bloated from an ill humor, looking like a dead gopher left in the hot sun."

"No, Easom!" said Oreleana.

"There is no other way," insisted the Druid.

"But how will you walk?" she asked.

"Much better than if I am dead. Doest thou not agree, Captain?"

Bowdin nodded, but his distaste for the matter was clearly evident in his eyes.

"Captain, I willst do it with mine own knife if I must, but the cut must be at least far enough up the foot to where there is some feeling, as I wast instructed pertaining to the matter I spoke of. Otherwise, the spread willst be worse. It wouldst be very difficult for me to do it with a knife...especially if there is bone outside of a joint involved. I wouldst count it a favor, a lifesaving favor, if thou wouldst do it with thine axe."

Bowdin sighed, resigned to his duty, knowing the Druid was right.

"Oreleana, doest thou know Woody Betany leaf?" asked Easom.

"Yes."

"See if thou canst gather some, as it is a good herb to help with pain. And also, Gnome's Rhubarb for a drawing poultice for the wound. It doest help draw ill from wounds and return blood to the flesh...."

Easom lay by the campfire, gazing into the night sky filled with stars as he chewed the Betany leaf for the pain that would follow. Oreleana sat at his side.

"See that dim star next to Orion?" asked the Druid, not waiting for a response. "It speaks of an ill omen pertaining to my future under this moon."

Oreleana remained silent. Her face spoke of anxiety and concern.

"Ready?" asked Bowdin.

Easom nodded, his eyes bleary with the drugging herb.

"Do you have the poultice ready, Oreleana?" asked Bowdin.

She nodded. "Are you sure, Easom?"

"Yes, my heart. It must be so. Captain?"

Bowdin grunted.

"Carve me a walking stick, if thou please."

"I will, boy. I will. Ready?" repeated the Dwarf.

"Let us get it over with. Lay your axe on my foot, Master Dwarf."

Bowdin rose from the fireside where one of his knives lay with its blade on the hot coals, the metal glowing red. Laying the axe-edge on the Druid's foot, he glanced up to meet the Human's eyes.

"No, I doest not feel that. Try a bit higher."

Bowdin repositioned the axe three-fingers' width above the joint of the great toe.

"I will not take more," the Captain panted.

"Do it then.... Didst thou know, Master Bowdin, that the sharp steel, thrust with sufficient *force and velocity*, willst penetrate the...."

Bowdin raised his axe, holding it in the air for a heartbeat and then with force, bought it down on its mark, cleaving through to the log that Easom's foot was positioned upon.

"Oooh!" cried the Dwarfess, gasping as if she had been wounded.

"I doest fear that there was no pain to the cut. Any blood?"

Bowdin shook his head, his mouth screwed up beneath his beard. The Dwarf did not need further instruction, knowing what was needed. He lay his axe above the cut another two fingers' width.

"Mayhapst that," said Easom, dizzy with the effect of the Betany leaf. "I doest feel the weight of the blade there. Try again, Dwarf-Friend."

The axe struck another blow, removing another dead segment of the Human's frostbitten foot.

Easom bolted up, eyes wide with pain, though he did not cry out. "I doest believe we have struck gold!" he rasped through clenched teeth.

Bowdin removed the knife from the coals and stared into Oreleana's eyes. She nodded, tears flowing freely down her cheeks, distress marring her face. She lay Easom back down and positioned herself across his chest. Her breathing was heavy with apprehension and anxiety, as if she had just finished their marathon across the snow-laden mountain pass. The Dwarf Captain straddled and sat on the Druid's legs, facing away from Easom's head. Without a word, he lay the blade to the open wound, searing the flesh.

Easom howled!

Oreleana held on, not releasing her grasp on the thrashing Human. Mercifully, Easom lost consciousness. Oreleana rose, got the poultice and dressed the foot.

Bowdin, sweat beaded on his brow, said, "I do hope the other foot recovers! That is about all of that which I have the stomach for."

Easom did not wake the next rising; the Human burned with fever. Oreleana attended to him, wiping his face, neck and torso with a moist towel and dripping water into his mouth. Bowdin sat off to the side in a disgruntled humor, even more unhappy about the turn that his "vacation" had taken, and even more angered by *ti-ord's* game and the Druid's insistence at playing it.

Two courses did Easom travail in fever, and on the morning of the third, he awoke, looking significantly better.

Sitting up, he looked down at his foot, asking, "Hast thou checked it?"

"No," answered Oreleana, looking somewhat abashed. "I did not want to see what I might find, especially since you have been two courses lost in fever."

"It might need to be cut higher," he groaned, obviously displeased. "It wouldst have been a better time to do it while I wast unconscious. Wouldst thou take the dressings down now, please?"

She nodded, shamed by her own aversion to taking necessary but distasteful measures. Once the bandages were off, Easom inspected the foot, slowly peeling away the rhubarb pulp.

"Pink!" he exclaimed. "Only this one little piece of dead flesh. Let us get more poultice on it and rebandage it." He trimmed the blackened flesh from the edge of the wound, wincing as he cut it away. "Master Bowdin," he called, "thou art to be commended on thine surgical skills; it doest appear that the amputation was successful."

The Dwarf turned to glare at the Druid, but a smile formed beneath his bush of whiskers instead. "Good to have you back. Would have hated to carry you three courses out of the mountain snows without stopping, all for nothing. Ready to travel?"

Easom smiled, fondness for the Dwarf swelling within. Undoing the dressings from his other foot to examine his toes, he removed sloughed skin in large layers, but this foot proved to be healing also. With his incantation to lessen pain and some Betany leaf, he expected to be able to get going again soon.

They remained camped by the springs for the next six courses, allowing Easom to rest and recover. On the seventh course, they were ready to depart. Easom now had an impressively carved walking staff in hand; its top was finished in the shape of an upside-down three-quarters of a foot. Dwarf runes were carved down the length of the staff. The travelers began their journey again, through the forest that separated them from the last mountain range of the Mystics, the last obstacle to the eastern coast.

Journeying was slow, Easom hobbling along with his staff, favoring his left foot, his right foot also painful. The skin on his fingers peeled in thick layers from having been severely frozen. At times, Bowdin forged ahead, found himself a mossy knoll or slope in the sun, and napped as he waited for Oreleana and Easom.

Their provisions held out well, for Bowdin had filled his entire pack with the elk-jerk and had even strapped a neat bundle of long strands of the dried meat on top. Water was in abundance in the mountain regions, and Oreleana had foraged more roots. The weather was warm by sun's course and only mildly cool at night.

It took them eight courses of the sun to cross the great pine forest, and at midcourse of the eighth, they emerged at the base of the next pass. This path began as a ravine set between two sharp cliffs. Fortunately, it appeared that there would be no need to climb.

Chapter 26

The second course into the pass was cool, for the mountain forbade direct sunlight on the trail. The travelers journeyed on. They had only been on the move for two spans when suddenly, a Moor Cat stood on the path before them.

"Mother-of-a-Troll!" growled Bowdin into his beard, sliding his war-axe from his belt. "I doubt that you are the same cat that did in Laskey, but I hope you are. Nevertheless, we will count it a score settled to have a go at you."

"No!" whispered Oreleana. "You cannot win!"

"We cannot leave or move unless he allows it," returned Bowdin. They stood staring at each other, two Dwarves and a Human opposite the cat who appeared not sure about how to proceed, being used to attacking running prey or its victim's backs.

"Well?" shouted Bowdin. "Let us have it over with, cat!"

A frightening rumbling rose in the beast's throat, as if in response. Bowdin stepped toward the cat and took a warm-up swing with his axe. The cat hissed, running gooseflesh down Easom's and Oreleana's arms and legs.

"Come on, cat! Cannot be waiting on you all course."

The Moor Cat, raising its right upper lip, snarled in reply, revealing a large canine tooth the length of two fingers. Then, quite unexpectedly, the feline sat, gazing at them rather indifferently.

And so, the three travelers stood in place and stared back at the beast. A full span of the sun passed, the four locked in a stare, the cat having eventually gone down to his belly, evidently ready to pounce at the slightest provocation.

Finally, Bowdin spoke. "Anything in that little bag of Druid tricks, Easom?" This brought the Human out of his paralyzed state; he had been hypnotized by the cat's stare.

"I couldst try. Doest not know what it willst accomplish. Anything I doest may provoke as much as repel the beast. Nothing to harm it with. It is said they doest have no fear."

"He will not let us go. He is waiting for one of us to bolt and is obviously not excessively hungry. But he will kill or be killed. Go on. Try something. Anything! I am ready for the damned beast."

"Do not provoke it," whispered Oreleana.

"What are we to do, wait till dark?" ask Bowdin, letting his pack slowly slip to the ground.

Oreleana did not respond.

"Do it, Druid. Try that flash of light you used on... Bobo. Slowly back yourselves, very slowly, against the boulders behind you but do not turn your backs to the cat."

When in position, Easom asked, "Ready?"

Bowdin nodded.

A bright flash of light briefly lit up the ravine; the cat suddenly stood on all fours and let out a loud, terrifying roar, causing Oreleana and Easom to tremble. Bowdin stood like a rock, like a bear ready to lash out.

"That didst not go very well," squeaked Easom through a fear-constricted throat.

"Gives me an idea, though," said Bowdin. "Set up a couple of flames in front of you and Oreleana. Might help keep him off of you. Let me know when you are done." The Dwarf remained locked in a stare with the cat, which had bellied down again, its head near the ground as if now considering a frontal attack. Its cycle-old-bullock-sized body rippled with tension.

"Fire is lit."

"Anything else in your bag of tricks, boy?"

"Not much. I am mostly a novice at magic...but mayhapst...."

"What? Anything. Let us just break this stalemate."

"I canst throw a ball of fire at him, but it hast no heat. It is just a visual effect. I suspect he willst attack if I doest, and it doest annoy him...."

"Do it!"

"Do not, Easom," protested Oreleana.

"Butt out, Oreleana. We cannot stay here until dark. Now is the time to settle this. I prefer the cat charge me than me it, which I am about to do."

"But why?" cried Oreleana, distressed beyond measure.

"Look, Oreleana. The cat is determined to kill...otherwise, he would be gone. I do not want to tangle with him in the dark, and if I am in a stance to receive the battle, my timing and my stroke will be better. If I have to attack, the advantage will belong to him. I do not instruct you in your cooking, nor the Druid in his magic...."

"Sorry," she uttered in a subdued voice. "It is just that I did not...."

"I know. Now, quiet! Easom, do it."

"The flame willst have to go around thee, so doest not be distracted by it, for thou art in my direct line to the cat. It willst think it came from thee...."

"I am ready. Do it!" growled the Dwarf, his hips lightly swinging, preparing for the only stoke he was likely to have.

A blue flame shot out, enveloping Bowdin for a heartbeat before exploding in front of the beast's face. Instantly, the feline was in the air, striking out like lightning. The swift broad strokes of Bowdin's blade caused it to pause and step back. The feline was now aware that the Dwarf presented a potential danger. It hissed and growled, swatting at the Dwarf, but from outside the axe's reach.

Bowdin charged it, but the cat leapt over him, turned back and rushed in for a kill as the Dwarf, surprisingly fast, met it again. Bowdin lunged forward. His blade opened the beast's cheek. Screaming with rage, the cat was on him in a heartbeat. The Dwarf flipped his axe, dropped onto his back, and with the long wooden handle and his feet, catapulted the cat over the top of him, using the animal's momentum to propel it.

The Moor Cat rolled and regained its feet. Terrifying screams emitted from its throat. It charged. The Dwarf was on his feet, waiting. The two rolled in a cloud of dust and separated again. Bowdin's meshed steel pant leg was torn open, blood flowing freely.

The Moor Cat circled, crouched...and hurled itself. Bowdin, with a limp, lost his balance but managed to catch the cat square on the cheek with a heavy blow from the flat of the axe blade. With a loud *crack!*, bones in the feline's face broke.

Again, the two rolled. The cat cradled Bowdin in its four paws, digging savagely with its hind claws at the Dwarf before howling and springing away. Bowdin's dirk was stuck in its left shoulder. The Dwarf's tunic was shredded down to his chain mail, and blood oozed from several large gashes in his face.

Biting at the knife in its shoulder, the cat growled furiously. Bowdin leapt at it, axe swinging in a wide arc as he sailed through the air, taking off the cat's ear. It sprang back like a screw and landed several paces away. Bowdin rounded on it, while it hissed at him, undecided whether to give its attention to the Dwarf or the knife protruding from its shoulder.

Again, the Dwarf threw himself at his opponent. The feline caught him between its forepaws and took a quick bite around the mailed chest. It released him and sprang away.

"Too fast," panted the Dwarf, rushing his quarry again. But this time Bowdin rolled, the cat having expected a straightforward lunge. The Dwarf passed right between its legs, stabbing another knife into a rear paw, and tumbled out between the cat's hind legs. The Moor Cat sprang into the air too late to avoid the blade. It was immediately on the Dwarf's back, teeth lashing down at the Dwarf's neck as the war-axe blade chopped into its mouth. The cat howled with pain as it bit into the sharp edges, cutting its upper and lower jaws, giving Bowdin enough time to roll onto his back. The Dwarf wound up and clove the animal's nose open, but the swing was a short and awkward one and lacked the power to do any real damage.

The two stood, merely three paces apart, panting heavily, blood flowing from each. The two were locked in a stare of hatred, the cat's remaining ear lay flat on its head.

It snarled at the Dwarf.

"Well, I do not like you either," the Dwarf snarled back.

Bowdin swung well before the cat moved. His blade clove deep into its neck as it sailed toward him. Both went down in a cloud, Bowdin's head came up, war-axe arcing down. All went still.

Bowdin fell to his knees, attempting a smile, but producing a grimace. Oreleana and Easom ran to him.

"Are you alright, Captain Bowdin?" cried Oreleana.

"No. I am not," whispered the Dwarf. "My leg is torn bad and my face, too, I think. And I hurt all over," he panted. "The ancestors be praised for steel mail! May their beards endure forever. His claw slit the steel mesh pants and the leg like an over-ripe tomato." Bowdin sat, opening his leggings, which were not the same strength as the mail coat he wore.

"How did you know when to strike the final blow?" asked Easom "He had not even flicked a whisker when you began the stroke."

"Saw it in his eye," puffed the Dwarf. "Knew he was coming in and meant to finish it. From there, it was luck that he jumped at the same time I swung. Oreleana? Got any more of that rhubarb poultice? I think that this leg needs some serious tending to. I think I got a couple of broken ribs, too."

"Oh, yes. Forgive me," she rushed off to get her supplies.

"Easom, help me off with these pants," grimaced the Dwarf as he began pulling at them. "Starting to burn like hot coals."

Between the two of them, they removed Bowdin's steel-fiber-meshed pants and his wool underlayer, revealing a gaping gash from his groin to his ankle.

"Well, that is not a pretty sight," said Bowdin, a bit pale. "Mostly skin and fat, not too much damage to the muscle," he said, inspecting the wound. "But it is a sure way to get infected and lose it. Easom, boil up some water. Oreleana, you got any of that Betany left over?"

"Yes, Captain Bowdin. I will get it."

"Easom, get me away from this beast first. He is dead enough, but I still do not like him any better." Easom lifted the Dwarf by the armpits, and hobbling, he dragged the Captain back to where the Druid flames still burned.

"We should camp here for the night," grunted Bowdin from where Easom had propped him against a cliff. He looked up into the sky. "Hmmm. Hardly a few heartbeats have passed since we started. Could have sworn that it all lasted a moon's cycle."

A span later, they had the Captain's wound washed and his leg poulticed and bandaged. Oreleana sewed the gashes on his face with a heavy needle and coarse thread.

"That wast quite impressive, Master Dwarf," said Easom after they had settled down. "I doest know a Human wouldst not have been fast enough to deal with such a beast."

"That is what Dwarves are for," grunted Bowdin. "Fighting, delving into rock and working stone. But to tell the truth, it was mostly luck...chain mail...catching him in a battle he was not familiar with and just some damned meanness on my part. Something about not wanting to end up like Laskey.... Sorry, Oreleana."

"I understand, Captain Bowdin. I did not want to see you there either." They thought it best not to sew the leg wound, lest it cause festering, and allowed it to heal with the poultice on it instead.

"Well, if any of us survive this walk in the wilds," said Bowdin that night as they sat about a fire of wood, the red coals adding an inner soul's warmth that the Druid flame lacked, "be sure that the tale of my conquest over the Moor Cat is written into the *Druid Histories*. To my knowledge, this is a first: A Dwarf (or Human) tangling with a Moor Cat and living to tell! I can see it now...." He paused to take in a deep draught of smoke from his gnarly pipe, the smoke mingling and twisting around his words as he continued to speak. "Bowdin, son of Duhlind, Moor Cat Slayer, Blessed Be His Beard! Has a nice ring to it. Do you not think?"

Easom smiled broadly and nodded.

"Oh, Captain Bowdin!" exclaimed Oreleana. "A bit more modesty would be in order!"

"It will take on its own modesty if it turns out to be the One-Legged Moor Cat Slayer," responded the Dwarf, 'tugging at her beard.'

"Let him have his glory, Oreleana," said Easom. "His feat of taking me out of the mountains the way he didst and slaying the Moor Cat doest command some recognition."

"Naw. Taking you out of the mountains was something any Dwarf could have done...but the Moor Cat!" he said dreamily. "That is what I want to be remembered for.... Anyone can lug a Human out of the mountains." He gave Easom a hard look but failed to hide the mischief that had returned to his eyes.

The next moon's quarter-cycle brought the travelers through the Mystic Mountains, following an easier trek across land much more desolate than the pine forests they had previously crossed. Midcourse of the following rising, they emerged on the foothills of the Mystics, bordering the southeastern side of the Inland Sea.

Easom's eyes narrowed. "This is a dangerous place," he said to the Dwarves.

"It is," responded Bowdin, "but it is the only way to the coast. Suggestions?"

"We hadst better check on our wounds before we have any thought of going down there. The terrain there is marshland, and we willst be walking though water. Last thing we doest need is infection setting into open wounds."

Having checked their injuries and rebandaging them, all were agreed that the cuts were still too fresh to expose to the hazards of the brackish marsh waters below.

"If we could grease them up somehow," mentioned Oreleana. "It would keep the water out."

"If we had grease," grumbled Bowdin.

"We can," she added. "With a bit of work." Both males looked at her.

"There are plenty of Tupelo-gum trees here. We could boil down leaves and make a thickened oil."

"Females do have their use at times!" volunteered Bowdin.

Oreleana frowned at him.

"He's pulling thine beard, Oreleana," whispered Easom.

"Oh," she said, pausing and then smiling a little. "Within a couple of courses, we should be able to have enough to cover your wounds and save some for a redressing."

The three set to work, first finding a suitable place to bivouac for their stay. Then they began to pluck leaves from the gum containing foliage. Easom set up a Druid flame for the boiling, and using the two cook pots they had, began the process. Bowdin hollowed out a bowl in a fallen tree to make a container for the product.

"War-axe does not bite well into wood," he complained as he worked. "If I had a chopping axe, it would go well. Explain that to me, Druid. I am using sufficient *force and velocity...*"

Easom smiled but did not respond.

The process of making the oily brew turned out to be more laborious and messy than they had expected. At the end of the third course, they had their ends.

"We shouldst apply this to the bandages tonight," said Easom as they sat about the wood-burning campfire. "I doest recall Queen Andreanna writing in her accounts of her journey that it took a full course of travel to cross the marsh. We doest not want to waste time at the rising."

The pale sunrising arrived. A light wind swept billowing clouds along high overhead. The group set out, down into the marsh, wading through the murky, tannic waters of the swamp that bordered the eastern Inland Sea. Using what remained of the materials they had used for making bandages, they tied their pant legs at the ankles to prevent leeches from swimming up into their clothes. The air around the marshland clung to them, a perpetual heavy humidity, permeated with the escaping fermenting gases from the decay of the fen. Mosquitoes blinded and choked them each step of the way. At midcourse, Oreleana suggested they smear a bit of the tupelo gum on their skin to deter the biting insects. The boiled sap worked in that it reduced the number of stings that they received, but the scent of it attracted the pests in swarms. It was not long before the sticky substance was coated with trapped mosquitoes pasted to their skin, making the ordeal utterly obnoxious.

Finally, at long last, they emerged from the marsh on the sea's northeast shore. They washed the insects and sap from their exposed skin, using the briny water of the sea, which left them feeling sticky with its minerals but relieved them from the insects. Moving deeper into the forest, they separated themselves from the worst of the mosquitoes' domain and settled down for a bit of a rest. The males redressed their wounds with the rhubarb poultice.

"Boy," said Bowdin. "You know where we are, do you not?"

Easom nodded.

"If you read the Queen's accounts, we lie in an area that is inhabited by creatures, both magical and dangerous."

"Most art not to us," interrupted the Druid. "Most art beings that doest feed on magic and art only attracted to magic."

"...And your magic?"

"That of spells, not the same as innate magic, which is what wouldst be the drawing factor to these beasts. But there are a few that art magical and dangerous to us, that doest eat flesh."

"I am comforted above measure," growled the Dwarf. "I think we should journey into the night and away from this place."

"But Easom needs to rest...he does not have a Dwarf's endurance," objected Oreleana.

"I will carry him. I want away from here. I read the Queen's accounts too!"

Gathering their belongings, Bowdin, Easom and Oreleana set out into the darkening night, following Bowdin's nose eastwardly, where he claimed there was a gulch that would take them out of the last of the mountains and to the coast. Slowly, they made their way. Easom leaned heavily on his staff again, an agonizing throbbing shooting into his feet with each step, in spite of his pain-deadening spell. Slowly, they progressed away from the Inland Sea. They traveled under a full moon's light, somewhat obscured by the pine forest. They crossed the very place where Andreanna and Daektoch had fought hundreds of cycles past, not realizing the marred terrain was the result of the battle.

Soon after midcourse of the moon, the trio became aware of a rasping breathing following behind them.

"Looks like we picked up a customer," grunted Bowdin. "You two walk ahead. I will pull up the rear."

Chapter 27

The Ranter, a magical creature, was one that did consume flesh; it was one of the creatures confined to the area of the sea at the end of the War of Magics some millennia past by the Faeries. As tall as a Cave Troll, its skin was covered with a blue-green, scaled hide, its reptilian face disturbingly Human-like in appearance. The beast's fiery-red eyes were lit with its evil, magical life force. Hands and feet resembled a lizard's. It walked upright. A long forked tongue flicked out through a mouthful of sharp, pointy teeth, tasting the air. Great fangs, much like a Moor Cat's, protruded over the edges of its closed mouth. It was hungry; cycles could go by before the Ranter had opportunity to feed. From a distance, in the dark, it looked far too Humanoid. It was one of the more intelligent beasts surviving in the enchanted prison.

The Ranter had smelled the three immediately when they emerged from the swamp, and it had followed from a distance, evaluating its prey, cautious but unfearful. Since the travelers were drawing near to the borders where the Ranter could not cross, it would have to make its move soon.

Bowdin listened carefully to the sound of the Ranter's breathing as they trekked through the night, it's tone turned ominous. Easom walked just ahead with Oreleana in the lead.

"It is moving in," grunted Bowdin in a whisper. "We had better find a place to make a stand...quickly. Move faster!"

They set off at as quick a pace as Easom could muster, painful groans escaping from his lips with each step he took. Rounding a stand of closely clustered trees, they found several large boulders, which they could use as a rearguard and formed a semicircle within a clearing.

"Up against the rocks," ordered the Captain. "We make our defense here!"

With rasping breath giving away its location, the Ranter closed in on them. It used the pines to conceal itself until only a few last trees towered between predator and prey. Bowdin stood, axe ready, monitoring his enemy's path with his ears.

"I do not suppose surprise is needed for it to catch something if it breathes like that," spoke Bowdin into the darkness. From the edge of an immense pine, two burning, narrow-slit eyes appeared, surveying the potential meal.

"Mother-of-a-Troll!" hissed Bowdin. "Anything with eyes like that is sure not to be an easy kill. I think I would prefer another Moor Cat."

"It is a Ranter," whispered Easom.

"And just what does a Ranter do?" inquired the Dwarf as the eyes stared, motionless and without blinking.

"Magical. Canst shift from solid to a mist in a couple of heartbeats but without disappearing like the Black wizards of King Jerhad's time. Teeth and claws art its weapons. If thou doest strike at it, it willst change to vapor and reform solid for its counterattack."

"Any way to kill it?" inquired the Dwarf, lifting his axe over his shoulder as if to warm up his muscles.

"If thou canst catch it as it solidifies again. But I doest not know how strong it is."

"So you are saying that applying the greatest possible *force and velocity*...it may not be enough."

Easom did not respond.

Crouching, the tall form of the Ranter emerged from behind the tree with a deliberate, measured stealth. It closed in on the Dwarf. Bowdin stepped out to meet it, grumbling under his breath. Just four paces apart, the two began to circle, sizing each other up.

"You are an ugly son-of-a-Troll," muttered Bowdin, as the Ranter crossed a moonlit expanse. "My guess is that you are just jealous of my good looks."

The Ranter hissed.

Suddenly, the Dwarf lunged, delivering two three, four powerful strokes of his axe, slashing clean through the Ranter. Unharmed, and with a venomous spitting, it retreated from the knee-high assailant, re-establishing the previous distance between the two.

"Like chopping the wind," complained Bowdin, circling, poised to strike again.

The combatants measured each other warily, as the heartbeats of time passed. Again, Bowdin shot forward. His axe swung back-and-forth like a blur in the night. The Ranter distanced itself and resumed its pattern. Behind Bowdin, Easom began muttering under his breath.

"What you doing, boy?" called Bowdin without interrupting his metered stalking.

"If I doest something...do not be distracted," answered the Druid.

"Someone might as well do something. I cannot touch him." With a lightning fast leap, the Ranter sailed toward the Dwarf, raking at him with its claws. Bowdin, at the same time, rolled aside and gained his feet, ready.

"Gives himself away," commented the Dwarf. "Moves fast but shows what he is going to do." Easom muttered under his breath, which somehow distracted the Ranter, burning eyes occasionally glancing at the Druid. Bowdin surged forward, five, six, seven, eight strokes whizzing though the lizard-man, without effect. The Ranter attacked quickly after Bowdin's last stroke, the blow hurling the Dwarf back to Easom's and Oreleana's feet. But he was up in an instant and met the creature as it rushed in for a kill. Bowdin drove it back.

"This is going to be a matter of wits and not strength, though he is as strong as a Troll," growled Bowdin. "And, he is pretty smart. But it will be a cold course in *Dolan's* furnaces before he can outwit a Dwarf!"

The Ranter hissed.

Bowdin lashed out purposefully, striking several blows in a row and then stepping back. The Ranter counterattacked at the end of the Dwarf's foray. Instead of retreating, Bowdin stepped forward again, axe arcing high, catching the surprised beast square in the chest before it could change to mist. The beast screamed, turning to mist at the last possible heartbeat. It hurled itself some twenty paces back to the edge of the clearing. Then, it rose from the ground with a blade's length gash where Bowdin had struck. Cloven scales dangled from the sides of the wound, and a fluorescing-orange fluid seeped from the opening.

"Well, it does something like bleed," observed the Dwarf with a slightly heightened hope. "Proved a bit smarter on that one, eh, Ranter?" The circling began again, the Ranter's caution increased as it refocused on the Dwarf.

Again, Bowdin lunged, repeating the same tactics, only actually retreating this time. The Ranter paused, slightly unnerved. Again, they engaged. With a great shout, Bowdin leapt into the air, axe sweeping through the beast. Bowdin flew through it as if it were but an apparition, tumbling, turning and rushing at it again with a repetition of the same, ending up next to Easom and Oreleana.

"Mother-of-a-Troll! If only he could stay put for a heartbeat. Here we go!" Bowdin rushed in again, but was caught by the lightning-fast strike of a clawed hand before his stroke fell. The Dwarf was hurled against a boulder. The *oomph* of air forced from his lungs echoed loud in the night stillness.

The Ranter was suddenly on the Dwarf as he rose, but the Ranter returned to vapor, Bowdin's hand sticking out through its back, a dirk in the Dwarf's fierce grip and axe swinging from the other, driving at the creature, bearing it back several paces. The creature jumped and sent itself flying to the perimeter of the battleground.

"Captain, are you alright?" cried Oreleana.

"Close one there, boys and girls...." The effort continued for nearly a quarter-span of the moon's course. The Dwarf now panted between his frequent assaults at the untouchable foe.

"I can keep this up till sunrising," complained the Dwarf. "But to what avail? He does not discourage easily." Bowdin charged again, ten, eleven strokes, chasing the retreating lizard around the clearing, cursing under his breath with each swipe of his blade.

Suddenly, a brilliant flash of blue flame erupted from Easom's hands and enveloped the Ranter. The creature's body arched back in pain. At the same time, Bowdin's blade caught flesh and cut deep into the creature's side. The Ranter screamed and fell back. The blue Druid-fire chased itself like a dog after its tail, coursing about the reptilian body.

Three, four, five strokes of the axe fell, severing limb from body. The Dwarf chased after the writhing foe, beating it from pillar to post. Finally, with one great stroke, Bowdin clove straight through the Ranter's face and through its skull, the axe sinking into the earth. The Ranter lay dead.

"Mother-of-a-Troll," bellowed Bowdin, rounding on the Druid in rage, "Why did you not do that with the damned Moor Cat?"

"A Moor Cat is not magical. The spell wouldst not have delivered...the correct...*force and velocity*," the Druid smiled.

"Well, then...you should have done it sooner here!" challenged the Dwarf.

"I didst have to gather sufficient...*force and velocity*."

"Save it for someone else, boy. Give me something to drink and...Oreleana, would you check my leg? I think that I tore my wound open." Oreleana and Easom helped the Dwarf to the boulder and sat him down. Easom pulled a water skin from his pack and handed it to Bowdin, and then, using a Druid flame, he kindled a wood fire for light and comfort.

"Mother-of-a-Troll, why did you wait so long if you could do that?" griped Bowdin. "I was working hard enough! What? Were you watching for entertainment?"

"I didst not think that thou wouldst want me to interfere with the making of another legend," answered the Druid.

Bowdin snorted! He gave his beard a sharp tug.

Easom laughed, relieved at their deliverance. "No, actually, it didst take a bit of time for me to recall the spell correctly, as I hadst not attempted it before. Then there was the casting of the spell, which is somewhat lengthy for a novice, and then the gathering of...*force and velocity*...before I couldst wield it. After that, I didst need to time its use as to give thee a clean advantage. Otherwise, it wouldst have transformed before thou wast able to strike."

"Humph! Sufficient *force and velocity*.... Bah! A likely Troll-sucking story," the Dwarf grumbled into his beard.

Once outside the magical confinement about the Inland Sea, Bowdin, Oreleana and Easom rested for two courses of the sun before heading east again and finally arriving at the borders of the Blue Mountains that lay to the north.

"This is it," said Bowdin surveying the pass between the peaks of the Blue Mountains and the northern Mystics. "That should bring much of this journey's troublesome spots to an end. Now, all we will need to deal with is Humans. Do not know if that is any safer, though." The Dwarf glanced at Easom.

"Do not worry thine beard, Captain. I am in agreement. We Humans art a dangerous lot. One canst predict a Moor

Cat or Troll's behavior, but one never doest know what to expect from a Human. Back in Breezon, we doest condition ourselves to expect the worst and art rarely disappointed. If one doest behave at a higher standard, it is seen as a gift."

"That is a mighty grim view, Easom," said Oreleana.

"Mayhapst, but one that deals with the reality of the matter. Those who doest hide behind optimism do not last long. There is the possibility that in other places, in other Human habitations, one wouldst be permitted a more hopeful outlook. But in Breezon, that outlook leads to death, for it is the most cunning and wicked who prey off those who doest think such thoughts."

"Even so," said the female Dwarf, "I for one could not survive within myself to see the world through such eyes. I would despair under such a cloak of suspicion."

"If your wards are set and perimeters secure, Easom, I, for one, am ready to retire for the night. If you two are not ready to sleep, I shall snore a bit louder so as not to be disturbed by your speaking." The Dwarf pulled a blanket over himself and was soon snoring, true to his word.

"What happens after we reach the coast?" asked Oreleana.

"That, I doest not know. *ti-ord* didst not say except that I must unite with Morlah somehow. To my knowledge, he wouldst be along the northern coast or, mayhapst, inland, somewhere between Heros and northern Canterhort.

"And once your quest is over...?"

"Breezon, I imagine, after I see thee home safely... unless...."

Their eyes met, the expression of love that words would not have communicated exchanged in their gaze. Several score spans of heartbeats passed before Easom spoke. His voice cracked with the strain of nervousness.

"As thou hast said, the Dwarves wouldst not accept our...ah...." The boy cleared his throat. "Our union...."

Oreleana blushed, but her eyes were lit with hope.

"No one among the Druids in Breezon wouldst take offense. But the city's population...they are frequently wicked for evil's sake. However, we couldst manage it if you were... willing to be separated from your kind. I mean family and friends...or even just the general populace of *Dolan*."

"I am willing. It is not as if they would be out of reach, for *Dolan* is but eight courses foot-journey from Breezon.

"Art thou sure?" asked the Human. "Life in Breezon is hard and, outside the Druid community, very unpleasant, even for one such as mineself who hast never known otherwise.... I wouldst not want thee to regret such a decision.

"There are other places in the world. The Homeland of the Giants, though distant, is a haven, and the Giants are a tolerant race.... They wouldst not begrudge us a union. And the Humans of Northern Canterhort, I have heard, are of a much more civilized and accepting manner.

"Let us think upon it," said Easom. "We doest have many troubles still before us if we art to make such choices. But...." The Druid paused, uncertain of how to proceed.

"What?"

Easom fidgeted. "Wouldst not mine having led you and Laskey out here, resulting in his death, come between us?" Easom averted his eyes.

"Easom! I thought we had agreed to share that burden and that we would not allow one to bear it alone. I would carry it myself if you were not so eager to have it all." She reached over and placed her hand upon his. "Truth be told, the Moor Cat didst kill Laskey, and we should perhaps lay the blame completely at its feet, though I am aware that the mind and heart do not permit this as easily as reason does.

"It is written in the *Histories*," spoke the Dwarfess, "that many cycles past, early in *Dolan's* being opened by the Dwarves, an earthquake collapsed a new tunnel before it had been shored up. The workers who had opened it fell into a deep depression due to their fallen fellows' deaths, taking the blame upon themselves for what had not been preventable. It is written that they did languish over it for four cycles of the moon until, as one, under a pact, they threw themselves into the river of molten rock which doest flow within *Dolan's* roots."

"But how could they? They couldst not have prevented an earthquake?" objected Easom.

"Nor could you a Moor Cat, Easom. Therefore, let it lie where it should."

"Thine meaning is taken.... We willst share the blame for now."

"I imagine that this is the best our minds may allow, though our hearts would argue otherwise. I love you, Easom, and would be with you if you will have me."

The Human looked into her eyes and nodded.

Chapter 28

At the summit of a small rise, the following midcourse of the sun, under a brilliant sky-blue heaven, the three travelers stopped to survey the view before them. The mountain was heavy with vegetation, and sparse clusters of hardwoods mixed with conifers dotted the grassy hills.

"That is a welcome view," said Bowdin. "After having seen so much bare stone for so long. I believe that I may even have become eager to cast my eyes upon the Maring Sea and to witness a landscape that moves, rather than one that stands so defiant to change."

Easom and Oreleana nodded in agreement.

As they walked along a small valley some time later, Bowdin, who was a short distance ahead of the still hobbling Human, let out a great shout and waved Oreleana and Easom forward. Looking behind them, they saw what the Captain had spied: four male Cave Trolls, known as bulls, were making their way down a steep incline, heading for the group.

Easom and Oreleana set out with all the speed he could muster. After they caught up to Bowdin, who took up the rear guard, they sped eastward, the male Dwarf monitoring the Trolls with an occasional glance over his shoulder. The Trolls were rapidly gaining on them, and though they did not relish Human flesh, they were quite fond of Dwarf flesh.

The three companions maneuvered around a group of boulders and climbed up a hill, though Easom slowed their progress. They emerged at the cliffs of a deep, narrow ravine, whose bottom lay almost out of view. The distant roar of water rose from its depths, and the mist from the falling water hung in the air. Moss covered the rocks and trees. The ravine, easily four times the width any of them could have jumped, lay as an impasse before them.

Bowdin's eyes surveyed the scene to each side. Then, the Dwarf pointed. "There! There is a tree in the distance, fallen across the chasm. Make for it quickly!"

They took off again. The bandages on Easom's left foot were blood soaked. Arriving at the large fallen pine, Bowdin took Oreleana by the scruff of the neck and the top of her pants and heaved her onto the log, repeating the same with Easom. With one knife in each hand, the Captain then pulled himself up, hand-over-hand, using the knives stuck into the bark to pull himself to the top. Within a matter of heartbeats, he was astride the massive timber.

"Move!" he cried, storing his knives and drawing his axe. "Good a place as any to make a stand. You two get across." The four Trolls emerged from the forest before he had finished speaking. They slowed, assessing their prey, as Oreleana made her way across the tree, weaving through the thick branches that protruded from its sides.

Bowdin positioned himself just where the ravine began, in order to force the Trolls to use the log as the only means of approach. One of the bulls did not hesitate and ran to the gulch's edge, clambering onto the log where Bowdin waited. With a forward rush and a mighty sweep of his axe, the Dwarf beheaded the Troll. Its body plummeted down to the stream below. The other three bulls hesitated, grunting to each other in their native tongue.

Oreleana was halfway across the ravine when she stopped and called back, "Easom, come quickly!"

Bowdin stole a look behind himself and found the Druid still standing with him. "Go, boy! What in the gods' names are you waiting for?"

"I might be able to assist thee."

"No!" hissed Bowdin. "Move!"

Easom turned to go. He had not taken two steps when the Trolls grabbed the tree by its massive fan of roots that spread into the air like a splaying sunset; with a mighty heave, they lifted the tree and dropped it. The tree shifted as it hit the ground, taking Bowdin's legs out from under him. Easom barely managed to save himself by latching on to two large branches that rose next to him. Bowdin swung his axe as he fell. The blade planted itself firmly into the pine, but the Dwarf was left dangling at the end of its long handle. Easom rushed back, extending his hand down to the Dwarf who, with a grip like a smith's vice, latched onto Easom's wrist.

Again, the Trolls jarred the tree. Easom, lying flat astride the massive log, was not thrown, but Bowdin had lost his grip on the axe handle and swung at the end of the Human's arm.

"Easom!" cried Oreleana. Bowdin and Easom turned their heads toward her, finding the female dangling dangerously from the end of a broken branch. Easom turned back and looked at Bowdin's eyes with despair in his. Quickly, Easom grabbed at Bowdin's wrist with his free hand, dropping his legs over the opposite side of the tree for balance just as Bowdin released his grip!

"Let go, boy. Save Oreleana!" whispered the Captain, shaking his head. Easom had anticipated the Dwarf's move from what he had seen in his eyes.

For a long heartbeat, Easom considered obeying. He considered allowing Bowdin to fall that he might attempt to save Oreleana. For a long heartbeat, Easom pictured the Dwarf plummeting to his death onto the rocks below. Finally, after what felt like spans of time later, but was, in truth, a score of heartbeats, Easom cried, "No, someone needs to ward the Trolls off. Come on! Climb up on my arms. Move, Captain!" Bowdin, laboring, hand-over-hand, hauled himself up along Easom's arms just as the Trolls dropped the tree again. Oreleana screamed. The males turned only to witness her plummet down into the chasm.

Easom gasped, crying out.

Bowdin retrieved his axe and rushed the Trolls who were lifting the tree again. The Dwarf opened the skull of the nearest bull. He hurtled himself to the opposite side of the roots, removed an arm at the shoulder from the second, but the third distanced itself before the Dwarf could inflict any damage on it. The bull that had lost its arm howled in pain and rage, thrashing an escape into the forest as blood gushed from the wound. It would not live long with such an injury.

Bowdin dropped from the log to the ground, rounding on the last Troll. It growled at him hesitating with confusion and dread. The Dwarf feigned a turn as if to climb back onto the log, provoking the bull into a charge. Moving like lightning, Bowdin turned to meet it, sending the war-axe whirling through the air, end over end, blade over handle. The axe embedded itself, cleaving open the Troll's skull. The bull lay dead.

The Dwarf rushed to the edge of the cliffs and looked down. Deep within the chasm, on an outcrop of rocks that protruded from the cliff, lay Oreleana's body, broken. Blood flowed heavily from her head.

Easom breathed heavily. Tears followed Oreleana's path into the ravine as he stared at the lifeless Dwarfess. Bowdin quickly retrieved his weapon, mounted the tree and made his way to Easom.

"Why?" cried the boy. "What sin have I committed that the gods shouldst hate me so! That they shouldst set their faces against me as they have since I didst leave my home!" He screamed into the heavens in pain and frustration, great choking sobs filling the air.

Placing a hand on the Human's shoulder, Bowdin said grimly, "I do not think it is the gods as much as that damned Faerie, *ti-ord*. The gods do not care about the comings and goings of puny creatures such as us. But that damned Faerie and her games...." Easom was not listening. His grief over losing his beloved Oreleana, was like a knife plunged into his heart and soul. He stared down at her lifeless body, shedding uncontrollable tears. He was inconsolable in his grief and anger.

After a span, when the Human had quieted and withdrawn deeply into himself, Bowdin lifted him to his feet. With one hand firmly gripping the Human's tunic, the

Dwarf propelled the boy across the chasm along the length of tree until they were again on firm terrain. There, Bowdin let the boy fall to the ground, where he wept into the night. Bowdin would have performed a release of the dead for Oreleana, but there was no possible way of getting to her body.

Three courses passed, the Human refusing to be consoled, refusing to communicate, not eating or drinking. Bowdin let it be. His own mood was not unlike the Human's.

Dismay had edged in upon Easom's spirit, at each step, each hardship, at every loss, with every wound they had sustained, at each disappointment they had endured. They were like millstones about his neck, dragging him down into the depths of despondency as into an abyss of agonizing hopelessness - as into the abyss that had claimed Oreleana. Self-hatred became a labyrinth of self-accusatory judgments. Self-pitying imaginations, blame-laden deliberations multiplied within him. Now, he himself wanted to die, to die and be done with his life, with his quest.

But the thought of the quest, of the Elves' plight, echoed in the recesses of his soul. He fought the notions it raised, refusing to be succored from dejection. Laskey was dead; Easom lay claim to the blame. Oreleana was dead! *That* was his too. His promise of love was destroyed. He was not worthy of being loved! Bowdin had his own injuries. Easom's fault. The Elves would perish in the Netherworld. The Human male shouldered the responsibility as if he himself had taken *soiccat*, opened the rift and hurled them there.

In sleep, in consciousness, Easom drifted in his disheartened desolation as if he were wandering the stark stone of the deep Mystics. His eyes refused to see, his ears to hear and his heart to hope. Then, one night as he slept, he dreamed.

*The naked, seductive **ti-ord** sauntered toward him as he lay in a velvet bed whose edges lay somewhere in the distance, far from view. Easom lashed out at her with Druid fire, without effect.*

*"Easom," she breathed seductively. "I thought that you...**desired** me."*

"The gods curse thine name," he spat. "Thou and thine accursed quest."

"But Easom," she pouted, "it was not my quest, but yours. I did not ask this of you. I only did warn you of the dangers if you set out to find me. I warned you that these matters do not belong to Humans...but you persisted." She drew near the seated boy, dropping to her knees, straddling his legs, her firm breasts before his face.

"Get away from me, harlot! Get away, temptress. I doest hate thee with all my being. Thou art uglier to me than a female Troll." He spat on her, struggling to lay hands on her that he might murder her, but she restrained him with her enchantments.

*"Easom," she whispered into his ear, wrapping her arms about his head, drawing it to her bosom. "Easom, didn't I tell you that if you desired the end of your quest, that you must want it as much as you...**wanted** me? Did I not tell you that you had to give... **everything**?"*

"Why! Why have you tormented me so!" he screamed.

She released him, put her hand to his forehead and pushed him onto his back. The Faerie was suddenly clothed.

"I tire of you, mortal!" she spat. "It wasn't me who sent you on your quest. It's not me, who handles and designs the path of fate. Enough of your ignorance and false accusations. I do not write the

*journey of life. I merely instructed you as to what the path held and what the outcome could be...if you persevered. I grow bored with you, but the path remains open. Persist on your quest, and you will find the stone **ti-ord**, and when you do, **soiccat** will be thine also. The cost placed upon this is not set by my hand. Trouble me no more,"* she said, and she vanished.

Easom awoke, his being raw with grief and pain, his utter hatred for *ti-ord* fueling his spirit. Somewhere in the recesses of his flesh, he *could* remember how intensely he had wanted, with great lust, the naked Human apparition of the Faerie, but now, his anger and hate equaled the former passion.

And...what of the Elves and their plight? Did it matter to him anymore? Did he no longer thirst to see them freed from their prison? Was it possible that they were alive? Yes, they were. He remembered *ti-ord* saying that they were when he had first encountered her. Could they be rescued? *ti-ord* had said he would have his end if he persevered. The Faerie had never lied to him. What she had spoken in his last dream was true. She had made him no promises. She **had** warned of the dangers. Nevertheless, he chose to hate her as if she were to blame, even if he sequestered and held all the blame for himself. *And what of the Elves?* With vehemence, Easom's anger and hatred of himself and *ti-ord* rekindled his desire to see their restoration to Mildra.

Bowdin sat by a fire whose flame licked at the early dawn when Easom rose, the Human aware of the world once more. Bowdin's reddened eyes and grim, somber face turned to the Druid.

"I am sorry, boy. Sorry about this whole damned mess. Sorry that I did not take you children by the ear and drive you back to your homes while there was still time. Just plain sorry...."

"Dwarf-Friend," whispered Easom. "With or without thee, I wast going to attempt this quest. This fool's mission, as you so wisely name it.... I wouldst be dead if thou hadst not accompanied me. For that I am forever in thine debt. Mine only regret is that I didst not force Oreleana to turn back when it was time.

"I doest remember reading once of the individuality of each thinking being and how dignity is given to our fellow man...and Dwarves...in allowing them to be masters of their own fate. I doest remember how moved I wast by these thoughts that the author didst place into mine head at that time. I hadst endeavored within mineself that I shouldst live my life, bestowing such dignity upon my fellow man. I didst not understand at that time how severe a price couldst be attached to it," he said, casting his gaze to the ground.

The Dwarf sat in silence. Easom's words apparently had found purchase within the Dwarf. As the sun rose over the foothills of the eastern Mystics, casting its rays of gold, the Dwarf sighed and nodded.

"There is a measure of wisdom in what you speak, Human...and I had thought all wisdom to lie and originate with the Dwarves...or was this author a Dwarf?" he asked hopefully.

Easom shook his head.

"Well, then," surrendered the Dwarf, "let us make a pact together. You can retain your portion of guilt, and I will claim Oreleana's that we may share in this, and if we achieve our end and find these Elfstones, then we will take our burdens and burn them on a pyre and be rid of them."

"Agreed," Easom said with a weak smile. "But now, my stomach grumbles with appetite. How long has it been since...."

"This is the fourth rising, boy. I thought you would die in your grief.... Once to the coast, will it be north or south?"

"North," stated Easom, emerging from his reflections. "Morlah set out to go into northern Canterhort. *ti-ord's* directions were that I seek him out as the next step of our journey. I think we shouldst attempt to at least get as far as the canal in Heros before making any further plans."

Chapter 29

⚜

Easom and Bowdin slipped off the back end of an empty mule-drawn cart that did not stop to let them off. Easom shouted thanks to the driver as the man continued along the docks.

"Here we art at last," said Easom, turning to Bowdin.

The Dwarf gazed about, slightly unnerved. "I have never seen so many Humans piled up in one hole."

Easom smiled and patted him on the shoulder. "Come, Dwarf-Friend. Let us find a haven for the night...and some food."

They had not taken more than a couple of steps when Easom stopped and found himself gazing up at a woman on the deck of a ship. *Capt's Lady* was back in the Port of Heros, looking to load a new shipment of slaves. Star was leaning against the rail of the silent ship, a single stone suspended on a cord dangling from her neck It had slipped from within her clothing where it normally rested with the other she had from her mother.

Easom gasped, grabbing at Bowdin's shoulder to stop the Dwarf.

"*ti-ord*!" he hissed into the Dwarf's ear.

"What? Where?" grumbled the Dwarf, not believing the Human.

"Up on that ship," Easom indicated. "That woman... around her neck...."

"You sure of this, Druid?"

Easom nodded his head vigorously.

"How?"

"I recognize the stone from my dream."

"Looks like a stone, low-grade agate, to me. No value to it other than that this one is polished."

"It is *ti-ord*. Trust me! It is *ti-ord,* the stone we seek."

The Dwarf acquiesced and stepped toward the ship. "Ho! Missy, up on the deck," he called.

Star looked down at the travel-stained, journey-worn pair.

"What ship is this?" the Dwarf continued.

She shrugged. "*Lady*. What of it?"

"What manner of vessel is she?"

With a frown, Star gazed at the two, thinking they were beggars, and not understanding exactly what the Dwarf asked. Looking around to see that none of the crew were about, and she replied in a lowered voice. "Slaver. Best you stay clear if you value your freedom."

"Thanks, Missy," answered the Dwarf. He took Easom by the elbow and ushered him down along the dock, propelling the resisting Human along without difficulty.

"Where art we going?" insisted Easom.

"Not on board a slaver. Dwarves are sold and put to the oars until they die."

"But what of *ti-ord*?"

Bowdin turned Easom around a corner and into the next side street.

"Adding folly to a fool's mission?" grunted the displeased Dwarf, chancing a glimpse down the street they had left to see if they were being followed.

"I am going back."

"No. Wait, boy!"

"Maybe I canst buy it from her. She canst not know what it is."

"Alright, but do not board the ship; do it from the dock."

Easom limped back to *Lady,* where Star still stood at the rail, looking over the docks.

"Miss!" called Easom. Looking down at the Human, she motioned that he should continue with a lift of her chin. "That stone about thine neck...I willst purchase it from thee!"

Star glanced down and saw *ti-ord* dangling out from its usual hidden location and quickly delivered it back to its proper place, within her clothes.

"Not for sale," she stated.

"What is it?"

"Sort of a family heirloom. Passed down to me from mother to daughter. Worthless except for that...it's all I have of any family ties. Not for sale," she repeated. "Get lost or I'll put the crew on you." Easom turned and quickly departed. Returning to Bowdin, Easom told the Dwarf of his plan.

"I must get on board. She will not be parted from the stone. This is where we part company, my friend."

Bowdin's face contorted, and he huffed into his beard, glaring at the Human. Finally, he stood a mite taller and responded. "No, I think not. I have too much invested in this to turn away now. Besides, methinks that you will have need of a Dwarf's assistance before this ends. I am coming with you, boy."

"No. I willst not permit it!"

"What was all that Troll-dung about allowing others to be masters of their own fate?"

Reddening, Easom bit his lip.

"I wouldst rather that I didst accompany thee, boy!" the Dwarf mocking him by speaking in the ancient dialect.

Easom surrendered.

"Besides, we have a burden to bear together, one we must bring to an end."

The Human bowed low before the Dwarf. "Forever at thine service, mine friend! How doest we get on the ship?"

"Oh, that is the easy part. Come with me."

Late that night, with all activity on the docks at a standstill, a drunken Dwarf and a Human staggered along the boardwalk by the ship, singing slurred songs, laughing and falling over each other. The watch up on *Lady* called to someone behind him, and soon eight men stood at the rail staring down at the drunken duo.

"Two free 'uns, Capt," said Martie.

"Dwarf has a battle-axe; might not be *free*."

"True, Capt. But they sure looks drunk.... I doubts he could use it."

"Never! Never! Never underestimate a Dwarf!" replied Capt. The sots now passed abreast of *Lady*. The Dwarf looked up at the crew and yelled, stumbling and catching himself on the Human.

"Ho! You boys gotsh any corndrippings? Powerful shirsty work, emptying all thosh bottles." He laughed and slapped the Human on the back, sending him spinning across the dock.

Capt smiled and said, "Just up the gang plank...all you can drink."

"Naw!" huffed the Dwarf in disbelief, "You cannot have *that* much?" Then, he roared with laughter and took off on a crooked line that led them to the gangplank. "Come on, boy," he called to Easom. "More for the tummy!" Easom followed, unsure of the path; Bowdin caught him by the arm and lugged him up onto the deck.

One of the sailors met them and offered them a bottle.

"Thanks, mates," laughed the Dwarf. His friend appeared to unwind and fell sitting on the deck. Each took a deep draught at the bottle offered to them; Easom stretched out on the deck and did not move again. The Dwarf joined him after having drained half the bottle.

"Well, that was easy," said Martie, kicking the Dwarf to see if he could elicit a response. "Take 'em to the hold, boys...and double check the Dwarf for knives.

Later, alone in the hold, Easom sat up.

"Easy as stealing eggs from pigeons," said Bowdin in the dark. "Did not even have to take a bump to the head."

"I doest not know about that," replied Easom "These corndrippings willst provide me with all the bump to the head that I doest need."

"Told you to go easy at it. Not my fault you drank so much."

"I didst want to look and smell the part more than just act it."

"You liked it too much," protested Bowdin. "Well, let us get some sleep. What a stench of a hole. Smells like a Troll-cave."

It would appear that fortune had her hand upon Easom at this point, for he found himself not only in the presence of *ti-ord* but upon Capt's ship as well. Several courses later, out on the Maring Sea, with a hold more than half-full of captives, *Lady* made her way north. As was his manner, Capt allowed the prisoners to remain on deck in order to prevent disease from establishing a grip in the hold. However, Capt was leery of Bowdin and only allowed him out with shackles on his legs and a square iron mass linked to him. The iron was so heavy that the Dwarf could barely carry it alone, and it took two of the crew to assist him to move it; but the Dwarf had decided to go peacefully as the more time spent outside of the hold the better, as far as he was concerned. But he soon decided that he was not fond of the sea and her fluidity, and he was found staring out toward land all the course long.

With a routine established on deck, the prisoners settled in. A few risings later, Easom saw Star meandering about the ship and poised himself to happen upon her. Easom stood along the rail to the rear of the foredeck, staring out at the vast expanse of water. Star strolled past.

"Miss?' he asked, glancing about. "May I have a word with thee?"

She eyed him suspiciously, obviously not afraid. "Aren't you that boy that I told to get lost?"

"I am. But I wouldst forever be in thine debt if, for a little, thou didst give me thine ear."

"You talk funny.... Where you from?"

"Breezon. The speech is that of the ancient language of the Druids."

"Breezon...I never heard of any Druids in Breezon."

"We doest keep a low profile...."

"I'm from Breezon too...."

"Then, thou art a long way from home, also."

She shrugged.

"Everythin' alright, Miss Star?" called Pig.

She turned and waved at the sailor. "I can handle it. Thanks, Pig. What do you want with me?" she asked, her attention again on Easom.

"Please, hear me out before thou doest make a decision. The stone about thine neck," he said. Her hand reflexively moved to her clothes, where the stones lay beneath.

"It is magic, an Elfstone, a very rare Elfstone that I have been in search of for several cycles of the moon."

"Elfstone." She shook her head. "Naw. It's just an old piece of rock."

"Please hear me. I doest seek the stone thou doest wear; *ti-ord* it is named in the ancient Elven tongue, meaning seeker. With it, it is hoped that we canst find the stone *soiccat* by which the Elves of Mildra canst be returned from the Netherworld. They were cast there by the use of *soiccat*. But to locate *soiccat*, we need *ti-ord* and one who canst wield her."

Star pouted with a twist of her lips, wondering if she wanted to listen to any more of this gibberish. Finally, she spoke. "There's no such thing as magic...and the Elves, well who knows. Most likely just another myth."

Easom extended his hand and lit a blue flame in his palm for but a heartbeat before closing it and extinguishing the fire. "So much for there not being any magic," he grinned. "My friend, the Dwarf, is Captain of the King's Guard in *Dolan*. He hast accompanied me on this quest for the Elfstone. We feigned being drunk and walked onto the ship of our own accord, and you know that we were aware that it is a slaver. What other purpose couldst we have to put our lives into such a state?"

He had her there. She remembered telling them that *Lady* was a slaver. What other explanation could there be?

"Alright. Tell me the whole story. I wasn't going anywhere just now anyway."

So, propped up at the rail, Easom told Star the entire story from start to finish over the sun's course, even his dream of *ti-ord*. Finally, his tale was finished.

"Ever think of being a bard?" asked Star. "They'd pay you a lot of coin in some of Breezon's brothels to hear stories like that! So, you just want me to hand over the only tie I have to my family, just like that?"

"I am afraid so."

"Then what? You can't just walk off the ship...."

"First things first. I wouldst pay thee handsomely. I doest have gold hidden upon me."

"I'll think about it," she said, turning and leaving the Druid. But for the remainder of the voyage, Star did not allow Easom near her and took great measures to avoid him. The Druid feared that all was lost, even when his goals were at hand.

Lady continued north, holding over for a couple of courses in each port, loading more slave cargo. After she reached Mallion, *Lady* turned west along northern Canterhort and sailed directly to Consists Isle, the center of the slave trade, with the largest auction of the cycle at hand. Folk, almost exclusively Human, came from everywhere to buy and sell slaves at this market. Upon arrival at Consists Isle, the slaves were unloaded and put into open corrals for each boat's cargo, somewhat like an open warehouse. There, thousands of penned slaves suffered under the heat of the sun and in the cold of the nights.

There was quite a variety of slaves: Humans of different colored skin, some as short as Gnomes some tall as Trolls. In a deep stone-lined pit, there were Cave Trolls. Rock Trolls were kept in thick iron-barred cages; how a slaver got hold of these was hard to imagine. There were Dwarves, but not from Frontmire, except the one, as well as Gnomes, horses, mules, oxen, small green smooth-skinned lizard-like men and a large variety of beasts and Humanoids of a wide variety of descriptions.

About the market, on three sides, was a tall stone wall that easily measured ten paces in height. On the four corners of the great enclosure, archers were posted in wooden towers. The front wall facing a small trading arena was a heavy wooden fence. Large fires burned at night to give the guards light and as a deterrent to escapes, even though most prisoners were shackled.

There were guards everywhere, heavily armed. Customers also traveled with their own entourages of mercenaries to protect gold and purchased goods. It was not a place to cause trouble; it would have taken an army to breach it.

Easom and Bowdin stood staring out of their pen, like livestock awaiting slaughter.

"Well, boy. It is at this point that I say that our quest is over. If we get sold, most likely we will be separated and could end up in some distant country and never return. If I get an opening, I am running for it."

"Think thou wouldst get far?"

"Humph! With sufficient *force and velocity*, you would be amazed at what a Dwarf can do...."

"I am sorry I got...."

"Shut up, boy. We have been over this a hundred times...one hundred and one, now. I give you the dignity of your choices.... You give me the dignity to make mine, and we both steal what guilt we can and hold it fast, but privately."

Easom exhaled deeply.

"You coming if I break for it?" asked the Dwarf.

The Druid nodded. "We canst not accomplish anything here. I guess thou hast reason. It is over. Didst I tell thee that I know a spell to unlock shackles?"

"What! Why did you not tell me sooner? That, my boy, could come in handy indeed!"

The first course of the auction had arrived, buyers milling about by the hundreds, inspecting the wares. Slaves were taken from pens, brought down into the arena and put out for bids.

Surrounded by *Lady's* crew, Star and Capt wandered about, waiting to collect the return from the sale of their goods.

Star worried the stones about her neck. The woman had been in turmoil ever since she had spoken with Easom. The stones meant so much to her; she had no ties, no family, no friends, only these stones. How could she be asked to part with them? Yet, that was not what bothered her most. Somehow, the whole of Easom's quest haunted her. Here were a Human and a Dwarf, given to this mission, giving of themselves, risking life and limb out of concern for others.

Actually, the whole thing had scared her; it was too foreign a concept - giving, service, bonds of friendship and sacrifice, magic and the quest. The thought of it all struck a deep chord within her, speaking to her of nobility, dignity and pride, which were foreign to her experience but true to her spirit.

Star had retreated to the safety of things familiar, avoiding Easom for the remainder of the voyage, obsessed by the Druid's tale. Sleep eluded her, and she lay awake many a night, lying next to Capt, listening to his soft breathing, staring into the darkness that closed in about her and called out to her, a darkness that knew her.

Something of Destiny brushed against her in the night. Purpose and decision beckoned to her. The entirety of Easom's tale lay at her feet, making it her responsibility. She despaired, fearing to enter into what was so alien to her, fearing to make a decision.

The auction was well under way. Star stood next to Capt, but her gaze was riveted on Easom penned some distance away. Time rolled on, and finally, Capt's merchandise was brought forward to the auction block, as another ship's wares were held in the chute, awaiting their turn. The auction continued as normal, Star's gaze fixed on Easom.

Easom, scanning the crowd, somehow found Star's eyes, as Capt moved in closer to the block to watch the sale of his goods, the eyes of the boy and the woman locked on each other. Star's breathing grew fast. Anxiety mounted within her. Easom was at the end of the line of slaves, followed by the Dwarf.

Two women in front of the Druid and the Dwarf were set out, and the bidding began. Then, appearing out of nowhere, pushing through the crowd and stopping a few steps away from Star and Capt, were Morlah and a Gypsy!

Easom tugged at the chain that connected him to Bowdin, grabbing the Dwarf's attention. "That is Morlah the Druid standing there! I have to tell him. He has to know about *ti-ord*!"

"Hold, boy. You cannot get there."

"There willst not be other opportunity." Easom muttered and the shackles about his wrists and ankles fell open.

"Get the boy for me, would you, lover?" Star asked Capt.

"What? What do yer want him fer?" he asked suspiciously.

"No! It's not that, you big ox," she said punching his arm. "He knows some good tales and does little magic tricks; could be entertaining on board ship. We could use him as cabin boy."

"Yer should have said somethin' earlier," complained Capt. "Now I'll have to buy him to get 'im back and pay the auction fees on 'im."

Suddenly, Easom lunged forward, running through the arena toward Morlah, shouting at him through the auction's din, desperately trying to draw the Druid's attention. Bowdin quickly outpaced and blazed trail for the Human. Guards were bowled over. Barricades splintered at the Dwarf's passing. The crowd parted as wheat under the scythe. Bowdin, appearing dangerous, as if gone mad, led Easom toward Morlah.

The guards in the towers, quickly, accurately released two arrows. Bowdin fell face down, no longer protected by chain mail, an arrow in the center of his back. Easom fell onto his side and screamed in pain. Bowdin did not move. Easom, arrow protruding from his shoulder, staggered to his feet and surged toward Morlah again. The whole of the auction ground to a halt to watch the spectacle. Easom hurdled the last fence and ran toward Morlah, calling his name.

Morlah turned to see what the commotion was about and saw Easom a few paces away. Star ran toward Easom, followed by Capt and the *Lady's* crew. Finally recognizing Easom, Morlah stepped forward while the guards, at the same time, released two more arrows into the back of the fleeing slave.

Easom fell headlong, face-first into the mud at Morlah's feet. Star stopped and gazed down, her fear and turmoil at a boil. Easom lifted his head, weakly.

"Morlah," he whispered, blood trickling from his mouth. Then Easom saw Star. "Morlah!" Easom grasped Star's ankle with an outstretched arm. "Morlah...*ti-ord. ti-ord*. She has...." The guards, satisfied they had made an example of the two escapees, returned to their posts as Easom released his last breath. Morlah was in shock. He rose from Easom, turning to meet Star's eyes. The girl looked as shaken as he felt. She abruptly pulled her ankle away from the dead boy's hand, with revulsion. Revulsion at herself. Revulsion at herself for not having intervened sooner. She bore the guilt of his death.

"Do you know this boy?" Morlah asked.

Faintly, she nodded, her face pale, as Capt cursed at the loss of his merchandise, hollering at the guards about the cost of his goods.

"*ti-ord*? Is it true?"

The woman shrugged. "He said so," she said, removing the stone, at which a second stone on a different cord was pulled out along with the first. Removing them from her neck, they became tangled in her hair for a heartbeat, and she dropped them. They fell toward the ground and into Easom's dead, outstretched hand, as *ti-ord* herself had spoken of in his dream, saying, *If you endure, the time will come when you will lay your hand on me, but not as you would now. And when you find me,* **soiccat** *will also fall into your hand, and you will have your desire for the Elves."*

Morlah retrieved the stones and gasped. "Not only *ti-ord* but *soiccat*!"

"That's what he said he was looking for...*soiccat*! That's the name of the Elfstone, but how can it be?" She cast about looking for comfort from Capt, but he was engaged in an argument with the auction officials and the guards.

"Witch!" elbowed Petrosis, finally becoming involved. "Witch! Look!"

Morlah took a heartbeat to refocus. When he followed the aim of the Gypsy's pointing finger, his eyes fell on the auction block where three Gypsy women and an Elf girl stood.

Pulling a pouch of gold from his mantle, Morlah instructed Petrosis, "Bid on them. Buy them back at any cost! Hurry, lead-post!"

Petrosis gaped into the bag of large golds. "Had I known you had these, we would have tried your hand at cards, my friend." He looked up with a broad smile on his lips and a bright gleam in his eyes.

"Go, lead-post. Go!" Turning back to Star, Morlah asked, "Can I have these? Name your price!"

Down at the arena, Capt and the crew were locked in a shouting match that appeared to be about to develop into something dangerous. The tower guards and other nearby guards had arrows and swords at the ready. Star glanced in Capt's direction.

"Maybe...if you can stop them before they fight. Maybe...its just that the stones are all I have of family and heritage."

Morlah glared at Capt. "Stay here. Do not move!" he said to Star, placing the stones in her hand, folding her fingers over them. Star went down on one knee in the muddy soil and stroked Easom's hair, lost in a grief that she did not understand, as Morlah rushed down to Petrosis who had his purchase strung behind him on a chain. Lohlitah wept at the sight of Morlah.

"I like this, witch! Buying women! Has a certain something about it," exclaimed Petrosis.

"Where's the rest of the gold?"

Petrosis' face dropped. "Oh! You want that back? Alright then. I will win it off you at cards." He beamed and handed Morlah the purse.

Morlah ran down to the argument and stepped in. "Friends!" he yelled. "Can I buy the two dead slaves?" All turmoil ceased, the men staring at the Druid as if he were mad.

"How much? My offer stands once...twice...and is gon...."

"Five golds," interrupted Capt, elbowing the guard and auctioneer official aside. "They're yer's fer five golds!"

Suddenly, the auctioneer looked angry, wanting in on the transaction. Morlah turned to him and gave him one gold, folding it into the man's hand but hanging on tightly to his arm.

"Let it be, friend," he said dangerously, sending a sharp charge of electrical power up the man's arm. "If you anger me, I will cook you right where you stand! Do you get my meaning?"

The auctioneer's eyes grew wide with terror. The man pulled away as Morlah released him. He fled.

Morlah turned to Capt. "Finish your business here, my friend, and join me. I will buy you and your crew all you can drink." Morlah turned toward Star, but Capt swung him back around.

"What are yer up to, man? No one buys dead slaves."

"I have matters of concern that are of greater worth and importance, and I fear that they may involve you somehow. Humor me, and I will make it worth your while, in gold." Capt followed Morlah eagerly to where the Gypsy women stood with Star and Petrosis.

Arriving to where Star knelt by Easom, Morlah put his hand on her shoulder. "Come. We have much to speak of."

Lohlitah jumped Morlah, arms and legs still in shackles wrapping them tightly around the Druid. "Witch! You have come for me. Oh, I could love you right here! You wonderful man!" she cried, and she kissed him forcefully. Slowly, with difficulty, Morlah peeled her away and asked Petrosis to undo the women's shackles with the key the Gypsy had obtained with his purchase.

"Not yet," grinned the lead-post. "I like a string of women behind me, like a string of horses!" The women did not object, just glad to be freed from their captors.

"What of your dead slaves?" asked Capt.

"Have your crew take them aboard ship. We will get them away from this place and give them a proper burial."

Capt glanced at Martie, who commanded, "Alright lads, let's get these goods back on board."

Chapter 30

Late that night, aboard *Lady*, anchored out in the harbor, Morlah, with Lohlitah fused to his side, Star and Capt sat about the table in the captain's quarters. Petrosis was playing cards with the sailors below deck. The two Elfstones sat in the center of the table.

"Let's take it from the beginning," said the Druid. "How did you get these, Star?"

"My mother. Her mother gave them to her. Said they were family heirlooms of some kind. She didn't know... or didn't say." Star trembled, still apprehensive, still unnerved. Capt reached over and took her hand in his.

"These are Elfstones, stones of power and magic." Morlah picked up the first. "This is *ti-ord*, the seeker. It has the power to find that which was lost. However, in this case, it wasn't needed, as what was sought was with the seeker." Morlah returned the stone to the table and picked up the other. "This is *soiccat*. Its meaning is unknown, but it has the power to open a passage between us and the Netherworld, allowing those focused on by the one who wields this magic to be crossed from or to the Netherworld."

Capt looked skeptical and Star, afraid.

"Easom did seek the stones so that the Elves of Mildra might be returned to this world. It is possible that they are alive."

"They are," whispered a wide-eyed Star. The silence in the room was heavy for a score of heartbeats.

"They are?" prompted Morlah.

"Easom told me about the dream he had of *ti-ord*. She said they are alive."

"Perhaps you could tell me what it is that you learned from Easom...and about the Dwarf."

"The Dwarf was Captain of the King's Guard from *Dolan*," she began, recounting her own tale in escaping from Breezon and telling the story of Easom's quest and how he got on board *Lady*, which led to his death.

It was the third watch of the night when they ceased from their talking.

"Captain," said Morlah, "let us sleep, and I will propose my plan to you once we have slept."

Capt nodded, stood up and opened the door. "Find someone on watch and have them give you a bunk."

The following course, Morlah laid out his proposal to the captain. "I doest not need Star's stone, *ti-ord*, but I doest need *soiccat*. I willst hire your ship to take us to Mildra where the stone is needed. If Star allows, we willst use it to rescue the Elves. Then, we canst decide what is to be done. But, may I advise thee...? The stone would be very dangerous in the wrong hands. She wast used of the Elves, millennia past, to push all manner of evil beings and demons through to the Netherworld. In the wrong hands, the stone couldst be used to allow them to return. It wouldst be a dire time for the inhabitants of this world shouldst this come to pass."

After burying Easom and Bowdin at the far end of a nearby island, *Lady* set sail for Mildra. Capt was open to any tale that allowed him to prosper in gold. They sailed east around the cape of Mallion, where Petrosis, Syndrill and the third woman, Anndine, disembarked, returning to be reunited with the Gypsies.

Lohlitah was glued to Morlah.

Capt and Star were introduced to Andreanna.

"This," said Morlah, "...is the only living heir to the throne of the Elves, unless some remain alive within the Nethers. Andreanna has asked if she might see the stones."

Star, without hesitation, removed them from her neck and gave them to Andreanna, who briefly studied *ti-ord* and handed it back. The Elf had glowed with a radiant power as she examined the stone. When she examined *soiccat*, the intensity of power about the female Elf rose to a pitch that caused apprehension in Star, Capt, and his crew.

Andreanna exclaimed, the magic instructing her, "*soiccat*, Opener of the Cleft of Evil." She turned to Morlah. "Morlah, I can use this. The stone communes with me of her power and use!"

"Are you sure?"

"Yes. I could do it now...."

"I think we had better wait until we get to Mildra."

Andreanna returned the stone to Star, who gaped in wonder at the Elven girl. Star had become cooperative upon Easom's death. If she had heeded him, both he and the Dwarf would still be alive. And, Fate seemed to stir in the depths of her being, making her feel more lost than she ever had felt. Assisting Morlah was an attempt to ease her upheaval.

No one who had not previously seen it would have believed the city was such, even if words could have described the Magnificent City. Morlah led the group up into the castle and onto the porches off of the Royal Quarters.

"May I?" asked Andreanna of Star.

Star nodded and handed *soiccat* to the Elf.

"Morlah, I need to use your knife. I lost Gildar when we were captured."

The Druid, untangling himself from Lohlitah's grasp, handed the Elf the blade of Earthen magic, the knife immediately glowing with power in the future Queen's hand. Andreanna, with a tilt of her head, as if listening, eyed Star and then smiled.

"Elendaire, descendant of Stanton, Commander of the Elven Armies and of Ahliene his wife, The Mother of those who Heal, for the power of *acrch* that she had. That is who you are, Star - Elendaire."

"What?" asked Morlah incredulously.

"She's Stanton's heir," cried Andreanna. "That's how she got the stones. *ti-ord* was passed down in Stanton's line, given to him and Ahliene for their part in the first quest for *soiccat*. Then at the *salong*, the magic wrested *soiccat* from Daektoch and transferred the stone to be with *ti-ord* where it remained onto this course of the sun."

"How do you know this," asked Star, her head swimming as if in a dream.

"This is what the magic speaks to me of, pertaining to you and *soiccat*. The remainder is written in the *Elven Histories*."

"Oh, my! Oh, my!" said Star putting her hand to her throat. "Oh, my. This is all too much...like a dream. Does that mean...that I am an Elf?"

Andreanna nodded happily.

"Are you sure?"

"Yes, Star, or should I say Elendaire? Take my hands."

The two females held hands for a heartbeat and Star's eyes radiated with Elfish power, her face brightened as understanding registered upon her countenance; and it was then that Morlah noticed how Star's ears were *almost* like an Elf's. And the shape of her eyes.

"I knew your ancestors, Stanton and Ahliene," said Morlah to Star. "They were as fine as thou couldst find among mortals. Now, I doest see thee for what thou art, I canst see Ahliene's eyes in thee, and thou doest bear the color of Stanton's hair...and his chin."

Star turned to Capt, who stepped away from her and bowed. "I did not realize that I was in the presence of nobility. But I do see it in your eyes, my lady. I had mistaken the air of nobility for a whore's defiance. You have come home, my lady! You have come home."

"But, let us return to our cause," said Morlah, Star lost in confusion. "The Elves of Mildra." Andreanna was a step ahead of him, her eyes closed in concentration, her hand gripping the glowing argentus knife, *soiccat* in her opposite hand, held in open palm. Her breathing grew deep, and she paled a little.

"tis orla cntola tuma soiccat. enpal. rndo. ommolista cristi lastin enoi," she spoke under the power of the Elfstone and magic, continuing for a long time. Those who observed were lost in the sphere of the magic's power, not noting the heartbeats of time passing them by. The intensity of the Elfish power grew until the entire city throbbed with its might. From within the magic, within himself, Morlah heard Andreanna's voice.

"I need more power, Morlah. Your staff, quickly." It took a span of heartbeats for the Druid to move, for though he had clearly heard her, he was lost in the rhythm of the magic, as if in the *dance*.

"Elendaire, Star. I need you, too," Star heard Andreanna call from within. "Take my hand, for you also are entwined in this. Come quickly to my aid."

The three stood, hand-in-hand, Morlah with staff blazing in his right hand. The argentus knife, spitting power, was held between the Druid's and Andreanna's hands. Elendaire and Andreanna clutched *soiccat* together, until the whole of the south of Frontmire pulsed to the magic.

The Elves along the coast stopped and gazed toward the capitol city, aware of *soiccat's* presence, aware of the might being wielded, aware that the rift was about to be opened, but not knowing to what end. What would come or go through the tear?

Then, it felt as if the breath was drawn from all the living under *soiccat's* reach. The midcourse sun dimmed. Sound ceased. Minds numbed. Fear threatened at the edge of consciousness. With a tremendous release of power that rocked the city, a gaping black hole ruptured the heavens and a tendril of might sped toward the sphere sheltering the Elves in the Nethers, seeking to return them to the living.

The Elves in the Nethers languished and hope failed. Hundreds upon hundreds of cycles in the land of the living had passed them by. What hope could there be? What remedy could be found? It was likely that they were forgotten, a myth, a legend in the land of the living. Perhaps they should quit. Quit. Just let go and allow what may follow to be. It was all fruitless. There was no escape. Why did they linger on and on? What insanity demanded that they continue?

These thoughts were an insidious cancer, for they not only diminished the morale of the Elven collective, but unobserved, these thoughts caused the Elves' strength to falter. Were these thoughts their thoughts. Or were they planted there by a foe, perhaps *Kravorctiva*, the sorceress, herself? With each heartbeat of their failing hope, the sphere that contained the Elves dimmed in strength, equally to their diminishing resolve, until, as one, the Elves were sure that the only way was to surrender and let fall what might. The Elves knew they would not be inhabited by the spirits of the evil dead, for these denizens would tear limb from body to claim them. But what of the Elves' spirits? What torments would be ravaged upon these?

As long as they could remember, it felt as if the Elves had drifted in this unholy limbo, attacked savagely and repeatedly by the stained spirits that dwelt there. Again and again, the Elves had repelled them with mighty heavings of power, each assault foiled. Of late, the attacks came more frequently and ferociously.

The heart of the Elves faltered.

And then, first, like a star, a light shone in the darkness; it grew, glowing like a beacon from afar. It was an opening, a rift into the land of the living! But to which world? Who could tell? Nevertheless, to the land of the living!

As one, the Elves and their foes surged toward the distant beacon shining in the blackness. A tendril of white light lashed through the darkness and secured itself to the sphere of Elves. Hateful, terrible spirits raged at the light, mounting a horrific assault on it and the sphere from which, within, the Elves faintly resisted, all strength abating.

And then, the sphere hurled toward the rift, the denizens of the Netherworld in frenzied pursuit, hoping against hope, Elf and demon, that they might escape this hellish nightmare of a habitation.

Andreanna's tone changed; her voice grated with fury. Her voice rang with the resonance of a roaring waterfall. Power burst forth from her as she separated herself from Morlah and Elendaire. She stepped forward. Those about her cowered at her unleashed fury, the terrible majesty of the Elf girl come into her might. The ominous manifestation of the terrible Dark Queen of old was returned in her fullness!

"*kata, kata,*" she cried, her words as if turned evil, ominous and terrifying. "*bata balin balat bahal. coudo pasi stelra.*" The mortals around Andreanna quavered in fear as the Elven Queen rebuked her enemies. The air turned as dark as night. The essence of the evil dead was felt keenly. Foremost in the foray from the Nethers was *Kravorctiva*, the evil sorceress, gathering her minions, uniting them in their power against the Elven girl. The Elf's eyes became raven-black and grew increasingly menacing. Her face became skeletal. She rapidly rose to the height of a Rock Troll. She clothed herself in darkness, and her skin became dark like the color of oiled coal. Elongated obsidian, skeletal fingers were poised within her cloak, ready to strike with fearsome strength. Her hair, long and ink-black, undulated as if in the wind. Long pitch-black robes rippled in the still coastal air.

"*bacto balak. bacto balak. bacto balat,*" shrieked the descendant of the Dark Queen of centuries past. The inherited magic of her ancestor spewed forth, unleashed. It came to life, into the fullness and magnitude of its potency. Her friends lay paralyzed in terror about her feet. Dark clouds swept in from all horizons, and thunder rolled continuously as lightning filled the air. The earth beneath them shook. Far to the north, the volcano, Mount Bahal, belched lava. The Korkaran Sea churned violently to the south.

The evil dead lashed at the Elf with all the power they possessed. The Dark Queen, Andreanna, grew in stature again, to twice the size of a Giant, her might increasing proportionally to her size. The magnitude of her strength rose to heights never before witnessed in the realms of magic.

"*tacto balak,*" she hissed, unleashing her terrible might.

The souls of the Netherworld slashed at her in fury.

The Dark Queen's power erupted, its intensity climaxing, the Elf cursing her foes.

"*anonat tombilista hano!*" she hissed with a cyclonic vehemence.

A screech followed her last command, a cry of dismay that echoed across the entire continent. Even in distant lands, as the malevolent dead were subdued, some turned frightened eyes toward Mildra as if threatened by a great malice as well as by a majestic power. *Kravorctiva* and her minions were hurtled back into the Nethers. With a loud snap, the rift was closed and sealed.

Andreanna, spent, fell to the ground, again a mere Elven girl.

Not long after, a small solitary figure slowly moved onto the balcony and gazed at the unconscious group. It was Sannae, the Elf girl that Morlah had first met when he arrived in Frontmire. Moving from person to person, one at a time, she revived them, healed them with her gentle and gracious power: Andreanna from her spent exhaustion and her companions from the paralysis of terror-stricken minds, having been in the presence of the Dark Queen in the magnitude of her fury.

As they rose and looked out over the balcony's railing, they saw that the Elves of Mildra were returned. A loud cheer, a cry of tremendous joy from the returned Elves, rang in the city streets!

Epilogue
Of The Elves

Southern Frontmire flourished with the return of the Elves' to Mildra; and for centuries to come, the Elves prospered in the Earthen magic, the magic never again taken for granted, and the power never being allowed to return to dormancy.

Andreanna was wholeheartedly accepted as Queen of the Elves and reigned for several hundred cycles in peace. She opened an area of the castle for Star, who was treated as royalty by the Elves. Capt became Commander of the Royal Fleet, *Lady* being transformed into the Queen's Galleon. Capt had not been able to refuse the wealth the Queen offered him; neither did he dare to refuse her request after the display of her might to which he had been witness.

Every two or three cycles, the Queen, accompanied by Star and Capt, would board *Capt's Lady* and sail to Mallion to meet with Petrosis and the Gypsies again. These were times of great joy for all involved.

From their lands, the Elves reached out to the other inhabitants of Frontmire, the Parintians, the Dwarves, the Gnomes and the Humans of Breezon and Heros, even attempting to tame the Trolls; and though they were never actually domesticated, the Trolls did live on in peace with their neighbors, while continuing to love a good brawl among themselves.

Elendaire, Star, offered *soiccat* to the Elves, who hid it with many magical wards in the depths of the castle, never to be seen again. She retained *ti-ord*.

Of the Druids and Parintia

Morlah persuaded the Breezon Druids to abandon Breezon, and on the *Capt's Lady*, they returned to *seilstri* in Parintia. There, with the Elves' assistance, the island's soil was healed and made fertile, and it began to flourish once more. The ground was tilled, the Elves setting enchantments that would deter vermin, rot and disease. And with an effort of great magic, the entire island enjoyed an abundant harvest within one moon's cycle of the end of their labors. Parintia soon took its place in the world markets and grew to be a thriving country.

Jat, the fisherman who had given Morlah passage on his ship, with the Druid at the nets, trolled the outer reef and returned to the Parintian docks with a boatload of Blue Gill.

The Druids were restored to favor with the Parintians, and not long after, the archives were opened again. *seilstri* took its first step to once again becoming a center of knowledge and learning as it had been some sixteen hundred cycles past.

Of Morlah and Lohlitah

Morlah made a final quest, that of recovering the lost *Gildar*. With use of his argentus orb, the Elven blade was easily located and bought by the Druid for two coppers from a market table. From there, he returned it to the Queen of the Elves.

All having been said and done, the Faeries' purposes fulfilled and Morlah's mission finally over, Morlah and Lohlitah went north along the Maring Sea on the *Capt's Lady*, accompanied by Queen Andreanna, Star and Capt. Upon leaving Mildra, Morlah, by apparition, appeared to Petrosis, who was back in the deserts with the Gypsies.

"Petrosis, we art coming home," spoke the shimmering manifestation of Morlah that night, standing before the Gypsy.

"Ye gods, witch! You are dead?"

Morlah laughed. "No. Just some...witching. Lohlitah and I art coming to live with the Gypsies. Queen Andreanna willst accompany us by ship, for she desires to see you again...though it puzzles me why she wouldst want to," the Druid teased the Gypsy. "Willst thou meet us in Mallion where we willst arrive?"

"Yes, yes. Are you sure that you are not dead? You scared me like the *gatalopie* we hunted together." Then he grinned broadly. "Will we go hunt the *gatalopie* again, witch?"

"That we willst, my friend. That we willst."

"...And do you bring your gold?" The Gypsy grinned, and his eyes sparkled.

And so, having been reunited with the Gypsies, Morlah and Lohlitah remained with the nomads. Lohlitah stopped taking the elixir of stinkweed and bore a daughter, though they named her after the Queen of the Elves, Andreanna, and not "Little Lohlitah" as her mother had wanted. But the girl did grow up to have straight black hair and dark eyes, and she stole the hearts of all men, to Lohlitah's great delight and to Morlah's infinite dismay.

Morlah no longer partook of the Druid Sleep, intending to let his life end naturally. And, as much as is possible, they were happy to the end of their courses.

Of Oreleana, Easom, Bowdin and Laskey

Oreleana and Easom were reunited in the afterworld. The power of their love, pure and great, would not allow them to remain apart.

Neither Oreleana or Bowdin had been given the release of the dead normally given by the Dwarves, which allowed the dead to achieve the Final Journey. However, *ti-ord* intervened. With the Earthen magic wielded by the Faerie, the love that Easom, Oreleana, Laskey and Bowdin had for each other, and perhaps some of Destiny's own hand, as a reward for their selfless service, in that they gave of themselves onto the end to see the Elves of Mildra restored, they were finally, as one, sent through the White Gates. The first step of the road to eternal bliss.

Bowdin, through Star's account of the story that Easom had told, did go down in the *Dwarf Histories* as the only Dwarf ever to have slain a Moor Cat and a Ranter!

The Frontmire Histories - Book IV

Final: Of Daektoch

Daektoch was struck with terror when the *salong* was undone and he found himself in the midst of the Elves of Mildra. He was locked in a cell for a time, but the Elves pitied him, and so, built a stone-walled enclosure with a house in the midst. However, the enclosure was an insurmountable magical barrier, and there, under the constant vigilance of Elven guards, Daektoch was to live out the remainder of his time.

In many ways, the mage's prison was the most beautiful and innovative of the Elves' constructions. As the mage wandered about the interior perimeter of the circular structure, the scene magically changed after he passed, so that he never returned to the same setting. As Daektoch followed the wall, which frequently simply appeared as the edge of a forest trail or lake, he would encounter gardens, ponds, meadows full of wildlife, hills, mountain scenes, streams and beaches in an ever-changing array.

If he chose to, Daektoch could return to any scene he had enjoyed simply by thinking of the place. Then, after a short walk up a stone path, he would be back at his house.

This prison happened to be not far from where Sannae lived. Daily, she visited with the mage and, in her twentieth cycle of life, moved into the enclosure with the mage, caring for him and keeping his insanity from spiraling out of control, saving the mage from himself.

In her four hundred thirty-eighth cycle, a crimson sun-setting on the horizon, Sannae sat with Daektoch, watching the brilliant-red sky dim toward darkness from the porch of the mage's residence.

"Sannae," said the shriven wizard. "Your kindness toward...me and the magic you've cleverly washed me...in, over the cycles, since I knew you as a child, has changed me...I think."

"How so, Master Daektoch?" Sannae inquired, her eyes fixed on the sunset, absently smelling a flower picked from the mage's gardens.

"The magic you so cunningly...cleansed me with has made me feel...almost Human again. But now, I abhor myself for the crimes that I've perpetuated...in my thousands of cycles of existence. I am sorry above measure...but what I have done, I grieve...can't be undone."

Sannae turned to him, tears streaming down her face. "It does my soul good to hear you say this, Master Daektoch."

"Is it unnatural to live as...long as I have?"

"In the manner you have...yes."

"I must be quite a hideous...beast to look at."

"To some, but not to me."

"Child, I love you like I have...loved none other, not even my family in Pernham, though...I had quite forgotten...of them until recently...though I had also forgotten of love...."

"I love you too, Master Daektoch."

"How? How can you love such an...evil cur?"

"It was not really you, Master Daektoch, but the magic of the dark sylph who taught you the path of darkness. But now, it appears that you've at last come to your senses."

"Perhaps, but with it I've come to...loathe myself. Never again will I utter a spell of...the Dark Arts; that I vow before you, my...Sannae. But alas, I am weary of my existence...."

"Then let go," she said.

"Let go?"

She waved her hand before his face, her magic opening his mind.

"Ah...*let go*. I do see your meaning, little one. But...if I do, the Netherworld awaits this evil soul and...I'll never know the joy of your presence...again."

"I think not," responded Sannae. "I believe that your change of heart will allow you to undertake the Final Journey."

"No, that would be...too much to ask. It can't...be."

"Hope, Master Daektoch. There is hope for one who leaves his evil deeds and expresses a genuine sorrow over a wasted life. Surely you know this."

"Yes, but not for me. How...many thousands have died at my...."

"Shush, Master Daektoch. Do not speak of those things. There is hope for even you. Look." Leaning down she passed her hand over the marble floor, opening as it were a window into another dimension. "Look within and tell me what you see, Master Daektoch."

Daektoch looked at her for a heartbeat and then leaned forward and peered into the distant land.

"I see nothing but...white, radiant gates."

"And what do they speak to you of?"

"I hear nothing...but they do ring with...joy in my heart."

"Then go. You will be received."

Daektoch stood, a skeletal, ghoulish figure, folded in two with age, and he stretched out his arms. Sannae went to her knees and hugged the ancient mage.

"I have great love for you, Master Daektoch."

"And I for you, dear...little Elf."

"Let go," she repeated. "You will be received; I swear it, for *this has been my destiny.* And I'm overjoyed to see it come to pass...for your sake. Many hearts did I heal in my time, all in preparation for this *one,* for yours, Master Daektoch.

"The first time I looked upon you, Master Daektoch, I saw within your heart an ember that was about to go out, a remnant of the boy from Pernham, City of the Mountain. From that time on, I sought to flame it to life, which I did...except the time I visited you with Morlah, seeking *soiccat.*"

"Ah yes, Morlah.... I guess in some ways he was...a likable fellow, don't you think?"

"Yes, quite likable, though I didn't know you thought of him that way."

"I hadn't then. Never did learn...how he put wings on that horse he flew when we last fought."

"It was a White spell, Master Daektoch. That is why you're unfamiliar with it."

The two rose, hand-in-hand, and she led the repentant mage to his room where he lay on the bed, Sannae sitting next to him, holding his hand in both of hers. She kissed the mage on the cheek. The wizard cried out faintly in surprise.

"Farewell, Master Daektoch. We will meet again, by and by. *Let go,*" she whispered, her green Elven eyes burning brightly with Earthen magic. One lone tear stood at the corner of Daektoch's eye, the sole tear to have done so in thousands of cycles.

And then, he did let go; the mage released the spell that had kept him alive for centuries, and instantly...he turned to dust.

"*acrch evandol, ponday cantalti*. Be at peace, Master Daektoch. Be glad."

The *Druid Queen*, though not visited in this account of The *Frontmire Histories*, was released into the Final Journey upon Daektoch's passing. Morlah did have cause in his thoughts of their state of mind and had done well in not visiting them as he had travelled to the Dwarves in his earlier visit to Frontmire. They had not forgiven him. But with their passing through the White Gates, they were healed of all wounds and ills.

They went on in peace.

Made in the USA
Charleston, SC
04 June 2010